Tricia Sullivan was born in New Jersey in 1968 and studied in the pioneering Music Program Zero program at Bard College. She later received a Master's in Education from Columbia University and taught in Manhattan and New Jersey before moving to the UK in 1995. *Dreaming in Smoke* won the Arthur C. Clarke award.

MAUL

TRICIA SULLIVAN

www.orbitbooks.co.uk

An *Orbit* Book

First published in Great Britain by Orbit 2003
This edition published by Orbit 2004

Copyright © Tricia Sullivan 2003

The moral right of the author has been asserted.

A CIP catalogue record for this book
is available from the British Library.

ISBN 1 84149 108 X

Typeset in Palatino by M Rules
Printed and bound in Great Britain by
Mackays of Chatham plc, Chatham, Kent

Orbit
An imprint of
Time Warner Book Group UK
Brettenham House
Lancaster Place
London WC2E 7EN

For Steve and Tyrone,
my Everything.

ACKNOWLEDGEMENTS

My deepest thanks to Mic Cheetham for being this book's champion for *years* – I 'd never have done it without you, Mic. Thanks also to Tim Holman for taking a chance on an early partial and for enormous *patience*; to Simon Kavanagh and everyone at Orbit; to Lily Liang for grammatical advice; and to Denis B. Sullivan and Denis J. Sullivan for filling me in on the truck tunnel and stock passages at the real Garden State Plaza.

I also want to thank my family, especially my mother, Marion, and my father, Denis, for emotional and sometimes financial support. I'm also profoundly grateful to my partner, Steve, for the untold riches he has given me in terms of both inspiration and actual narrative problem-solving, not to mention making it physically and psychologically possible for me to work during the difficult personal circumstances that surrounded the writing of this book.

I read a lot of stuff that drove, influenced, informed and affected this story. I was too lazy to keep a real list, but I am aware of the direct influence of these texts (in no special order): *The Red Queen* by Matt Ridley; *A New Science of Life* by Rupert Sheldrake; *Guns, Germs and Steel* by Jared Diamond; *Gyn/Ecology* by Mary Daly; *Confessions of a Gender Defender* by Randi Ettner and *The Gate to Women's Country* by Sheri S. Tepper. Of course, the science in this book is pure fudge.

In the work process I was aided enormously by Julia Cameron's book, *The Right to Write* as well as the audio recordings *The Creative Fire* by Clarissa Pinkola Estes, *Writing Down the Bones* by Natalie Goldberg and *Creative Writing* by Barrie Konikov.

I had a lot of help. I'm very grateful.

!

I T FEELS SMOOTH and heavy and warm when I stroke it because I've been sleeping with it between my legs. I like to inhale its grey infinite smell for a while before I pass my lips down its length, courting it with the tip of my tongue, until my mouth has come to the wider part near the tip. This I suck, and blow gently into the hole. It becomes wet in my mouth but doesn't soften. It remains achingly solid and I put it between my legs. Its tip snuggles around my clit. On the day I bought it, I had to test out several models before I found one that fitted, and Suk Hee's gangster cousin Woo kept trying to look around the side of the van to see what I was doing. Woo was afraid someone would come and he'd get caught with the van and everything. *I* came. It was the only way to be sure I had the right one.

1

It's narrow enough that I can slide it into my cunt without breaking the hymen. I grope around for a while trying to find my G-spot but the urge to pee is too great when I press there and anyway I think the whole thing's gotta be a myth so I go back to where I started.

Astronomy.

Bodies of light fence and entwine on a mantle of blue. Leo and the Hydra.

The fine hairs on my arms are electric and there's a tingling down my legs and up the back of my head. It's a tropical kind of feeling. *The Lynx, and Ursa Major,* which looks like a reindeer not a bear. My nipples are standing up and rubbing against the sheet. My clit gets more sensitive first in one spot, then in another: but it can't elude the round metal that encircles the glans and works every aspect at once.

Orion, Orion, Cassiopeia and Auriga buried deep in the milky way.

It's good if I twirl the cylinder, a spinning circle around my flesh sinking also into, and. Come in. Its muzzle seeks me out: *Factory made in New Mexico,* it noses toward its original home. Deep deep. Into the danger; the curves, the trigger. Its steel pin has butterflied me: I'm spread out on a card. The metal wraps me and I wrap the earth in starpaper. I can see myself now in the third person. She is splayed across the planet: a contortionist, her hands and feet meet behind her head, *she is whirling fast and the stars become lines become a ribbon of light becomes a curtain.* Her body. MY. Appearing, the taut, her legs

SEE HER a torn place, there's a dark SHE'S darkness beginning to split open now tears the curtain THE GOLDEN a wet rending sound the consequences if seen I AM

a deep place of no light. NOW yeah yeah yeah

the missile, it's—YEAH.

A deep PLACE. Something's THERE. It's really BIG and it's going to, deep in the Earth where it's hot there's a core of IRON it's coming towards sliding metal on metal black black fire

LYRA! SCORPIUS!

IRON Fe chemical number 26 which is made of the original matter of the SUN a great gob that split away in the primordial moments of *deep in the* consequences if seen a rending *Plieades like a doll's veil*

YOU ARE MADE OF STARS

and here comes the big missile *past the point of recall* it's it's it's it's it's

TOO LATE now oh it's much too late you CAN'T stop YEAH **YEAH**

yeah!

!!!!!!!!!!!!!!

don't end

!!!!!!!

!!!!!!

PLEASE stay

!!!!!

!!!!

no. oh. no. don't go.

!!!

Hmm. Not bad.

!

Not bad.

Pretty good.

What time is it? Late. Better quit here. Stay hungry.

I lie back in bed and grope for a cigarette.

I smile.

I used to wish I had a boyfriend but now I know better.

Even a hypothetical boyfriend wouldn't understand.

3

How I feel.
About my gun.

Finish cigarette. Late. Too lazy think good English now. Get up. Legs feel rubber, *chowdery* and I nasty juicy but no time shower. 11:30 a.m. Clean gun, splash on CK1, load gun, whip bra from hanging place on telescope arm, get dressed. Think about Mom who I know lurking nearby. Hear Mom small voice taking me through routine: dropped articles & shitty grammar. Shut up, inner Mom.

That's better. The gun straps to the inside of my leg with Velcro. It's not the absolute zenith of fashion any more to do this, but girls who wear theirs with leather straps and buckles aren't serious: with Velcro, you can get at the thing when you need it.

I have a pink ammo belt. It's heavy, but who said fashion was easy?

Ken is playing piano down the hall in the music room. Scriabin. I'm beginning to feel slightly more alert. I kick open the door, take a flying leap across the room, and land on the piano bench, bringing my hands down on his shoulders like creepy-crawlies.

'Boris the Spider!' I shriek, and he hunches and goes rigid, his clever hands pausing mid-stroke, his face at once blank and angry.

'Get off, you fucking bitch,' he squeals, flapping his elbows.

'You,' I hiss in his ear, 'are the result of a tragically misinterpreted amniocentesis. Did anyone ever tell you about that?'

'Sun!' Mom, in doorway, dressed in golf clothes. Holding entire pitcher of fresh-squeezed orange juice. Shit. 'Sun, breakfast!'

'Mom, she called me amniocentesis, can you get her away from me, please? She's ruining my life.'

Down the hall to the kitchen, trying to step on the backs of Ken's sneakers as he trots after Mom, who having abandoned the orange juice pitcher on an occasional table now whips out her English pocket dictionary to look up 'amniocentesis'.

'No, it's M-N-I, Mom, but never mind—'

'Sun, what you do? Tell me what you say little-brother.' Mom getting all flustered, waving the dictionary in my face. In a minute she'll break into Korean, which must be prevented at all costs.

'Mom, it's a new band, all right, G?'

'What you want breakfast? Egg? Pancake?'

'Forget it,' I say. 'I have to meet Suk Hee. We're going to the maul.'

I hear Ken mutter something like 'Losers' but he's too far away to kick.

After I leave I feel guilty because I used to be nice, or at least some of the time I was nice, or at least I wasn't a complete mean bastard at all times like lately; but the weight of my piece drags at my thigh and I know it's just nerves. Nerves. I'll be much better once today's over. I'm sure of this. I'll take an interest in Mom's horticulture and I might even give Ken some of my old George Clinton CDs in hope of teaching him some real culture. But later. Later. Not now.

Standing outside the Cyprus Towers apartment complex, squinting up into the half-rain. Piles of uncontemplated homework in my backpack, crumpled money in my pocket, about to slip onto the conveyor belt of Saturday in New Jersey. Thinking, *Please not to let me get fucked up today*.

Suk Hee's waiting at the bus stop.

Let's get it over with straight away: Suk Hee is beautiful. There's really no point in describing her. She's

5

just beautiful, end of story. As she stands in the bus shelter under a little yellow silk umbrella I feel all the usual pangs of jealousy and resentment and at the same time I want to go stand next to her as if it will somehow rub off.

Turning, she sees me and gives a fetching scowl.

'Did you see the Whackback highlights this morning?'

'No.'

'Could you believe it when Xacto bit Python on the tooshie?'

'I didn't see it,' I repeated. 'Where's Keri?'

'It was so fake. As if Python would ever let him do a thing like that. And now they're trying to make out like Helga and Cowgirl Jobeth are fighting over The Reaper so what's up with that, Katz?'

'Maybe we should call her,' I mused.

'What's the matter?' Suk Hee said suddenly, gazing hard at me as if she'd only just noticed me. 'You look awful.'

Suk Hee doesn't seem to be aware that she's a boytrap. I've known her since eighth grade and in that time she's had seven boyfriends. One of them was a 24-year-old stockbroker she met at a record store in the medieval-music section. He was kind of an asshole but he did take us all clubbing. This 38-year-old friend of his tried to get me to sit on his lap.

'I attract pervs and old men,' I said, recalling the incident. Suk Hee always reads my mind. Today she was right on top of it.

'How many times do I have to tell you I'm sorry about that?' Suk Hee got out her phone and frowned at it. 'I mean, thirty-eight, that's disgusting. People should stop having sex after a certain age. Like when my grandma got her driver's licence revoked 'cos she couldn't see.'

6

Anyway, I lifted up my skirt and showed him my gun and he desisted.

Suk Hee is speed-dialling.

'*Keri?*' She reached out and played with the ends of my hair as she listened to the phone. She said, 'Where are you? Katz and Dogs is worried.'

'I'm not *worried*,' I snapped, and bit savagely into an overgrown cuticle, drawing blood. SH started talking to Keri about calculus. I was thinking about something Suk Hee said yesterday. We were standing in the parking lot at lunchtime and I was smoking a cigarette and shivering and I had this thought. Mr Beardsley made us watch this film on the Holocaust and they showed bulldozers ploughing the bodies. I turned to Keri – who is also half-Jewish but doesn't smoke so she was only keeping me company – and I said, 'Where were the girlz when this was happening?' and she said, 'They were oppressed and having babies,' and started going on about it, and Suk Hee in a small voice goes, 'They were watching.'

I didn't think much of it at the time but for some reason it started bugging me now.

'Iggh,' Suk Hee said into the cellphone. 'I think I'm breaking out.'

I said, 'Why didn't they do something?', thinking about the women who watched every war and mended their husbands' battlefield socks or however it worked but of course Suk Hee didn't know what I was talking about so she covered the mouthpiece of the phone and said, 'I think you'd look good in Dusky Pearl.'

The bus came and we moved out of the way to let people on. Suk Hee hung up the phone and craned her neck to see around the bus. Keri must be on her way.

It turns us on when you fight, I thought. That must be why. We get off on it. It's OK with us if you don't give head or haven't historically – we don't need orgasms as

7

much as we need wars. Otherwise why would you guys be fighting them?

After WWII the Allies tried a bunch of Japanese bigchiefs on the grounds that even if they didn't perpetrate the atrocities directly, they were part of a giant fascist machine, a giant human meat-grinder and they were to blame. Actually, the Allies put the entire Japanese Imperial culture on trial in a certain sense. But how come nobody tried the women? I don't mean the comfort women who were literally captives, I mean the ones who made tea for the guys who ordered the rape of Nanking.

We're the engines of life. We're it. And men think we're their victims. How did that happen?

Are we really that sneaky?

& could we get away with this for ever?

A black Saab pulled up to the bus stop and flashed its lights at us. Suk Hee squealed delightedly and dashed through the rain to jump in the back seat, beckoning me to follow. There was a burst of music when she opened the door; I recognised the bass line of 'Birthday' by the Sugar Cubes.

'Whose car?' I said, getting in the passenger seat. Keri was at the wheel, looking uptight. With one manicured thumb she turned down the stereo as though squashing a bug.

'Sandra got it when she passed the bar. She's pissed at Mom so she's letting me drive it.'

I sank back into the leather seat and enjoyed the acceleration. The car had a moonroof and I was thinking how nice it would be to drive out into the middle of the desert and lie back and look at the stars while some particularly awesome man was driving, going about 115 and some P. J. Harvey maybe was playing on the stereo. As I storyboarded the Saab commercial I couldn't figure out who the man would be. I tried out several models in my mind but I couldn't work out what kind of man would be dangerous enough and dark enough and hot enough to be next to me in the car commercial, and yet not be totally repulsed by me. Or for that matter who I'd trust to drive my Saab, if I had a Saab (because it definitely wouldn't be *his* Saab). This is the main reason there are never any men in my sexual fantasies. I just can't seem to construct one that fits me. So now as I lean back in the seat and watch raindrops accumulate on the moonroof while we crawl past Yaohan market through the Saturday traffic, in addition to feeling nervous and tense and scared I feel thwarted.

All this despite having gotten myself off this morning. I squeeze the piece gently between my legs to remind myself: whatever happens, I've got my little friend.

We're approaching the entrance ramp to the George Washington Bridge.

'Let's go to the city,' I say suddenly. 'C'mon. Fuck the maul. We'll go to SoHo.'

'I'm not allowed to drive in the city,' Keri answered. 'Besides . . .'

She shot me a sidelong look.

'Besides what?'

'*Besides*, Sun. You know as well as I do.'

Yeah, I do but I don't wanna think about 10Esha's cryptic e-mail right now. We're past the bridge; we have achieved Route 4. I'm not feeling too happy.

'They should have a thing,' Suk Hee is saying from the back seat, 'to make the windshield wipers stay in sync with the music, you know?'

Keri stalks a Lexus, pulling up behind it, flashing. She tailgates it until it moves over. She turns up the stereo, probably to drown out Suk Hee. Björk is shrieking about spoons.

'Seriously.' Suk Hee doesn't give up so easy. 'And what about direction signals? Yours are out of sync with the wipers *and* the stereo.'

'How can you tell?' I've never known Keri to use signals.

'Shut up, Sun. At least I passed my test.'

'I think I'm dyslexic,' Suk Hee added.

'Yeah. That's relevant.'

'I've decided,' I said suddenly in a last-ditch attempt to distract myself from the fact that we'd almost reached the maul, 'to give up on sex.'

'You've never had sex,' Keri reminded me.

'I mean, trying.'

'Get thee to a nunnery,' said Keri. She offered me some bubblegum, which I refused. She chewed hers noisily and began blowing a bubble. 'I hope you're not planning on going lesbo.'

'I'm serious,' I protested. 'I don't need men in my life.'

'Boys,' said Suk Hee.

'Whatever. I don't need them. I really don't. I'm going to concentrate on intellectual things from now on. That's what I've decided.'

Keri's bubble was getting so big I couldn't work out how she could see to steer the car.

'Intellectual things?' Suk Hee said it slowly as if pronouncing a foreign language. 'You mean like books?'

'Yeah, among other things, books—'

'But Katz, you only read to know stuff to impress *them.*'

'That's not true,' I said weakly.

Keri snorted and slammed on the brakes to avoid a lopsided station wagon. The bubble popped and Keri peeled it off her face, zagging through lanes.

'I have lots of my own academic pursuits,' I said.

'Oh, give it up, you limp twat,' Keri said, stuffing the

gum back in her mouth. 'Let's list your intellectual interests. World War II – that would be Mark Stein in eighth grade, right? Entomology—'

'Myrmecology, actually.'

'Bug stuff, whatever, anyway that's Kevin Handley. Then we have computers. Tommy Green.'

'That lasted, like, one day. The computer hated me.'

'OK. What about astronomy? Alex Russo. And you know the really sick thing? You always end up being better at their hobbies than they are.'

'Yeah, that's like whatyoucallit,' Suk Hee added. 'That spider who eats her mate after her gazz.'

'Spiders don't come, S-H.'

'How do you know? How does she know when to eat him if she doesn't come?'

'Look,' I said. 'I admit I only took up astronomy so I could go lie on my back on Alex Russo's lawn and look for the Hyades with binoculars. I thought it might lead to something. But since then I've developed a genuine—'

'Why didn't you just go over there and say, Alex, I realise I'm a freshman and you're a senior, but I want to lick you and I hope you reciprocate. Why did you have to take a summer course at *Columbia*, Sun? And then he goes out with Kristi Kaleri.'

'I have a bigger telescope than him.' I smirked.

Suk Hee has been looking preoccupied. Now she gives a tiny moan.

'What's the matter?'

'I forgot to line up my stuffed animals.'

'*What?*'

'In alphabetical order. I always line them up before I leave my room in the morning. I put Alpha the wolf in charge, and then I go out. But I forgot and I think Gerald the crocodile is in front. Fuck. I can't believe I did that.'

'It's OK,' Keri said. 'Maybe Alpha needed a day off.'

'Yeah. That's possible.' Suk Hee brightened. 'Good. For a second there I thought it was an omen.'

Keri pulled into the maul entrance.

I put my finger on the moonroof.

'So did I,' I whispered.

BONUS GIFT

THE BUGS ARE eating him alive. They live in the iridescent blue stain that Naomi painted upon his skin in a snaky pattern: down his back, across one thigh and up his abdomen, where her brush stopped. But the bugs do not stop. They march onward, sidling around his flank and aiming for his right kidney, leaving an azure trail where they go. The colour of the Az79 Y-assassins is very beautiful, for which he is grateful because they are after all consuming him cell by cell. He appreciates beauty and doesn't want for it here: through the glass of his habitat's walls and ceiling he can see the snapdragons by the Fun Park's lake, the arc of gold sky, and best of all the brilliant coloured beads of cars slippering through *DNA Xpress*. At precise intervals of forty seconds, bursts of screaming are blown to him on the wind in a never-changing rhythm, the respiration of his life outside Mall. At night the ride lights up and he can see the cars whipping through the helices, trains crossing magically. They look like phosphorescent animals. They are abstract and soothing. It is not always so easy to sleep.

Here come the little girls.

'This is Meniscus,' says the guide, planting herself in his line of vision; the spiral of the roller coaster crawls through her windblown hairs, violating the rules of perspective. Right on time come the screams: *eeeee!*

'Can anyone tell me what Meniscus is?' the guide asks.

Small hands are raised.

'Bonnie?'

'A man, he's a man!'

The guide tilts her head, 'Yes, well, that's true.'

Giggles and little whoops of excitement.

'But could you be more specific? Tabitha.'

'A charity clone?'

'Yes, Tabitha, that's right. Meniscus is a male clone, and he was donated by his father for an experiment. Can anyone tell me why male clones are so rare and important?'

'Ooh! Ooh!'

'Yes, Crystal?'

'Because of the legishun . . . ?'

'Legislation.'

'Because of the legislation changing after the Y-plagues killed men.'

'Yes. Very good. The legislation changing meant what, Margot?'

'I forgot.'

'You forgot. Well, does somebody else remember – Kimba! Are you *biting* Angel?'

'Sorry.'

14

'Kimba, can you answer my question?'

Kimba twists a cornrow between her gappy front teeth, speechless. From the back of the pack, a tiny voice pipes up. 'We can only use clones dedicated for science while their fathers were still alive to give permission. And there isn't much of that tissue left.'

Meniscus can't see where the tiny voice comes from, and the Hibridge tour guide doesn't seem to hear it. Two teachers are standing off to one side, smoking and comparing fingernails, equally oblivious. One of them points to Meniscus's display of reward stones, meticulously arranged on a shelving unit by him; he often moves them around as he plays the game. To the viewers, his reward stones are part of some weird Y-autistic ritual. To Meniscus, they are his own private solar system. They are special beyond anything else.

'Come on, Kimba,' prompts the tour guide. 'Your teacher tells me your class has been studying the Y-plagues. What did the change in legislation mean?'

Kimba clears her throat and parrots the phrases exactly as spoken by the tiny voice: 'We can only use clones dedicated for science while their fathers were still alive to give permission. And . . . and . . . there isn't much of that tissue left.'

'Ah, that's more like it! So you *have* been listening.'

Somebody raises her hand and asks, 'But – why can't the men who live in the castellations make clones of themselves?'

'That's not in the lesson plan for today, Margot.'

'Oh, please tell us!' It's the tiny voice again, a little louder now so that the teacher can hear it from behind Kimba's shoulder. She squints a little, puzzled. Meniscus is still straining to see where the voice came from. Its tone tugs at him. He lets Mall drift to the back of his awareness, tuning in to the moment despite the fact that

15

he feels the bugs in his skin more without the cushion of Mall to protect him. His left forefinger rests on the malachite, third planet from the Sun. It shifts slightly beneath the pressure, like a Ouija board.

'Well, briefly, the answer is that clones are genetically unstable and we can't risk the weakening of the species by letting them reproduce. And we need the uninfected castellation males for the Programme, but their clones would only be a burden on society because they'd be vulnerable to Y-plagues without being able to provide quality sperm. A clone like Meniscus, on the other hand, can serve a valuable purpose.'

In the time it has taken the guide to explain, the girls have begun poking each other and giggling.

'But why's his skin all funny colours?'

'Because he's a farm, right, Ms Kang?'

'People can't be farms, you stupid shit.'

Giggles, before Ms Kang can shout, 'Children! Language! Kimba, don't you dare bite—'

A violent shiver gripped Meniscus, an impossible sort of feeling as if the stained area on his body were moving the muscles beneath his skin. The bugs were up to something.

Meniscus sat down. He let his eyes roll back in his head so that his consciousness could drift deeper into Mall. He had heard the tour guide give talks like this one a thousand times before. They offered no real distraction from the bugs in the blue stain, which were attacking nerve endings, teasing his immune system. He breathed deeply, trying not to react. Being Y-autistic made this easier for Meniscus than for other people. He had lived this long because he remained physically passive. He used Mall as a distraction and an outlet for his energy; to temper the pain; to reconcile himself to the deadly invasion and survive in spite of it. What happened outside his body shouldn't matter to him. But even now, deeply engaged in the game, he could not help overhearing the tour guide's occasional phrase. *Neurochemical harvesting. Pig testes. Legal rights of Pigwalk contestants. Prevent extinction. Mitochondrial DNA. Inevitable.*

Mall is really useful at times like this. When he first started playing it, he could do nothing but regulate the heat and electricity and water services, occasionally managing to subtly influence buying patterns. But since Naomi started painting him with Set 10E, Dr Baldino's newest Azure design, the sensory detail has become richer, so that sometimes Mall seems more real than his familiar habitat. And he is getting to know the people who inhabit it, especially the employees. Security guards, salesgirls, janitors have become transparent to him. He moves them around so as to make himself feel better; just as he moves around the planets of the reward stones. It is all play.

And no one seems to mind if he plays a lot, even if he racks up big expenses in the process. Last week there was even a visit from Ralf of NoSystems – The Pioneers in Do-It-Yourself Adventure Gaming® and her lime-green Kangoo van. Ralf spoke to Naomi, the chief manhandler.

'Tell Dr Baldino we'll add more modules for her. The game's eating up all its space. A lot of people don't realise how much processing power is needed with NoSystems products. The self-engendered thing really throws them for a loop and so they miscalculate when they're making their initial purchase. It's OK. I'm going to upgrade you for $299,999.99 and the rest on instalment. You won't regret it.'

'OK, as long as you charge it to Dr Taktarov's account,' Naomi answered. 'I should be so lucky to have the guy for a patron. I could spend every weekend in Neiman Marcus.'

'Hi, Meniscus,' Ralf said.

17

Meniscus didn't answer, but he studied her covertly. Ralf had on jeans and a faded Red Hot Chilli Peppers T-shirt. She had big pecs but practically no breasts, and her moustache was always immaculately trimmed. She had a deep voice and swollen muscles that she liked to flash, and a prominent Bicyclefish tattoo. Meniscus had often heard her and Dr Baldino talking politics; Ralf claimed that castellations were no more than harems, and asked Dr Baldino how she felt about experimenting on a human subject. Dr Baldino always retorted that men had gotten themselves into this situation and women were left to clean up the mess, as usual, and that Meniscus wouldn't be alive if it weren't for the experiment because a wild Y-plague would have got him by now. And Ralf would say, 'Hmm' and fold her arms across her chest, flexing the Bicyclefish tattoo. Meniscus wondered what it was like driving around in the Kangoo all day. He's sure he would far rather hang out in Mall than have to listen to WYNY and pay tolls every few miles on the Parkway. Especially now that he can use the people in Mall to taste the tacos in the food court, or smell the garbage in the dumpster behind Borders if he really feels like showing off.

Too bad he can't stop the bugs from scarfing up his skin, though.

At first Meniscus doesn't notice when the Piscataway fourth-grade class moves away, nor that one child, smaller than the rest, has stayed behind. Then the chime sounds on his pass-thru chute, as if lunch has arrived early. He pivots on his seat bones and sees the child watching him. She has placed something in his pass-thru, which has sterilised the object before presenting it to Meniscus.

He feels nervous, bites back bile. He adjusts the planets slightly to make himself more comfortable; Mall

18

obliges by shifting focus a little, and for a few moments he can almost forget about the Az79. Then he stands up and goes across to the child. He recognises her now. She is featured in the pictures that Dr Baldino keeps in the lab. She's Bonus, Dr Baldino's clone daughter, and he doesn't think she goes to Piscataway fourth grade at all. Dr Baldino has Hibridge Education Privileges – Silver Class, meaning that Bonus is being expensively educated via a NoSystems Kid Trix Adventures in Cognition® MuSE package. She has wide-set brownish eyes and the kind of blonde hair that will turn brown at puberty. She wears a green T-shirt with the word 'Spoonfed' scrawled across it and a picture of the band etched on the sleeve. It hangs to her knees. Looking at her face makes his whole body go suddenly dark, and when she leans against the glass and speaks the stars come out in him.

'There's a wolf loose in the Meadowlands.' The tiny voice belongs to her. Her voice finds an echo in his neurochemistry. His planets tremble. Invisible tensions tug at the bug colonies inside him, like gravities.

When he doesn't answer she rolls her shoulder against the glass as if she's nudging him, even though they're not touching nor could he even imagine it.

'I saw it on the news this morning. I cheated on my Learning Adventure and snuck out early. I'm not really supposed to be here.'

The confession made him uneasy. Why would Bonus want to be here without her mother? Why would anyone want to be here if they didn't have to? His feet itched, and the vague ache in his spinal column grew more pronounced. Maybe she saw this occur. Her brows wrinkled cutely.

'You're really blue. Is it tattoos?'

Meniscus shivered. Her voice rose sweet as a bird's on the question.

19

'I'm a clone, too,' she said. 'I don't get to reproduce either. It's not fair, is it? Meniscus, have you seen a mouse around here? They keep talking about exterminating her, but I'm going to find her first and let her go.'

He was hurting. He ought to take his senses back to Mall, where the pain would translate into something more cognitive, less physical. Something abstract. Something he could cope with. But she fixed his attention as surely as if she'd pinned his skin in place with a nail gun.

'I'm going to find that mouse. But you have to be quiet, OK? Or I'll get caught.' She starts to turn away, then thinks again. Her tone becomes almost accusing and her eyes flash. 'Why do you let my mom do this to you? Why don't you run away?'

The sound of her voice is high and whispery through the intercom: the metallic overtones intensify the little-girl quality almost beyond his endurance. Meniscus doesn't want her to leave. But he never speaks. To anyone. Ever. It's part of his pathology, a law that he always thought was physical.

Now he surprises himself. He answers, and although his voice sounds hunched, muted, and grotesquely deep, he can speak. He tongues the syllables awkwardly.

'Where would I go.'

'You could live in the mountains. With the animals.' She trails one finger over the glass. 'Humans are the only animals that control their males. My Adventure says we used to be the only ones who had wars but now we're the only ones who subjugate the males. Except ants, maybe. I think animals are better than us.'

'I am not an animal.' But his voice is a dragony growl.

It isn't the answer she's looking for. Her eyes rest on his face – then a wisp of fear scuds across her irises. She has probably remembered what everyone knows: that Meniscus doesn't talk. He expects her to run but she

20

doesn't. She stays, fixed in a hemisphere of sunlight, head tilted.

'We're both clones,' she said. 'You and me. But I'm free, and you're not. It isn't fair.'

She is whispering now. Inside Mall the bugs are restless. Something's going to happen.

'That's why I brought you it. I know you collect rocks and things, but this isn't a rock. It used to be alive. It's my favourite thing.'

He looks down at the pass-thru chute and a volcanic shudder passes up his spine. A yellowy oblong lies there, lumpy at one end and pointed at the other. He picks it up. Mall is loud in his mind but he doesn't want to be there any more, he wants to be here. He fights to hear Bonus's small voice.

'It's a wolf's tooth. Wolves are free. That's why people are so afraid of them. Because they're mysterious and free.'

Now, that's done it. In Mall, pain comes running out of the hidden corners and starts rioting. Chaos balloons and explodes. He tries to keep Mall out of his awareness, but he can't. He clutches the tooth so hard it bites into his palm. His neurochemistry surges and falters. Blood and lymph are re-routed. A cascade of effects flows from the actions of the Azure bugs like silk thread and weaves a tapestry of responses in him. Statistical functions too small and fast to see accrue and send agents across cell membranes, rearranging his molecules. He fights not to drown in the bugs' otherness – fights to retain his self-awareness. They want control, but – *wolves are mysterious and free*.

Bonus's whole posture says that she has no idea of the effect she's having on him, and on his bugs. She can't possibly understand the consequences of standing there talking to him. Of looking at him that way.

What way?

21

As if he is another child, or otherwise akin to her.

As if he is something other than a feature of the Educational Fun Park.

The human retina is so sensitive that it can perceive even one photon of light. Out of Meniscus's years of blindness, past all hope of sight, Bonus's photon is seized by his mind, magnified until it becomes a sun. A sun in the world of the blind.

'We'll save the mouse. Then we'll save you. Don't you want to escape?'

He has forgotten himself utterly.

'I can't,' he whispers. 'I can't get out.'

'Bonus?' Naomi has come into the lab, unusually pinch-faced and tense. 'Bonus, what are you doing here? Your mom's not in yet. How did you get here?'

'I came with Piscataway. Naomi, can you bring me a Snapple?'

'No, sweetie, you shouldn't be in the lab by yourself. How did you get in, anyway?'

With only a casual glance at the stricken Meniscus, Naomi leads Bonus away; the child looks over her shoulder at Meniscus and mouths, '*Save the mouse!*'

Meniscus stands there while Naomi removes Bonus. He presses his hands on the glass barrier as if he would touch her if he could – which is crazy because he would rather die than touch anyone. He's Y-autistic. Everyone says so. The psychic detachment of this inherited condition is all that saves his personality from disintegrating when the bugs enter his body. They seed him and they make him grow neurochemicals, and then Dr Baldino harvests them. But now Set 10E, a new breed of Azure, roams his tissues. It hears Bonus's words. It feels his feelings. It takes the abstraction of a thought like a relay racer takes a baton. It takes the thought of escape, and it runs. 10E gnaws at the twig-tips of his peripheral

22

nervous system, sending powerful bursts of commands up the line to alter his brain patterns.

He's scared. 10E likes it. 10E takes his fear and turns it to poison. He turns to Mall in hope of exerting some control, but 10E knows about Mall. It's there, waiting for him. The 10E bugs want to talk to him. Want to own him, enfold him.

They are poisoning him. They don't care if they die, too; they are making his brain make poison that attacks his nerves. He observes this, just as he has always observed them while they eat him, slowly, alive. Only this time, they don't want only his flesh to digest. They want his feelings. His thoughts. They like the taste of Bonus's suggestions. They want more.

They want *him*, and they like it when he hurts, because now he and they know that he's alive.

And it hurts a lot. It hurts so much that he can't think. Old, ancestral instinct stands up inside him and looks around. Something must be done. He cannot stand by. *Wolves are mysterious and free.* He must fight the bugs.

Naomi's voice reaches him through the sound of roaring blood.

'Curator Gould! I can't reach Dr Baldino and the subject is in distress. I need help!'

The I-MAGE flashes its green light over him. Women's voices, conferring. In Mall it's all a violence of moments breaking over one another like waves on rocks. He has the feeling of trying to wake up from a dream and finding himself in another dream that encloses the first one. The smell of many perfumes commingles in his nostrils. He gags and tries to come out of Mall but he can't because the game is getting bigger and bigger, around him, over him, under him.

The crack of bullets. Falling. Time to rest. Then: words. The voices of hard reality forming out of white noise.

23

'I don't *know* how to reduce the pain, Dr Gould. All I can do is cut off the juice but I don't know if I should do that. Dr Baldino wouldn't like – what? I can't reach her, that's why I called you.'

Naomi is near to tears. Meniscus is far beyond them. His body is moving in fits and jerks; he performs coordinated actions, reeling around the habitat, beating his head against the wall, ripping at the bedclothes with his hands and feet. But it doesn't feel intentional. It feels automatic, desperate. He loses control of his legs and falls. He wonders if this is dying.

'Will you authorise removal from the game, Dr Gould? *Please.*'

Can't get enough air. Heart doing all it can, but too feeble by far . . .

'Thank you. *Thank you.* That's very compassionate of you, Jennifer.'

Mall goes spiralling away, leaving him plastered against the habitat's tile floor, his cheek slipping in a pool of his own saliva. Lost planets vanish into darkness, and he's floating.

It doesn't hurt any more. For a long time there is peace. But he opens his eyes and sees that he is not floating. His back has gone into spasm, arching, making his legs kick. He can't feel anything but the wolf's tooth biting into his palm. He can see his legs thrashing but can't feel a thing, not even his breath.

He observes his body from a still point of inertia, within. 10E rampages and there is nothing he can do.

'What the fuck is happening?' Dr Baldino is here. *Help.* 'Turn the fucking game on before you kill the subject.'

'But he can't handle it, he was freaking—'

'Well, put it on subliminal, then. Naomi, for god's sake what does Gould know about our study? I said put it on sub—'

24

The roaring in his head subsides. But the pain is coming back, an ache in the deep and ancient parts of his bones. He knows Mall is still there, like a ghost. On the level of his bones he can feel the white curves and polished floors of its structure, a syncytium in which the Azure now swarm. His body sends in signals, damage reports, complaints of abuse.

'I'm sorry, Maddie, we didn't know what to do, he was going to shit himself in a minute.'

'Shitting himself is the least of it, Jennifer. What possessed you to turn off the game, Naomi? You've nearly lost him to the bugs. Let me see that I-MAGE.'

So it's true. The Azure are taking over, and too late he has realised that he can't accept this conquest because they don't just want his skin, they want *him*. He has to fight. There can be no more appeasement. His face rubber with liquid grief, his teeth bald in the afternoon light and his rectum goes taut with anguish, wells or portals of despair opening all over his torso, and maybe he's alive but the pain is bigger than he is. Meniscus wide-eyed stares straight through Dr Baldino, Curator Gould and manhandler Naomi as they huddle in the observation area, monitoring their instrument panels. He's on his feet, consumed with agony, and he starts tearing at his treacherous skin. Even as it turns blue, he attacks it with his own nails and teeth.

MAUL

I'M TREMBLING AS we leave the car. We all got the same challenge via e-mail from bullit-video artist 10Esha, and although it was brief, it was deep. 10Esha had the makings of a real poet.

Saturday is Bonus Gift Day at Estée Lauder, it said.

'Sun, you look like shit.'

'Thanks, Keri.'

She stood in front of me, blocking my view of Taco Bell where I'd swear I saw Alex Russo loping along the sidewalk towards the Macy's entrance. Yummmm . . .

'You better tell us what you think is going to happen.'

'I have no idea, Keri, honestly.'

'All you did is beat her at chess, right? On-line, right? So she doesn't even know who you are, right?'

'Yeah.'

'And that's *all* you did.'

I nodded untruthfully.

'And the zine,' Suk Hee corrected. 'You bragged on the zine.'

'So? Bragging's not a crime. Neither is reviewing her bullits.'

'Good reviews?' said Keri hopefully.

Actually, I'd panned two of them: the one with the drive-by in Hasbrook Heights and the one with the little kids torturing the dirty old man.

'Well . . . I like *some* of her stuff a lot. But some of it's a little over the top.'

Keri groaned. 'I can see I'm going to have to do some diplomacy on your behalf. *As usual*. Do you know what labels she likes? Can we buy her off?'

'I doubt it.'

'Well, why's she challenging us like this? *Saturday is Bonus Gift Day*. My god, that's so flagrant. What does she want from us?'

Keri stalked ahead, waving her arms at the air in general. I could see the maul pulling at her like a little filing to a big horseshoe magnet.

'Who are you dating these days, Suk Hee?' I asked as we crossed the parking lot toward Nordstrom. The jealousies of Suk Hee's boyfriends' other girlfriends has gotten us in trouble in the past.

'No one,' Suk Hee said cheerfully. 'I'm not allowed to until I get to Harvard, remember?'

'That makes no sense,' Keri put in. 'What difference does it make whether you have a boyfriend here or a boyfriend at Harvard?'

'I'm supposed to be concentrating on my work. My father says that if I'm mature enough to go out with boys I'm mature enough to be in the PhD programme at Harvard and then he threatens to throw away my stuffies.' She looked genuinely distressed. 'He says that as long as I live at home and go to high school—'

'Never mind,' Keri said. 'It makes me sick but you know that.' Then: 'Are you going next year? To Harvard?'

I restrain myself from remarking on Keri's wetdreams about getting into Harvard herself – and dreams are all they will ever be.

Suk Hee shrugged. 'Ooh! Pussies, can we look at shoes? I'm dying for shoes.'

'That depends on whether or not you want to get ambushed by 10Esha,' I said. 'If we're not careful, we could be shopping at Caldor next weekend.'

'*That* will never happen,' Keri said confidently. 'It's probably a joke.'

'And if it isn't?' I hear myself saying weakly.

'Aggression on the net never adds up to anything in real life.'

'Female wolves,' Suk Hee observed, gliding through the automatic doors and into Nordstrom, 'can be pack leaders. Did you know that?'

'Nope,' Keri said, and deftly steered Suk Hee away from the shoe display. 'What else?'

'The alpha female fights the other females to compete for who gets to mate with the alpha male. The alpha males sometimes fend off other males who want to mate the females, but not as ferociously as the females fight.'

'Hmm,' I said, not listening at all.

'Young female wolves are faster than young males so they are the best hunters. And black wolves are always male. That's why Alpha – my stuffy – is a he, even though he has a name like a she. Oh. And if one wolf howls, all the others start howling. And they howl to get in emotional synchrony with each other. They howl to celebrate.'

28

'Is there a point to this?'

Suk Hee fell silent. We all stopped outside the Norstrom men's department. Last chance to run away before we're on Maul Security TV.

'What do you think?' Keri said.

'Not here.' I jiggled my thighs to make sure the gun was secure. Keri and I locked gazes.

'Neiman Marcus?' she said.

'Lord & Taylor,' I corrected, and she nodded. 'Let's get this over with.'

The maul was full of shuffling figures carrying plastic bags. We came out of Nordstrom and my heart was pounding. The thing I really hate about fear is how it makes you see shit like it truly is. I looked down the length of the maul and suddenly I could see everything. I was the hunter and the gun against my bare leg told me that I was looking at trees and fruits and animals and nests and rivers and every kind of ecological structure there is: all of it was there, mocked in the tile and glass and shop-window displays. Like somebody did a really crappy imitation of reality all moulded in Fisher-Price plastic and there it was all arrayed to headfuck me. It's all here, I thought, to fuck me into buying things instead of ripping up raw meat with my teeth and you know what? I'm more in the mood for raw meat. I don't fucking wanna shop at the Nature Company.

Fear of course doesn't stop me from being too dumb to realise I wouldn't last ten seconds in a real jungle. I was totally caught up in my fantasy and anyway I could smell Route 4's truck exhaust mingled with L'Oréal mousse in my own hair, plus a kind of tertiary scent of frying oil from the food court and I very nearly came to some kind of epiphany right then and there. But it wasn't meant to be because at that very moment Suk Hee saw the shoes.

'Oh baby,' she cried, running towards the display. She runs with tiny cute little steps as if her feet are still bound in some kind of race-memory thing. Smiling, she points a slender finger at a pair of pink sneakers. I have to admit they're pretty sweet. In fact, if I didn't know I'd look stupid in them, I might even buy a pair myself. I started looking around for something I could walk in without breaking an ankle.

The thing about it is that it's almost enough. It's so close to being enough you lose track of what enough really is and you feel satisfied by a new pair of earrings and you're mesmerised by some craftily shot footage of another girl's legs as she scampers through the latest tampon commercial. You believe there's a world in which she really lives, being so complete, so satisfied, where everything's so much more fascinating than your world with your stupid mother and your boring school and your lack of yummy males and overall drama shortage. So you aspire to get into that commercial somehow, you think it's waiting for you and meanwhile you lose track of yourself or I do anyway.

'Come on, girlz,' says Keri. 'We'll buy them after. Let's go to L&T.'

Suk Hee pouts. She hates being told what to do but she never rebels because she would be less cute if she were in any way disagreeable. So she trailed after Keri and me, gazing lingeringly at some puppy stationery.

As we were approaching Lord & Taylor's SH suddenly gave a squeal and began to pull hard toward the Vinnie's Video Xtravaganza next to Banana Republic. 'I want to play *When Pigs Fly*,' she wailed.

'Prada,' Keri sang as though dangling cherries.

'Morphic Pig,' SH countered. 'I want Morphic Pig.'

'You can't have him today,' I muttered. 'We have an appointment.'

'After?' said Suk Hee. 'After can we play?'

'Yeah. Sure. But you're going to have to fight off the eight-year-olds. Why don't you get the CD for home?'

'Because I like pressing those big buttons. And I like being inside that chair thingie.'

'It's gross,' I said. 'Ken left his bubblegum in there one time, it was like a bubblegum graveyard.'

Suk Hee doesn't cheer up until we reach the cosmetics department at Neiman Marcus, where of course I'm now feeling so doomed I want to laugh.

But the cosmetics section is awfully middle-aged. I don't see any of *us* here: just a lot of forty-something women with Coach bags and sunglasses on their heads. The muzak dj is a real amateur: whatever's playing sounds like Henry Mancini or some other junk. The smell of perfume and the sight of all the crystally displays and colour-coordinated packages make me feel completely disordered and inferior. All the clerks are made up like goddesses and they look so clean, like they should work at a spa.

No wonder I can't get a boyfriend.

'We're getting you that Dusky Pearl eyeshadow I was telling you about,' Suk Hee informs me, and tugs my arm. I don't see anyone who looks like she could be 10Esha. I feel strange. My mind keeps going back to Friday afternoon in History. There were bulldozers moving piles of human bodies. There were hollow-eyed people, the soon-to-be dead who knew they were already dead but clung to life like a kid to a doll. When I saw it I thought: I will never be the same after this. I will be different.

But here I am in Lord & Taylor while Keri picks out perfume and anti-feather lipstick. Shopping is like preparing for a show that never goes on.

'Prada,' says Suk Hee. 'We got to check that out. Here, try this.'

31

She hands me a tester and I obediently apply the eyeshadow. Suk Hee does the same and we look at ourselves in the magnifying mirror.

'It's too blue for you. It makes you look like a corpse.' Keri laughs, surveying me. She gazes critically at Suk Hee. 'It's gorgeous on you, though, SH.'

I have to agree. I start wiping off the make-up, feeling disaffected. Every new outfit, and I think I'll be different. But who cares? I might as well be invisible. There are mirrors everywhere, so I will feel important. I don't. Why is 10Esha doing this? I'm only a critic. You've got to learn to take criticism, if you're going to call yourself an artist.

'I think I'll shave my head,' I say. Nobody pays attention to me. I scowl at myself in the mirror. My bangs cut too sharply across my face, exaggerating the flatness of my eyes. I have a Jewish nose via Seoul, a nose like a Lipizzaner stallion pulling on the bit. It's the only feature of my face that has any real character. I wish I had Suk Hee's lips but I don't.

Under her breath she is filling in words to the muzak that seems to come part and parcel with the perfume in the Lord & Taylor pricey air. *'I just called – to say – I love you . . .'*

The salesgirl brings SH her eyeshadow. 'It's the last one I have,' she tells us. 'These have been selling like hot cakes. You want the mascara that comes with it?'

SH considers this carefully. Under my ammunition belt, my stomach began to growl. Suddenly Keri's nails bit into my arm.

'Tabitha at two o'clock,' she said. I froze for a second. Suk Hee hadn't heard her; she was deep in conversation with the salesgirl about the relative merits of waterproof eyeliner.

I turned slightly on the pretext of pulling my backpack off my shoulder to get something out of it. 'Tabitha' is a code word for enemy, and when I saw what Keri was referring to I realised she should have said 'Tabithas' because there were seven of them.

Now I know why I've wanted to pee on myself all morning. 10 isn't just a bullit artist in her own right. She's got connections. Her pack is coming after us.

Shit. I mean, who do we think we're kidding with our miniskirts and guns? Sure we're a hotsite on the net, and my zine's buttlicking good, but we can't cut it out here in the maul. Let's face it – we're not that attractive, collectively, and the whole fashion thing kind of means you gotta be. I've never seen these players before but they are dropdead. Look at those Latina chix with their big tits, and that Swedish-looking emaciated blonde they cut out of a J. Crew catalogue. And the fat one – of course, the obligatory fat one who is all attitude and Heavy Style. I mean yeah we got Suk Hee, but Keri & me, we're not in this league.

'You little kids get your Bonus Gift yet?' The leader was tall and mocha and sloe-eyed. I had never seen 10 before, and I expected her to be hot, but not *this* hot. If this was 10, I wished I'd panned *all* her bullits – even my ultrafave, the really surreal one with the Jewish grandmothers fighting over a blouse at Kaufman's while a seeing-eye dog steals the purse of one of them.

Suk Hee was deep in conversation with the salesgirl, who gave a wan smile when 10's crew arrived reeking of free perfume samples. Suk Hee didn't even look up. I don't know whether or not this is strategy – always hard to tell with SH – but her oblivion has a perceptible effect on the crew that otherwise outclasses, outguns and outbra-sizes us. Nobody can look spacy and disconnected like Suk Hee.

That's my girl.

I said carefully, 'I heard it was Bonus Gift day. But we just came by . . . out of curiosity.' I wanted 10 to know I

33

respected her. Maybe there was still a way to get out of this without having shots of us being made to look like idiots all over the net. I'm proud of my zine. I don't want my subscribers to think I'm a dweeb.

I think affectionate thoughts of my gun to cheer myself up.

The leader now poked at SH's collection of purchases, spread across the counter.

'You not seriously spend your daddy money on that shit?'

Keri looked alarmed. The girl behind the counter made signs she wanted to squirm away and serve some middle-aged ladies with pixie haircuts, but Suk Hee kept asking to see things. She ignored everything else, and the tall girl didn't like it.

'That so bony and no good I wouldn't feed it to my goldfish Fred,' the tall girl went on. The others who were ranged behind her were gradually outflanking us. One of them was geeky – she had glasses and, true to form, she was filming us with a hot pink digital palmcorder. I felt about one inch tall. We were going to come out of this looking really stupid.

The leader said, 'Which one of you be Sucky?'

I felt my nostrils flare. Suk Hee hadn't even indexed the question.

'The name is Suk Hee,' I said coldly. 'Who wants to know?'

In the middle of the pack, the blonde J. Crew one was throwing her skinny self against the fat one, trying to get to Suk Hee. A hot pink flush came up in her chiselled cheeks.

'Lemme at the sow!' she shrieks in a horrible central Jersey accent. 'Lemme at her, KrayZglu!'

KrayZglu gave a toss of her head and the fat girl grabbed the blonde and shut her up. I could see her wild blue eyes over the grip of the fat girl's hand, which had a gold ring on it with a matte blue stone inlaid with some kind of, like, cockroach.

Oh, shit. The Bugaboos.

Right about now I'm going fuck, they're not for fashion, they're a *real gang* and we are *screwed*. The 'boos *own* the maul.

'Are you Suk Hee?' KrayZglu repeated, getting right up all in my face. Suk Hee is talking to the salesgirl about blushers. The Latina behind KrayZglu nudges her and whispers something in her ear. A slow smile spreads across KrayZglu's face. She is very pretty.

'Hey! Why you pussies lookin so nervous? Why you carrying?' While KrayZglu speaks, a petite black girl is already moving. A dark, swift hand slips behind Keri's back and disarms her neatly.

'Nice piece.'

'It's a Smith and Wesson – hey, wait, don't show that around. We'll get kicked out of the store.'

'I do what I want, poo,' said the little black girl, twirling Keri's weapon like a six-gun.

'Hey, I give you respect,' said Keri. 'I can relate to your situation, I really—'

Without ever taking her eyes off me, KrayZglu reached over and pinched Keri's face between two sharp nails. Keri muffled a cry, tears starting in her eyes. KrayZglu spoke in a very soft voice.

'And don't you fucking empafize w/me, Mz Psychologist why don't you empafize w/a fuckin cow cuz that's what you *are*.'

Keri pulls her hair over her face to hide her tears.

The black girl passes Keri's gun to the videographer, the curvy babe with pink-framed glasses. 'Chex it out, 10,' she says. 'Should we get 'em kicked out the store or should we be goo-girlz?'

So the geeky one with the camera was 10. So much for all my illusions. She looked back at me and softly said, 'Smile for the camera, Sun.'

SH tapped me on the arm before I could answer. 'Um . . . I bought my lipstick so maybe we can go?'

The tall girl in front gave Suk Hee a shove and said, 'Don't interrupt, Barbie.'

Suk Hee looked cowed. She said nothing. Out of the corner of my eye I saw a woman with a sales-associate badge moving towards us. She went up to 10 and said, 'You can't have that running in the store.'

'Sorry,' said 10 in a deep soul-singer voice. She drops her eyes. The woman is white and repressive. She's not exactly giving off Welcome to Lord & Taylor vibes towards KrayZglu's crew.

Keri's antennae stand up straight and she goes, 'Why can't she use her camera?' Keri's eyes flash. Her Tommy style screams bigbucks, as does her accent and her whole posture towards the sales associate, who is probably pulling down less in salary than Keri's allowance-plus-good-grades-bonus.

'Store policy,' says the woman firmly. 'Security.' Her glance takes us all in and she looks a little disturbed until Suk Hee gives her a big, gorgeous smile. 'For all we know you could be casing the place out.'

Keri snorts to show what she thinks of this.

'You want the tape?' she says condescendingly.

'That won't be necessary. Just keep the camera off and you're welcome to continue shopping.'

She moved away, still eyeing us, and I took the opportunity to turn to KrayZglu and say quietly,

'Look, can we just forget it? There's been a misunderstanding, that's all. We're sorry, we didn't know this was your turf.'

For some reason the word 'turf' made them all start

giggling. 'You hear that?' said the big fat one to the salesgirl, who smiled weakly as she handed Suk Hee her receipt. 'Turf?'

But KrayZglu's attention had left me and fixed on Suk Hee. 10's camera was running again, but the sales-associate woman had turned away to respond to a little old lady with a Gucci bag. Another squaddie passed KrayZglu something pink, which she held clenched in her left fist like a grenade. 'You been fucking with Snowcone man Layback,' said KrayZglu. Snowcone began to wriggle in the grip of the fat girl again, and all of a sudden KrayZglu was dangling a pink lace G-string in front of Suk Hee's nose.

'Those are not my panties,' Suk Hee said.

'Yeah, right. Snowcone got e-mail says you was with him.'

'Layback? I don't even *know* him.'

'Snowcone got a digital pitcher,' said KrayZglu. She held out her hand and the girl who had disarmed Keri put the photo in it. Suk Hee peered at it. It showed Suk Hee giving some admittedly very well-endowed chunk of boyness a blow job. Suk Hee sniffed.

'That's an obvious fake. You can do that on PhotoOp5.' She turned to the salesgirl, who had been getting Suk Hee's bonus gift and now proferred it across the counter.

'Sisterhood,' Keri was saying, 'is the point. We're carrying to be strong, not to shoot other girlz. Especially over men. Please.'

She was a few degrees too white and condescending. KrayZglu said, 'O, yeah is that right Previous?'

The Latina touched her shoulder and whispered something in her ear.

'Awright, Larissa,' she said. 'I can be reasonable.' Turning to Suk Hee, she added, 'So you say you don't

37

even know Layback. I guess I should take your word of honour.'

Larissa now picked up Suk Hee's lipstick from where it rested on the glass case.

'Um . . . that's mine,' Suk Hee said in a small voice.

'I think I'm go keep it,' said the other girl.

'Go on, Larissa, you keep that pumpkin,' chorused the others. 10 was looking over her left shoulder. I followed her gaze to a security camera. She caught my look and smiled.

Suk Hee said, 'Ah . . . it's the last one and it's nice isn't it, but I really need it and besides I already paid.'

'That's good cos I don't wa' spend my money on this junk.'

'You could have my bonus gift.' She offered the tub of Perpetua anti-wrinkle eye cream. Larissa's lip curled.

'How about Beaujolais Nights?' suggested SH. 'It would go better with your outfit.'

I could see that they were all totally baffled by Suk Hee. They couldn't figure out whether she was for real or not. So I didn't interfere. I wish I had. Larissa reached out and fingered the wolf button that SH had on her backpack.

'That one ugly dog,' she said, winking at 10's video camera.

'It's not a dog!' Suk Hee screamed. 'So bite my dick, okay?'

Her gun came out fast and everybody scattered.

'That some seriously disturbed pussy,' said KrayZglu to Keri. 'I don't think any of y'all want to live.'

'Put the gun down, Suk Hee,' Keri shrieked. 'We'll get in *trouble*.'

I think we already are in trouble. In fact, looking at those seven sets of Bugaboo eyes, I am remembering the stories about the number of Bugaboos in cemeteries and pens. Last summer the rapper Charisse Shark used a Bugaboo funeral chant in one of her joints, you know, what they sing when they're burying one of their members; the track went to number eight on the Pepsi chart.

I try to calculate how much cred my firing-range experience gives me and make it to be about a molecule. Ah, what the fuck? Gotta do something.

I make a decision. A woman screamed and two pseudolabcoated male-model types started toward Suk Hee. They froze when they saw me. My trusty piece had migrated into my hand.

'Get out of here, Suk Hee!' I cry. 'Run for it. Just run!'

It's a line from about fifty different movies, and it pops into my mouth like a reflex. I feel hot. I keep the male models in my peripheral vision, but my sights are on KrayZglu. Now that it's really happening, it's just like I knew it would be. I move fast and without thinking. I find myself standing on the counter top, legs spread, thighs flexed, with the gun in both hands held out straight in front of me. I can feel the air rushing up under my skirt and tickling as it meets the residual moisture from this morning's fun. I can feel the tension in my deltoids and the back of my neck. I have an unarmed probably-gay retail-therapy prettyboy in my sights.

Hitler was a woman.

It's funny the things you think when you're on the verge of getting arrested or shooting somebody. I hear myself shouting.

'Now get the fuck out of here, KrayZglu!'

KrayZglu and Co scatter, ducking expertly for cover. Suk Hee isn't moving so I decide to draw attention away from her, to buy her time to collect herself because I know that wolf remark really hurt her. I start to run across the counter tops, kicking aside bottles and displays, hoping my legs look good from below, deeply grateful that I don't have varicose veins like Keri. Security guards are popping up everywhere and everyone's shouting. I skidded to a halt and ducked around the back of one of the islands: Clinique.

DROP YOUR WEAPONS, the guards are saying. And other stuff like PUT YOUR HANDS UP and all the usual. Suk Hee doesn't seem to hear them. I waver. I'm not dropping my weapon. No way. That's my *gun* you're talking about.

Suk Hee is gazing up at a whole wall of cleansers and skincare. As two security guards came barrelling towards her she cried out in a five-year-old's voice.

'It's so pretty!'

She tossed her bonus gift up in the air and shot it. Then she kept shooting, taking out pyramids and columns of fragrance and colour. Estée Lauder, Nina Ricci, Lancôme, Gucci, Calvin Klein, Clinique, Chanel, Ralph Lauren . . . a crystalline gazz of the highest order for Suk Hee.

I realised then that a gun is not an extension of the hand.

It's an extension of the eye.

I-MAGE IS
EVERYTHING

MADELEINE BALDINO'S HAIR looks like a team of racoons have been playing field hockey in it. And it isn't on purpose. She looks at her half-reflection in the habitat plexi, and while her subject sits hunched and shivering on his bed, passing reward stones from one hand to another with classic Y-autistic repetitive patterning, Maddie focuses on her frizzy dark hair and how shitty it looks under the MUSE headset. Her hair is the safest thing to think about. The rest of her mind is frozen – maybe in disbelief, maybe in denial, or maybe even in relief – because her subject is succumbing to the bugs too soon, and it isn't what she planned.

'I tried to get you,' Naomi keeps saying. 'I couldn't get through.' Implicit in the remarks is the question,

Where were you? – but Naomi wouldn't ask that in front of Jennifer Gould because that would be, to use one of her favourite expressions, 'unplugged' – and Naomi was nothing if not plugged in. Maddie's assistant had skin the colour of wet sand, chemically straightened pink-champagne hair that she wore in a long braid, and a tuft of fuzzy spikes where her bangs would otherwise be. Today she wore kung fu pants and a little golden corset that gave her cleavage you couldn't take your eyes off. She had long gym-sculpted arms enhanced by body art, and she moved like a Pilates manual. Maddie suspected that at least some of the body art was camouflage for the skin drugs Naomi took, but since the Hibridge mandatory substance tests always came up negative, Maddie had to assume that whatever Naomi was using was new enough not to be illegal – or even detectable.

'I can't understand how this step could have been taken without my approval,' Maddie said. She was shaking all over, she could see it in the plexiglass. She wanted to scream and throw things, but that wasn't her style. 'If he dies . . .' She let the sentence trail off unfinished. She wanted to say that it would be Jennifer's fault, but again, that would be too direct. And she's stunned into silence by Jennifer's attitude. Because the curator hasn't uttered a word of apology since Maddie arrived on the scene to find that Jennifer and Naomi had pulled the plug on Meniscus's game and all that it implied, thereby ruining the data and possibly also giving the bugs a foothold in his system that was beyond his ability to tolerate. Jennifer seems to feel that she's done the right thing – after all, it's what she does best – and now, far from being upset about the situation, Jennifer almost seems to be enjoying herself. Which is very strange because, of all the bureaucrats Maddie has

42

known (and in her years at Hibridge she has known many) Jennifer is categorically the most tight-assed. Especially about protocols and procedures. Yet she's broken with protocol and interfered with Maddie's experiment, and she's so damned relaxed about it that if Maddie didn't know better, she might suspect the curator of sampling some of Naomi's skinwares.

'*If* he dies?' Maddie heard Naomi mutter. 'More like *when*.'

Jennifer was middle-aged and skinny, always well-dressed and well groomed, but she had a mouthful of rotting brown teeth that gave her projectile halitosis – she could take a horse down from a distance of fifteen feet – and sometimes Maddie felt she would rather let Jennifer have the last word than risk passing out from the stench of having an argument with her. Or that was how she justified to herself the fact that she could never bring herself to openly challenge Jennifer. Now the curator folded her thin arms across her chest. 'Come on, Maddie, what was I supposed to do? He was in terrible pain – he still is. Your instructions expressly forbade introducing tranks.'

'Damn straight,' replied Maddie, startled into bluntness at the very thought. 'Ruin the delicate balance of his brain chemistry.'

'Right, well, Naomi said that he started drawing more processing power at the same time that the infection kicked up to a higher level.'

'Yeah, but that doesn't mean one caused the other. He's got a new strain of bug in there, he's only had it a few days and I'm not even sure what it does yet. Now you've broken the I-MAGE continuity, you've taken him out of the driver's seat—'

'It was only temporary! And he was feeling a lot less pain.'

'Not as little as he'll feel when he's dead, which he will be if the 10E get too strong.'

'But wasn't that only a matter of time?' Jennifer suggested gently. 'Every assassin-bug study reaches the point where the bugs . . . assassinate.'

This was so patronising that Maddie ignored it, calling up her MUSE instead and checking out the I-MAGE visual results. Meniscus's immune system was a mess. It had been conditioned to look the other way at the incursion of Az79, but now his tissues were inflamed and his nervous system on red alert. He was no longer passive in the face of invasion. He was fighting the bugs.

Jennifer said, 'You can't let him go on like this, Maddie. He's in agony. What about our customers? They're going to ask questions. He's a popular exhibit; people come off the Dendrite Drop and want to check him out. I've got to think about PR control. How about some nitrous oxide?'

'Not one molecule of any drug, Jennifer – shit, not even lemonade until I figure out what's happening here. What's the situation with the video records?' She wanted the videos so she could document the fuck-up, but she didn't want to say as much.

'Video records?' Jennifer said, as if she didn't understand.

'Yeah, I want to see what happened for myself.'

'I'll see if I can pull them up,' Naomi said.

Jennifer looked at her watch. No one looked at Meniscus, now rolling on the floor and making terrible mewling sounds. A patch of blue covered his nose and part of his mouth so that he looked like a skewbald horse. Only his tongue was still pink – red, in fact, where he had bitten it. The I-MAGE was doing a constant scan of the biofactions in his tissues but nobody had had time to analyse the results. Except for the undersea glow of the I-MAGE, there wasn't much light in the Habitat. Naomi had run outside and dragged a tarpaulin from a nearby renovation site to cover the public window on the Meniscus exhibition. Now she made mute signs to Maddie that it would be better to shut up; but Maddie wasn't paying attention.

'You know, Jennifer,' Maddie finally managed to say, while Naomi was occupied at the system console, 'I feel a little uncomfortable with the way this is unfolding.'

'Uncomfortable? With me?' Jennifer had adopted her best Avon-lady voice. Maddie tried her best not to recoil from her breath. 'But I was only trying to help. Naomi couldn't reach you.'

'But that doesn't make sense, I was only window-shopping at—' Never mind, she'd been at Babyshop.org but Jennifer needn't know that. 'What kind of flag did you send me?'

'It wasn't just a flag, I sent an urgent breaker message—' Naomi began.

Jennifer cut in. 'Naomi was beside herself. Like I said, the subject was in agony. We had no way of knowing that taking him out of Mall would make him worse.'

Naomi didn't meet Maddie's gaze. 'Nobody ever warned me that this could happen.'

'That's because I didn't *know* it could happen,' Maddie said through clenched teeth. She was at least as angry at herself as at Naomi and Jennifer.

'There, you see? Nobody meant any harm.'

'But why was he in crisis in the first place? Until this morning he was perfectly stable except for a little extra activity in his spine, and he's *never* gone like this before because I take pains to make sure he isn't over-stimulated. He might seem stoical and unresponsive, but – Doctor Gould – I shouldn't have to tell you that in

45

their own way, Y-autistics are emotionally delicate, and Mall makes him even more impressionable.' Maddie threw in Jennifer's academic title in hope of shaming the Curator into admitting she'd been stupid; then she remembered Jennifer's doctorate was in something like Organisational Administration. Maddie changed tack. 'There must have been *something* that set him off. Some kind of external stimulus. What was it, another tour group from LA? Anti-science activists spitting on the glass? What got him started?'

Naomi cleared her throat and piled the toes of her right foot over the toes of her left foot, staring down at them like a naughty child.

'What, Naomi?'

'Dr Baldino, could I talk to you in private?'

Maddie was getting hot under the collar so she said impatiently, 'Whatever you have to say, Naomi, you'd better just say it now.'

Naomi looked pained. 'Like, Dr Baldino, I don't know how it happened. I was doing my prostrations, like I do every morning during break. I turned my back for maybe two minutes while the Piscataway Fourth Grade tour was going on. Like two minutes, OK?'

Maddie took a deep breath. She knew she could check Naomi's story on the video records. 'Go on.'

'And when I come back, the school group is gone and . . . and . . .'

Naomi looked around the lab frantically, as if by finding the right object to fix her gaze upon she could escape the admission that she was about to make. Meniscus let out a squeal and Naomi flinched.

'And what, Naomi?'

'And Bonus was standing there talking to Meniscus.'

Maddie went still. That didn't make sense; but Naomi met her gaze as she said it, and there could be no doubt that it was true. Jennifer's mouth twitched in what Maddie took for a suppressed smile. *Goddamit*.

'Bonus?' she said faintly. 'As in, *my* daughter?'

'Yeah, Bonus. She was hanging around and he was . . . I don't know how to describe it. He was acting really weird.'

'Weird?' snapped Maddie. 'Weird how?'

'Well . . . for one thing he was talking back to her.'

Maddie started to laugh. This was too unreal. While she stood there, speechless and on the verge of hysteria, Jennifer turned to Naomi and made a jerking movement with her head. Naomi left. Jennifer went to the security controls and turned off the video recorders that monitored the lab. Maddie was still laughing and shaking her head in disbelief and contemplating suicide when Jennifer grabbed her arm and blasted her with foul breath. Her words were uncharacteristically direct.

'Why don't we keep the situation simple, Maddie? I mean, you don't want your subject to be out of control like this. I don't want the park compromised. And if it *is* compromised, then I'll have no choice but to launch an investigation. You don't want Bonus caught up in an inquiry, do you?'

Maddie said nothing. The thing had gone ballistic. She could accept the fact that somehow Jennifer had gazumped her: unless she cooperated with Jennifer, Meniscus would be kicked out of the park and Maddie would find herself teaching at a Midwestern technical college. But what really rankled was the way Jennifer pretended to be sympathetic.

'Maddie. Come on. Look at him. This is turning into an ethical violation by anybody's standards.'

'If you're suggesting we sacrifice, forget it. I'll get the pain under control, all right, but I have to find a way to do it through the I-MAGE. Drugs don't behave normally in his system.'

Even as she spoke, Meniscus let out more screams. He had ripped the bedding off his mattress and broken a built-in light fixture with his head. Maddie looked at the I-MAGE read-out and saw that she had a catch-22. Meniscus remained vividly conscious. Despite the fact that Mall was set to subliminal now, he was drawing unprecedented amounts of processing power to the game. But if she took him out of Mall, the bugs would surely have their way with him – they had multiplied rapidly during the brief period when Jennifer had removed him from the game.

'Never mind the bugs, I think you'd better get the drugs going *now*,' said Jennifer in something closer to her usual officious tone. 'Otherwise I'll have no choice but to step in. I can't turn a blind eye to this.'

Maddie looked around the lab. Millions of Hibridge investment dollars and years of Maddie's life had gone into this study. Her whole career depended on it. She was so close to achieving her objectives with Meniscus, and now everything was coming down like a landslide, and she didn't know why. If she left Meniscus alone to cope with the pain, the infection might slow down, but he'd destroy himself. But if she pumped analgesics into him, who knew how the bugs might react?

From around the corner of the I-MAGE, a white mouse poked its head, squeaked once, and then shot away again into the shadows.

'All right,' Maddie said at last. 'I'll medicate him. I'll put him in a coma if I have to, OK? Shit, it's not like I'm inhumane. I just want to know what's happening.'

Jennifer favoured her with a brown smile. 'I know. It's hard to let go. Look, this isn't the time to go into it, but once you've got your subject stabilised, come up to my

48

office, all right'? There's something I need to talk to you about.'

Maddie must have looked aggrieved, because Jennifer smiled again.

'I know you'll find it hard to believe, but what I have to say just might cheer you up.'

Glowering, Maddie seated herself in front of the I-MAGE. She was close to tears. She said:

'You guys want to cheer me up? Get the goddam exterminator in here pronto. I don't want to see that fucking mouse again.'

EXTRA SPOOKY
WITH SAUCE

LIPSTICKED WHITE-SMOCKED *parfumeuses* dived for cover. Shoppers in their jeans and loafers crouched down.

Everybody who had a gun started to shoot it. Just like wolves howling to synchronise the mood, I thought – only I nearly got hit in the first five seconds, which was not very funny. I saw the 'Boo who had fired on me and without even thinking about it I shot her in the leg. It was weird, how connected I felt to that bullet. Like that bullet was me, piercing the Bugaboo's muscle and bumping hard into her femur. I leaped off the counter and got down on my belly. There was more screaming and shooting, and glass breaking, and larger crashes of various kinds. It wasn't as loud as it is in the movies because there were no digitally enhanced sound effects and there was no music track. I could smell the cordite. Keri was calling my name but I didn't answer. I was panting. I kept crawling, trying to remember which way to Accessories. I cut my knees on broken glass. I could still hear men bellowing for us to put down our guns and all that, and there were footsteps all around, but for some reason there was nobody in my immediate vicinity.

I didn't know whether or not to feel left out.

I'd reached the edge of the Estée Lauder island and I could see the Origins island across the aisle. The Origins counter must have been custom-built because its formica sides came up higher than the others' and the glass display cases were closer to eye level. It had a raised platform inside where the salesgirls stood lording it over everybody else; I remembered this because I'm short enough to begin with, you know? And also I don't really get the beauty appeal of looking up the inside of people's nostrils. Anyway, Origins looked like shelter to me now, and I started looking up and down the aisle to see whether I could get there from here without being shot. I was just about to make my dive to safety when Keri came backing into the aisle between Estée Lauder and Calvin Klein.

She's moving much slower than I've ever seen her move, holding the gun out in front of her like a pair of smelly gym socks someone's handed her but she doesn't want to touch them.

'Go on!' she croaks in a sort of whisper-shriek. I can't see who she's talking to. She waves the gun vaguely in a spastic, I-don't-know-how-to-use-this way, and I want to groan. 'Go on, *go on*, get out you stupid bitch!' she cries again, and then a whole family goes by, mother and three little kids, one in a stroller, all of them in a bright huddle of purple and orange fleeces and hiking boots. What they

51

were doing in Lord & Taylor cosmetics is beyond me, and I giggled inadvertently at the notion that Keri was probably kicking them out on fashion principles, and Keri looked towards me.

Her stare fixes on me and then beyond me. Suddenly she grips the gun firmly in both hands and she's looking down the barrel. Keri has this weird look of concentration on her face, one eye all screwed up and her head tilted so that her right earring splays against her neck like a spinnaker in a calm, and the left is suspended into free space, swinging ever-so-slightly counter-clockwise over her left shoulder, which is dropped so that her left hand can support her firing wrist and steady the shot. Little stray frizzy hairs that have come out of her French braid are interfering with the geometry of the earring and acting as tell-tale wind signals. Her mascara still looks OK but her blusher is clashing with the real tone of the blood that's rising towards the surface of her skin. Her real blood is less bronze, more piggy-pink. She has a lavender-and-yellow friendship bracelet on her left wrist and a Tommy Hilfiger watch on her right. Anyone who can see style can see Keri.

Don't get me wrong. She doesn't look cool. She doesn't look indifferent or ironic or above it all. She's pigeon-toed and terrified. Her face is all squidgy and damp and her left leg is twitching and quivering rhythmically. I'm thinking we could have a new attitude here, like the heroin look in the late seventies, we could have the adrenalin look. Nobody buys clothes to be happy in them, anyway. Nobody under twenty, I mean. I start picturing a whole photo shoot, Keri as a Tommy Hilfiger girl, with her big sweatshirt and her accessories and her gun, standing just like this, about to pee herself, and the flash coming out the barrel while behind her all the shattered perfume bottles look sort of magical because you can't tell by looking how raucous it all smells . . . it could work.

Her bullets pass over my head. I hear four shots but only three of them come from Keri's gun. By the time I get the concept to turn my head and look where she's shooting, the security guard is on his way down.

I remember one time my mom and I and Suk Hee were driving back from Tower Records and we took a back road because she doesn't like driving on Route 17, and it was a summer night and my mom's headlights suddenly hit these animals in the middle of the road and she slammed on the brakes just in time. There were two racoons in the road, a mother and a baby. The mother had been hit and the baby was there nuzzling it and sniffing and making these high-pitched calling noises. My mom pulled over and we got out. The mother racoon was in the middle of the road, and its head was totally smashed and crushed but its body was making these arching movements like I usually make with a really good come, and the baby had scurried away, but we could see it in the bushes, and there were two more little ones beside it.

We stood there for a second, my mom squinting and going, 'Ssss' and shit while the mother racoon went through her long-drawn-out Hollywood Old West death throes. Suk Hee hurried over to the nearest house, which was set very close to the road. I followed, hoping she wasn't going to cry too much because SH is very sensitive.

'What you doing?' my mother cried.

'It's OK, Suk Hee,' I called. 'Come on back to the car.'

Suk Hee was already knocking on the door. Mom came rushing up after us.

'I'm going to ask them for a shovel,' Suk Hee said.

'You kill it? Ah, that horrible! Stay away! It dying anyway.'

53

I was struggling to formulate the concept of Suk Hee bludgeoning a racoon to death. She said, 'I'm going to move it off the road. Otherwise the babies are going to get killed, too.'

Suk Hee rang the bell and knocked again. A white girl a few years older than us answered. Suk Hee explained the situation and asked for a shovel, my mother blinking and standing with her legs clenched together in the background, like she was about to wet herself. The girl went inside and meanwhile several cars went by, braking when they saw my mother's hazard lights and then continuing on around the carnage. The baby racoons kept going out into the road and then retreating.

'They think I hit it,' my mother kept saying as the cars passed, their occupants peering accusingly at us. She hid her face, on the verge of tears. 'Sun, come! We leave now. Sun, they think I drive over—'

'Fuck them,' I muttered. The girl came back, looking embarrassed.

'My father says we can't give you a shovel because if it bites you or something happens, we could get sued.'

'Bite me?' Suk Hee said. 'It has no head! Its skull has been crushed. How can it bite me?'

The girl looked horrified and said, 'I'm really sorry.'

She closed the door in our faces. By now the mother racoon was still. My mother came and grabbed us with her wicked strong little hands and dragged us to the car. Suk Hee broke away and dashed towards the baby racoons in the bushes. She was saying something to them but I couldn't hear because cars had pulled up and started hitting their horns and shit. My mother was hiding behind the driver's seat.

Suk Hee came running back and jumped in the car.

'I hope those little guys have the sense to listen to me,' she said. My mother stepped on the gas and peeled away,

54

testing the 0–60 on her Nissan Camry. Suk Hee kept looking back. In the moonroof I saw Orion.

But the thing I don't get is the death-throes part. The racoon was lying there with essentially no brain, and it looked like it was having a big orgasm which made the whole thing extra spooky, with sauce.

But now, in the confusion of the maul, when the security guard went down he just dropped, without a twitch or a sound, and the blood was really dark and slow as it came out of his body, and there was also somewhat of a smell of shit. I think he was dead.

I looked for Keri to see her reaction to the fact that she just killed a guy, but she had disappeared again. I was just beginning my rapid crawl toward the safety of Origins when I glimpsed something beyond the fallen security guard. I squinted and recognised the neon stripe of Suk Hee's book bag lying in a dark splotch of bloodspill I couldn't really handle the input. I changed direction to go toward the book bag and climbed over the guard's body, getting tangled in the legs slightly.

There was Suk Hee's book bag, but there was no Suk Hee. I crouched there, clutching my chest and breathing really hard, wondering if I was going to have a heart attack. My whole body was tingling and everything was so sharp and clear and slow.

The shooting had stopped. There was a blood trail leading from the book bag. 'Suk Hee,' I whispered. 'Suk Hee?'

Oh my god. I don't like this. I made myself slither through the blood, unheeding of the fact that my hindquarters were poking out from under my skirt and that if I got shot it would be an ignominious ass-shooting probably. There had been multiple bullet impacts into a corner in the glass casing, which housed a bunch of Christian Dior. A bullet had passed through the glass and lodged in the plywood beyond. One bottle of cellulite cream had been damaged and was leaking. There was quite a bit of blood on the floor. I looked at all this but I still didn't know if Suk Hee was OK or not. The strange silence continued. I knew that everyone else couldn't be dead, but they weren't talking and this made me feel nervous, as if they had a plan and I didn't know what it was and I was about to get caught. I reloaded the gun.

My phone vibrated.

I had no intention of answering it; all I could think was thank God it wasn't set to ring. Then I realised it could be Suk Hee, and I grabbed it and checked the display to see who was calling me.

ALEX

The phone vibrated in my hand, my hand shook, my mouth was dry, my armpits were cold and stinking.

'Hello?' I whispered.

'Hey,' he said.

'Where are you?'

'The Sharper Image. You're never going to believe this.'

Oh my god. Now what do I do.

'I can't talk right now,' I whispered. 'Can I call you back?'

My heart was doing backflips. In between syllables of Alex's words I scanned the mirrors, the displays, my nostrils trembling. My legs were shaking like a lotto machine.

'Aw, c'mon Sun, get this, I'm in the middle of a *shoot-out*!'

'Really?' I hear myself say. 'That sounds pretty fucked-up.'

'It is, it's totally fucked up, I can't go anywhere, we're like trapped in here—'

I have to take the phone away from my ear because I can hear something moving behind the Origins counter. Panting, I go racing over there, only to see the breeze stirring some plastic bags. Numbly I put the phone back to my ear. Alex is rattling away. '—Stuck here with nothing to do, and I called Kristi but her line was busy and anyway, well, you know. She probably just wants to talk about clothes or something anyway.'

Typical. Complain to me about his girlfriend being too girlie. Never noticing I have a cunt too.

'I see.' My good pal Alex apparently didn't catch the grim note in my voice. He sounded very fucking cheerful. I wonder if that's why I like him so much. How could anyone be so cheerful when the world is so fucked? 'Alex, can I call you later?'

'So what's up with you, you sound like kind of funny.'

I pressed the kill button with my thumb. Doing that was pretty exciting. Normally I'd rather die than stop talking to Alex. Here I am, with something *more important than Alex* going on. Maybe this will impress him. Maybe he'll see me getting arrested on the news and will think that's sexy enough.

Suk Hee says boyz don't work that way. She says it doesn't matter what we do or say. She says it's only looks. I guess she would know but it's easy for her. She's beautiful. I gotta find another way. I'm just not attracted to geeky types. I need somebody hot, with muscles, so drastic measures might be called for. And I don't mean a wonderbra, although it probably couldn't hurt.

I had to put the gun down for a second to switch off my phone, but I grabbed it again when once more I heard a tiny noise from around the side of the Origins island. Another plastic bag, I thought, going to check it out.

I was almost quick enough. 10Esha and I pointed our guns at each other at the same time. Except her other

57

hand was holding the Sony, and she was already shooting me with it. She was on her elbows and knees and I jealously noted her generous cleavage.

'Freeze,' she said. She was smiling.

JUST LIE BACK AND THINK OF VEGETABLES

(MB/Lab notes/comments)

Subject has been stabilised in Delta. However, the AZ79-10E infection is persisting, with no signs yet of the subject's immune system mustering an effective response. Even if the immune system does defeat AZ79-10E, the balance between host and bug has been destabilised.

Therefore the effectiveness of this subject is almost certainly at an end. I was sure that we were close to achieving a homeostasis with the AZ79 that would have allowed for continuous live harvesting of rare biochemicals with a minimum of distress for the subject. We have indeed made substantial progress in the use of assassin bugs to command neurochemical response, but I didn't foresee the present setback.

There appears to be considerable diversity in the 10-series offspring, and I will harvest a series of samples, collecting as many live strains as possible. Sacrifice will be postponed for as long as humanely possible in order to achieve some clarification as to what went wrong.

Lab video evidence shows the subject engaging in unprecedented verbal communication behaviour immediately prior to the crisis. This is a curious point considering that my predecessor, Bernard Taktarov, once used this subject in his unfinished work on a cure for Y-autism. I am going to bring him in on this – if I can find him. So far he has made no response to my e-mails, but I 'm hoping this is just Bernie being eccentric.

Maddie slapped an endorphin patch on her arm and closed her eyes, leaning back in her chair. She could feel the static electricity coming off the housing of the I-MAGE. She could smell the panicked sweat where it had dried in her armpits. Outside the habitat, most of the lab equipment was hooded for the night, dust-protected and moisture-shielded. The observation area was stuffy, redolent of the Tibetan incense that Naomi habitually burned. Only in the soft curves of the I-MAGE unit was anything apparently at work: there the NoSystems liveware performed its incessant coupling with Maddie's subject on a cellular level, sending shivering spurts of data into the I-MAGE. Everything about Meniscus – every *detectable* thing, Maddie corrected herself – was being read off him and recorded. The footprints of his thought tracked across the receiving centres of the MUSE in the form of intimate physiological truths that would play their own tuneless chorus in Maddie's MUSE when she distilled them, tomorrow.

Six hours of wrestling with the data collected by the I-MAGE's lights as they played across Meniscus's tortured skin had left her chasing her own tail. She knew that Meniscus's crisis had begun at 11:58, and a simple cross-reference to the lab's video records at that time showed Meniscus examining the wolf's tooth that Bonus had given him. Mall usage also shot up at that time, as Meniscus's subconscious demanded more processing power.

But why?

And what about Mall? How did it fit in? She had never paid that much attention to the game: Taktarov had sworn by its therapeutic value in keeping the subject alive under stress, but Maddie had never understood why it worked for Meniscus. She recalled the NoSystems promotional material for the game.

NoSystems Mall is the first VR system to permit the direct expression of unconscious material in a tangible form that is essentially invented by the game-user. Popular because it recreates the halcyon days of turn-of-the-mill consumerism and sexual freedom pre Y-plagues, the Mall series has been used to successfully integrate multiple personality patients; it has been employed in therapy for post-traumatic stress disorder, post-partum depression, stress-related infertility, eating disorders . . . and, most dramatically, Mall has worked to confront and dismantle hard physical addictions including heroin, cocaine, alcohol, c-based hallucinogens, nicotine, and virus-delivered intoxicants. In the case of substance abuse, Mall was instrumental in the relearning process that is critical to recovery. In the case of viral infiltrations, NoSystems Mall7 was effective due to its unique ability to render both psychological complexes and chemical influences as virtual personalities, enabling the subject to literally confront his demons.

This stuff had all sounded lyrically proactive, ground-breaking – very California in its approach – and nine years ago when she'd accepted Bernie Taktarov's terms, Maddie had wanted to believe in the possibilities of Mall. But the studies that NoSystems was so proud of all involved close work between therapist and patient *outside* the game scenario. The patient's accounts of what she was experiencing in the game could then be critically processed with the therapist, who was able to provide insight and guidance to her patient.

But Meniscus was Y-autistic. He didn't talk. He also refused to paint, play music, engage in expressive movement, perform therapeutic doll games, or keyboard. And as for the stones: who could make head or tail of what they meant to him?

No one knew what he was thinking. Meniscus's private version of Mall was opaque to everyone but him.

Today he had spoken to Bonus. And now, as he approached death, he was using an enormous amount of Mall processing power – but for what?

Maddie stood up. The endorphins had started kicking in, and her headache was fading. But her mind was racing in wild ellipses. She looked around the lab helplessly.

Naomi was sitting on a lab desk in the lotus position, subvocalising a mantra and gazing upwards. Meniscus's habitat was a shambles: cushions were strewn everywhere and his stuffed animals lay scattered on the floor among the stones he collected. Ollie Oliphaunt® was standing on his trunk. The subject himself lay prone on his bed, bathed in the I-MAGE lights. Even from here, Maddie could see that the new Az79 colony had begun to send tendrils up his shoulders and around towards his left kidney.

Naomi stirred, and without looking at her Maddie said, 'He's going to die. As sure as if we shot him in the head. It's only a matter of time. Keep the I-MAGE running continually – fuck the costs, I don't care – so that we can at least collect information right up until the very end. And prepare containment units for the samples.'

Maddie turned away from the I-MAGE and the evidence of its read-outs. She hated the brutal finality of her own words. She had to say them, get the truth out in the open, force herself to face it – but that didn't make it hurt any less. She was losing her subject and she didn't know why.

And she couldn't even beat her head against the wall as she wanted to. Like a good scientist, she had to stand by and take notes.

'I looked at the video,' Naomi said softly. 'He definitely spoke to her. But I didn't have audio activated, and the camera angle doesn't show what she said.'

'I know. I asked her what she said. Just something about this wolf in the Meadowlands. She's obsessed with it.'

'So you don't think she created some kind of impression on him?'

'I'm sure that she did – but so did the Piscataway girls, for that matter. So does everyone he sees. So do the bugs, so does the game he plays. I can't winnow out a single cause from all of those things, and I can't link any of them to that kind of bug reaction.'

Naomi gave her a half-smile.

'I know what you're thinking,' Maddie said.

'What am I thinking?'

'That because she's my kid I don't want to involve her.'

Naomi shrugged.

'And that's true enough. But it also happens that she's not relevant. It has to be something brewing with those 10Es we planted.'

'Are you going home, then?'

'Not yet. I'm taking a walk, though. Maybe I can get some sense out of this.'

Maddie activated her MUSE and logged on to the lab mainframe so that she could take her work with her; then she stepped out into the darkened Fun Park, lifting her hair off her sweaty neck to pick up the breeze.

She felt a strange sense of relief; but she had to rationalise furiously to justify it. She told herself that she had never wanted this project in the first place. Meniscus had been a remnant of Bernie Taktarov's unfinished work on Y-autism, to which, on her arrival, Maddie had been expected to graft her own experiments – a necessity born of the scarcity of male research clones. For many researchers, the Meniscus assignment would have been a plum. But Maddie was a bug designer: she had never worked with a live subject before; she had neither knowledge of nor interest in Y-autism; and as for working in the Educational Fun Park – talk about Oxymoron City! – well, that too had been a necessary evil. Or so she had thought at the time.

Not that Maddie could be sure why she did anything any more, having lost the magnetic north of herself while beating back the offers of several defence interests and one food multinational when her dissertation had been published nine years ago. Her work, 'Some Dermato-Specific Techniques in Product-Driven Colonisation of the Human Male Somatic Tissue by Harvestable Assassin Bugs', possessed a higher market value than she'd ever expected. Each offer had topped the next until Peach Tree Baby Foods, a subsidiary of Hibridge Global, offered her Silver-level executive status with all the privileges that implied, including self-cloning and, ultimately, eligibility for designer sperm if her project came good in the end. That was how she'd found herself here in the unlikely setting of the Hibridge Educational Fun Park, which was the only private site in New Jersey licensed for human male wetwork thanks to some loophole in the zoning laws from twenty years back.

Maddie hadn't been prepared for the stresses of working with a live subject, though. Maybe that was why she threw herself into the work with such self-immolating fervour, as if to say: you really want me to *do* this? Well, fuck you, I will, and then you'll see how it's *done* and we'll all be sorry.

Nine years of infecting Meniscus's tissues had rendered her cold. If she had ever really known that he was a person, she had long ago forgotten it. But for all that, she hadn't cut a good deal, because now her sold soul was ruined, and still her work had come to nothing. Her subject was dying, her design was incomplete, and her own clone daughter had interfered with the study . . . she shunted aside that last thought. It was not that she really believed Bonus's visit could have affected Meniscus; no, she was privately convinced that when she combed through all the bug data that the I-MAGE had collected, she would see that Bonus's presence had been coincidental to the crisis. Surely some unanticipated evolutionary leap on the part of the bugs had been the cause of today's incident. But this new evidence of her clone daughter's insubordination and independence was unwelcome.

Maddie passed the Cardio-coaster, temporarily closed for repairs, the Gut Zoom and the Dendrite Drop. She crossed the food court and made for the vast parking lot. She was beginning to feel ill, and the flow from the MUSE made her a little ataxic so that she kept reeling off to the left and then correcting herself. Her MUSE was tuned a few degrees above subliminal to allow Meniscus's tissue readings to feed into her senses on a

65

low level, like a TV turned on in the background. Just as Meniscus could be present to Mall without being consciously engaged in it, so could Maddie take in large amounts of data without attempting to analyse anything yet. She wanted to get a feel for the overall picture of what had been going on in Meniscus before, during and after the crisis point, and she didn't want her own conscious assumptions to prejudice her perceptions. This was where a MUSE could come in really handy.

The MUltiSEnsory wasn't simply a more intimate projection of the graphs and sims that you could do on a visual monitor, although the same data that came through a MUSE could also be processed in that linear way. A MUltiSEnsory was far more sophisticated, subtle, and therefore more chaotic. Yet, equally, the MUSE was not as subjective as a game like Mall, with its sense-tickling, dreamlike VR interpretations of cold data. The name, MUSE, might mean multisensory, but Maddie suspected that its makers had also chosen the name because of its allusion to music. A MUSE presentation of data came into the 'space' of your head like a piece of music. You could 'hear' different parts that seemed to have their own identity, like voices or instruments; but you could also hear the orchestrated whole. A MUSE sent data into your mind through sound, colour, shapes, motion, and sometimes smell, all at the same time.

Only the data seldom possessed the integrity or interest of music. To continue the analogy, MUSE data at its best came across about as aesthetically pleasing as the sound of a flock of sheep wandering amongst a drunken gamelan orchestra. Yet Maddie found there were times, in working with colonies of bugs, when you had a large amount of data to process and it was changing at such a rate that you couldn't hope to look at everything unless you took it in just like this, raw. And sometimes you could pick out a little piece of sense in all the chaos, and focus on that. And sometimes that little piece of sense was something you never expected, never would have thought to look for.

Sometimes.

But not tonight. Tonight, the MUSE gave away no secrets. It just made her nauseous.

She felt pregnant. The thought spasmed across her mind before she could stop it. She knew for a fact that she wasn't pregnant – ironically, when Meniscus had been having his crisis she had been window-shopping for pigs – because she hadn't been anywhere near live sperm, ever. Yet this was that same nagging, bottomless feeling she'd had when Bonus was an embryo. Seasick on dry land.

Now, Maddie supposed, even the option of securing designer sperm for her banked eggs would be out of the question. Everything she'd worked for was in ruins. How ironic it would be if her own clone ended up being the instrument by which she failed to achieve her life's ambition: Hibridge designer sperm, Pigwalk-selected, the elite of the elite. Ooh, but it was too painful to think about that consequence.

She made a mental note to stop at the liquor store and stock up on something nasty and 100-proof and habit-forming. Hey – if Bonus was going to act like a delinquent little shit, Maddie might as well give her a reason.

Her MUSE pinched her with a phone message; automatically, she started to dismiss the icon, and then remembered that she'd been too distracted by the MUSE to answer when Naomi had been desperately trying to get help with Meniscus. Maddie had never missed an urgent call before, no matter how deep she'd MUSEd. Now there was something else to feel miserable about!

Maybe if she'd answered Naomi on time, none of this would have happened. She picked up the call.

It was Jennifer.

'I see you've logged out of the lab. Remember what I said? Coming by my office?'

'I really need to look over this material, Jennifer. Whatever it is, can't it wait until morning?'

'No. It can't. I see your subject is hanging in there.'

'For now.'

'Good. Just come up here, all right?'

There were cheap prints of circus clowns on Jennifer's office walls, and a disused mountain-climbing machine was tucked in one corner. A whole wall was devoted to Hibridge service awards and certificates of official qualification for whatever it was that Jennifer did – which Maddie had never been able to figure out beyond the fact that Jennifer was always sending out memos about policy changes and employee picnics. There was a pyramid of Play-Doh tubs on Jennifer's desk: blatant advertising of the fact that Jennifer had not one but *two* daughters, both conceived with her partner Giselle in the heinously expensive female-female design process that Hibridge Diamond privileges provided for – no mere clones for Jennifer Gould. She smiled when she saw Maddie looking at the Play-Doh. Then she offered Maddie a Dunkin' Donuts bag containing several mini-muffins. Maddie was miserable, so she took two.

Jennifer said, 'You know they're gearing up for the Pigwalks down at Atlantis Castellation?'

'Who doesn't? The coverage is everywhere.' Maddie took a glum blueberry bite.

'Have you been following it?'

Chewing, Maddie shrugged. She stared at the Play-Doh containers. Until today, her study had been going

68

well. She had expected to make a killing from it, and therefore had hoped to be awarded some high-level sperm sometime in the next year or two, before her ovaries completely packed it in and she had to resort to her egg bank. Of course she was aware of the candidates. But for Jennifer to mention it now, when Maddie's chances of ever fulfilling her ambition to be the mother of a designer baby looked to be destroyed – well, that was just cruel.

'Have you heard of Arnie Henshaw?' Jennifer was watching her.

Maddie snorted. 'Of course.' Henshaw was one of the hot-list candidates, heavily tipped to Pigwalk. He was as yet unproven, but that didn't stop otherwise sober Hibridge women from wetting their panties over him in advance.

'Arnie asked me to do him a favour, and I need your help.'

'*My* help? Is this a joke?' Maddie ate the chocolate muffin, too.

'Not at all. It concerns your subject, Meniscus. You see, Arnie's manager wants to ship me an SE that Atlantis is having problems with.' Maddie was surprised by Jennifer's use of the crude term. 'SE', or *swinus erectus*, had originated in a fairly recent monologue from *The Tonight Show With Corinne Davis*; it was a joke label that had stuck. The socially correct euphemism for a castellation male was 'aspirant pig', but maybe Jennifer was trying to get hip at this late stage. She certainly wasn't acting like her usual uptight self. 'Now . . . Maddie, what I'm going to say is totally confidential. I need you to promise that whatever you decide, you won't mention this conversation to anyone. Ever.'

Maddie sighed and wiped chocolate off her mouth. 'I don't know, Jennifer, I wish you wouldn't . . . it's been a shit day. I really don't want to get involved in anything slippery.'

'Don't worry, this is going to make you feel a whole lot better.'

Jennifer suddenly made a face as her phone pinched her. 'Excuse me – I forgot to tell my system to hold my calls.' She muttered something into her headset, then tugged it off her head, tousling her short, practical hair as she dropped the headset on the desk. Maddie had a sudden feeling of menace.

Jennifer leaned across her desk and put her palms on the plastic tops of the Play-Doh tubs. Maddie held her breath to avoid inhaling Jennifer's.

'I'm involved in an . . . exchange. An exchange of favours. I can get you designer sperm. I can get you Henshaw's sperm. I can get it *before* he hits it big – the first samples, no grafting involved, no middle-pig, straight from the dick – as they say. *And* I can put in a good word for you with Charlotte, save you from getting shipped off to Alaska or something now that your study is pretty much kaput.'

Maddie winced at the term 'kaput.'

'So? So how does that sound, Maddie? Well? Say something!'

Maddie noted the wild gleam in Jennifer's eye, and for the second time that day wondered what was up with the curator. Jennifer was usually so insipid. Maddie's curiosity was piqued.

'All right. All right, tell me, then, but I'm not actually agreeing to anything . . .'

Jennifer cocked her head expectantly.

'. . . And I promise not to disclose this conversation.'

'Good.' Jennifer sat back, folding her hands somewhat prissily on her blotter. 'Now, your part in the exchange of favours is very simple. There is going to be an accidental

70

breach of the airlocks between habitats, and all you have to do is not report it. Look the other way.'

'Airlocks? You can't be thinking of releasing the AZ79? They're not dangerous to women, but all the same I don't think I can collude in that kind of pollution.'

'It's nothing like that. All I need is for Henshaw's SE to get infected with your assassin bugs. Inadvertently, of course.'

Now Maddie laughed. 'You know we can't do that.'

But Jennifer just gave her a clueless look.

'Jennifer, I'm serious. Look what they've done to Meniscus – and *his* body has been trained to coexist with them. If you give the AZ79 to a natural male, the bugs will kill him right away.'

Jennifer picked up a can of Play-Doh and pinched off a clump. Her fingers worked at it rapidly.

'What you're suggesting is tantamount to murder,' Maddie added.

Jennifer handed Maddie a little yellow Play-Doh flower.

'I told you. It's an exchange of favours. These things happen to SEs all the time. It's unfortunate, but they happen.'

Maddie squashed the flower between her fingers and thumb. 'I feel like I'm in a Mafia movie. Jennifer, if I go along with you this so-called SE is going to be *dead* and it will be our fault. How are you going to cover that up?'

'I don't have to cover it up. No one cares. Look, obviously he's run afoul of the powers that be at Atlantis Castellation. It's not my problem, or yours. All we're doing is acting as agents. If we didn't do it, somebody else would. Grow up, Maddie. That's the world and you know it.'

Maddie just sat there, unable to erase the shocked expression from her face. She had never suspected

71

Jennifer of such ruthlessness. It was just too incongruous, as though in the middle of showing you the latest anti-blemish virus the Avon Lady had whipped out a howitzer and blown away half your living room.

'I can't understand you,' Maddie said at last. 'You've always played everything by the book.'

Jennifer chuckled. 'That's the reason you and I have never gotten along. Ironic, isn't it?'

Jennifer still had that brightness in her gaze; the revelation of this other side of the curator's personality reminded Maddie why she herself worked with bugs. It was because she didn't like people. Especially when they revealed themselves like this. She didn't want to know what made Jennifer hot and bothered. She didn't want to scratch Jennifer's back.

'I don't think I can go along with this, Jennifer. You'll have to . . . find some other way.'

Jennifer sighed and sat back in her reclining chair. 'That's too bad. But if that's the way you feel, so be it.'

Maddie stood up. Well, that had been too easy.

'I'd better go,' she said. 'I have a lot of material to work through tonight.'

'OK,' Jennifer said, turning away and reactivating her headset. She started to take a call, then excused herself again to the caller. 'Oh, Maddie?'

Maddie, halfway to the door, turned.

'Security will be up to your place in the morning to collect Bonus.'

Maddie's eyes narrowed. Jennifer turned her attention back to the caller as though what she had just said had no significance.

'Hi, sorry about that. Did you get my – wait – oh, forgive me, I've got another interruption, can I call you back in five minutes? Sorry.'

Maddie was standing over Jennifer's desk, barely

resisting the primitive urge to pick up the tubs of Play-Doh and pelt the curator with them.

'You *wouldn't* involve Bonus,' she hissed as soon as Jennifer had hung up.

'That's up to you. I have to put something in my incident report.' Jennifer tilted her head and favoured Maddie with an umber smile. 'I mean, we agreed I should play it by the book. Right?'

Maddie was dumb with rage. She could see no way out of Jennifer's trap.

'Just tell me one thing. Did you do something to my subject, so that I'd have no choice but to go along with you? Did you plan this?'

Jennifer looked shocked. 'I would never sabotage your study!'

'OK, OK, I was just asking.'

'Really, Maddie, after all these years we've worked together . . .'

And hated each other, Maddie thought.

'But what if I'd said no?' Maddie said. 'What if Bonus had never come down here, and today had never happened, and you approached me and I said no?'

'I'd tell you to go home and look at Arnie Henshaw's package. And eventually you would have come around.'

'It just seems like too much of a coincidence.'

'If you really want to know, I only just received this offer myself. This morning. I was considering how to approach you – and then this happened.'

Maddie wasn't inclined to believe in such a coincidence, but she did remember how oddly Jennifer had been acting. Maybe the headrush of Henshaw's offer had been the cause of her odd gaiety.

'You're saying it just fell in your lap.'

'I wouldn't put it quite that way. Your subject being on the skids means we have to move fast, Maddie. That's why I have to put you under a little bit of pressure. But – as you said – that's all down to your management of your clone child. If your subject wasn't in critical condition, there wouldn't be such a rush. But I can't hold up my end of the bargain with Arnie Henshaw if I have an empty habitat where Meniscus is now.'

'Because he's dying.'

'You said it, not me. Oh, go home, Maddie. You look exhausted. You don't have to do anything. I'll arrange for the airlock failure. All you have to do is keep quiet. How hard can that be?'

When Maddie was seventeen her girlfriend had tried to find her G-spot by fucking her from behind with a cucumber. She hadn't liked it then and she didn't like it now.

'Arnie Henshaw is a sure thing,' Jennifer said. 'You're going to be really happy at the outcome, and then you can forget all about today.'

In other words: just lie back and think of vegetables.

DESCARTES A.K.A. TERRY

1 OEsha HAD A NEAT little .22 in her left hand, which pressed against my temple so hard my eyeballs turned neon on the inside. She put the camera down and gripped my wrist, hard. Her fingers felt like little electric eels and I had no choice. I let go of my piece.

'You doofus amateurs,' she said, collecting my gun with her video hand. She shoved it in her bra and then continued filming. 'You really going to be the end of me.'

The first strains of 'I Will Always Love You' started coming in on synthetic violins. I had started to back up but now both camera and gun were directed at my face. It was very weird because even from a distance of three feet I could actually feel the metal extending out from the barrel and pinning my cheek. It was an indirect feeling, like you get through novocaine when the dentist is halfway down your throat asking you what sports you play at school but your favourite sport is drinking six espressos and playing in traffic, and your tongue is too numb to talk but you can still feel that metal penetrating, drilling the girders of your body with a kind of fine, high-pitched shiver – it was like that. Sort of. And I knew 10Esha really would shoot me, which was more than I could have said for myself – after seeing Keri off that guy I'm kind of freaked out and definitely having less fun than before.

I could hear someone female panting and sniffling and shuffling around somewhere behind 10Esha, who glanced over her shoulder at the noise. One of those females in a stewardess outfit who normally try to assault you with crap like Organza and Dune as soon as you walk in the store, she was crawling between the islands, bleeding from one leg. She hadn't had the presence of mind to go for waterproof mascara this morning, which when you think about it was an act of great optimism because even if she wasn't anticipating getting shot in the leg during the Saturday-morning Estée Lauder rush, what was to say her boyfriend wasn't going to break up with her or her boss yell at her or for that matter she could pass by *Schindler's List* or something playing on a TV in the window of Vinnie's Video Xtravaganza on her way to I Can't Believe It's Yogurt at break time and then where would she be? Like Rocky Racoon is what, mascara-wise. Speaking of racoons.

'Suk Hee? Suk Hee? Where you at pussy?'

Keri's voice. I made out that she was somewhere behind the Polo shaving kits about fifty feet away. At the sound of her voice the crawling girl paused, sniffled loudly, saw 10Esha and me. 10Esha hesitated. Stimuli were coming from several directions at once and I was glad I wasn't expected to handle them all: that was 10Esha's job now that she had the guns. Just to get the flava of not being responsible I looked 10Esha in the eye and defiantly flicked a piece of glass across the polished floor in Keri's direction, like in fourth grade when K.C. Jones used to look Mrs Diaz right in the eye and shoot spitballs at Angela Balboni. Like K.C. I smiled hugely after I did it. 10Esha didn't smile back but she also didn't shoot. Keri must have got my message because she shut up.

The crawlgirl was less subtle. She gave a self-contained shriek and started to scurry faster. I could see 10Esha for about .25 of a second trying to decide whether to go after her or stay with me, and at the same time something moved in a mirror behind 10Esha and without thinking about it I gasped. Crouching around the corner of the island between Shiseido and Aveda was an armed guard, black-haired, slightly overweight, sweating, hairy-armed. He was beckoning to crawlgirl, who began crying harder when she realised someone was trying to save her. I despised her then.

10Esha looked, still covering me with one gun. The guy must not have realised we could see him in the mirror. 10Esha's eyes flashed from one mirror to the other, calculating the angles rapidly, and she suddenly leaped up and darted around the Shiseido island. I saw her appear in the mirror and she said, 'Put the gun down and kick it away.'

She must have come up behind him. I couldn't see her but his reflection stood up. Crawlgirl stopped in her tracks and drew breath to scream.

He dropped the gun and kicked it away. 10Esha appeared in the mirror, the video camera hanging unused from her neck. She put the gun against the back of his head. She pointed my gun at the girl and made a shooing motion with it straight out of *Miami Vice*. Crawlgirl staggered to her feet and stumbled sideways into Small Leathers, and at the same moment Keri made a run for it.

I was disgusted with her, really. If I'd had a gun in my hand I probably would have shot her, that was the state I was in. What she did was she ran right in the path of 10Esha and the man, put her hands up, and inserted herself into 10Esha's custody. There are a lot of things about Keri that are really magnum, but her absurd fascination with authority isn't one of them. She actually thinks she can be inside it and outside it at the same time. She flirts with the basketball coach to avoid running laps in gym. She does all her homework but she does it sarcastically and gets As even when she's dissing the teachers behind their back. She's very good at it but it's dishonest, isn't it? (Or am I just jealous because of her GPA. But I could have her GPA if I wanted, really I could, I swear.) When in truth she never had to obey at all. I really can't stand this about her, I can't I can't I can't I can't.

10Esha didn't seem to have a problem with it. She never batted an eyelash at Keri's surrender.

'Walk,' she said.

The guy walked stiffly around the corner towards us, holding his hands up and rolling his eyes from side to side.

'Don't shoot,' he whispered. 'I'll cooperate.'

Bayonne, I thought. He's probably from somewhere like that. House with a pool but not an in-ground pool. One-car garage.

10Esha was holding the gun steady against the guard but the rest of her was shaking. I began to refer to him mentally as Descartes for reasons that are nothing to do with anybody but me. I nodded in the direction of the Clinique sales register.

'Let's go back there. It's safer.'

10Esha and I eyed each other. I knew she was preparing to say 'fuck you' but suddenly the Whitney Houston cut off, and she startled, shoved her prisoners ahead of her and dived behind the Origins counter. The music cutting off was genuinely scary, like a loud noise not its opposite, so I threw myself after them. All that happened was that the loudspeaker crackled and a man's voice said,

'GIRLS WE DON'T WANT ANY MORE BLOODSHED. I'M LIEUTENANT STRZWICKY' (or something) 'FORMERLY OF THE ORADELL POLICE DEPARTMENT. I'M THE HEAD OF SECURITY HERE AT THE MALL. I JUST WANNA TALK TO YOU, OKAY?'

All of a sudden we were allies, all of us huddling under the cash register, among miscellaneous paper supplies and different sizes of plastic bags and the salesgirls' purses. We looked at each other and Keri started giggling. 'Is this for real?' she hissed.

Lieutenant Swizzlestick was talking:

'MELANIE SMALLS WE JUST WANT TO TALK TO YOU. THERE'S NO NEED TO SHOOT ANYBODY ELSE. LET'S SEE WHAT WE CAN WORK OUT HERE.'

'I didn't shoot nobody,' 10Esha muttered. 'Racist dogshit.'

'Is your name really Melanie?' I asked 10Esha, who seemed inordinately preoccupied with the intricacies of her Sony. She was fiddling with it but getting no joy.

'It Lamar fault. Now my crew been shot, they must of.' She was crying all of a sudden. Oh no, I thought. Don't break down.

'We have time,' I said. 'So let's just think.'

'*Time? Think?*' 10 started looking like a wild animal. 'I lost my goddamn cell link, wachoo mean, think? I got to get my shit Out There, you know what I'm sayin?'

'They're cops,' I soothed. 'Or ex-cops. Or wannabe cops. Same difference. There's going to be a lot of standing around. It's a cop thing they do. Like doughnuts. They stand around a lot and talk in radios. And then other people come and stand around carrying their groceries and watching, it's an obsessive standing-around thing—'

'Shut up, Sun. You're making her agitated.'

10Esha's gun hand looked very steady but her lower lip was trembling and her feet were twitching as if to a very fast ragtime. I don't like to see anybody panic.

I raised my head and yelled at the ceiling, 'DON'T FUCK W/US WE GOT A WALTHER PPK, TWO SPECTRES, AN H&K 5.56MM ASSAULT RIFLE AND FORTY BOTTLES OF OBSESSION SO KEEP IT IN YOUR PANTS UNTIL WE'RE READY YOU SHITHEADS.'

'Oh fuck,' said Keri relevantly. There was a spittle-ridden blast of static and then the answer came back.

'LET'S NOT GET HASTY, LET'S JUST TALK GIRLS.'

'10Esha I think it's time you put the gun away don't you?'

I recognised Keri's best borrowed-from-TV-game-show-hostess voice. It made me want to become hysterical, so I shouted, 'I NEVER GOT MY BONUS GIFT YOU FASCIST PIGS,' which made me feel more centred. Hah.

'Why don't they talk to your nutty friend? You girlz takin' shit too serious. Oh sweet baby Jesus she shouldn't of messed w/my crew—'

'WE'D LIKE TO SEND SOMEBODY IN TO HEAR WHAT YOU HAVE TO SAY—'

'I'VE HAD ENOUGH!' I screamed, warming to my task. 'YOUR CELLULITE CREAM DOESN'T WORK!'

'Sun you don't have cellulite.'

'No but my mom does and it's gross.'

Keri's ignoring me in favour of 10Esha. 'Use your head, videobitch. You shoot us and they definitely will shoot you. And you go have to shoot us cuz you outnumbered and your crew gone bye-bye.'

I cocked my head at her and squinted.

'Why are you talking like that?'

'They're going to kill us,' Keri said in clipped suburban. 'I'll talk any way I want.'

'They'll never kill you,' 10Esha said. 'Cute little overachieving upper-middle-class sweethearts like you—'

'Hey—' I began.

'They gonna kill me easy as spit but not you even though it be all your fault. Here.' Suddenly 10Esha tossed Keri her piece. Descartes's gaze followed its flight path like it was a football. 'Now I'm *your* hostage. Since your chick Puppylove started all this you girlz might as well take the fall. I sujjest you get a plan and quick or they be nerve-gassing us outta here.' She sniffed and resumed filming.

'That's not nerve gas, that's *Joy*,' Keri said.

I hollered, 'DON'T EVEN THINK ABOUT GAS BECAUSE HITLER—'

Keri grabbed me and pulled me back down.

'*Shut up!*' she hissed, her brown eyes going all adult and bossy on me. 'This is fucked. I'm starving, I've got a major chocolate craving, I have to study for a physics test, and this is no way to spend a Saturday. Let's just turn ourselves in before somebody gets hurt.'

'Somebody did get hurt,' I retorted. 'Did you see that guy's body out there?'

81

'I didn't shoot anybody,' Keri lied with wide eyes.

'GIRLS RIGHT NOW WE'RE JUST TRYING TO GET EVERYBODY OUT ALIVE. MELANIE WOULD YOU RATHER I CALLED YOU 10ESHA? I HAVE THE REVEREND VAN EMBERG HERE AND HE WANTS TO SAY A FEW WORDS.'

'Why are they after you?' I rounded on 10Esha. 'Suk Hee started it. How do they even know your name?'

'Long story,' 10Esha said. 'Ask me some other time. We'll do lunch.'

'10ESHA MY NAME'S MIKE VAN EMBERG, AND I'D JUST LIKE TO SAY THAT NOBODY WANTS THIS TO GET ANY WORSE THAN IT ALREADY IS. GOD WILLING—'

I seized the nearest gun and shot out an Aveda display.

'EVERYBODY SHUT UP. WE CAN'T THINK WITH YOU TALKING. JUST SHUT UP. AND PUT ON SOME BETTER MUSIC.'

There was a shuffling. After a couple of seconds Boyz II Men came on hesitantly. As a kind of informal consumer-feedback response, I located a speaker and took it out. Shooting the gun was proving to be almost as addictive as when you use it for sex. I saw myself in a mirror and was I smiling. Descartes had his hands over his ears. I desisted.

'They shot all my chix didn't they?' 10Esha's low voice penetrated the aftershock of the shots. She was addressing Keri.

Keri bit her lip. 'I saw two get caught. The others got cover, I guess they split.'

'They left me.' 10Esha was shaking her head. She poked Descartes in the shoulder pugnaciously. 'They left me. You fire on any my pussies?'

Descartes licked his lips. 'I don't have a gun. I'm not your enemy.'

82

10Esha gave him a long, low look. Surprisingly, Descartes didn't back down. He said, 'Can you hand me my wallet, please? It's in my back pocket.'

There was something kind of calming about the way he said that, like pass the butter or here's your receipt. 10Esha pried the wallet out and opened it.

'You don't got enough here to buy a Elvis record.'

'Look at the pictures.'

10Esha looked and then passed the wallet to me.

'That's my little girl, Katie,' said Descartes as I looked. Bangs, straight teeth – shiteating little thing, if you ask me. 'She'll be at ballet class – no, no. Correction. Jen probably picked her up by now, it's one o'clock but anyway . . .'

His voice broke slightly and he cleared his throat. I started to feel bad.

'You know,' he said – and the way he said it was sincere and with his hands and all that, kind of stumblingly as if he didn't feel up to speaking the words because they were really his or some of them anyway, which is unusual because most people just parrot back the lines they hear on TV – 'I'd hate to think of my Katie ever being so angry or so desperate she'd resort to violence.'

I started to feel really bad.

Keri pointed the gun at his face and closed in. 'Hey. Did you or did you not download that free realtime of Buffy giving Dog Jam a blow job?'

'What are you talking about?' Startled, he was trying to squirm further back against the cabinets. The glass doors rattled.

'Answer the question. And I'll know if you're lying. You did, didn't you? Every man with a modem snapped that one up. Don't try to deny it because I'll just blow your brains out.'

Keri would have made a good Kempeitai interrogator, I thought. She had exactly the right blend of conviction and irrationality. Now she shoved the gun up his left nostril. Sweat beaded on his forehead, and his face twisted. He looked like a horse resisting the bridle. It was just like in a movie only he was flabbier.

'OK OK I did.'

'And was it good?'

'Well . . . yeah I mean Buffy come on . . . but fuckit I didn't mean any harm, it was just—'

Keri laughed and took the gun away.

'Bet you can't tell me what colour lipstick she was wearing,' she challenged, snapping her fingers.

'Huh?'

'You're not a woman. That's your main problem Gonzo.'

'Naked Coral,' supplied 10Esha.

'No it was Mandarin Rose,' I said. 'Close but no smoke.'

'OK, I downloaded it but that's not violence,' Descartes retorted – unwisely I thought. 'I see where you're going with this. You radical feminists you think pornography is so evil but—'

'Actually it was Tawny Sunset,' Keri said to 10Esha, and then cocked her head at Descartes. 'I *love* pornography. How do you think I knew about Buff? I had to check out her style, didn't I?' She licked her lips. I covered my eyes, which were filling with tears because of suppressed laughter.

Descartes looked at me.

'Don't cry,' he said softly. 'It'll be all right.'

'What's your name?' I sniffed.

'Terry – what's yours?'

'Sun.'

'That's a pretty name. Sun please don't let her shoot me.'

Looking at Descartes I knew I ought to tell Keri to back off because I was afraid he'd pee himself and I hate the smell of men's pee. But I said, 'I don't know. She's in kind of a bad mood. Dusky Pearl doesn't look good on her either.'

You could tell Descartes was about at the end of it, assuming he'd had any to begin with which was a point subject to contention IMO.

'OK shut up now,' I told him. 'Bitch and me got to talk.'

'AHEM . . . THIS IS THE REVEREND VAN EMBERG AGAIN. PLEASE DON'T SHOOT! NOW, WE HAVE SOME INJURED FOLKS NEEDING MEDICAL ATTENTION IN THE COSMETICS DEPARTMENT, AND WHAT I WANT TO DO IS I WANT TO COME IN, OKAY, AND JUST SEE IF THERE'S ANYBODY WHO NEEDS HELP. ALL RIGHT? I MEAN, I'M UNARMED, I'VE GOT A DOCTOR WITH ME, AND ALL WE WANT TO DO IS HELP OUT ANYBODY WHO'S INJURED.'

Me and Keri looked at each other.

'Don't do it,' sang 10 under her breath.

'We're discussing it,' Keri hollered. 'Just hold on to your hoohah.'

She turned to me. 'Sun, let's give up and get some Dairy Queen. It's 10 they want, not us.'

'What about Suk Hee?'

'They probably got her already.'

'I don't think so. I saw her in Small Leathers, near the entrance. She could have got out before security closed in.'

'Great! Then she's free. Which is pretty ironic, considering she should be the one surrendering, not us, since she started it . . .'

'Keri, if she's out in the maul she's going to get caught. But I'm talking about her state of mind. I want to go after her . . .'

'No way.'

10 is pointing the camera at me. 'Don't you need a strategy for that shit?'

'Mine is the strategy of no strategy,' I said automatically. Zen can find you out in the funniest places, can't it?

'Is that like the Knicks last season?'

'10Esha, you're the one calling us doofus amateurs. So, uh, you're some kind of pro?'

10's beautifully manicured stick-on nails tapped her chest importantly. 'Hey, I'm a artist. But . . . if I had to give advice?'

'*Yes . . .?*' We all leaned towards 10 and her camera.

'Use the hostage, stupid. And do it quick, before back-up gets here.'

'How?'

'Just walk out there with him and go where you want to go.'

'The car's miles from here,' Keri wailed.

'Yeah, and can't they pick you off through a scope from like two miles away around a corner at night in a high wind? I've seen the ads in *Soldier of Fortune*.'

'I wonder how much money they losing every minute we here,' mused 10Esha. 'Big sales day today, Saturday.'

'Who cares?'

'I'm just trying to calculate your worth.'

'It's only a minor 20%-off-selected-items sale,' Keri said. 'If this was Thanksgiving weekend we'd have a problem.'

'What about Suk Hee?'

'Every girl for herself,' said Keri.

I stared at her in disbelief and she elaborated. 'They expect us to sacrifice ourselves for each other,' Keri said. 'So we're not going to.'

Again I wondered if Keri had been studying Japanese

86

imperial policy in the first half of the twentieth century and again I decided that no, it must be low blood sugar. Speaking of which—

'Anybody got a cigarette?' I said. 'No? Right. I'll be back in a second.'

Keri hissed and cursed at me, but I squashed past her and Descartes undeterred, crawling sideways down the aisle towards Suk Hee's abandoned book bag.

'ATTENTION SHOPPERS.' This time the voice was female and came from the main maul. 'WE APOLOGISE FOR THE INCONVENIENCE. WE ARE EXPERIENCING POWER FAILURES IN THE MALL. ALL SHOPPERS ARE ASKED TO MAKE YOUR WAY TO THE NEAREST EXIT.'

I didn't look up. When I reached for the book bag, a shot rang out, missed my hand by about a centimetre, and sent me flying back to cover with the book bag in tow.

'Hah!' I shouted, waving the book bag above the counter. 'Missed me, fuckers!'

Triumphant, I rummaged in the book bag. Then I burst into tears. Suk Hee had left her phone in her book bag – meaning she had no way to communicate with us.

And I couldn't find any cigarettes.

'UH, THIS IS REVEREND VAN EMBERG AGAIN, COULD WE GET AN UPDATE ON THAT PLAN? WE JUST WANT TO COME IN AND REMOVE THE WOUNDED, OK?' *Pause.* 'OK, I'M GONNA START WALKING, YOU CAN SEE MY HANDS, THE TWO LADIES BEHIND ME ARE GOING TO HELP ME WITH THE INJURED, NOBODY HAS ANY WEAPONS.'

I couldn't see him, but somebody could. There was a delay of about four seconds, then a flurry of gunfire from the direction of Hosiery. A bullet whizzed past between me and Keri; I thought it was a hornet for a second and cringed, then made a rapid scurry over to Calvin Klein, seeking refuge. 10Esha's phone was ringing, 'Another One Bites the Dust'.

'YOU AREN'T DOING YOURSELVES ANY FAVOURS, GIRLS,' said Swizzlestick. The little half-door to the CK island was swinging open, and I whipped inside and shut it behind me before I saw the salesgirls. Swizzlestick was busy talking tough but I no longer paid any attention. I was staring.

There were three cosmetix chix, two Latinas and one white, bound and gagged with their own pantyhose, stripped to their underwear. Their little white dresses and pink lab coats were nowhere to be seen.

'What is this, a Spanish porno movie?' I muttered as their eyes widened and one of them began to kick away from me. They were grouped in a little huddle that made them look particularly vulnerable. Their belongings were scattered on the floor, spilling from the clear plastic cosmetic bags that they have to carry so they can't shoplift.

Benson & Hedges!!

There is a God.

I lunged for the pack, visible inside the plastic bag, and the captives squealed into their gags. I guess they were pretty pissed off. I would be. I lit up and inhaled.

Van Emberg had been persuaded to shut up and 'Like a Prayer' came on the musak.

Outside in the maul, the lights started flicking on and off like in study hall when the teacher's trying to make the class quiet down but the class is so loud no one can hear her screaming, so she flashes the lights. I wasn't totally sure how much time had passed since Suk Hee first went berserk, but by now I would have expected more in the way of sirens and possibly helicopters. Instead, the lights flickered and went out, then came back on.

I could hear 10 on the phone.

'Chantelle? Good Pooky. Got the stuff? How much? Good. Later.'

Van Emberg must have strayed too close to Origins because Keri fired off a round into the sunglasses rack in Accessories and they started the tape over. Cher.

'There's a pile-up on the Parkway causing a delay with the state police getting here,' 10 announced, punching in a speed dial. 'We just might have a little bit of time – Mama?'

I crawled to the doorway and looked around. About twenty feet back into the store, I could see what I assumed was Van Emberg, a skinny balding guy in chinos and last year's Adidas Pogo cross-trainers bending over a body. He was talking to a black woman in a maroon sports-coat store uniform whose back was to me. I looked the other way and saw whole groups of uniformed males standing guard over the cul-de-sac where Lord & Taylor meets the rest of the maul. They were already erecting barriers in the form of janitors' yellow and black stripy 'Caution – wet floor' sawhorses. I noticed that the security door between Sharper Image and Lord & Taylor's was open; as I watched, two men in boiler suits emerged, carrying more of these barriers. It must be a janitor's closet or something back there.

We were quickly being walled in.

I glanced across the aisle into Origins. Keri was mouthing something at me but I suck at reading lips. 10 said, 'I gotta talk to Uncle G. Yeah, I'm OK. No, we didn't have no lunch yet.' Her face contorted as her throat went tight and her eyelids squashed a tear. 'Could you put Uncle G on? Bye Mama. I love you too. Yo G it's Mel. Hi. Yeah I need a favour.'

We watched her bite her lip.

'*Mel?*' I marvelled. *Melanie Smalls.* How did store security know her name? I looked at 10. She looked more like a Melanie than a Teneesha, I guess. Still, I got a kind of vertigo watching her talking to her mother. I became absorbed in examining her tight baby-blue acrylic-mix sweater, which had a scallopy edge on the sleeves and was starting to pill. I couldn't work out whether she was ahead of or behind fashion. She seemed somehow beside fashion. I still couldn't believe this was 10Esha the Bullit Artist. Not to mention a Bugaboo. I moaned a little, softly.

'No, boo it ain't no thing except I need you to git the truck and come pick me up. They be cops all over me.'

I whipped around and pressed my pistol into the nose of the white girl. 'I'm gonna take your gag out for a second and if you scream I don't know what I'll do, so don't scream. OK?'

She nodded. She was about 25 I guess, heavily made up, with her hair pulled back in a smooth ponytail. 'Don't look so grumpy,' I added. 'You're a good-looking chick meaning 98% of the time you have more fun than me, so live w/it.'

I took the gag out. The girl wiggled her reddened mouth around, her eyes darting all over the place. I could hear 10 saying,

'Look, I know I'm a little outta line. This the only time I ever ask. I don't fux w/u, I make my own lux, but baby I need the trux. Cross my heart.'

What is 10Esha up to? Who's Uncle G? The *trucks*? She looks like a Catholic schoolgirl with those brown loafers.

'Who tied you up like this?' I interrogated. 'And keep your voice down.'

'Some girl with a gun,' said the white girl, and the other two nodded. I avoided looking at them. They both had big, liquid dark eyes with a lot of mascara and girlz like that scare me, they're all soft and shit. 'She shot out that camera, then took our stuff and left.'

I followed her gaze to a broken camera on the wall near the edge of the department, right next to a black security door adjacent to The Sharper Image, next door.

'When?'

'Right in the middle of like, you know. The guns going off.'

'What the fuck was that all about?' I wondered aloud, replacing the gag before she started hollering.

'Hey Sun get yo ass back over here, little queenie.'

10.

I glanced into the aisle, checked to see whether I was safe but Keri was already covering me. I dived across the aisle.

I probably should have explained about 10 before but at the time I was in denial. I mean, the idea of 10 being flesh and blood was kind of inconceivable and if I expected anything it was probably along the lines of Tina Turner in *Mad Max: Beyond Thunderdome*. But the real 10 wasn't that derivative; in fact, there was nothing fashionable or cool about her. Definitely not like Keri with the Tommy watch and the gun. When I squeezed back behind the counter again, she'd hung up and all of a sudden she was lecturing me like a Sunday School teacher. She had set the camera on the counter so that it took in our whole little scene behind the register. Descartes kept looking into the lens.

'Don't you get it that you can't be shooting people? I am a bullit artist, not a bullet artist!' She waved the gun @ the camera. 'Check my barrel for GSR. I carry for fashion only. I ain't fired it like some crazy bitches.'

'Leave SHee alone,' I snapped. 'She's very smart.'

10 snorted. 'She ain't connected.'

'Maybe not, but you don't know her so just don't be talking about her.'

'Yeah, fine, ah'ite.' She picked imaginary dirt from under her nail. There was a volley of further shots and we all startled and dropped reflexively lower behind the counter. The commotion was coming from deeper within the store (Small Leathers, I'd have guessed; maybe Hosiery) and, in addition to the pistol reports, involved a certain amount of enraged-bitch screaming followed by baritone shouts. The screaming turned to the spitting of insults ('YOU FUCKERS I'M ON A FUCK YOU UP DON'T *TOUCH* ME YOU SCUMSUCKING PIECE OF SHIT' etc) went on in a prolonged, pissed-off way that told us at least two of 10's girlz were getting captured. I was heartened by the implication that they hadn't been shot, but didn't say anything about it. I wanted to appear unafraid of death.

'Shouldn't we decide what to do?' Keri pestered. 'Why waste time with this shit. They're watching us on the security cameras. We need a plan.'

'What security cameras?' 10 snapped. 'You girlz shot most of 'em out already. Especially psycho-puppy – she a good shot.'

'So am I,' I said in a threatening tone. 10 shrugged. 'Why did you call us out?' I demanded. 'If you didn't want to fight, then what? Why?'

'I wanted to meet you,' 10 said, pouting. 'I was thinking of using your little zine for some shorts. Larissa was only fooling. Why you bitch hadda go Melrose Place on us?'

'I don't know,' I mumbled. So much for my chance at greatness. 10 would never want to use my site now. She was really upset. So upset that her ghetto accent was breaking down.

'I'm going to lose my job. I'm going to get arrested. And my scholarship —'

'Job?' I blurted incredulously. 10 was a famous bullit artist on the Net. What did she need money for? I thought everybody on the Net was a millionaire.

'At Godiva. Assistant manager.'

Keri made a sad strangled sound and looked wistful. She rummaged around under the cash register and came up with a pen and some register tape. She pulled her knees up to her chest, put the tape across her legs and started to scribble something on it.

'I,' declared 10, tapping her chest with her gun and adopting an adult tone of voice, 'have plans. I'm going to be a lawyer. Then I'm going to marry one of the NY Knicks, preferably Moses Andrews, and drive a Ferrari. Why would I want to shoot anybody?'

There was a noise from behind a pyramid-shaped display of Gucci body sprays and I leapt up and aimed.

It was Rev Van Emberg. He looked at me, I looked at him, he put his hands up and—

'Back the fuck up!'

—backed off. I waited until he was out of our zone, checked my perimeter, and sank back down. 10 was still looking at me, expecting me to answer for Suk Hee's behaviour.

'It all just got sort of outta hand,' I said lamely.

'You got to learn to master your hostility, puss. You got to get some manners, some control.'

It belatedly occurred to me that 10 was just putting on an act for the camera. Of all the stupid things – we're surrounded by store police and any minute now Lt Swizzlestick is gonna take matters into his own hands. And 10's being an artist. I was mad. I said, 'Who are you, Obi Fucking Kenobi?'

10 is looking at me with some kind of sadness. Or maybe it's just the way she looks. She has shiny brown eyes like most of SH's stuffies.

'Girl, you got problems.'

I laughed.

'I've got a file in the school counsellor's computer bigger than Dungeonmaster,' I said.

It's strange how shit sometimes never comes out the way you mean it. As soon as the words were out of my mouth and absorbed into 10's calm large-breasted J. C. Penny sweater aura, they no longer sounded like the boast I'd meant them to be, they sounded pathetic and childish and disturbed, but not disturbed in a Good Scooby way.

Lt Swizzlestick said, 'WE HAVE APPREHENDED SEVERAL YOUNG WOMEN WITH WEAPONS AND THEY ARE IN CUSTODY. YOU ARE NOT IN DANGER FROM ANYONE. YOU WILL NOT BE FIRED UPON. REPEAT, YOU WILL NOT BE FIRED UPON. PLEASE SHOW YOURSELVES IMMEDIATELY.'

'Come on, ladies,' Descartes said in a thick voice. 'Just think of the future.'

Without looking up from her scribbling, Keri pressed her left forefinger into his temple like it was a gun and said, 'Shh.' Descartes looked sideways at her as though she were a giant bug.

'Fuck,' I said after a while, because like a little black dress it's the old standby.

10's phone rang again. 'Annette, am I glad to hear your voice,' 10 said. 'Where you at? Gap? Dressing room? How many items? Just kidding.' She laughed. 'Yeah, I know. They gotta be evacuating. They flash the lights here, too. It's to make everybody think it's a power failure. Just stay there. You got somewhere you can hide? When they come in to look for you you going to have to take them out. Yeeh. How much stuff you say you got? Hee, hee, good girl. You all right. Call me when you free. OK boo.' 10 hung up and smiled at us. 'She's going to make a big pile of clothes and hide until they gone.'

Keri paused in her hurried writing and looked up with a wrinkled brow. 'Do you think my sister would look good in that orange jacket I have, the one with the zippers?'

'What the fuck are you doing, Keri?'

'Making my will.' She held up the register tape she was writing on. It spiralled around her like toilet paper. 'Oh shit, the car. My mother will freak. I'm going to call her.' She reached into her bag and rummaged desperately, producing three scrunchies, a pack of Wrigley's, some receipts and finally her phone. It played 'The Ride of the Valkyries' in Casiosound when she turned it on.

10Esha snatched the phone away with a wordless frown. Her look said *fuck off*.

Keri looked at me, at the phone, at 10Esha. She was actually speechless.

10 said, 'Terence, just do like we tell you and you won't get hurt.'

Descartes stiffened at this formal use of his name.

'No,' I said. 'Keri, don't trust her.'

But they all stood up. Keri kicked me in the process. '*Come on!*'

Keri looked down on me. She has double chins, I realised with shock. Does everybody at that angle, or has Keri been burgering to excess? 'Come on, Sun, you can't keep telling them you have an M-80—'

'H&K 5.56mm,' I corrected automatically. 'Should I start shooting now?'

'Yeah,' said 10. 'You go on and shoot, now.'

I was getting to like this part. As I came up over the edge of the counter I glimpsed a whole phalanx of plump security guards silhouetted against the doors to the parking lot. They ducked big-time while I took out most of Clarins and then changed clips. The counter was getting pretty torn up, but we hadn't been shot yet. Maybe that was because they weren't shooting back at us. I did them the same courtesy and made an effort not to kill anybody.

There was only one problem. 10 wasn't taking Keri and Descartes to the exit, she was making for the escalators. I bolted after them, realising I had lost precious seconds of running time in my firearms orgy.

The security guards were shouting at each other and spitting into radios. I saw a couple break from cover to my left and then disappear behind the damaged Chanel counter.

I rounded the Clinique corner and mounted the escalator to the crackle of static as Swizzlestick got ready to reopen negotiations. There were security guards at the top of the escalators.

'What the fuck? What the fucking fuck?' I screamed at 10 as I raced after the trio. Descartes looked over his shoulder at me, wild-eyed. 10 and Keri were crammed to either side of him, 10 one step above him, Keri one step below but with her foot on the same tread as Descartes. His head was about level with 10's and with Keri's gun in his right kidney he was choked up, the muscles of his face oddly flaccid with fear. I glanced up and around and saw that the whole upper level was lined with guards, looking down on the escalator from behind the glass balustrades.

You got to bite being a terrorist. I mean, passing through a threat like that, just a few of us weaklings against all of them, and they don't dare take us out. It's a rush. It's like a moral balancing act, a deadlock between their power and their vulnerability, i.e. their morality/mortality in the form of Descartes.

Hmm, nice thought. Almost makes it seem like we are balancing an equation, correcting the power skew. I feel weirdly noble, for a second. Then I looked back down on the cosmetics department and saw the destruction. There was the guard's body I'd crawled over. There was Suk Hee's book bag. I couldn't see into the Origins counter where we'd been hiding; it was protected from view by a pillar and three large potted plants. But I could see the legs of the three salesgirls in their underwear.

Then I saw Suk Hee. She was cast out limp on her side, facing away from me, her head thrown back like a deer on an Isuzu roof in November. A display of cheap scarves had fallen across her legs. Her head was in a puddle of blood.

I started to go back.

10 got to the top of the escalator and the wall of guards did not part. They had body armour. 10 started shooting at their legs and they scattered; shots hit the escalator at my feet and shattered the glass sides. I covered my head with my arms and threw myself down on the moving stairs. They carried me up and into the mayhem. The next thing I knew I was following 10, all of us running like shitheads around the edge of the upper level, back towards the maul.

I had no idea what 10 thought she was doing, but I followed, spinning around every so often to try to cover our backs. I was expecting to be shot at any moment. I couldn't really understand why we weren't being fired on, actually. We came to the edge of the girlz department and began to swerve left towards the wide exit to the maul where yet another rank of guards had been stationed to cover our escape.

In that moment, several things happened all at once. Out in the upper level of the maul, a squad of bitches with automatic weapons came flying out of Godiva and across the bridge towards Lord & Taylor. Seeing them, 10 grabbed Keri and jerked her to the right, into a small hallway with telephones and bathroom signs. Descartes was released and went barrelling across my path, standing there for a second like a big mushroom as he tried to decide which direction to break in. Now that I was clear of the pack, I could almost smell the bullet with my name on it flying towards me.

I threw myself at Descartes's legs from behind and he went sprawling face-down across the marble floor. The girlz with the big gunz were in bloodbath mode. For all the noise and mess that we had made downstairs, as far as I could tell only one person had actually died. (I'm not counting Suk Hee because I don't want to think about that.) But there before my eyes as I grabbed on to Descartes and tried to use him as a shield, I saw four or five men go down like Barbie dolls and Coke cans at BB gun practice. One 'Boo got shot in the stomach and fell to her knees, her forehead leaning against the glass barrier that protected you from the drop to the marble forecourt of the lower level with its palm trees and fountains.

I just wanted to hide, but everything was open space and glass. Descartes got to his feet and tried to shake me off, but I shoved the gun against him. There was a scramble as he tried to wrest the gun away from me. He obviously believed I would not really shoot him and he was right – I didn't have time to. We were still struggling when the bullets hit him in a thudding triplet rhythm. I felt like I'd taken the shots myself, through the thickness of a telephone book. He staggered towards the glass balustrade, which had several bullet holes in it. I crouched behind his back as he continued to move forward with my gun in his hands now. He fired it wildly, hitting nobody, and the answering volley came back like vicious laughter. I danced across the floor. We smacked into the balustrade, which shattered. I fell down among the broken glass; Descartes turned around and grabbed at me as he fell over the edge.

It took too long to fall.

I landed very fucking hard in a planter full of fernlike palm things and fake gravel. Descartes smacked into the marble side of the crescent-shaped planter and then rolled over me. It was blurry pain in all directions. A series of big Chinese gongs went off inside my head. Then nothing.

STARRY
EYES

To: bernie@taktarov.com
From: mbaldino@edufunparknj.org
Re: trigger for M's crisis
Att: I-MAGE 712M–715M
Subject unexpectedly still alive, but infection now raging at levels I've never seen. 10E has taken some of the older sister strains along for the ride – whole thing muddy as hell, see attached I-MAGEs Moreover, cannot identify the trigger for 10E explosion here. Have tried to livewire, phone & courier you to no avail. Badly need your advice, please respond.
MB

When Meniscus woke from fevered dreams of Bonus and Mall and a display of nail polish exploding and turning the whole world pink, the first thing he saw was the open door in the wall of his habitat.

The last time he had seen this door open was the day he had been transferred from Dr Taktarov's hospital to the Fun Park. He had been carried through that door in a sealed suit. It was like the door of a submarine, with a wheel that spun metal bars into the walls, keeping each habitat hermetically shielded from the others. It had an electronic lock built into the wall, which had winked red at Meniscus night and day for nine years. Now a steady green light shone from the box, the door yawned open, and through the aperture he could see a bed just like his own. The bed contained a man.

Another first.

Meniscus sat up, sweaty and confused. The pain was bad yesterday; less so now, but he feels like a cloth that's been squeezed out then shaken, and when he examines his body he sees that the Azure is pushing into new territories. He looks at the man, who wears shabby grey sweatpants and a yellow T-shirt with faded letters stencilled across the back.

S   E CARRERA 4465 ATL   TIS

The man gives himself to sleep with such abandon that his enormous, doughy body drapes the bed completely, whereas Meniscus has always tended to huddle in one corner of his bed like a curled anemone.

He's grateful that he isn't actually immersed in Mall today; he can feel it under the skin, but it doesn't consume his senses. He absorbs the sight of the stranger. The man has long black hair like an Indian. He has great, bare feet. His face is squashed into the pillow, which is drool-stained. His habitat is empty, and his snores echo. The air smells of garlicky breath.

Meniscus glances around his own home. Someone has cleaned it up, and they've done it wrong because Ollie Elephant® is sitting on Tigger's head, and that shouldn't be. Also his reward stones have been piled in a heap.

101

There is no longer a solar system, just a pile of rocks. He gathers them to him and holds them tight against his belly. Their disarray makes him feel queasy.

The strange man produced a sound like a drain that has suddenly been cleared and lurched out of bed, stumbling over the sheets. He rushed through the open portal and past Meniscus, leaving a musky smell in his wake. Then he slammed into the plexiglas barrier that separated subjects from observers. Meniscus watched him sorrowfully. When the glass was really clean it did look like you could pass through it into the lab beyond.

When the man realised he couldn't get out, he went to Meniscus's toilet and urinated. The urine was black.

The man turned and said, 'What the fuck you looking at?'

Before Meniscus could respond, the man stumbled over to him and grabbed him by the throat.

'Don't you fucking look at me,' he ordered, gazing at Meniscus – who tried to look away but wasn't permitted to – and gripping his trachea between a hot, callused palm and finger pads. A blunt nail scored Meniscus's depilated throat. Meniscus doesn't flinch because he's used to pain. His eyes close and he goes limp like a rabbit. The man shakes him.

'You fucking sick? What they infect you with you miserable son of a bitch?'

His voice was harsh and forceful with a slight accent: south-west, Meniscus thought. His body was not exactly fat but it was big, like a horse. He smelled dangerous. He held Meniscus at arm's length, still pinned to the bed, and gave him the once-over.

Meniscus was wearing light grey scrubs so that most of the Azure stain was obscured without any chafing against his skin. He supposed what did show could be taken for bruising. The ID bracelet on his ankle was utterly plain; you needed a scanner to read it. Every day Dr Baldino uploaded her lab notes, but you needed a MUSE to read them. The new man quickly saw that there was no information to be gleaned visually.

'Who are you? Why are you here? What is this place?'

Still Meniscus didn't answer. Eye to eye, he and the stranger took one another in. After a minute the man said disgustedly, 'Ah, fuck!' and shoved Meniscus away. Then he started picking up objects and throwing them.

'Where's my stuff?' he screamed. 'I want my stuff. And I want some cigarettes. Gimme my stuff goddamn it.'

Greta, the night minder, glanced up from the Tupperware box containing the meal she had brought from home because she was always on a diet. Greta is everything that Naomi isn't: dumpy and old and unkind. She has a flat alligator face that always wears a totem-pole expression of threat. She looked at the stranger and let out a rough guffaw, then returned her attention to her food without answering him.

The man had a tantrum while Greta ate tofu. First he ripped the faucet out of Meniscus's sink. In the process of doing this he turned purple and the veins in his neck came out like pissed-off snakes. His right hand, holding the faucet, came back for a big wind-up. In a fluid, animal movement, he let the fixtures fly at the glass barrier.

Meniscus started flinching early. He knew the barrier was bulletproof, and he expected the faucet to come bouncing back, but it didn't.

The faucet *exploded*.

At least, put it this way: it went towards the glass as a single object and came back in a whole lot of smaller pieces. Meniscus was too shocked to count them. He watched the big man's body engaged in the throw, watched his breathing and the play of muscles across his back and the way his weight was transferred across his feet during and after the effort. Meniscus's eyes took in the sheer power of the physical release. Then there was a brief hiatus while the arm came back to the man's side after throwing the item, while little bits of metal were flying everywhere and Greta on the other side of the glass was disappearing under her workstation.

After that the stranger started wrecking the joint for real. When he was through nothing was recognisable for what it had been before except for Meniscus who had been driven against the back wall next to the air-conditioning vent, which was too small to accommodate him or he would have squeezed into it to escape.

'Where's my stuff?' the man said again, quietly.

Greta said something into her headset. Then she raised herself up over the edge of the workstation with a spooked look on her face.

'Dr Baldino will be right back,' she said. 'She's just getting some c-c-coffee OK? They're trying to locate your . . . stuff.'

She then scurried out of the lab, red-lighting the door as she went. Cameras swivelled to track the stranger as he whirled around, moving with more agility than his size should have permitted. Sparks glittered in the darkness of his eyes and he zeroed in on Meniscus again.

'What the fuck is that?'

Meniscus had been just about to try to escape into the game. Now he dutifully offered the MUSE. He wasn't surprised that the stranger wanted it. It was the only valuable thing he possessed.

'What does it do?'

The man was handling the components with an air of distant revulsion, as though examining Meniscus's used toilet paper. When Meniscus didn't answer his question, he repeated it. Meniscus picked up the malachite and nervously fingered the smooth stone. The last time he'd talked to someone, he'd got into big trouble with the bugs. There was no way he was talking to this guy, and he set his face into a blank mask.

The next thing that occurred went off so fast that Meniscus could never piece the sequence together afterwards, no matter how hard he tried to visualise it. One moment he was sitting on his bed with the big man standing over him; the next he was halfway across the habitat with his feet dangling off the floor and an elbow pinning his gut to the glass. The hand returned to his throat, steadying him when he tried to wriggle sideways away from the pressure of the elbow.

'WHAT DOES IT DO?'

Shadowy grey eyes were boring into him. They were eyes like stones spangled with mica: dark and bright at once. The room turned colours. Meniscus couldn't breathe. Starry Eyes gave a frustrated snort and Meniscus felt himself slide down the glass and slump in a heap on the floor. There was a little respite while he tried to get his breath back.

'*What does it do?*' The whisper came through the surf of his own blood returning to his brain. Hot breath was in his ear. He cleared his throat.

'System access. Multisensory.'

Interest flashed on the unshaven face.

Meniscus added hastily, 'Only education modules. And recreation. Games.'

An eyebrow quirked.

'Games? Any good?'

The change of tone was so rapid that Meniscus wanted to laugh, but he didn't dare. So Starry Eyes liked games. Meniscus shrugged in reply.

'Dr Baldino, he's interacting again.'

Naomi's whisper came over the intercom and Meniscus's head shot up to see Dr Baldino's assistant crouching over the I-MAGE panel. The lab door was open again, and Greta was standing in the background, wringing her hands. Naomi saw Meniscus watching her, added 'Oops,' covered her mouth, and killed the sound.

Starry Eyes's attention had not wavered from the MUSE.

'You need an inboard with this, right?'

Meniscus nodded.

SE looked at it a little longer and then threw it down at Meniscus.

'Piece of shit.' He turned to Naomi. 'Where the fuck is my stuff? And I want an account with Cycle Freek, I got work to do.'

Meniscus examined the MUSE. It appeared undamaged. He told himself to relax and get his blood pressure down. The stress hormones were feeding the bugs, he could feel it in the form of tiny pinpricks in the post-Bonus bright zones of his body: one under his right armpit, one at the base of his spine, one between his solar plexus and his navel on the left side.

He wondered what Dr Baldino's lab notes would have to say about this.

'I think your new settings are working, Mads.' Naomi, summoned when Dr Baldino realised that Meniscus was awake, was now using the lab's MUSE to ride the I-MAGE's reports of Meniscus's current status, while Greta, eyes downcast, operated the robot cleaning team to remove the debris from the two connected habitats. 'He's drug-free, awake, Mall's on subliminal, and the pain's under control.'

Maddie, slumping over her latte, grunted. It had been a long fight, and she knew the victory wasn't real; this was just a brief respite intended to buy her time to figure out what was going on before the subject croaked. Her head hurt, her eyes felt itchy in their sockets, and the dull ache in her lower back that had visited her like a migrant bird ever since the parturition of Bonus now seemed to be settling in for the winter.

'What about the bugs?'

Naomi deactivated the MUSE, frowning. 'Well, you can't have everything. At least the fever's down.'

'Meaning his immune system is accepting them. Not even putting up a fight.' Maddie was disconsolate. 'I ought to get on the phone and call some folks back at Stanford. I know about five people there who would kill to be where I am now. They'd find this whole thing fascinating. But I just feel sick.'

Naomi took off her headset and turned to face Maddie.

'It all happened real sudden,' she cooed in saccharine Southern tones. 'You're probably in shock. You should go home.'

'No, no. I'm fine.'

'But it's silly. You can't put in any more MUSE time, the system won't let you break the health regulations. Go home. I'll watch over them.'

'I'd rather stay . . .'

'And what about Bonus? Don't you want to make sure she's OK?'

'She's with her grandmother.' But Maddie stood up. 'I'll let you know if anything changes.'

'It will. They'll start to get to his organs soon. Oh – did the exterminator come yet?'

'I cancelled.'

Maddie looked at Naomi through narrowed eyes.

'Well, we couldn't have people around, not with the way Meniscus was acting – we'd get reported to the state.'

'Did you reschedule?'

'You know I can't do that.' Naomi twirled her lip stud.

'Goddamn it, Naomi – first Bonus and now you! Listen, that mouse has got a nest in the wires between the habitat and the I-MAGE unit. If we lose the I-MAGE link we're in a big mess, because right now that's the only way we've got a prayer of finding out what's going on with 10E.'

Naomi switched her weight to one hip, folded her arms, and flexed her biceps, making the jungle foliage of her body art shiver as if in a breeze. She said calmly, 'I told Hibridge when they hired me that I can't break my bodhisattva vow.'

'Your *what*?'

'It's a thing where you promise among other things not to harm beings.'

Maddie rolled her eyes. 'Oh, give me a break.'

'I won't kill a spider. I try not to kill mosquitoes. If you want an exterminator, *you* call. I'll make myself scarce while they're here. I don't want to be a party to it.'

'How can you work in a lab and have a vow not to harm beings? What about the organisms inside Meniscus? And where do you draw the line at *beings*? What about *rocks*?'

'I like rocks,' Naomi said. 'So does Meniscus.'

'Uh-huh. And if you get a cold, what do you do, refuse to destroy the invaders? Apologise to the monkey god for your own T-cells killing the virus?'

'If I get a cold I fast and go in the sauna until I'm better,' Naomi said, completely missing the point. She swung her lithe body around the side of the I-MAGE cabinet and could be heard next to the lab sink, operating the $40,000 precision centrifuge. She called, 'You feel like a seaweed shake?'

Maddie went to Wipeout.com and booked an exterminator for the next morning. Naomi reappeared holding a centrifuge beaker and licking algae off her lips. She started to say something more when there was a loud thump against the glass of the habitat. Maddie jumped. The SE was beating on the divider with his closed fists again, demanding his 'stuff' and blowing through flared nostrils like an aroused horse.

She muffled a curse at her complicity with Jennifer in the matter of the SE. What had begun as an 'airlock breach' had turned into cohabitation between the two males, and Maddie hated the unpredictability of the situation. So far the SE was asymptomatic. It seemed like about every ten minutes that Jennifer called to ask, 'Is he dead yet?' – which made Maddie feel progressively shittier. She wished he would die quickly so that she could pretend none of it had ever happened. She refused to feel sorry for him because that would open up too big a can of worms.

'You better take an I-MAGE of the SE, too, and get samples of whatever tissues you can.'

Naomi looked at her curiously. 'He's clean,' she said. 'He's been through the works before he got here. He can't infect Meniscus.'

'Yeah, I know that. But it would still be useful for us to see how the bugs behave in virgin tissue. As long as he's alive, he's a second subject.'

'OK. If you say so. But you know we could never publish.'

Maddie often wished she could have a more dominant personality. Naomi was always questioning her and pushing her around. Maddie told herself she tolerated it because Naomi was sexy. When Jennifer was around, Naomi called Maddie 'Dr Baldino' and cast her eyes down, which Maddie interpreted as a sign that the rest of the time Naomi was flirting with her by being so familiar. Still. There were limits.

'Naomi, I don't need you to remind me that this is a confidential project.'

'OK, OK, sorry.' Naomi leaned on the I-MAGE and stretched luxuriously, showing off her triceps.

Maddie added, 'All I *meant* was that I could learn a lot from the SE. It might help me to formulate a new approach, the next time I try working with the Azure bugs.'

There was an awkward silence. Maddie knew Naomi believed that once Meniscus was dead, there would be no hope for Maddie's work to continue. And she was probably right. But Maddie didn't find it so easy to let go. She had invested too many years in this project; she wouldn't abandon it as long as there was any hope of salvaging some piece of marketable bug talent.

'I'll do a full work-up,' Naomi said at last.

'And don't tell Jennifer about it. This is between you and me, just like your . . . tattoos.'

Naomi smiled at Maddie's reference to her skin-drug addiction.

'I can get you some any time you want,' she offered, winking. But Maddie was watching the two males in the unit. She could swear that Meniscus had just moved his mouth, made some sort of noise, as if he were talking.

The SE had noticed, too.

'What's that, monkey?' he asked, cocking his head at Meniscus's wordless vocalisations. 'You want cookie? Here you go, buddy.'

A yellow box of Mallomars went sailing across the habitat. Instead of catching it, Meniscus cringed. The Mallomars spilled on the floor. Meniscus stared at them helplessly, blinking to activate the summons for Naomi; but when Naomi moved towards the habitat, Maddie

110

shook her head to restrain her. The summons buzzer sounded seven times as Meniscus called for help.

'Don't go to him. I want to see if he'll speak,' Maddie said, glancing at the I-MAGE read-outs to see if something dramatic was happening with the bugs. She didn't notice anything obvious on the visual, but there was a definite spike in Mall processing power, which made her uneasy – it might mean the Az79 were about to make another reproductive surge.

The SE resumed his chant. 'Where's my fucking stuff? I want my stuff. This is illegal, you can't do this. You girls better bring me my stuff or else MonkeyCMonkeyDo buys it!'

He moved toward Meniscus threateningly, but Naomi went to the pass-thru hatch and spoke into the intercom. 'See this panel? This controls the atmosphere of the habitat. I can gas you unconscious any time I want, you big oaf, so lay off Meniscus and behave yourself.'

The SE's black eyes widened. His nostrils flared in challenge and he seemed to grow bigger, like a cat with its fur standing on end. Naomi put her weight on one hip and gave him a Marilyn Monroe pout. 'Come on,' she said, crooking her finger. 'Try me.'

Maddie clenched her fists nervously. Naomi couldn't gas the habitat because she would pollute the study; but hopefully the SE didn't know that. Maddie had been so busy thinking about the ethical implications of murdering the SE with her assassin bugs that she hadn't really thought about Meniscus's vulnerability when confronted with a full male – especially an unsocialised specimen like this one. She didn't know what she would do if the SE attacked Meniscus.

Meniscus must have been thinking the same thing because he hurriedly began picking up the Mallomars and sweeping the crumbs away. He cancelled his summons buzzer and assumed a beatific expression. The SE turned his manic gaze on Meniscus, who shoved two Mallomars in his mouth and tried to chew and smile at the same time.

'Fanks,' he burbled at the SE.

The SE grunted and picked up some rolls of toilet paper. He started juggling as if nothing had happened.

Maddie and Naomi looked at each other.

'Did he just say *thanks*?' Naomi queried, jerking her head toward Meniscus. But the subject retreated into his MUSE, curling up inside himself in the classic Y-autistic response to stress.

'I think so. Write it up in the report, will you?' Maddie said. 'And let's try to keep the SE quiet, OK? Give him what he wants, within reason. He's only going to be in here until he gets infected.'

'Or until Meniscus . . . er . . .'

'Dies, I know. Whichever comes first. They're both goners, anyway.' Maddie picked up her jacket and headed for the door, clicking her tongue with pity.

'I'll be nice to them, Mads.'

'Yeah, well, for starters, find out from Gould where his damn *stuff* is at.'

Meniscus observes Starry Eyes as he is reunited with his stuff. It's in a tan duffel bag, which Starry Eyes upends on his bed. Meniscus notes a bicycle chain, a bicycle reflector, an anachronistic three-pack of Trojans (Extra Large), a tube of Right Guard, a battered king-sized Snickers, and about fifty magazines. It's the magazines that Starry Eyes falls upon like a hit-denied addict. He sits in Meniscus's canvas director's chair and flips through them. They have the dented and shiny look of having been handled many times, and the pages make crinkling noises when turned in Starry Eyes's huge hands. They have titles like Racing Bike and Cycle Freek. Starry Eyes seems mostly to look at the pictures.

Unfortunately, on the first morning after Meniscus woke up from his coma, Naomi left a fax for Curator Gould lying around just outside the plexiglas, where Starry Eyes could read it. He read it out loud, whether for Meniscus's benefit or just because he liked to make noise, Meniscus couldn't have said. It was a fax about Starry Eyes, from Arnie Henshaw. How was the SE getting on? Was he healthy?

'That fucking Arnie Blonde Barbie-doll Henshaw!' Starry Eyes cried. 'I'll feed his shit to him with a spoon. Wouldn't take me on. *Couldn't* take me on. Balls the size of spaghetti-Os. Calls himself an Aspirant Swine. Who *aspires* to be a pig, huh? Are y'all loony out the butthole? Is he your idea of a prospective *mate*? What are you girlz *thinking*?'

Whenever anything pissed Starry Eyes off, he took it out on Meniscus, who was already so inured to pain on the inside that it scarcely mattered what the SE did to the outside. He would make like a rag doll while Starry Eyes flung him about, until the big man got bored and desisted.

Incidents like this occurred frequently in the early days. The manhandlers looked on in horror. Naomi's threats to gas Starry Eyes came to nothing. Instead, she refused Starry Eyes food, thinking this would make him more compliant. Instead he became even angrier, but with a hungry edge. 'I'll break every bone in his fucking body,' he commented, spittle flying from his mouth and the whites of his eyes gleaming as he smacked Meniscus almost playfully from one end of the habitat to the other. 'I want two cheeseburgers and a chocolate shake and a six-pack of Miller or else I'll cut his tongue out with a shoehorn.'

113

Meniscus, having long ago assumed the foetal position, took the opportunity to peek out and see how this performance was being received in the lab. On this particular occasion, Dr Baldino was there, and when Naomi begged her for tranks to bring down SE, Dr Baldino shook her head solemnly: No. Meniscus closed his eyes. No. The answer was always No: you will not be saved.

Starry Eyes got his food in the end. After he'd eaten it he sat back in the director's chair, which creaked beneath his weight, and his eyes took on a dull, sated look. Meniscus saw the subtle beams of the I-MAGE light centre on Starry Eyes as Naomi, her face half-concealed beneath the MUSE that linked her to the I-MAGE, scanned him. Starry Eyes took no notice of the lights. He flipped through his magazines in a desultory manner, occasionally making a note in one with a black indelible marker. Meniscus began to relax; but the détente was only temporary. After about ten minutes, Starry Eyes stood up and walked over to the pass-thru. He tore a page out of the magazine – it was an order form with writing scribbled on it – and stuck it in the hatch. The lab camera automatically zoomed in for a close-up on him.

'I need this stuff delivered,' he said to the camera eye. 'Sooner I get it, less I have to improvise.'

No one answered him.

'Hey!' he yelled, banging on the glass. 'I'm not a fucking pig so how about a little attention over here?'

The door opened and Naomi came in.

'Watch – now that she knows starving me don't work, she's gonna try to *bribe* me with food. They always do.'

Naomi had a selection of snacks and drinks on a tray.

'I'm doing the best I can in a complex moral situation,' she said. 'This is my way of showing compassion. Have a doughnut hole.'

114

Starry Eyes snorted and said to Meniscus, 'She thinks it's a petting zoo. That's how she'll justify her disrespect to us. See, the more domesticated the animal, the less it needs its survival skills and the stupider and weaker it becomes. And the stupider it becomes, the less respect people have for it. People have no problem killing sheep or cows because they figure the sheep and cows have entered into a contract with them that ends up with meat on the table. But kill a wild animal, and everybody gets upset. Wild animals are respected.'

'What about dogs?' said Naomi. 'People love their dogs but they hate the big bad wolf.'

'People like dogs but they *respect* wolves,' Starry Eyes replied, looking at the ceiling as if Naomi's question had come out of thin air. 'Now take us guys. Women figure they got us domesticated. They can do everything we can do. Thanks to assassin bugs they can even protect themselves against other men, which was always our big selling point as, like, a gender. We need them more than they need us. And that's why we're reproducing through pigs and they've got a thriving market in vibrators. We screwed ourselves, Squeak. All that technology made an end to us. Now we're weak and we're ruled by pussies.'

Naomi shook her fist. 'Yeah! Pussy power! We women know best, and you know it, Carrera. Why don't you lie back and enjoy it?'

'Enjoy *this*.' He took out his cock and waved it at her. Meniscus had the impression Naomi was supposed to squeal or giggle or something, but she just squinted, tilted her head to one side, and said, 'It really is the funniest of all the human organs, don't you think?'

Glowering, Starry Eyes put it away.

'Respect,' he said to Naomi. 'Get some.'

She made a face at him.

'Am I getting the parts on this form or not? Otherwise I got to improvise.'

'So improvise. I'm not your servant.'

She stalked away.

Starry Eyes spent the afternoon taking apart Meniscus's new furniture, which had been installed only hours after Starry Eyes had destroyed the original units. Meniscus's stuffed animals got tossed on the bed, and the planets were scooped up in Starry Eyes's big fist and dumped on the floor.

Meniscus let out a scream, then muffled the sound by shoving his face into the soft synthetic fur of Junko the Lion as soon as Starry Eyes looked at him. He sat on his bed, shaking, while Starry Eyes used his bare hands and teeth to take apart the shelving unit. He tossed the boards aside, showing an interest only in the aluminium tubing that supported them.

When Starry Eyes's back was turned, Meniscus began rescuing the scattered planets from the floor. He cupped them in his hands and crooned to them. You couldn't just hurl a planet out of orbit without expecting consequences. Meniscus felt the terrible burden of responsibility for letting the planets be treated this way. He put them on his bedspread in their original positions, with the stuffed animals arranged in a protective circle around them.

He found the lapis, the malachite, the mica, the flint, the sandstone and put them in their places. Each of the stones had been given to him in acknowledgement of a successful phase of the Azure study. Most of them had come from the first Doctor but when Doctor left, Naomi had kept up the practice of rewarding Meniscus every time a new bug was introduced to his tissues: hence, the lapis, which at eight years old was the youngest of the stones and represented the first incursion of Dr Baldino's Azure series.

But now he had an extra stone. Well, not a stone, actually. Bonus had given him a wolf's tooth, she said. But it looked like a stone, and it felt like a stone. And it had done something to the bugs, something worse than anything Dr Baldino had yet designed with her MUSE. It had made something happen inside him. He had reacted to the tooth, and they had reacted to him, and now everything was different. Soon they would kill him.

Yet Bonus had said she was trying to help him.

Meniscus hesitated, wrestling with this paradox and wondering where to put the tooth. He would have to rearrange the other planets, and maybe even the Sun, to accommodate this newcomer. But he didn't know how to do it. Usually he played with the planets at the same time as he roamed Mall, and the simple stone-game acted like a reflecting agent of the sophisticated virtual game – the stones were physical place-holders in a mathematics only he understood. Now he couldn't reach deeply enough into Mall to perceive it clearly. Like his solar system, Mall had been changed since he talked to Bonus.

He was pretty sure the lapis planet was now the dominant element in the system; maybe even it was making a bid to become the Sun. The Az79 were surely having their way with him. He was fevered and thirsty, and aftershocks of the pain came at him every so often like lightning bolts from within. He couldn't do anything to help himself, because he wasn't fully conscious of Mall. Now the game was playing itself, using him, and there was nothing for Meniscus to do but wait to die.

Meniscus gazed around himself in vacant self-pity. Starry Eyes was totally ignoring Meniscus now. He was busy messing around with the tubes and screws he'd recovered from the furniture. While Meniscus watched, presently Starry Eyes began to reassemble these elements into some kind of contraption whose purpose Meniscus couldn't begin to guess.

Everything Meniscus could remember learning, even in childhood, had been learned in a simulation. He had never actually watched someone work. The vision of Starry Eyes using his teeth to shape a rectangular piece of pine into a hammer head caught him up completely. He had a pretty good idea that Starry Eyes's hammer was inferior to a factory-manufactured one in various ways; still, Starry Eyes had made his out of the arm of a chair and that seemed quite creative.

Meniscus made a few tentative squeaking noises in a belated effort to communicate, but Starry Eyes ignored him. The wolf's tooth lay in his palm, begging for a place in the scheme of things. He looked at his planets again. The sun used to be a lump of gold from the second experiment, but there was a power struggle between the gold and the malachite people who lived on the fifth planet, so now the malachite is the Sun and the gold has been reduced to second-moon status around the now-abandoned Planet 5. He knows some of the planets wanted to let the lapis move in as the new people of Planet 5, which is obsidian, but the lapis doesn't feel like people at all, it feels like an exiled planet and so it will be.

You dark-hearted planet, Meniscus whispers to it. You are the hunter of the cold reaches, you old one, your fire is burned away but still you rove.

He puts it far out in orbit. Then, with tremulous fingers, he puts the wolf's tooth in the centre and sends the malachite people back to the lonely fifth planet.

Then he stands up, goes to the disposal unit, and vomits.

His veins ache Azure. When he returns to his bed, there is a tingling sensation in his fingertips.

118

He can feel his nails growing. They want to grow faster. Their moons are blue.

It's dawning on him that he has an ability he never noticed, like a new muscle only it's not a muscle. The discovery is a little like when he realised that he could flex his penis. He'd never remarked much upon the ability as a child; it was only in adolescence when plagued with erections that he learned to bounce his member up and down with the muscle that had always been there. Now that the Mall-induced pain has retreated, he is beginning to wonder. The big pink explosion reeking of perfume has aroused a suspicion in him. He suspects that he can affect what the bugs do. He has discovered a muscle that he never knew he had.

If only he knew how to use it. If only he could see what it did.

Starry Eyes is pulling screws out of formica with his teeth, pausing every so often to yell, 'When am I getting my cigarettes?' He notices Meniscus eyeing him. 'You wanna help me? Find me something I can use for a chisel.'

Meniscus only stared.

'Come on, Squeak, move it along. What are you gonna do, sit there and think about your disease? You really wanna spend your life moving these stupid little rocks around and pretending they're planets?'

'How did you know they're planets?'

'I got no choice but to hear you talking to them.'

'I don't talk to them.' Then he started to say, *I don't talk to anyone* but remembered it wasn't true any more.

'Yeah, you do. In your sleep, even.'

'They're presents. Rewards. For the experiments.'

'Some reward. How about a condo in Key West?'

'This one's the oldest. He gave it to me before I was sent here. He said we're the same so I have to be brave.'

119

'Who said?' Starry Eyes grunted, but didn't really seem to care.

Meniscus didn't answer.

Doctor had dark eyes and hands like Meniscus's hands, a man's voice and a woman's perfume.

'I love you no matter what happens and I'll be watching out for you even though you can't see me.'

Doctor's face is an odd face, its gender identifiers mixed in his memories, though at the time it was the only face he knew. Tapered at the jaw and Adam's apple-less like a woman's, yet stubbly like a man's, Doctor's face had been smiling at him since he was a baby. It spoke in a soft tenor.

'It doesn't matter what they do to you,' Doctor said. 'They can't touch the planets. After every phase you get a planet, and no one can take them away, and no one can affect what happens on the planets, except you. Watch the planets and you'll see whole histories unfold.'

Meniscus said, 'Why are you going?'

'Because I must. And it will be better for you. You'll be protected this way. You'll stay male, you won't become a half-thing, neither girl nor boy.'

Is it so bad? Meniscus wanted to ask, but didn't because he was a boy and boys don't want to be girls, or half-things.

'There's no other way,' added Doctor. 'You'd spend your life in an institution, otherwise, and sooner or later you'd die of Y-plague. You don't qualify for a castellation because you're a clone, and this way you'll be safe. The bugs they seed in you will be attenuated; they're derived from Y-plagues but they're many generations evolved and they won't destroy you. Not if I can help it.'

'I don't want you to go.'

'They say I have to.'

'They? Who are they?'

'You wouldn't understand, Meniscus, you're too young.'

'Well don't listen to them!'

'I must. They *are our future, our destiny.*'

Now Meniscus answered Starry Eyes.

'My clone-father. He's the only male I ever knew. Until you. Don't trust Dr Baldino, he said. Don't trust any of them. Don't tell them anything. These women think they're using you but *we're* using *them.*' He paused. 'Do you know, the day you came I almost died? If Doctor was coming to rescue me shouldn't he be here by now? I think he sold me down the river. So why shouldn't I talk?'

'You mean you didn't talk for nine years just on this guy's say-so? Well, shit, that's pretty good. Still, no point in acting all wounded about it. Come on, find me a chisel already.'

But Meniscus doesn't want to help. He curls up on the bed as far away from Starry Eyes as he can. With his new-found mental muscle, shakily, he eggs his fingernails on.

I WONDER IF
I'M DEAD

I WOKE UP UNDER Descartes's big cowlike body. I could hear people around me. My head thundered and I could hardly breathe. I'd never noticed before how flexible ribs are. Mine were totally squashed but didn't seem to be broken. I fought the urge to freak out and scrabble frantically to get out from under Descartes's corpse. I opened my eyes. The only light came from the skylight above. I could hear a helicopter as a bass backbeat to the gunfire and shouting but I couldn't see it. Descartes and I had rolled almost to the black glass walls of Sharper Image, where I'd been wedged beneath him.

After a minute there was a draught and a rush of noise from the parking lot beyond Sharper Image at the north entrance near the parking garage. Cops were running past me; they paused for a perfunctory check of Descartes's body, and then they kept running. I kept expecting to be noticed or remarked upon, but it didn't happen.

I'm used to being invisible at parties, but this is a little weirder.

Then, for a minute, nobody seemed to be around. All the guards had gone to the upper level. Sirens shrieked outside and I could hear the dull *thuk-thuk* of the helicopter getting closer. I was alone. Farther along the wide halls I could see a few guards moving semi-randomly. They all had their backs to me and seemed to be headed out towards the rest of the maul, like they were clearing the area from the epicentre outwards.

I wondered how much time had passed. I wondered what I was supposed to do now.

Then two men and a woman approached, walking fast and talking.

'. . . Tied them up, stole their uniforms, shot out the camera links, and made a break for it.'

'Which picture is the girl who started it all?' interrupted a nasal female voice.

'That one. No, *that* one.'

'Pretty girl.'

'No shit. From the camera history and the eyewitnesses, we're thinking yeah. This is her. But she had two friends, and the Estée Lauder witness says the three weren't Bugaboos. There was three uniforms gone missing.'

Oh my god. They think we planned this. They think we've escaped . . .

'How neat and tidy,' the woman remarked.

'We didn't even know about it until the three failed to show up at the employee fire-assembly point,' laughed the second man nervously. 'Then we were afraid they'd been shot. Thank God—'

'So these gangbangers walked right out of here as if they were employees?' shrieked the woman in outraged Jewish tones. (Remember, I'm allowed to say this shit, I'm half Jewish.)

'Ran, more likely,' said the first. 'Probably got out with the first load of evacuees.'

'You let them get away?' barrelled the woman. I covered my eyes and mouth and tried not to crack up. They've got it *all wrong*. I wish Suk Hee was with me right now so we could elbow each other in the ribs and giggle.

Probably better if I don't think about Suk Hee. The paramedics will have gotten to her by now . . . no, I'm not going to think about it.

'We'll find them, ma'am. If they were dressed as employees, they would have stood out in a crowd of shoppers. Someone will have seen them. They won't get far.'

The woman honked derisively.

'Whole thing smacks of a purpose,' she said. They were moving away now, into the wreckage of Lord & Taylor. 'The way the Bugaboos came running out of Godiva, it was like a military ambush. We gotta figure out how they got into Godiva, in case they have access to other secure areas.'

I knew how the 'Boos got into Godiva. 10 works there, she probably hid them in the stockroom. It's a good thing Keri's not a 'Boo, all the chocolate would be eaten by now.

'OK, what about the electricity in Section F?'

'Still down. Engineer though it was a fuse in Sony, but no.'

'Just as well – with any luck, these bad girls are afraid of the dark . . .'

The three of them had moved beyond my hearing now, and just in time. I couldn't have stayed that intimate with Descartes for another second. I wriggled away from him, slithering along the wall of Sharper Image. I can see guards milling around up above, in the area I fell from. There are two photographers up there, flashing away.

Why don't they see me?

Omigod. I wonder if I'm dead and don't know it, like in that movie with that annoying whispery kid. I creep *really* slowly towards the entrance of L&T, resting for a minute beside a couple of tall black iron Gothicky free make-over stools. Then I made a rush for the better cover of a formica plinth with the store map on it. The security door where I saw men moving sawhorses and *Caution* signs is still open a crack. I come up on my knees, dizzy, looking around in disbelief that nobody has spotted me. I can see myself in a cracked mirror over by Christian Dior. I look like absolute shit. There's all kinds of black stuff that I guess is blood from where I went through the glass. I guess I should be glad I'm not like carrying my head under my left arm or anything.

Here come a whole bunch of booted guys, I can hear them. I didn't really want to test the 'I wonder if I'm dead' theory, so I dived at the metal door, it yielded, I slammed it behind me, felt the latch catch. I was in a narrow passage, alone. I stood up shakily. I wanted to be sick. I staggered deeper into the corridor, coming upon a scratched and battered door on my right. I cracked it open. The stockroom of Sharper Image.

Alex, I thought with a pang. Did he say he was calling from Sharper Image? If I could just bring myself to casually infiltrate the scene there, maybe I could pass myself off as one of them and I could get out with Alex.

Fat chance. The image in the mirror looked like Swamp Thing meets Bruise Factory. I shut the door silently and continued along the passage. The corridor

125

eventually bent west, towards Lord & Taylor and the high-rise parking lot, and I followed it hopefully until I came to a set of double doors leading to a loading bay. I heard voices, cars, highway, and wind. I stood trembling and hesitating as the sirens drew so close I had to cover my ears.

If I went that way I'd walk right into custody. I introspected briefly and figured that no matter how well I might act terrified and pitiful, I had GSR on my hands and a holster strapped to my leg, and they probably had my face on security camera anyway when I was standing up there on the Estée Lauder counter playing Lara Croft . . . in a flash I retreated along the passage, scanning for air ducts and finding none, thinking that I was probably fucked but you know what? I liked this. I liked the fear. I liked the adrenalin. I liked the stupidity of it, the way it was totally OOB.

Alex was in Sharper Image.

Yum yum yum, now that's gotta be fate. I crept into the stockroom.

Outside in the store I could hear a male voice saying, 'Everybody stay down, try to remain calm. Please realise you are safer in here than out there.'

'How much longer is this going to go on?' another man asked in a deep voice, his tone more authoritative than the first.

'The police say they need to interview everyone before you can go, and right now they are still securing the immediate area for your safety.'

A scratchy female voice spoke up, arking and whining.

'Rodney how many times have I said they need metal detectors at these malls?' *Ark ark ark.* 'The number of gangs—'

'Shh, Rachel—'

Ark, ark, whine, 'Don't shush me you idiot, I told you we shouldn't come on a Saturday—'

'Ma'am, please, everyone please stay quiet so we can listen for instructions.'

'Shut up you skinny twerp, you think because you're a sales clerk, Derek is it, my god you think you can tell *us* what to do?'

'Actually I'm Assistant Manager.'

'Assistant Manager,' boomed another scornful voice, this one all chest and beard, but with a tweedy Harvard inflection. 'One feels deeply reassured to be entrusting life and limb to an assistant manager.'

Whoa, *peace*, people, I felt like saying. Instead I had a quick, almost-silent rummage and came up with a clock radio-cum-blackjack and some night-vision goggles. The not-silent part came when I accidentally knocked over a styrofoam cup half full of coffee. It hardly made a noise, especially in light of the arguing of the customers outside, but the coffee did start to seep under the door and I was afraid our alert assistant manager Derek would notice it.

I opened the door a crack. It was dark inside and everybody was clustered in the empty space between the aromatherapy chair and the robot lawnmower. I slid into the store and ducked behind the counter, letting the door swing gently shut behind me. So far, so good.

OK, but you got to remember my adrenalin was running pretty high, and this is the point at which I basically screwed up.

The way it happened was, I heard Alex's voice and stuck my head up over the counter to see if it was really him, and the Ark Ark lady caught sight of me and went, 'Stewart, look, it's—'

And I put my gun up, so incredibly tempted to shoot her just to shut her up. She was red-headed and short and

127

wore too much jewellery. Alex saw me, went, 'Sun—' and in a flash I flicked the gun at him and said,

'Get over here Alex!' and he *did* and then everybody else was backing away and I was going, 'Get out get out get the fuck out' and me and Alex were alone in The Sharper Image.

I guess it doesn't matter why people listen to you when you have a pistol in your hand. The point is, they do.

'Into the chair,' I commanded, and Alex slithered sideways into the aromatherapy chair. It's black leather like practically everything in this store, looks a lot like the astronomical chair in *Myst*, except instead of a viewscreen it has a kind of vent thing that blows scented steam or some such shit. Alex had no choice but to recline in it, his legs slightly apart displaying his cock and balls in a pair of black sweatpants. The bottoms of his sneakers are clean and almost new. His eyes are . . . I'm not gonna look at his face. I've got to check my perimeter.

From where I'm standing, I can see out through the black glass of the storefront and into the skylit maul. Outside of Lord & Taylor is an expanse of marble floor with the crescent-shaped fountain and some palm-tree things where Descartes and I plunged from the upper level. From this plaza, the maul splits in two directions at right angles. In the third direction, the west, is L&T, and in the fourth is an escalator. The escalator is between me and Continental Coffee. I could see Ark Ark and Co being herded out past the escalator to the north exit, near where I'd heard the sirens from the back passage. A whole bunch of cops were assembling behind various different pillars and below the rim of the fountain.

I was so relieved that I wasn't dead and that people

could see me, I hardly took in the fact that I'd just made things a whole lot worse for myself.

Keeping Alex covered and ignoring what he was saying ('Sun are you OK? I had no idea when I called you that . . . that . . . holy shit, Sun what happened, talk to me—' etc, etc) I slithered between the robot lawnmower and the therapeutic-sound-wave baby-mesmeriser, and peered out into the hallway. All I had to do was make it into Continental opposite. Then, if nothing else, I would die with espresso in my hand. But what about Alex?

Things hadn't gone very well for my first hostage. I wasn't going to think about that or I'd probably become hysterical. Still, I knew that when I did think about it I was going to be upset, and I was going to be a lot more upset if I got Alex killed.

'Alex, I started this whole thing OK?' I said, retreating to a position of relative cover behind a display of intelligent golf clubs. I looked at him then. There wasn't too much light in here, but my eyes had adjusted well enough by now. Alex isn't very tall, only about 5'9", but he's put together like a Greek statue and he's got skier's quadriceps. His hair is black and his eyes are dark, dark, dark with the longest lashes. He's got cheekbones. He's got a smile that – well, not at the moment, he doesn't.

'You don't believe me, do you?' I said, wiggling my back a little because the NiteEyes goggles were digging into my kidneys. Looking at him down my gun barrel I was getting wet, actually. I read somewhere that the clit loves power. 'So whassup, what you shopping for?'

He laughed uneasily. I didn't like the way he was looking at me any more. Shit, wasn't he impressed with me? *I* would be.

I put the gun back in its holster, wishing I had cleavage to show when I bent over. 'Sorry, is this making you

129

nervous? Look, I guess I just had to get it out of my system. I swear, this is my first and last time. No more telescopes or firing ranges. I'm going to concentrate on my wardrobe. I'm gonna learn to dance. Maybe I'll join a gym. Take aerobics. And I'm giving up cappuccino because it makes me all edgy and bitchy.'

He was smiling again like the old Alex I knew and loved. Well, OK the smile looked a little terrified but he was obviously making an effort to be nice.

'Bitchy?' he said. 'You got a long way to go before you hit bitchy. You should hear Jennifer when she's on the rag. "Don't touch me I need chocolate do I have zits I hate myself!"' he mocked in a high voice.

'Oh, I'm like that too,' I said airily, hoisting myself onto the counter and crossing my legs. Behind Alex I could see figures moving around.

'Really?'

'Yeah, totally.'

(*Not*. I don't even like chocolate and I've never had a zit in my life. Go, me.)

Now he was looking @ me like he never really saw me b4.

'I wouldn't have guessed that,' he said thoughtfully. He leaned forward like Regis Philbin and said, 'See, now, I don't have sisters and basically I think girls are pretty weird. Not you!' he added, holding up a hand. 'Just girls.'

OK let me get this straight.

:Girls=weird.

:Sun≠weird

: :Sun≠girl.

No matter how you shake it, I'm insulted.

I stood up. 'You don't think I'm weird?' I said in a low voice.

'AHEM GRR GRRR OK TESTING OK THIS IS CAPTAIN MONTEVIDEO FROM THE NJ STATE PD, I

130

KNOW YOU ARE SUN KASTZ AND ALEX RUSSO. SUN BEFORE THIS WHOLE THING GOES ANY FURTHER I'D LIKE TO SEND SOMEBODY IN TO TALK TO YOU.'

My piece came back out. I checked my ammunition. I was OK for the moment.

'They'll probably try to draw my fire and get me to use all my bullets on them, since they know I won't shoot you,' I said to Alex.

'Do they?'

'Do they what?' I was already moving him out of the chair and towards the door to the maul.

'Do they know you won't shoot me?'

'Probably. I called your name, didn't I? They might even think you're an accomplice. Go into the doorway, move real slow, keep your hands up. I'll be right behind you.'

He did just what I said.

'Say what I tell you to say. Don't get creative. Understand?'

I put the barrel in the back of his head under the occipital bone. If you shoot somebody there they'll die. Forehead and they might only end up brain-damaged. So I'm told, anyway. I'm not exactly Vinnie the Snooze here.

I told him what to say, right in his ear, softly.

'*Sun Katz says I am a hostage. I am unarmed. Hold your fire and please, PLEASE turn off the megaphones. The noise makes her really upset.*'

Alex said his piece and I paused, thinking. '*She says she will release me provided she is not placed under pressure. Stay back and stay quiet and I won't be hurt.*'

'ALL WE WANT TO DO IS TALK TO SUN,' called Captain Video, his megaphone hanging slack at his side. Boy these guys sure do act different when you've got a

131

gun than they do when they catch you driving around in Keri's sister's Saab with no headlights on Goosie Night and a half-bottle of Smirnoff's under the passenger seat. Then, they are comparatively cuddly.

'*No talking*,' Alex parroted.

'Put your finger over your lips,' I added.

'*Put your finger*— oops.' He did as I said.

I could see Captain Video conferring with his buddies. Then he shouted, 'ALL RIGHT, WE'LL GIVE YOU FIFTEEN MINUTES OF SILENCE.'

'Now back slowly away. Come on back to the stockroom. They're going to be in that hallway but the door is locked from the inside so we can have a little privacy.'

I knew that Captain Video would be happy to have fifteen minutes to get more plans in place, so I hadn't really gained anything. But I've got a splitting headache and I don't know how I'm going to get to Continental without getting Alex shot, and I just need to postpone the inevitable a little while.

While we moved through the store, I pointed an anti-your-neighbour's-dog warning system across the gap between the counter and the store and activated it, so that I'd get an alarm if anyone tripped the electric eye while we were back there. I didn't think the cops could really see us in the store, but I still felt too exposed out there.

Once in the stockroom, Alex sat on an ultrasound joint-therapy Roman chair and I leaned against the shelves. He's got a lot of shit to say, working on me the whole time with those big dark eyes and I'm not listening to any of it. I'm trying frantically to think. He keeps talking anyway. He must be trying to get through to me.

I think one of the reasons Alex and me always got along so good was because his mom's a guidance

132

counsellor and she makes him talk about stuff so he's a lot more articulate than your average teenage boy even though he's heterosexual. He once bitched at me that he was embarrassed when she sent him down to CVS to get her some tampons and the girl behind the counter looked at him funny. 'That's sick,' I said at the time because it was the desired response but privately I thought his mom sounded pretty cool. Now here I am holding a gun on him and he's going, 'I really liked you, I never thought it would end up like this.'

'It doesn't have to end,' I said. 'Think of this as like a transitional moment in a whole series of like moments that is like your life.'

'Like, *no*,' he said. 'Do you want to explain why you're doing this or am I supposed to shut up like a good hostage?'

'Because I got no fuckin' choice, my friend flipped out and now I'm gonna get blown away and I didn't *do* anything really—'

'Excuse me but why don't you turn yourself in?'

'No way. I'd be disloyal to Suk Hee. Besides, it's gone too far.'

'That doesn't make sense. You're a little off-centre Sun but you're basically OK, and this what you're doing now is going to fuck up your whole life.'

'How do you know it wasn't fucked already.'

Alex has Bambi eyes, really thick black eyelashes. I can see the layers of him in those eyes: the part that goes soft imagining what I mean by fucked – have I been abused, is my mother a drug addict, what? – and the part that watches with a detached light, the part behind the sympathy. And the part that's just shitscared but not showing it much. God he's cute.

'It couldn't be that bad . . . could it? What are you saying Sun? Is this some kind of cry for help?'

133

'Oh, save it. Look, you don't know me, all right. I have a . . . a . . . dark side and – *don't laugh!*'

'I'm not laughing.'

No he isn't. The gaze clings to me like water. His gaze makes me shine.

'I'm a lot more twisted than you know. You have no idea what goes on in my head. What I think about. I think about blowing shit up all the time. I think about killing people in disgusting ways. I think about the downfall of *everything*. Shit, in disaster movies I'm always rooting for the tidal wave.'

'Yeah, well everybody thinks weird shit sometimes.' He picks at the plastic coating on the ultrasound chair.

'I hang out at the firing range. I subscribe to astronomy magazines. I read *Soldier of Fortune*. I surf for hardcore porn. If I was a guy somebody in the CIA would have my name on a list of potential terrorists.'

I sounded pretty good, come to think of it. Alex thought so too. 'I had no idea,' he breathed, shifting his weight edgily.

'Yeah, well. I'm not like proud of it,' I lied.

He rallied. 'It's not what you think about, it's—'

'—Whether you act on it,' I finished, laughing. I waved the gun a little so he would remember I had it. 'It's good being evil,' I added. 'Better to be evil than to be nobody, a victim.'

'I disagree.'

'You'd rather be a nobody?'

'I disagree that you're evil.'

'That's nice of you, but like I said, you don't know me.'

'I think you're scared.'

'*What?*'

'I think you're someone who's really fragile and vulnerable and you don't want to show it so you put up this tough-guy façade.'

I had this major urge to blow his head off.

'Façade, huh? You get that from your SAT vocabulary-study list? Why not just say "you frontin" like everybody else? Or is that Mommy talking through you?'

I saw the barb go in. Saw him pluck it out and examine it, bleeding.

'My mom,' he said in a low voice, 'taught me to give people the benefit of the doubt. Not to judge them right away.'

'Thanks for that patronising remark,' I sneered.

'No problem. I'm sorry if I hurt your feelings.'

'What?'

'When I said you were vulnerable. It wasn't meant as an insult. It's not a crime, you know.'

'Look, could we check the cheesy Psych 101 at the door?'

There was a little silence. Alex shifted his weight. He's edgy, not very good at sitting still even in his favourite class, Precalculus. Now he looks around the stockroom with an alert, restless air.

'Do they have any luminous clipboards back here?'

'What?' I laughed.

'Luminous clipboards . . . can I look for one? Don't worry, I won't try to escape. See, I was just starting to check this thing out before. I figure when I go out in the country to stargaze with my dad I can keep my notes where I can see them without using a flashlight – it would free up my other hand for a beer!'

'That's a good idea,' I agreed. Stargazing. Alex got me into stargazing, and I've been waiting and waiting for him to invite me to come up to Woodstock with him and his dad to look at the sky without ground light. We were supposed to go last summer but the weather turned bad and then it got too cold.

'You should get one, too,' he said, standing with his head tilted back, scanning the shelves. 'Ah, here we go.

135

Otherwise you'd have to hold my beer and I wouldn't trust you.'

'You can trust me,' I said as he reseated himself, opening the package like a little kid at Christmas. 'I don't like beer, I like vodka. Don't you feel any sense of guilt for stealing that merchandise?'

'I'm not stealing it, I'm just checking it out. Look, it's got a little chip in it, you can run it off your computer and get an LED display, or use this nifty pen. Or you can use regular paper and the edges illuminate. Turn off the lights, will you?'

There is a single fluorescent unit burning in the stockroom. If I turn it off, I am vulnerable. Then again . . . I have my goggles.

'Wait a second,' I said, dragging off my backpack and putting on the goggles, ever mindful of the gun on my lap. Alex kept his distance, though. I started to feel guilty for mistrusting him. He wasn't going to try to get the gun off me.

'OK, here goes.' I turned the goggles on, turned off the light, and there we were, Alex's clipboard glowing away, and me with big bug-eyes.

'I can see you!' I cried.

'Well, I can't see you. Where are you?'

He's lost interest in the clipboard.

'Over here.'

'Over here *where*?'

'Here,' I said, going closer. He reached out and waved his hands around, trying to touch me. I evaded him a few times until we were both laughing; then accidentally on purpose I backed into his groping hand.

'That's my ass!' I shrieked.

'Oops. OK, c'mere, c'mere, just come here,' he said, and I found myself on his lap.

136

SCRATCH 'N' SNIFF

(Mbaldino/Lab Notes/Private-Encrypted)

To my amazement, the subject is still alive. Condition remains stable and there is no sign of organ failure despite the fact that Az79 infection continues as per last week's incident. Immune response is muted.

We have confirmed that Set 10E is the dominant organism within all tissues. We are looking at its metabolic products to assess its harvest value. SE 4465, our charming guest, shows no sign of Az79 infection. As yet.

Still no response from Bernie. I keep sending him stuff anyway. Have also set up a data feed to Kaitlin at DVL labs in California. What Jennifer doesn't know won't hurt her, I mean fuck all this sworn-to-secrecy crap. If I'd known Meniscus would survive I never would have agreed to this stupid idea of using Az79 to kill the SE. I'd rather get my sperm by legitimate means.

Anyway, Kaitlin knows her shit with assassin-bug network. I'm hoping she'll spot something I've missed.

'If you don't cut his goddamn nails, I will,' Starry Eyes hollered at Naomi. 'Gimme a pair of scissors or I'll make him bite them off.'

Naomi was on the phone. She called over her shoulder, 'Don't be so grumpy. I'm going to get your snack in a minute.'

She was acting funny, Meniscus thought. All flirtatious and cosy, no matter how rude Starry Eyes was. She was jumping to his beck and call. Most days she brought Yoo Hoo and Chips Ahoy!, which were Starry Eyes' favourites. She tried to get him into Pepperidge Farm and he had gobbled a whole package of Double Chocolate Mint Milano cookies once before pronouncing them 'pussy cookies'. After that he remained faithful to Chips Ahoy! with at least seventeen chips per cookie (Meniscus had counted, and deemed the advertising to be accurate). By snack time Starry Eyes was usually finished with his push-ups and sit-ups and jumping rope, this last using a piece of electrical cable torn from inside the wall of his habitat – exercises that he performed after he had woken up and taken a protracted shit while reading Cycle Freek. Then he usually fiddled around with the alleged bike (which resembled a praying mantis more than a vehicle to Meniscus's eyes) until he got frustrated, harassed Meniscus and told him to clean up the habitat and cuffed him around some. As far as Meniscus was able to determine, this routine violence was more or less recreational in tone. Sometimes it actually took on an air of levity and fun – for Starry Eyes, at least.

'Come on, Squeak!' SE would say, bobbing and weaving to the degree that his bulk would permit, extending an open-palmed hand slowly enough so that Meniscus was meant to be able to duck under it or cover his head. Meniscus, elbows clasped firmly in front of his face and his shoulders turtled up protectively, never attempted to put this advice into action. He was too terrified. He merely wanted to live. Usually he ended up on the floor in the foetal position.

'Cut that shit out!' Starry Eyes said this morning upon Meniscus's prompt collapse. 'You want to be in the foetal position? You're gonna be if I kill you and you get reincarnated as a newt.'

It was Round Two of the daily altercation/rout; SE had finished attaching the brake lines to the handlebars and Naomi was occupied on the phone. (*'No, Mads, the exterminator hasn't been. No. No, I didn't cancel; actually, I thought you did. They said the order came from your account. I am not being funny, I swear . . .'*) Starry Eyes had been amusing himself by trying to engage Meniscus in a boxing match, but every time he glimpsed Meniscus's fingernails he cringed and almost seemed to gag. Meniscus, a very small ball on the floor, remarked, 'Newts lay eggs. They don't have a foetal position.'

Starry Eyes hesitated. He was grossed-out by Meniscus's fingernails, which were not only a necrotic shade of blue but had begun to corkscrew, having grown to extraordinary lengths in the past couple of days. Meniscus was finding it hard to do things like eat and get dressed, but he was afraid that if he stopped making the nails grow he might lose the use of his new internal ability. He was working on his hair, too, and it now streamed over his shoulders, black streaked with tell-tale strands of azure.

139

Starry Eyes yelled again for Naomi. 'Hey bitch, this is your last warning – if he touches me with those fuckers I don't know what I'll do.'

But Naomi was busy talking to Dr Baldino on the phone. They could hear her through the lab's intercom system.

'How should I know what Bonus does? She's your kid. Yeah, the game's still working OK, I don't think the mice have actually chewed through the wires yet.'

Starry Eyes kicked Meniscus lightly in the kidneys and said, 'Wuss. Stand up for yourself, Wally.'

And how was he supposed to do that? He was a bug farm, not a tiger. Meniscus wanted to disappear. His nails rattled against one another as he tried to hide his face from Starry Eyes's scrutiny.

'What I want to know is why your toenails ain't long, too. You weird motherfucker.'

'Yoo-hoo!' Naomi called from the other side of the plexiglas. Her voice echoed a little. She waved the eponymous drink cans cutely. SE stepped back to let Meniscus up. He was wearing a Hawaiian shirt, which made him look Polynesian, some cut-off grey sweatpants and red canvas basketball Keds, size 14. He took in Naomi's bright expression.

'It's about time, baby,' Starry Eyes said. 'Let me see your tits.'

'No!' she said angrily. She glanced around to see if anyone was watching. Then she retreated to her cubicle and did something to the camera that monitored the habitat. The red light went off. She came back out, shucking off her T-shirt.

'Oh yeah Naomi baby I like that,' SE had his cock out. Meniscus tried to dive into his MUSE and escape to Mall, but the settings had restricted his access to subliminal. He couldn't override his real senses with the game. He

140

closed his eyes and wished himself away. It was no good.

'When you gonna come in here and pay me a little visit? I know you want my cock in you. Don't you baby.'

An odd squeaking noise made Meniscus open his eyes. At first he thought it was the renegade mouse, but it was Naomi's skin. She was fogging up the plexiglas, rubbing against it sweatily and stroking her nipples, panting. Starry Eyes yelled encouragement. Meniscus developed a painful hard-on and his back bubbled and sparked with bug activity. He could feel the azure monsters that lived within him. They ate and excreted at a furious rate. They reproduced.

He wanted to try to quell them, but he couldn't get into Mall. He couldn't know what was happening there. Meniscus thought his teeth would fall out. His insides were going berserk. Again he clenched his eyes shut but Naomi's teasing voice reached him.

'So tell me. Why do your pheromones match Arnie Henshaw's Scratch 'n' Sniff kit *exactly*?'

Starry Eyes sounded gruff and distracted when he replied. 'How'd you get Henshaw's Scratch 'n' Sniff?'

'It's in the promotional kit Curator Gould gave to Dr Baldino. I think Maddie's pig-shopping.'

'And you open her mail?'

'That's nothing to do with you. Come on, answer the question. How can you have the same pheromones as him?' Meniscus opened his eyes. Naomi was leaning against the barrier and so was Starry Eyes.

'If I tell you, will you let me out?'

'As if!' Naomi grinned and backed off, replacing her T-shirt.

Starry Eyes put his cock away sulkily. Suddenly he spun around and kicked at a loose bicycle pedal that was lying on the floor. The blow generated a surprising amount of force, because the pedal bounced off the plexiglas, taking a chunk out of it before shooting across the floor like a hockey puck and vanishing under the toilet unit. The shard landed amongst the planets. Meniscus flinched and felt his skin creep ominously.

Naomi made a face and called Starry Eyes a beast.

'I mean, are you *related* to him or something?'

'Do we look like we're related?'

'You smell the same.'

'Piss off. Henshaw's a piece of shit but you go right ahead and vote for him, I hope his pig fucks you senseless. Hey – Squeak! *Here*. Now.' The summons was addressed to Meniscus, who obeyed, trying not to look at either of them. Starry Eyes pointed to the toilet and Meniscus crawled over and retrieved the bike pedal, like a dog. As he fetched it he was remembering the wolf that still wandered, uncaptured, amid the sports stadia and factory-outlet stores of the Meadowlands.

Naomi looked shocked at Starry Eyes's crudeness, but she gave as good as she got: 'I'd rather fuck a pig than fuck you.'

'Oh, sorry to disappoint you, but I was only kidding. You don't get a cock in you, poor bitch. Not even a pig cock. You get inseminated, don't you know? Hell, girl, anything else would be cruelty to animals.'

Not to be outdone, apparently, Naomi turned her back, bent over, and farted.

'I can't smell your stench. That's what the glass is for, remember? Give me that piece of wire, Squeak. No, the green one. Ugh, and don't touch me with those claws . . .'

Starry Eyes made a good show of ignoring Naomi. But Meniscus noticed that Starry Eyes's sweatpants still contained a tent pole. For his part, Meniscus was giving out irregular panting grunts, and his muscles were twitching spasmodically.

142

'Whoa, hey, Dr Baldino, breaker breaker, this is Naomi – we've got a testosterone surge and it's provoked a major Az response. I'm not gonna do anything until I hear from you just in case you know like I don't want to screw up or anything like the other day but whoa I think you better call me, Meniscus is acting real weird. Bye.'

Naomi, acting like a firefighter sliding down a greased pole, dived under the I-MAGE headset and started processing madly. But the damage was done. Meniscus's bugs were up to something dirty with his body. Blue shudders passed across him.

When the mouse ran across his foot the first time, he didn't even notice it. The second time, he withdrew his foot. The third time, he slipped out of the game because Starry Eyes had shaken him.

'Look, Squeak, it's Naomi's mouse!'

The white mouse was sniffing around an empty bag of Cheez Doodles. Starry Eyes, without any indication he was up to something, suddenly snaked out an arm and grabbed it.

Meniscus cringed, but Starry Eyes just said, 'He's cute. Let's call him Genghis and keep him as a pet.'

'Why?' said Meniscus blankly; he was understandably preoccupied with himself and failed to see the appeal of a pet mouse.

'Because Dr Baldino wants to exterminate him, that's why. He's one of us.'

He put Genghis into an empty jumbo-sized Oreo box. 'He must be coming in and out of the habitat through a broken seal near the I-MAGE cables.' Starry Eyes chuckled and added, 'No need to report that!'

Meniscus was too agonised to have a moral protest. Anyway, only males could catch Dr Baldino's plagues, and all the precautions that the staff always took seemed a bit much.

The bugs were munching on Meniscus's nerve endings. He saw himself in the plexi and he was blue like a djinn; the bugs were going to grant his wishes but only if he'd serve them. He couldn't tell their desires apart from his own any more. He couldn't tell Starry Eyes and Naomi from himself any more. It was like he had no skin, nothing to separate interior and exterior; his skin was a blue sky of possibilities and the bugs were going to write on it. Squatting on the end of his bed, he pulled the blankets over his head like a hood.

'Help me,' he whispered to no one in particular.

SE turned a night sky gaze on him. For a moment Meniscus thought Starry Eyes could give him the thing he needed: the word, the sound, the insight. For a moment Meniscus thought Starry Eyes had really come to save him, that he would finally utter the profound words that surely were waiting, folded potentials like unborn birds in their eggs, waiting in the orbs of those eyes.

Starry Eyes said, 'I can't find the Allen wrenches. Did you see them?'

Meniscus bunched his fingernails together and shoved them in his mouth. A burning pain rippled across his shoulder blades. He bit down, hard.

STARRY NITE
EYES

'I NEED TO ASK you something embarrassing,' I
said.

'No, that is not a gun in my pocket.'

We both laughed nervously.

'It's about the sky,' I said. 'Do stars ever make you
feel . . . you know . . .'

'What, romantic?' He combed his hair back off his face
with his fingers and started to gear up his 1940s generic
Leading Man impersonation, but I punched him on the
arm.

'No, just sexual.' The gun in my hand was hot and
sweaty.

'Sexual? They're giant balls of gas and atomic—'

'I know that, I know, but there's something about them.
When I'm watching them I feel like they're watching me
back, and that's kind of you know erotic.'

'Ho, ho, the truth comes out Sun. Not so cool after all, are we?'

'Cool? Me?' We had both dropped our voices since the lights went out. I pictured armoured agents with submachine guns creeping along the access corridor from the parking lot, about to jump in the stockroom any second.

'Yeah, I mean, it's like you're above it all sometimes. I mean, we get along pretty good, don't we?'

I shrugged and then realised he couldn't see it.

'Sure.'

'But I don't feel like I really know you.'

'Know? In what sense?'

'See? That's what I mean. Why don't you just put it down for a second?'

Actually, I *had* put it down. Unknown to Alex, I'd laid the gun carefully on a shelf just over his head. But of course that wasn't what he meant.

'Maybe I don't know how,' I whispered. There was a lot of body heat going on between us, and even though I'd come only just this morning I was practically dripping. My aches and pains sort of faded away. He slid his hand up my arm and curled it around the back of my neck, turned his face up towards me and—

'Ow!' He startled and jolted back, rubbing his nose. 'What was that?'

'My night-vision goggles,' I answered sheepishly. 'Sorry about that.'

Now his hands were groping over my face.

'I can't believe the stars make you horny.'

'They do. When I masturbate I always—'

He had evidently worked out where my mouth was because he kissed me. His tongue pushed into my mouth and slowly probed around.

Suddenly the lights came on.

I flicked the goggles into daytime mode and looked

146

around nervously, but he held me down, pulling me closer.

'I wonder what they're up to,' I muttered, but Alex passed his hand over my breasts and I couldn't concentrate. I shifted so I was straddling him and I could feel the shaft of his cock through his sweatpants against my open cunt. I wrapped my arms around his head, watching the gun the whole time. The only way he could get it would be if he reached back over his head with his left hand, and even then it would be chancy. Since his left hand now was inside my T-shirt and unhooking my bra, I figured it wasn't a major problem.

I threw my head back when his mouth connected with my left nipple. I can't even believe this is actually happening to me. It's the last thing I could have predicted, and today of all days … I'm starting to feel like the world has fundamentally changed and will never be the same place. Like I'm finally in the movie, and I'll never eat or shit or be bored ever ever again.

'Do you wanna take those goggles off? They look pretty weird.'

'Then close your eyes,' I said. If I took them off and the lights went out again, I'd be fucked.

His left hand was now messing around pretty inexpertly under my skirt. He pressed too hard on everything. He stuck his fingers inside me but it was nothing like a gun barrel, and he didn't seem to even register the concept that I had a clitoris. 'My god your pussy is wet,' he whispered. After about thirty seconds, I pulled away and said, 'What about Kristi?'

He was bucking his hips up and down under me, which was very nice, but when he answered he didn't seem too with it.

'She won't,' he answered. 'She keeps her legs shut. It's a real drag but that's her thing.'

That hadn't been what I meant by the question, he must have known that but was avoiding the moral problem of his girlfriend. How I hate Kristi. She doesn't put out and this boy *still* goes out with her. How can she turn him down? He's so *hot*, it's a crime not to fuck him.

I don't feel even slightly guilty. I feel smug. I pull his fly down. 'Do you have a condom?'

He's busy getting his wallet out, I've got my right eye on the gun although I have to keep my head back to avoid bashing him with my goggles again. I'm going to *do* this. Yeah, I'm going to do it.

'I'm a virgin, so you gotta be patient with me,' Alex says with no sign of shame. He's tearing the condom package with his teeth, he's putting it on.

'Ribbed for her pleasure,' he says, trying his best to leer. I stand up to give him clearance for his cock. It's hard to tell its exact size because it's *glowing* in my NiteEyes goggles.

I've been stretching my hymen for about six months with various objects, trying to improve my chances of orgasm while losing my virginity. It was all a total waste of time, because (a) it took a long time to get his chocolate lined up with my peanut butter and (b) in the end he just had to shove really hard and once he got in there it hurt like hell. It was worse than they tell you in *Cosmo*. A lot worse. I jerked my head forward and butted him in the face with my NiteEyes. Whenever I feel pain, I always lash out, and in this case the fact that he was feeling ecstatic while I was feeling like I was being ripped apart made me even less considerate of others than usual. The goggles connected satisfyingly with the bridge of his nose and he grunted. Then he thrust his cock into me again and I considered elbowing him in the eyeball. He was oblivious to how I felt. He actually reached up and shoved my head absently to one side while he banged his thing in and out of me, groaning, grabbing the flesh on either side of my hips and wringing it, grabbing my butt, and more or less doing excruciating things to me right up my snatch.

'Ow, you shithead!' I squeaked. He stopped.

'Sorry. Oh, sorry, sorry, are you OK?'

'Yeah, yeah, never mind.' I'm glad the goggles hide my tears.

'Are you a virgin too?' he said incredulously.

'Duh!' I said.

'Oh. You should have said. Do you want me to stop?'

Why does he have to be so *nice*? I really can't in good conscience shoot him. Still. So much for a nice fat gazz. This is more like a root canal. I just wanted it to be over. As Alex carried on enjoying himself I scanned the shelves, looking for something to focus my attention on, and that was when I noticed the security camera high on the left-hand wall. It was pointed straight at me and the red light was on.

Alex's whole body went tense and the most incredible expression came over his face, and then all at once he'd stopped. He was kissing my neck and face and gasping and saying things like, 'Oh my god Sun, my god that was incredible' etc, etc, insert hyperbole of your choice, the point is he was pretty well-glossed about the whole thing. Gingerly I picked myself up off him, expecting a colossal rush of blood but there were just a few pink marks on the condom, that was all.

Shit, how embarrassing. It hurts so much I could cry and I'm barely even bleeding.

My phone started ringing. I jumped, then grabbed the gun and took the safety off, and reached into my backpack with my other hand and answered the phone.

'Congratulations, Sun, you broke your Tootsie Roll. Smile for the camera.'

It was 10's voice.

'What?' I said faintly, turning towards the red light. 'How do *you* . . .?'

'Your fifteen minutes is almost up. You better do something quick.'

She hung up.

BIKE

'Now you would think that with the constant danger of Y-plague exposure, even the bravest male would have to think twice about becoming a firefighter. Yet Khari Lee, our guest and a semi-finalist in the upcoming Climb 'n' Dive mixed competition, chose to do just that. Khari, can you explain why you are willing to risk your life, not only as a Los Angeles firefighter, but also as a man in a woman's world?'

Meniscus was pretending to be out of it, but in truth he was listening to the Pigwalk Previews, courtesy of Naomi, who played the coverage almost incessantly in the lab. He was sitting on his bed with his knees drawn up to his chest and swinging his head from side to side like a metronome, and every so often he took a swift glance at the screen. He took in Khari, who was lean and broad-shouldered with a flat nose, a receding hairline, and bad skin.

151

'Well, Chevette, the way I see it the two things go together. You risk your life putting out fires, so it'd be stupid to sit home and be safe from Y-plagues, too. I mean, I'm a strong guy, you know?'

Appreciative noises from Chevette and crew.

'It's a real rough job, even with all the technology we've got these days. Requires a lot of strength and toughness. Very few females can even get near me in terms of physical ability. Can't even get near me, even the elite athletes. That's just a fact.'

'Ooh, we sure appreciate that, Khari,' said Chevette. 'But what about risking exposure to Y-plagues? Obviously you're not the only male firefighter out there, but you're the only who's made it this far in the run-up to the Pigwalk.'

'That's partly because the Y-plagues have taken out a number of my colleagues over the years. You suit up, you do your best to avoid exposure, but it's always a risk leaving the castellation. But the other reason there aren't more us here, Chevette, is because we don't make the glamour cut.'

Raised eyebrows, half-hearted laughter. Starry Eyes was nodding his agreement.

'The glamour cut?'

'Yeah, you know, we're not good-looking enough or smart enough to get into a castellation, we don't have a seat on the stock market, we didn't cut a hit joint, we're just regular guys. A lot of the contestants here tonight have all kinds of education and experience going for them. And they have a whole team behind them, to push them to the audience.'

'Word up!' yelled Starry Eyes. 'It's about time somebody said it!'

'So you've lived outside a castellation, taking your chances. Do you think it's unfair, Khari?'

Khari shrugged. 'Fair, unfair, that's life. I just figure I better take a shot at it. I was born Accidentally, but I don't think my life's been a waste.'

'Neither do we, Khari,' chorused the studio admirers.

152

'Yeah, and I just figure I'd like to be a dad, you know.'
Embarrassed shrugs, muscles all over the place.
Meniscus noticed that Dr Baldino wasn't looking at the I-MAGE read-outs any more, she was looking at Khari.
'You can't do that the old-fashioned way any more. You can't just get a girlfriend and go out. Women want to see a brand name. So I thought I'd take a shot at it.'

'Well, good luck to you, Khari, and I can tell you that during the course of this interview your standing in the polls jumped seventeen per cent, a huge leap. So everybody watching can see, this Pigwalk really is an open competition.'

'Awesome,' Dr Baldino breathed, but now she wasn't talking about the firefighter. She was swimming in the I-MAGE of Meniscus during the testosterone surge. 'You know, I think he's holding his own? I can work with this.'

Meniscus continued rocking back and forth on the bed. He listened to everything Dr Baldino said. He had long ago learned how to listen without showing it. He looked, but only in sidelong glances, when they didn't expect it. He was afraid.

'He seemed awful freaked-out to me,' Naomi put in.

'I imagine he would be. Look at these colonies.'

In the I-MAGE display, the Az79 10E camps looked like whirling spiral galaxies.

'Ooh,' Naomi hummed. 'Bug chakras.'

A commercial for Evian water came on. It showed three babes in the depths of an automobile pit, taking a break from welding with some 500ml mini-bottles of Evian.

'This is the strangest thing I've ever seen. It's an actual DNA exchange between 10E and human. See, I've labelled the relevant blocks where the bugs are picking up pieces of the subject's DNA. Dammit, when is Bernie going to answer my calls?'

153

Meniscus heard the clicking of her fingers on a keyboard.

'Meniscus reads those lab reports, you know,' Naomi said.

'Of course he reads them. It's a condition of the study.'

'What's the point of that?'

Maddie snorted. 'I dunno. It's a bee in Bernie's bonnet. He says it makes him feel better, like if the subject doesn't actually object, then silence can be taken for tacit consent. I don't think he really believes that any more than you or I do, he's just trying to hold on to this idea that Meniscus is his clone and since Bernie's a scientist who would want to read the lab reports, Meniscus should read them too.'

'Weird. And Bernie doesn't mind paying for the SE's bike parts?'

'I'll ask him when I see him. Why?'

'It's just that he's ordering some exotic stuff. Cycle Freek has been making deliveries round the clock, and he keeps ordering more. I wonder what Meniscus thinks. You know, what does he think when he reads about what's happening to him?'

'I wish he'd tell me,' Dr Baldino said. 'Maybe he could shed some light on the situation.'

Meniscus made sure he didn't look at her then. He rocked and rocked, like seaweed in a tide; he rocked to the surge of bug impulses in his blood.

'*Yeah*,' muttered Naomi into the intercom, so that only Meniscus and SE could hear her. '*Or maybe he'd tell you to get stuffed.*'

'Now what I really want to know,' said Dr Baldino, 'is what was going on when the camera was down. And, naturally, why it was turned off in the first place. Naomi?'

Naomi and Starry Eyes were looking at each other. Starry Eyes looked like he might crack up laughing any second. Naomi looked pale and confused.

'Oh, that. I was afraid you were going to ask about that.' She went bustling back into the kitchen and started cleaning the centrifuge.

Dr Baldino raised her voice without taking her attention away from the I-MAGE console. 'This is the second time my subject has had some sort of incident on your shift and this time the camera's been deactivated. But you can't pin this one on my daughter. I checked with KidTrix before I came down here, and Bonus is busy doing team-building exercises with her core age-mates. So what's your excuse this time? That video was shut down manually.'

Naomi came out of the kitchen, red-faced.

'Anitra was here,' she said softly. 'I didn't want Security to see, so I turned the camera off. Then, when Meniscus started acting weird, I forgot all about turning it back on again.'

Dr Baldino made a frog face. 'Who is Anitra?'

'An old flame. I didn't think ... didn't expect ... but ... you know how it is, things just ... got started.'

Meniscus forgot to be secretive and stared at Dr Baldino to see her reaction. Flashbacks of Naomi throwing herself against the glass darted through his mind, and his skin prickled. His teeth sang.

'Whoa, look out!' Naomi cried. 'There it goes again! He's off!'

Meniscus struggled to shut down his reaction this time. It was only sex, only sex, only sex – nothing to do with him. He buried his face in the blanket, clutched the faithful old sun, and counted backwards from ten thousand. He could hear Dr Baldino warning Naomi about losing her job but what he really wanted was to get into Mall and try to assert some control. He made his mind go as smooth as he could amid the seething activity of the bugs. He could sense the activity in Mall ticking over beneath his skin, like a whisper just below the threshold of hearing. He tried to lean into it but instead of seeing the familiar polished corridors and the flash of credit cards passing across glass counters, he saw the smoky starshot eyes of the wild man as he grabbed Meniscus by the throat. The stars in Meniscus's body smouldered in recognition. Blue rivers coursed like veins beneath his skin. The muscle that was not a muscle flexed, feeling its new power.

Like a rower straining against the tide, he pulls for control and slowly, exhaustingly, he gets it. He feels the bugs coming into line with his thought, and the emotions start to subside as the receptors take their cues. He opens his eyes.

Some time must have passed.

Naomi, kicking back with her bare feet crossed at the ankles on the I-MAGE console and her finger up her nose, is reading a grubby paperback called *More Than Masturbation: a Post-Boypower Guide to Chinese Internal Alchemy*.

The Atlantis Pigwalk Previews have broken off to make way for a midday news update. The wolf has been sighted in the Ikea parking lot but state rangers are no closer to capturing it than they were last week. Several crates of brass curtain rods have been peed on.

Dr Baldino argues with Curator Gould on the phone.

'Until I know why my subject is still alive in the face of certain death, I can't be sure your SE has nothing to do with it. Meaning that you can't remove him from the habitat . . .' She pauses, rolls her eyes, drums her fingers on her litre-sized take-out latte. 'I know you say he was clean when he arrived, but there are other kinds of influences than bug influences. Meniscus is a sensitive, Y-autistic subject and he seems to be reacting— What? Look, this was your idea, not mine . . . *Yes*, I'm doing tests

156

and then I have to get the results. What's your rush anyway? Well maybe if Arnie Henshaw would take my calls we could resolve this quicker. I can't find out *anything* about this SE of yours.'

Starry Eyes, who has just received a large shipment of bike parts and is now examining them and making notes on his magazines, begins to chuckle. Meniscus wonders whether Starry Eyes knows why Meniscus's immune system is acting so funny. He has a way of acting like he knows more than Dr Baldino. But all he does is make Meniscus box and wrestle, even though Meniscus is terrible at it. All Starry Eyes does is engage Meniscus as audience for his totally inane performances ('Look, Squeak, I can bend this crowbar with my psychic powers'; 'Count how many seconds I can hold my breath standing on my head'; 'I bet you two beers I can put six twinkies in my mouth at once without chewing'). All Starry Eyes does is stress Meniscus out, asking questions about cataphoresis treatments and aluminium 6061 tubing and the advantages of a 37-112-inch gear range, and when Meniscus answers, 'I don't know,' then Starry Eyes swats him around and insults him and makes him look it up.

Starry Eyes acts like building his stupid bike is the Manhattan Project.

Bike bike bike bike.

Meniscus thinks about it but does not grasp it.

The bicycle, a most unlikely extension of the human body. Especially Starry Eyes's body. Meniscus wants to stand back from Starry Eyes and understand, but everything Starry Eyes does has him under a kind of spell of admiration and perplexity. If he could step back he would have to ask himself what the hell SE intended to *do* w/the bike & he would have to ask himself what the bike in itself meant.

The bike *qua* the bike. Well, the idea that there could be a mechanical addendum to the human form doesn't seem to have raised many eyebrows but when you think about it the bicycle is a scary and mind-expanding creation. It recognises the cyclical nature of walking and then transforms it into something more effective. The idea that you could mechanically improve on nature is nothing new.

But punch through it and the Wheel = Female Domination. Because the Wheel led to everything else tech-wise, which led to the emancipation of women and their ultimate ascendancy. And it all happened because someone could perceive the cyclonic qualities of human movement and idealise this in the form of the bike. Hey, Bike-Designer Guys: we salute you!

That's what Meniscus was thinking as Dr Baldino, having hung up on Curator Gould, stood beside the I-MAGE unit and nodded to Naomi to proceed. The examination lights began their probe of Meniscus's passive dermis. The examination is the neurochemostimulative equivalent of an electrician checking the connections of a device using a couple of those negative/postive thingies like battery cables that probe and quickly zing and either the connection is made or it isn't; like checking for faults on a telephone line. So his hormones were stimulated each in turn, raising their associated words and sense images, as each little assassin-bug colony or subcolony was roused from slumber just long enough for a headcount. Then on to the next one. He felt like a marionette.

When the probe of Meniscus was finished, Dr Baldino and Naomi directed the I-MAGE light on Starry Eyes, who didn't even seem to notice.

Meniscus wished he knew what they could see. Without conscious access to Mall, he couldn't spy on their

I-MAGE files using the monitors at Vinnie's Video on the Lower Level next to Lenscrafters II. Mall was an iceberg, ninety-nine per cent submerged beneath the Arctic of Meniscus's awareness. In the realworld SE ratcheted away on the bike, and sometimes rumours of Mall rose up white and blue to the surface where Meniscus could perceive them, but only as omens. He knew that ghostly people fabricated from his imagination were acting out the drama of Azure and antibodies, thought and chemicals. Yet he couldn't sense these characters clearly any more, and he couldn't control them – Dr Baldino had taken that ability away when she reduced his access to the game to subliminal. Since the absence of consciousness also meant the absence of pain, he should theoretically be happy about this inner blindness.

He isn't happy. He is uneasy. He is changing. His skin, encroached upon more and more every day, conditioned and coloured by Azure79, has become permeable to every thought, every feeling, every impulse. He can feel everything. He belongs to everything.

His planets ride their new orbits, full of mystery.

He got bored of growing his nails, and besides, something else is going on in him: the execution of a wish so deep he can't speak its name or look at it straight on. Yet he carries it out, under the cold waters of the game. It makes him feel always hungry. He has been finding it hard to keep still, and sometimes when Starry Eyes is asleep, Meniscus, made bold, has taken to prowling the habitat like the wolf that roams the empty parking lot of Ikea. In his imagination he heard the breath of the wolf as it ran, and he smelt the oil and dirt and dead grass that bordered the turnpike slip road, and a polluted mist off the river stung his eyes.

But when Dr Baldino, having finished both scans, comes right up to the plexiglas and scrutinises her subjects he doesn't feel like the wolf. He feels like the mouse that they have failed to corner: granted a temporary reprieve, maybe, by default – but only until matters can be organised better. Dr Baldino looks at his blue face.

'Just what are you two up to?' she says. 'I know you can talk, Meniscus. I know you two are plotting something, and I'm going to find out what it is. You wait.'

Meniscus shivers and avoids eye contact.

'Ah, fuck off,' Starry Eyes remarks to her from behind the bike. 'Leave him alone. He's all right.'

She turns to Starry Eyes, bristling. She pays no attention to Meniscus now, and he is left clutching at the still air in the wake of the vibrations made by her voice, addressing him, Meniscus.

She spoke to him.

She spoke to him, and he hasn't curled up and gone Inside.

She spoke to him and he survived.

Now, hands on hips, she addresses Starry Eyes. 'Do you want to tell me why Arnie Henshaw is trying to kill you? I might be able to help you if you'd stop acting like such a jerk.'

Starry Eyes shrugs, picks his nose and rubs it on the edge of the wheel rim. Then he polishes this with a dirty rag. He stands up and adjusts his balls, sporting a partial erection. What else is new?

'Doc, you're just like the others,' he laughs. 'You want to help me. Isn't that sweet? I was wondering when you were gonna shake your ass my way. Don't be shy. I ain't that picky. I'll give you the same deal I give everybody: help me on my way, and I'm willing to fuck you.'

Dr Baldino's cheeks go red and white and red again. A big grin crosses Starry Eyes's face. Meniscus, shocked, only stares at him at first.

'Or we could put it in a jar if you're not into cock.'

Dr Baldino looks even more mortified, if that were possible. Starry Eyes laughs at her.

Dr Baldino is the most powerful being in Meniscus's world and Starry Eyes is laughing at her.

Meniscus feels something he never felt. His eyes and nostrils are going wide, blood is storming through his heart and his muscles feel stiff and electric. He launches himself across the room at Starry Eyes, biting and pummelling and kicking and scratching.

He doesn't take in all the details. The fight only lasts a few seconds before Starry Eyes rolls him up in a ball and bounces him off the bed. He lands in the toolbox, badly bruised, bleeding from his nose.

'Cut that the fuck out,' Starry Eyes says, and picks up his rag. 'Go over there and shut up.'

Meniscus obeys, shocked at himself. Naomi goes scurrying for medical supplies. Dr Baldino is screaming imprecations at Starry Eyes but no one pays attention to her. Blood trickles down Meniscus's bare greenbluegold chest, diverted from its surest course by the dark hairs that are sprouting on newly swelling pectorals. He gets to the little nest he has made on his bed and curls up in it. He looks at Starry Eyes. Without looking back, Starry Eyes throws the snotty rag at him.

'That's more like it,' Starry Eyes grunts. 'Now clean yourself up, will you?'

BE
RATIONAL

ALL I REALLY WANT is for this not to be happening. I want Alex to say to me, 'Let's go grab a pizza,' and then we go back to his place and play video games and mess around, and maybe later try it again, the sex thing. I just want to spend time with him in a real way. Without the gun. Without the cops outside.

Without 10Esha, apparently, recording every second of the most intimate, shameful, disappointing, totally sucky moment of my life. I mean it's worse than being filmed taking a really loud wet shit. How am I going to live this down?

'I want to crawl under a rock,' I murmur, looking anywhere but at Alex. He on the other hand is in a generous, expansive mood. He is on top of the world.

'This is the most awesome day of my life. Come on, let's go to the police, you can explain everything. I'll vouch for you, I swear to god Sun.'

'Will you visit me in jail?' My voice breaks in a sob.

'Of course.' His arm going around my shoulders. 'Definitely.'

I feel limp and weak, I lean on him. He's kissing the side of my face softly, kissing my hair . . . I pull away, back up, turn around.

I got to get myself together here. Among other things my hair's a mess.

Woman can make everything she needs in her own body. How Xtra Gruesomely Iro that it is she who worships at the shrine of commerce. She throws herself away on the artifice of Man, who invented commerce to entice her. She never needed any of it. Credit cards discount outlets advertising and PR are unneeded by her, she can make human beings but this has escaped her larger notice.

I really think if women can't see this they don't deserve to rule the world.

Anyway I have this weird conviction there will be no tomorrow. Like, I just can't take it in. And the stuff I said to you before about jungles and hunting, I thought I was shitting you but really I wasn't.

I know what you're thinking. What is this girl doing here? How come they didn't catch her ages ago and why is it so odd and abstract? You're watching the pretentiousness quotient with an eagle eye. So am I but when I tell it to behave it threatens to have me on toast, it's like that sometimes, you gotta believe me.

Did you ever feel so much of something that you just couldn't control it? And you've tried shit like going to the basketball game and screaming your head off for hours and you had the orgasm or six or seven and you drank

163

the SuperSize Chocolate Shake from 7-11 but in the end you didn't feel as empty as you hoped to feel. Did you ever feel something so strong you thought it was a physical hunger but it couldn't be satisfied that way, it was thicker than physical, it stuffed your axons, it was a pregnant idea begging to be born and it was using you for that shit, but you just didn't know what it LOOKED LIKE or WHO inseminated you or how to get it OUT.

Did you ever feel that? It feels like being slapped upside the head about 20,000 times a day and you'll do anything to escape it but you CAN'T.

Subversive behaviour. What a fucking world. It's like everyone's flowing along and the only ones stopping are the ones who can't hack it, they are the ones you stumble over in the street surrounded by plastic bags full of their worldly possessions **it hurts** YOU ARE ALL SO FUCKING DELUDED & HELPLESS and I'm reduced to paying $18.99 for a CD to express this for me because you won't let me do anything REAL until **after** I've been indoctrinated broken down and seduced into submitting to the same CIVILISING WILL that's **sitting on your face**.

Sniffling, I grab Suk Hee's phone with my free hand and speed dial Keri. All I get is her voicemail, which consists of a blurry recording of 'Snap My Drawers,' the cover version by Snack Size Weiner.

'Call me bitch,' I blurt, and hang up. When I turn around, the camera's still running. I put the phone away and give it the finger. If I was a cat my fur would be the size of Barbados. I'm starting to shake.

Alex is fiddling with the luminous clipboard. 'Does it still hurt? I'm really sorry, I didn't know . . .'

He does look really sorry, his eyes are all extra dark and soft. He doesn't even know why I'm pissed off, he thinks I'm ashamed because I gave it up for him, but I . . .

164

AAAAAARGGGHHH obviously that is NOT the problem.

I know there are two choices for me. Self-pity is one of them, and I need to save the self-pity for jail. And the more he looks at me like I'm pitiful, the madder I get, until he stretches out an imploring hand at me and I shoot at it.

Alex springs back, the bullet ricochets off the metal frame of the ultrasound healing Roman chair and disappears into a cardboard Rid Ye Pest bug-zapper box.

'Turn the fuck around,' I snarl, just as I hear what sounds like a Monster Truck slamming into the stockroom door from the back. I shove Alex into the main part of the store with my foot, keeping the gun on him but not so close that he can turn and grab it, which is the mistake they always make in TV movies. A glance over my shoulder confirms that it's not a Monster Truck, it's a guy with a blowtorch.

Fuck.

Alex has tripped over some virtual reality golf clubs but he gets up quick enough when I fire a shot into the baby mesmeriser. He careers through the store, then hesitates in the doorway when he sees what's beyond.

'We're coming out!' I shriek, pushing Alex into the open maul. It's bright out here.

'Don't shoot!' Alex keeps yelling in a high, cracking voice and I don't know whether he's talking to me or them.

I'm in another world. There is the pale grey speckly tile floor, gleaming. There is the curving sweep of the balcony that delineates the corner of the plaza. There are the riflemen behind the cracked glass balustrades and at the top of the stilled escalator. I glance at the maul doors and over the tops of the riot shields I notice the helicopter parked in front of Nordstrom.

'Don't shoot, please don't shoot! It's all a terrible mistake!' Alex is saying. I admire his presence of mind but you know what? Even if he had made me come I don't think I could still like a guy who let me do this gunpoint thing. Especially the way he's crumbling at the edges.

'C'mon Sun, just give it up,' he's mouthing over his shoulder. 'It's not too late. Be rational.'

Be rational.

I kick him in the back and he stumbles forward. Every rifle in the joint shifts aim but no one fires. I grab Alex again, hold him as a shield just like I did w/Descartes only Alex is much smaller.

'Be rational' is what they tell you when you are having a sane reaction to an insane situation, and the rationale behind their conception of reason is FUCKED. *Be rational.* What it really means is assume your position in the status quo. Assume the position.

There is only one place I can go, and it's a dead end.

Continental Cappuccino is a deep, narrow, Manhattan-style store. It has black glass all along its left-hand side, matching Sharper Image across the mall. There's a bar-type counter on the right where people can order coffee and goodies, and near the door there's a bunch of racks of assorted imported yummies.

'Keep walking,' I said. 'When we get to the coffee place you will take these keys and open the door.' I passed him Descartes's keys. Lucky for him, he has realised he better shut up. Besides, Captain Video is making speeches.

'BLAH BLAH BLAH Sun Katz for your own good YADDA YADDA YADDA long life ahead of you don't BLAH BLAH.'

We're at the door. I can feel all those rifle sights set on me. I've got my body angled so it's really hard to take a shot at me without endangering Alex.

The door swings open. Releasing Alex, I lunge for the counter, scrambling over it and falling into the space behind in a complicated crash as coffee cups, pastries and spoons go flying. Captain Video is making more demands even as booted feet close in on the store.

I know this is the end. I mean, my *head* knows this is the end but my body doesn't believe me. I feel high. I can hear them running towards me and I really want to come up over that counter like a little submarine surfacing and fire.

My father started taking me to the firing range when I was twelve. He knew somebody there, we'd go after hours and he'd pay the attendant $100 a day to let me practise. I don't think my father is fully cognisant of what he does. He's very intellectual, you see. He taught me how to shoot, even bought me a gun for personal protection (it sucked for masturbation, barrel was too narrow) before he fucked off for Sumatra. That was almost a year ago. My dad's 'in' corporate finance. You just know he's sloshing with money. But does he take us with him? No. He leaves us here, something to do with citizenship for my mother, I can't keep track of it. Anyway, I'm a hell of a shot.

I want to take out as many as I can before they get me. I felt bad for Descartes because he was kind of an innocent but these guys I'm dealing with now, they are trained for it and they *like* it so that means we're in a mutually gratifying situation here.

Then I jump, startling so suddenly that I find myself flat on the floor and stiff as hell with fear before I even realise what's happened. About two seconds later – sacks of coffee toppling down on my head, a whole shelf unit collapsing, napkins feathering in the air, plastic coffee-stirrers going *sssss* as they fall and my ears filling up with terrible, teeth-shaking pressure – I get it.

Something just blew up.

TRIGGER
HAPPY

To: bernie@taktarov.com
From: mbaldino@edufunparknj.org
Re: trigger for M's crisis
Att: summary.m/3; summary.4465/1
PRIVACY LOCKED – ENCRYPTED

Where are you, Bernie? Are you reading my messages? I'm going to keep reporting in the hope that something is delaying you from getting back to me.

4465 is clearly influencing Meniscus, but I have been unable to find meaningful correlates in the I-MAGE data collected on each male. Safe to say M can no longer be classified as Y-autistic.

You need to check this out. We've got muscle development approx. +300%, elevated testosterone, dopamine, DHEA;

gonad development similar to rate of early adolescence. And diversification of substrains w/in the five major Az79 colonies shows exponential increase. Detailed developmental data summary attached.

PLEASE contact me as soon as you get this. MB

'I can't do it,' Maddie said for the fiftieth time. Arnie Henshaw had finally called her back, catching her at home first thing in the morning. She sat up and ran her tongue around fuzzy teeth as she took the call. She had been sleeping on the couch because her bed was covered with a pile of laundry that had been clean until Zoom the cat had slept on it, shedding extensively and vomiting the occasional fur-ball. Maddie avoided that whole room. Outside, Route 4's rush hour was groaning into gear, while inside Maddie's Hibridge apartment the morning light exposed piles of dirty tissues, pizza boxes, Diet Snapple bottles and crayons scattered across the beige Stainmaster carpet. Purple remnants of stickijellispyderglu clung to the trim of the bathroom door, blowing like psychedelic spiderwebs in the air-conditioning breeze.

'I can't do it,' she kept saying to Henshaw, varying the words to *forget it* and *no blow* and *go fish* but making no impression on the Aspirant Swine. He was so clean and young and smiling, and her words didn't even seem to stir the air around his ears for all the heed he took of her.

Maddie felt at a distinct disadvantage. Arnie Henshaw was an influential piece of dick, as they said. The Next Next Big Pig whose face was plastered all over Hibridge cable and satellite was in fact a kid of no more than nineteen. He looked like a very young Burt Lancaster, but instead of fluffy blond hair he had a silver buzz-cut with some kind of design shaved into it, and a blob of scarlet dye a few inches above the middle of his forehead. He was deeply tanned and had diamond studs on his teeth; they caught the early-morning light that pierced the greenhouse glass of the Atlantis Castellation penthouse. He was sitting with his legs spread apart in an obscene 'V' on top of a conference table, its media units inactive and almost invisible beneath the black glass surface. Between his legs he dribbled a basketball. All of his movements were fidgety and adolescent. Over his shoulder the Hibridge logo was etched subtly into the glass so that it seemed to be carved into the sky itself.

"Course you can do it, Maddie. All we're looking for is a little cooperation among friends.' He smiled nicely. She knew it was a coached smile; knew he had a manager and a voice coach and a movement guru and a homeopathic astrologer and a whole battalion of other minders and guides. But even coached, it was a good smile. Henshaw was cute.

'I never agreed to collude in murder. Jennifer had an airlock breach, the SE got into my subject's habitat, and nothing happened to the SE—'

'Exactly! Nothing happened. We're disappointed, Maddie. Az79 is supposed to be lethal . . .'

'Ho, wait a second. I never promised you anything. I kept quiet just as I was asked. It's not my problem if your SE didn't get sick. But something *did* happen to my subject, and until I can be sure your SE isn't a factor, I can't authorise his removal. Not to mention the fact that although your guy shows no symptoms of Az79 infection, we can't be sure he isn't contaminated.'

'Well what good is that fancy I-MAGE of yours if you can't pinpoint his cellular reactions?'

Maddie sighed, bored by his ignorance. 'I would need a control sample for your SE. I-MAGE data is relative. Now, I keep asking for more data on this specimen and I keep getting stonewalled. If you want to know why the

Az79 hasn't worked yet, you're the one who needs to be cooperating with me.'

Henshaw jumped off the table and paced around the room, transferring his dribbling to the carpeted floor. His aquamarine kimono billowed behind him. He was still smiling.

'Let's not get bitchy, Mads. I think you must be forgetting who I am.'

Maddie said nothing. She was aware that she was trembling. The kid had charisma, she had to admit that.

'Come on, Maddie. Just let the SE go, and we'll handle it from there. I'll keep my end of the bargain.' He came up to the phone lens and Maddie couldn't help but glance south. Under his basketball shorts, Henshaw wiggled his penis at her. Then he laughed. 'But you've got to keep your side of the deal. It's no different than it was a week ago. You looked the other way once, now you'll look the other way again.'

Maddie had expected this tactic. But she had not ruled out the possibility that the whole murder business was a ruse, that what Henshaw and Jennifer really intended to do was to bootleg her Az79 using the SE as a carrier. Given that the bugs were doing such extraordinary things to Meniscus, it was possible that somebody out there was prepared to pay to get them before Maddie's study was complete. Paranoia wasn't really Maddie's brand of chocolate, but there was something suspicious about the way both Jennifer and Henshaw were acting. All she said was, 'I can't let an experimental organism loose on the environment. You should know better than to even ask me.'

'Then we can say the SE is dangerous to your subject – he is, isn't he? Isn't he beating the crap out of the poor subject?'

'Meniscus is all right.'

But Henshaw was on a roll. He was excited. While he was speaking, he dropped the ball, bending to retrieve it, and she noticed that the design cut into his hairstyle was a cock and balls. The twin lobes of the back of his skull were meant to be testicles and the shaft ran Mohawk-style up the middle of his head. The red splotch on his forehead was apparently meant to be blood on the glans. 'See, we can say he's dangerous, euthanise him there in the lab, and then take the sealed body to a cremation unit. I'll get Jennifer on it, she's good at logistics.'

Maddie took a deep breath before she answered.

'Like I said, I never agreed to collude in murder. Look, Henshaw, you and Jennifer thought you had me where you wanted me because my subject was in a crisis and my study was in trouble. But now I've got ten times the study I ever had before. I could be on the verge of a big breakthrough here. I have no intention of compromising, or of letting you fuck me up. You still haven't even attempted to justify this killing. I mean, your SE isn't very pleasant but I don't see how that means he's got to be killed.'

'You don't know the first thing about him, and you don't want to know. He's bad news.' He gave her the big pretty eyes.

'As in?'

'He's extremely violent.'

Maddie shrugged. 'That's obvious, but so what? He's just a big fat oaf.'

Henshaw's eyes flashed. 'That's not fat, it's muscle,' he said in a warning tone, and then seemed to remember himself. For an instant, it seemed as though Maddie had insulted Henshaw, not the SE. But it was only an instant; then he let out a chuckle. 'He's a throwback to another time – not a caveman, exactly, but . . . not castellation material. Sure, he's physically very talented, but he'll never go anywhere in life. He's a sort of tragic figure because he's socially inept and he can't handle living in the castellation. He's deeply self-destructive. He put himself where he is now.'

'Is that supposed to be a big revelation? I'm not looking for a personality profile. I'm looking for an immune history, among other things. There is no brand logo on this guy, no bar code, no identifiers of any kind. I can't even look him up on the system.'

'Ah, yes.' For the first time during the conversation, Henshaw stopped fidgeting. He stood still and watched her through the phone, holding the ball as if it were a ritual artefact. His manner changed, mellowed – coaching, again, but it was good coaching. He was about to sidestep her question. 'Immune history. Fashion, of course. The condition of the Y. You know what I find fascinating?'

Maddie frowned and didn't answer, hoping he wasn't going to try to distract her with a piece of amateur philosophy. Her hopes were in vain.

'The durability of the Y, that's what's amazing. Men may go in and out of fashion, but we'll never disappear. And people can't distinguish between what was important in the past and what's still important. They can't discriminate between substance and surface. Nowadays, no matter how skinny, a really good hacker is worth ten guys who can impale a mammoth with a spear, but you chicks would rather have a hacker with muscles, wouldn't you? You're stuck in primeval times. And what the industry tells you is sexy, you accept, whether or not it's really good for you, like some female bird going for a male with a red crest – it's totally arbitrary. Fashion! It's like, Hasidic Jews keep nineteenth-century clothes alive, don't they? What have long black coats got to do with God, right? So there you go.'

'Immortality among the Hasidim,' said Maddie drily. 'How wonderful for you. Are you saying that you don't mind if a woman has no breasts, then? I mean, we don't really *need* them any more.'

Henshaw shrugged. 'It doesn't matter what turns *me* on. You beavers call all the shots.'

Then he walked across the conference room to a window that looked out on a lounge full of women with recording devices and cups of coffee. He waved to them, and as one the women smiled adulatory smiles and waved back.

'I'm late for a strategy meeting,' he added, nodding at the crowd. 'We have to plan my Pigwalk exploits for maximum sex appeal. They're the focus group.'

There wasn't a trace of irony in his tone. In spite of herself, Maddie responded to his belief in his own authority. She had seen this sort of thing happen between men and women in old films but she'd never experienced it. With the Autumn Pigwalks right around the corner, Arnie Henshaw was already behaving like a king in his castle, and his act made Maddie all soft and melty inside. The fact of this got right up Maddie's butt.

What would a more aggressive person do in this situation? Maddie wondered. Pull rank, probably. But she didn't have any rank. What the hell, maybe she could pull somebody else's rank . . .

'I wonder what my predecessor Bernard Taktarov would make of this SE you've saddled me with,' Maddie said, and Henshaw actually blanched. He suddenly came over all queeny. He almost seemed to shudder, pulling his kimono closed with a defensive jerk.

'Bernard Taktarov is as good as dead. His generation are bug food.'

Maddie had pot-shotted the remark, and she was taken aback when it found a sore spot in Henshaw. She knew that all Aspirant Swines hated each other because they had to compete for Swine Model status, but that couldn't be the reason why Henshaw hated Taktarov, because Taktarov was no longer morphologically a competitive male.

No, it had to be that Taktarov reminded Henshaw of his own vulnerability. Taktarov's generation had not had the benefit of sophisticated plague-screening in the castellations, and few men of his age group were even alive; none were undamaged. Henshaw might be safe now, but the very lifestyle that gave Swine Models their status inevitably felled them in the end. Fashion demanded risk-taking in males, and sooner or later all the high-level Models ended up out of their castellations, out in the bad air taking their chances with the Y-plagues. Henshaw, as a leading candidate, had undoubtedly been exposed himself and it would only be a matter of time before some Y-plague or other got to him, delivering him the same fate as Taktarov's – or worse.

Whatever the reason, Henshaw was clearly unsettled by the reference to Maddie's famous predecessor. He was in a hurry to end the call. 'Look, I'm late for this meeting. This is getting us nowhere. What can I do to convince you? Have you seen my promo? I'll jack it to you.'

'My assistant has a copy.'

'You should look at it. Maybe then you'd reconsider your position.'

'I don't think so.'

'Ah, Maddie, Maddie. A bird in the hand is worth two in the bush . . .' and he made an obscene gesture.

Maddie frowned. 'Aren't you at all interested in the reason *why* your SE hasn't become ill? If I wasn't so busy with Meniscus, I know I'd have people on that question like the tan on your butt.'

She was aware as she said it that the subtext of the conversation was becoming increasingly sexual. He was getting to her.

'Look at my stuff, Maddie. Please. And really think about it. I am heavily tipped for Big Pig. *Heavily*. This is your chance to get in on the ground floor. Is that your kid?'

Bonus had passed by in the background on her way to the toilet.

'Clone.'

'Ah, you see? Tell you what, take my codes and go to Babyshop.org and see what our kids would look like. Then make your decision. OK? I've got to go. I'll call you later.'

Another gorgeous, blue-eyed smile, and he was gone. Maddie was hot and bothered. Actually, she was hot and bothered and angry, because she couldn't control what she felt. She should be thinking about work. She should be thinking about the bugs. But weren't they the source of all her troubles?

The war against the bugs had been going on down through time. Human sexuality is dependent on the intricate immune-lock-switching that the bugs' incessant attacks make necessary. Without the bugs, we wouldn't be here, wouldn't be what we are. They define us. The war against the bugs had created and then chewed up and spat out the concept of the male, which still lay on Maddie's species like a stain or shadow, some morphic echo, a ghost in her blueprint, a hunger – but she would not succumb to this particular necrophilia so early in the morning when her cortisol levels were high and she felt strong. No matter what Arnie Henshaw's deltoids looked like.

Besides, her cervix was still low and pointy and hostile in her dry cunt, so there was no way she was capable of conceiving today so STOP THINKING ABOUT SEX, MADDIE.

'There are lots of ways to propagate the species,' she muttered, 'that do not involve a human penis.'

She didn't say the rest aloud, but she thought it. A little desperately, she thought: And if there's a weird morphic field created by growing human gametes in pigs, then let us revel in it. Let's melt the species. Let's see what we can do. I can create and destroy dozens of species of bugs, and I can do it fast. The bugs aren't afraid to change. Their morphic resonance is so fleeting, they aren't weighed down with evolutionary baggage like us and they never needed male or female either. Not that I'm comparing us to them.

But what the hoo-hah are the bugs actually *doing* to Meniscus? Come on, try harder, Baldino. Stop thinking with your cunt and do your job.

Without even pausing to make coffee, Maddie switched the MUSE on and soaked herself in the data of Meniscus's incident with Bonus. She examined before/during/after the crisis, seeking an explanation. She smelt it, listened to it, looked at it: the bodyweave of Meniscus as the pain broke him down. But the answer was not obvious. Nothing about MUSEing was ever obvious. It was a different way of seeing. You could look at behaviours as if they were objects. You could stretch your senses artificially – but that meant they weren't your senses any more. You didn't know how to look, had to invent your way of seeing as you went along.

Kandinsky started it. Then, when photographers started exploiting and exploring the potentials of the macro lens, taking pictures of lichens and mosses and slime moulds, pictures that looked like abstract paintings. This pre-fractal recognition of the order principles of the microscopic world was the visual equivalent of some guy discovering how to use a wedge-shaped piece of wood pressed into wet clay to make cuneiform to keep track of grain tithes, a breakthrough that in no way predicted the development of, say, illuminated manuscripts. But somewhere implicit in that clay discovery was the precognition that we could really take this one and run with it, something could come of this baby and you know what – now we have the Library of Congress! Woo-hoo!

And, by analogy, now we have the MUSE that brings the meaning of micro-evolution to our eyes – statistics à la Monet – and breakthroughs can happen any time and any place. Like here in Maddie's Paramus apartment, with the rain falling on the green-and-white-striped awnings of Bennigan's below. Maddie fought with the data even as she rummaged under the sofa for her left sneaker. The sneaker emerged covered in dust bunnies.

'Some day I'll get a clean math out of this,' she muttered, sneezing. She must have accidentally blinked and shifted the focus on the data because all of a sudden, instead of reading patterns of chemical interaction, she was being bombarded with algorithms describing cell behaviour. She lowered the inputs because they made her queasy, but stayed with the new view out of curiosity. Now she could hear/see/feel/smell the data superimposed on her morning apartment with its odour of stale breath.

Bonus had wandered out of the bathroom still wearing footie pyjamas. She teased the cat with a toy fishing rod that had a feather on the end of it. 'What was there before Clean Math mommy?'

'There was dirty math, honey. There were construction workers dump trucks and guys with pencils behind their ears. There was calculation and aeronautics and flow charts and other nasty counter-intuitive stuff.' Maddie paused, tilting her head and watching the activity of

178

Meniscus's astrocytes, star-shaped cells in the skin. 'Design was a hobby you went to at William Paterson Adult Education courses, like ballroom dancing and flower arranging. It was an affectation. It had no market value. That was before we found out Fashion always drove evolution, from back in the primal soup.'

'Fashion,' Bonus echoed. 'Mom, do you think there are rats in the Meadowlands?'

'Yeah, probably lots of them. Why?'

'The wolf has to eat something.'

'I wish it would eat the damned mice in the lab,' Maddie muttered, turning up the inputs on the MUSE. It wasn't just Meniscus's fingernails that were growing. It was the astrocytes; they were developing into neurons.

Holy shit.

Bonus was on the verge of tears. 'That's so cruel. How can you be my clone-mother when you do such terrible things?'

'And how can you be my clone-daughter when you are insubordinate at every opportunity and throw my trust back in my face?'

'I hate you.'

'Go eat your breakfast.'

'Can I have a pop tart?'

'Only if it's an organic one. The junky ones are for me.'

'I can't believe the double standards in this house.'

Maddie ignored her. She kept replaying the relevant data patch. Astrocytes were *always* latent in the adult organism. During a crucial developmental window they could differentiate into neurons, but you certainly didn't go around growing brain cells in your skin under normal circumstances.

The idea of neurons growing in Meniscus's skin tissue made her flinch. She thought: of course. Meniscus's crisis had nothing to do with the SE. Or Bonus. He had been

179

building up to it for weeks. She just hadn't spotted it because astrocytes were big compared to, say, molecules of serotonin – so big that she hadn't even seen them. But they had been growing, completely out of phase with adult development, developing into an annexe of some sort to his central nervous system. Then, one day, the wrong stimulus had come along, and the new system kicked into action.

'You didn't do *anything* to him. You were just the trigger.' Maddie was addressing Bonus, but in a very low voice. Bonus was in the kitchen. Maddie raised her voice. 'Bo? Can I ask you something?'

'Can I play with stickijellispyderglu after I do my math adventure?'

'Are you going to get Zoom tangled up in it again? Because the vet is going to report me to the ASPCA if we have to go back there.'

'Is that the question?'

'What?'

'You said you were asking me a question.'

'Yes. I want to know what you said to my subject down at the lab. I know you gave him your wolf's tooth – that's a very valuable and special thing to give away, Bonus.'

'It's mine. I can give it away if I want. Ow, that's hot!'

'Put the pop tart on a plate, Bonus, and stop messing around. What did you say to Meniscus?'

'I already told you. I advised him of his rights. He wasn't interested, though.'

'But he talked to you, Bo. Do you understand how big a deal that is?'

'He didn't say much. Do you want me to talk to him again?'

'No! No, I do not, and you better keep your promise not to go down there again, or else.'

'Whatever.' Bonus munched her pop tart.

'I'm just trying to figure out if there was something in the *content* of your speech that acted as a trigger. Or if it was you. He nearly died that day, you know.'

'It's not my fault you put bugs in him!'

'I never said it was, sweetie. It's just that sometimes the things you do really throw me for a loop. Like this mouse thing. What possessed you to try to save the mouse?'

'Nobody else was going to do it. Why do you have to get an exterminator? Why can't you just take the mouse out in a cardboard box and let it go?'

'They're not that easy to catch, Bo, and where there's one there are probably twenty that I can't see. If they chew through the wires they could cause a lot of harm. They're vermin.'

'That's what people used to say about wolves.'

But Maddie didn't give a fuck about wolves. Instead, Bonus's observation sent her thoughts back to the sight of Henshaw. Why did men have to be so freaking rare – and rarefied? What happened to the good old days when men paid women for sex and not the other way around? The nerve of that disgusting SE. As if!

'People used to say wolves were vermin,' Bonus persisted. 'Until the wolves were almost gone.'

'Tell me about it, kid,' Maddie sighed, and now she wasn't thinking about astrocytes at all.

A MILE IN YOUR MOCCASINS

THEY SAY FEMALE aggression is classically expressed as vicious gossip, backbiting, snubbing and ostracism. When KrayZglu got all in Suk Hee's face about Snowcone's boyfriend, that was just normal girl stuff. If nobody had guns the whole thing would have ended in people scratching each other's faces and crying and calling names. But we all do have guns, and I have to admit I really enjoyed letting mine rip.

I guess that's what 10 was trying to say about mastering my hostility: that I don't have the discipline to know when to shoot and when to hold fire. But I had to back up my friend. I wasn't going to let Suk Hee go down alone, and once SHe fired those first bullets, there was no way anybody was going to be able to back down.

Why SHe started shooting is hard to say. I guess that somewhere along the line, she just lost it. She ceased to be able to distinguish between ritual warfare and the real thing. Her amygdala told her there was a fight on, and she started firing.

I think. It's hard to be sure, because the weird thing was how she just fired at the wall of perfume. She didn't actually try to kill anybody. She acted *happy*. But there's no point in rehashing it. I can say this: I'm not going down so easy. The way I see it, even if I survive today, I've got a criminal record. My best friend has been shot in the head and my other best friend is probably giving evidence against me at this very moment. And on top of that I've lost my virginity with Alex Russo but only at gunpoint and anyway it totally sucked. So the way I see it, I've got nothing to lose.

I'm going to take this as far as it can go.

After I change my underpants, which I've peed in.

I assume it was a bomb, or maybe a grenade. Like about fifteen feet away, in the back of the coffee shop, the metal door of the Continental stockroom has been blasted open from inside. It's balanced against the edge of the counter and while I watch, it slowly topples and slides to the floor, spattering bits of broken coffee cup into my face. I shut my eyes. I can't hear over the ocean in my head. I'm frozen.

Shit. These cops must be less stupid than I thought. They figured you'd go here so they friggin' booby-trapped the place.

Oh yeah? Well, fuck me.

I feel like a salmon jumping up waterfalls as I scramble towards the now open door, firing a couple of test shots around the corner to clear the area for myself.

I crash through the coffee shop's stockroom, which is a shambles. The door at the other end is wide open, leading to a plywood access corridor with some cartons of sugar and coffee on a dolly. No cameras that I can see. There's very little light and once you go around the bend there's no light at all. I flip down my NiteEyes. I'm guessing maybe this passageway runs along behind the stockrooms but since I've never worked in a maul I couldn't say for sure what it's all about. It's funny the things you don't learn in school: like how all the *stuff* gets into the stores.

Everything hurts. I tell myself I'm a long way from a concentration camp. I know I keep referring to this holocaust thing but the film has stayed with me like a filter over everything I do since I saw it. The images of the piles of bodies hover inside my eyes. Only the stars make it go away – the stars, or thinking about them.

Enough bullshit now. I wish I had my penlight because in the faint illumination of the blackjack-cum-clock radio it's hard to read the instructions for the night-vision goggles. Also, the goggles bleep and chatter when I turn them on, and the sound echoes loudly in the still hallway. I end up tottering down the hallway with my hands stretched out in front of me, groping. My knees crunch down a little so I'm not even walking fully upright but more like a 1950s movie mummy. I feel I want to be lower, safer.

They have let me get this far because it is a trap. I am walking right into it.

I think nice things like that to cheer myself up.

I had a jungle sweat going by the time I found an unlocked door in that corridor. It's labelled 'Lady Footlocker', but I can't remember a Lady Footlocker on the upper level, only downstairs next to Sbarro's. I go in cautiously, but the stockroom is empty except for a couple of boxes of tennis sneakers. Weird. I flip the NiteEyes out of the way and peek into the store itself.

184

I was right: it's not Lady Footlocker. For one thing, it was too bright: there was daylight filtering inside and I could see through the glass front of Guess! across the way. I can't immediately see any cops out in the maul walkway, so I open the door a little more and check for cameras. One, but the red light is off.

This must be a new store, I could swear there was a Papier Papier here, but not any more. The place has all shoes where the handmade rice-paper displays were, and behind the shoes I glimpse all kinds of clothes on racks. Everything's so densely packed that I feel reasonably secure about leaving the safety of the stockroom. I start moving from rack to rack, honestly curious because this is the weirdest store I've ever been in. Unlike Banana Republic or for that matter any other self-respecting fashion store, there are no neatly stacked tables w/sweaters in six colours or racks w/things that are meant to go together tastefully combined so you won't have to think. There's nowhere for the eye to rest on kindly identical rows of shirts. Instead, the racks are as eclectic as the J. C. Penney rock-bottom clearance rack. Totally mismatched and weird. It's like an Army-Navy thrift shop except for the prices. Those are twice what you'd pay anywhere else. The labels all said 'Miles Moccasins' in ornate lettering.

Cute, I thought. Sell junk and price it really high. Neat trick.

This *would* be a good time to find some clean underwear. I can't find any thongs, but I guess it doesn't matter and – ooh, look, I *am* bleeding a little, how gratifying! I slide on a pair of pink lace bikini panties labelled 'Open Mind'. Then I check my gun's ammo and creep to the front of the store. I can see armed men going up and down the corridor outside. I slip behind a rack of boots. Then I see a really nice lace nightie, but I realise that to try it on I'd not only have to disrobe but remove the NiteEyes, and I need those if I'm going back in the access corridor, which I better do pretty soon because they're going to be after me.

Those clogs are nice, though. Actual wood, painted green, with little daisy chains around the edges. The price tag says 'Happiclatter'. Hiding behind a rack of coats, I kick off my boots and slip on the left clog.

OK, this is gonna sound weird, but the godawful truth is I experienced a sudden, nearly uncontrollable urge to start singing and dancing. Specifically, I wanted to sing and dance tunes from *Oklahoma!*, which sadly I am familiar with because I had to help Keri rehearse last year, she was in the chorus. Wearing one clog, I started doing a little western dance and humming something about corn and elephants, before I caught myself, remembering the guys outside the store.

My leg kept twitching, though. I grabbed the coat rack to steady myself, clapping a hand over my mouth, horrified and freaked out. I couldn't stop my foot trying to dance. The only thing I could think to do was to trip myself with my opposite leg. My ass hit the carpet with a thud and the clog came off. I swear it was quivering like it wanted to dance all on its own, so I slammed my palm down on it.

As I sat there on the floor holding the stunned-to-submission clog in one hand and a lace nightie called 'Fruition' in the other, the potential didn't strike me right away. At first all I could think was how psycho and amazing it was to be manipulated by clothes like drugs. At first I only felt hopeless and lame, victimised by my threads.

Then it kind of lurked and shambled in my mind, the fact that if I found the right outfit I could actually change my personality.

I wouldn't be stuck being me any more.

I shuddered. Suk Hee always thinks it would be neat to be one of those brain-damaged people who because of some frontal-lobe lesion can't perceive a certain class of objects – say, cats. Or salami. The people that get studied in split-brain experiments and stuff. SHe seems to think it's glamorous to get a bunch of psychologists that interested in you. Or maybe she just wants to take a trip to the Land of No Salami.

'You'd still be *you*,' SHe said. 'But you'd have this funny thing in you all the time.'

'A funny thing?' Keri said disdainfully. 'Suk Hee a brain lesion isn't like a stuffy that you hug at night.'

'How do you know? Why do you have to be so left-brain?'

Left-brain? Suk Hee can do trigonometry in her head, but never mind.

Anyway, these clothes are my ticket outta here. I could become someone or something that can deal with this shit. Like maybe that was the idea of Suk Hee's tying up those cosmetix chix and pretending to be them. This is just a little more extreme. Instead of changing my clothes to suit my mood, I'll change my mood by the power of clothes. I'll change myself.

I found a T-shirt called 'Energy' and immediately felt much, much better. In fact, I feel so good I could drop to the ground and do some one-armed push-ups. Then I started trawling the racks in earnest. I grabbed a lot of stuff, but the only things I put on were 'Insight' socks and 'Lucky' leggings. Oh, and a pair of 'Anything is Possible' sneakers. There was a pair of 'Kickass' jeans but I look shitty in jeans so I shoved them in my backpack with some other goodies to use later, if necessary. I didn't want to get carried away.

I didn't know what to do w/my original clothes – I was reluctant to hide them anywhere the police might find them if they were conducting a store-to-store search. In the end I upended a mannequin and stuffed my clothes into its empty thorax.

Then I saw the poster. It had been obscured by the mannequin, which was propped against the wall wearing 'Compromise' pants and a 'Diplomacy' belt. It was a Nike poster, the kind of thing you *would* expect to see in Lady Footlocker. It had a picture of a woman running beside a black timber-wolf. The woman and the wolf are photographically morphing into one another like in a New Age painting by Susan Seddon Boulet. I remember Suk Hee saying that black wolves are always male, so I gotta laugh, realising that the designer has unknowingly done something rather naughty and hermaphroditic. (It's thoughts like these that guarantee my permanent geekhood, by the way.) The poster says, 'I run, therefore I am.'

My heart was thumping. *I think therefore I am.*

'Descartes,' I said. But it didn't make sense. 'That's impossible, nobody but me knows I was thinking of that guy as Descartes – his real name was Terry.'

Clearly I am touched if I think this poster being here means something. It can't. But I'm feeling kind of emotional about shit, and I get this fixation about it. I want that poster. Suk Hee would love it. I'm taking it.

I check to see if the cops have passed by – they have. Then I reach up and pull the poster off the wall with a loud shredding sound. It comes down on my head. I stumble backward and knock over a stack of 'Inspiration' sandals.

Behind the poster there's a recess in the wall. Something black and odd-shaped has been stuffed in there. I pull it out and turn it over in my hands several times. At first I think it's a piece of scuba gear; then I realise it's a gas mask.

This is creepy. I actually feel chilly, and the hairs on my arms are standing up. I pick up the nearest jacket. It says, 'Submission'. OK, does that mean you become submissive or bring other people to submission? Grammar, like I said before, I hate it. I wasn't born here and I can never be totally sure.

I put it on. I don't feel any different. Well, maybe a little more mellow, but—

Somebody grabs the back of my neck and the next thing I can't see because they've ripped off my NiteEyes. I'm expecting the cops, but the voice belongs to a girl.

HOTHOUSE
FLOWERS

To: bernie@taktarov.com
From: mbaldino@edufunparknj.org
Re: astrocyte DNA
PRIVACY LOCKED – ENCRYPTED

The astrocytes that have developed into neurons do not have the same DNA as Meniscus's other tissues. The firing patterns of the new 'dermal' neurons occur in synchrony with brain waves relevant to Mall. I can only speculate that the increase in Mall processing power observed in connection with Az79 crisis is a result of the demand of these new cells.

4465 displaying no visible signs of infection but there are Az79 cells present in skin scrapings taken this morning. I cannot explain this.

Bernie, I'm under a lot of pressure here. I've got Mall on subliminal while I wait to hear from NoSystems, and the I-MAGE is so expensive there's nothing in the budget to allow me to hire more help.

If this doesn't get you to answer me, I give up.

To: mbaldino@edufunparknj.org
From: bernie@taktarov.com
Re: Mall settings
PRIVACY LOCKED – ENCRYPTED

Subliminal won't be good enough. Give him full access. My credit with NoSystems is good. Tell them to call me if they need validation.

B.

Meniscus lurked on the edges of Mall like a nerd at a school dance. Without explaining why or even making a note of it in her lab reports, Dr Baldino had let him back into the game. He could approach it with all his senses now. He could immerse himself in it; but the first few times he tried, it freaked him out. There were new awarenesses running all over the place, and he wasn't even sure which points of view belonged to his own body, which to the bugs. The whole issue of the body/bug boundary had become marshy and unpredictable.

Dr Baldino didn't seem very interested in him any more. When he was in crisis, she paid attention, but the rest of the time she looked harried and distracted, and because she didn't like Starry Eyes she avoided looking in the habitat at all. Meniscus was disconcerted, and where once she had stared at him and he had been unresponsive, now it was the other way around.

'She doesn't think we're people,' Starry Eyes remarked, noticing the focus of Meniscus's attention. 'I thought the female world was supposed to be so intuitive and sensitive.'

Dr Baldino had come in looking harried and distracted as usual, sent Naomi out for iced lattes, and then without a glance at either of the males, she repositioned the lab's cameras so that she herself could not be seen at her workstation. She either didn't hear Starry Eyes, or pretended not to hear. She was making a call to Babyshop.org.

'You don't conduct private business in front of other people, but you'd do it in front of your dog,' Starry Eyes added in a lower voice. Meniscus had to agree that there was a furtive air about Dr Baldino today.

'I have a bone to pick with you people,' Dr Baldino said to a video image of the diminutive bronze-skinned blonde who womanned the swanky designer cell of Babyshop.org. 'I was in your shop earlier this month running some sims, and my office tried to contact me with an urgent message. The call was blocked by your MOAT, and as a consequence I wasn't able to handle an emergency at my lab.'

The dwarf chick frowned. 'I apologise, Dr Baldino. That oughtn't to have happened unless you specifically requested a privacy lock. Let me just look up your file and see if I can find the problem.'

Meniscus watched Baldino drum her nails on the I-MAGE console. 'Yes, I think you'd better do that. The incident caused me a lot of trouble. Unless you can promise it will never happen again, I'll have to go to another provider.'

'Bear with me, I'm just checking your records . . . ah! But on that date there *is* a privacy lock requesting no interruptions while shopping. Our MOAT would have screened your calls.'

'But I never asked for any such thing!'

192

'Let's see. The authorisation comes from your address in Paramus. Can I just confirm your password with you?'

'Password?' Dr Baldino's brow wrinkles and she looks upset. 'But I didn't authorise it. My password is Bonus.'

'Yep, that's what we've got. It was used to confirm the privacy request. Did you tell anyone else your password?'

'No!'

'Did you write it down?'

'No, no, of course not. It's my daughter's name, I don't need to write it down to remember it.'

'Ah, well, you see, someone must have guessed it. OK, so we'll remove the privacy lock which means you can be interrupted while at Babyshop. Do you want to change your password?'

'Yes. Yes, of course.'

'Fill out this form and send it back, and I'll activate that immediately, Dr Baldino .'

'Thank you. I can't believe this has happened.'

The brazen-skinned midget made a sympathetic moue.

'I am sure that no one at Babyshop could have been responsible, but as a courtesy, in light of the inconvenience this has caused you, I'd like to offer you a complimentary autumn preview. Did you have anything special in mind when you came today?'

'Yes, actually. Yes, I did. I have codes for Arnie Henshaw and I'd like to look at some of our kids . . .'

'Great, I can set that up for you. It will take a little while to make up the simulations. Do you want to look at the Runway reports? Or perhaps you'd like us to run Mr Henshaw's promotional package for you while you wait?'

Until now SE had been spinning the rear wheel of his bike, filling the habitat with a hypnotic clicky-clicky noise that made Meniscus want to sleep. SE let go the wheel and stood up. He was laughing silently, tears streaming down his face, his pectorals bouncing as he observed Dr Baldino. She had her feet up on the main video console now, and at the dwarf chick's suggestion one of her hands had dropped to her crotch, probably unconsciously. Starry Eyes laughed and laughed, but Meniscus glared at him. He did not find this funny. He stood as close to Dr Baldino as the plexiglas would allow, and stared at her. He wondered if she would take her clothes off.

Henshaw's promotional video came up on the screen. It was set to the music of his latest single; Starry Eyes started nodding his head to the beat.

'I wonder what poor fucker wrote that for him and never got the credit,' he remarked. But he wasn't laughing any more.

Henshaw's voice-over came on, working the audience with a rap-fugue of his various intellectual accomplishments and political good deeds, while the images did the real work. They began with clips of music videos and feature films starring the man; then they switched to real life. There was Henshaw boarding down the face of a moving glacier; demonstrating arcane brick-breaking techniques in the Shaolin Temple; fighting off a shark in the Great Barrier Reef. It had his arm in its mouth and was dragging him into deep water when the image cut to darkness and silence.

Starry Eyes gave a shudder and grabbed his right arm as though in total empathy with the struggling figure in the video.

A moment later, the music changed and the images resumed. There was Henshaw covered in blood and grinning from ear to ear, dragging the dead shark out of the water, a trophy; the story of the battle was melanged

194

in a series of strobe-fast cuts as Henshaw actually rode the thing and plunged his knife into its head and body again and again until it stopped thrashing. Starry Eyes made a small, high-pitched noise and gaped at the screen.

But the narrator had moved on to a discussion of Henshaw's famous abilities in mano à mano combat. *'Arnie Henshaw's preferred technique is the Dim Mak strike, an arcane Eastern method of disabling and even killing. Using the secret and subtle energy meridians of the body, you can disrupt your opponent's energy balance. The idea is that you touch someone and then, a day or a week later, they drop dead. Well, Arnie Henshaw wouldn't want to murder anyone, but his opponents have been known to lose consciousness after what appeared to be an innocuous touch on his part. Not that he can't mix it up with the best of them ...'*

A collage of fight scenes ensued, featuring Henshaw's ripped and near-nude body dominating a series of opponents. Starry Eyes made a noise like he was going to be sick.

'That's what I've been offered, in exchange for giving you up,' said Dr Baldino, turning to the big man. 'Considering that I never asked to be lumbered with you in the first place, I think I'm helping you out bigtime just by keeping you here. So don't you think you owe me some answers?'

Starry Eyes wiped Goop! off his hands with a rag and stood up. He laid one of those long, intense gazes on Dr Baldino, and then punctuated it with a belch. She flinched.

'Nope. Hey, I told you the deal. I go free, you get my come. There aren't any other questions to ask.'

The two of them stared needles at each other.

'Well,' said Dr Baldino finally. 'I guess I know what answer I can give Mr Henshaw, then. Since you obviously don't value your life.'

195

'No, it's you who don't value your cunt,' said Starry Eyes.

Meniscus couldn't take any more. 'You cad!' he cried, and leapt off the bed. Starry Eyes gave him a quelling look, reminding him of what had happened the last time Meniscus had tried to protect Dr Baldino's honour. Meniscus turned aside and busily scratched the back of his neck.

Dr Baldino was shaking her head sorrowfully.

'It's sad, what you and your kind have become,' she said. 'Hothouse flowers. I feel sorry for you, and I'd like to help you, but I can't in conscience let you go. You'd die. And as for your sperm, well . . . look, I'm very sorry for your situation but I can't help you to replicate your genes. You're just going to have to accept that you are an evolutionary dead end. Women want brand names. It's a dangerous world out there, and we have to stick with the tried and true.'

Meniscus hesitated, wondering how Starry Eyes would react. To his amazement, Starry Eyes chuckled.

'It's a dangerous world. You want Henshaw, yeah? Brand names, right? Well, have him. Go ahead and have him! Ah, the human race is fucked and nobody cares but me.'

Meniscus sat down on the bed. Dr Baldino turned her back and gathered her stuff to go, and Starry Eyes just stood beside his bike, gazing across the plexiglas barrier and shaking his head and laughing to himself. 'You can't tell people nothing, Squeak. Remember that. You can't tell them nothing, so you might as well keep yourself to yourself.'

Meniscus didn't answer. He felt embarrassed for Starry Eyes.

But Dr Baldino came back over to the glass, holding Arnie Henshaw's promotional packet. The Scratch 'n'

196

Sniff card with its pheromone load was in her left hand. She passed it absent-mindedly under her nose as she reached the glass. Meniscus thought that the blood rushed to her face when she did that. She certainly appeared to be distracted by whatever she smelled.

'*Why does Henshaw's Scratch 'n' Sniff have the same pheromones as you?*' Naomi had asked. Why did it, Meniscus now wondered as Starry Eyes went over to Dr Baldino and stood so close that only the plexiglas separated them.

Starry Eyes stuck his tongue out and put it against the glass. Dr Baldino recoiled.

'She wants me, Squeak,' he said. 'Look at her. Her pupils are dilated. Her nipples are hard. I bet she's wet, too. Take another sniff, baby!'

'I want to talk to Meniscus,' Dr Baldino said.

Meniscus sat up.

'He doesn't want to talk to you.'

'Let him tell me that himself.'

'Fuck off, bitch.'

The security system announced the arrival of Naomi. Dr Baldino, startled, turned to greet her. Meniscus strained in her direction. She wanted to talk to him. Was she going to explain what was happening to him?

'You're not on this shift, Naomi.'

'I traded with Greta. She's camping out to get Pigwalk tickets at Atlantis. Went down on the old-lady bus this afternoon.'

'Can you handle the sleep dep?'

'Me?' Naomi patted her heavily decorated arms coyly. 'No problem for me, Dr Mads. I got the power.'

Dr Baldino was definitely not herself, because she didn't even act uncomfortable the way she usually did when Naomi mentioned her skin cocktails or her sex life or Buddhism. Naomi's remarks hardly seemed to register. Meniscus looked at her, wishing she would address him again, because he didn't dare speak to her himself, especially with Starry Eyes physically interposing himself between them. But now that Naomi was back, Dr Baldino seemed to be in a hurry to leave. She pulled her jacket closed as though she had had a sudden chill. She checked the latest I-MAGE read-outs and gave Naomi some terse instructions. Then she left.

'Good riddance,' said Starry Eyes. 'Hey, Naomi, get us some tacos, willya?'

Meniscus could think of several nasty things he wanted to do but he still had a black eye from two days ago when he had dropped his cover while Starry Eyes was 'teaching' him to fight. Besides, SE had begun to juggle socket wrenches. So Meniscus said, 'I hate you.'

'Oh, that's rich.' Starry Eyes grabbed a roll of toilet paper and juggled it, too. 'Considering that you should hate *them*, not me.'

'*They* don't beat me up. *They* don't insult me.' Meniscus dodged a wrench thrown by Starry Eyes, surprised at the speed of his own reaction.

Starry Eyes said, 'That's reason enough to suspect them. You should be so lucky to get an honest beating; I've been saying that to you from day one.'

'This is stupid,' Meniscus said, not understanding and not wanting to. He climbed onto his bed and shut his eyes, looking for the game. SE bounded across the room and grabbed him by the shoulders.

'WAKE UP YOU SHIT.' Very round eyes were staring into Meniscus's. His throat caught.

'WHAT? WACHOO CRYING ABOUT NOW?'

'Why do you look at me like that?'

'Like what?'

'No one ever looked at me like that.'

'Like *what*, motherfucker?'

'Like they cared what I did. Like they were angry. Like I mattered.'

'Yeah, well, don't get carried away with yourself and start thinking you're a person,' said Starry Eyes dismissively, and walked away.

Meniscus began to sob. Loneliness overtook him, it was just like when the malachite people were exiled to the far reaches of his solar system, the rejection.

'Aw, come on – I was only being sarcastic, making a point, get it?'

Meniscus gulped down his tears.

Starry Eyes shook his head, watching Meniscus. 'Fuck, look who can dish it out but can't take it? Come on, quit hating me already. I'm helping you out, don't you know that?'

'Liar.'

'I am not a liar. What good were you before I came? You were like a wet noodle. You didn't even talk.'

'Are you saying *you* are doing this to me?'

'Doing what?'

'Giving me these powers. Like, me growing my fingernails. And I can do other things, too.'

'So you're saying we got Magneto and Wolverine and then we got Meniscus – he can grow his fingernails! Ha ha, wait, I gotta start knitting you a cape.'

'All right,' said Meniscus sulkily. 'So it's just a side effect of the bugs, so what? If only you knew—' He caught himself. He had been about to say, *If only you knew how much power I had in Mall now.* But Starry Eyes would probably laugh at that too. Anyway, whatever power he had, it was still operating mostly unconsciously because he was afraid to use it.

'Look, it's no big deal,' Starry Eyes said, tossing the toilet paper roll at him and catching the rest of the socket wrenches in one hand. 'I'm just teaching you to be a man.'

'But men are doomed. Hothouse flowers is right. The tour guide says so every day.'

Starry Eyes gave an effeminate little wave, saying in a high voice, 'I'm just a hothouse flower, don't breathe on me, I might wilt.' Then he snorted. 'Bull*shit*.'

Naomi cleared her throat. She was standing beside the pass-thru chute with a Taco Bell bag dangling from her left hand.

'So, uh, Carrera, remember what we were talking about the other day?'

Starry Eyes, wearing a smirk, turned slowly towards Naomi. 'Ye-es?' he said in the same faux-girlish tone. Naomi made a face.

'I was wondering if we could come to an arrangement.' She tugged her shirt over her head and threw her shoulders back, displaying cleavage in a red lace bra.

'I told you the arrangement,' said Starry Eyes coolly. 'Same as I offered Baldino. Sperm for freedom.'

While they were talking, Meniscus sat on the bed, holding Genghis's box on his lap to shield his erection from view. His bugs seethed as Naomi cavorted in front of Starry Eyes, never glancing at him once. He didn't know if he was jealous, or afraid.

'Maddie's got the same offer as me?' Naomi sounded offended. She looked down at her sculptured body and frowned. 'Are you crazy?'

SE laughed. 'I thought you weren't going to take me up on it. Every night you stand out there and show me your ass, like you think I'm gonna just grab a test tube and come into it and give you it for nothing. But you know the deal. When are you going to disable the security and let me out?'

Naomi shook her head. 'Number one, it's against my bodhisattva vow, and number two, I'd lose my job. And number three, I don't like fucking.'

'Who have you fucked that you know you don't like fucking.'

'Well, a dildo, obviously.'

SE snorted at the comparison. 'Well, you can have it in your precious little baggie if you want, but only after the door is open.'

'The bugs. I couldn't.' She dropped her pants and kicked them away. She hadn't shaved her pubic hair, which burst out from the edges of her g-string in bright red tufts like clown hair.

'Then you don't have a deal.'

'You're impossible!'

'No, I'm not. Why don't you take it by force if you want it so much.'

'Oh, typical male response. Dominate and control, right? Because that's what you'd do if you were in power. Unlike men, women are not rapists, Carrera. When we make laws they're to protect you, they're for your own good.'

'"We" aren't rapists? When you say "we" don't include your precious grandmother. I know why you won't come in here. You look at me and you're afraid I'll assault you and get off on you. But you don't know the first thing about rape. *I've* been raped. I don't mean butt-fucked, I mean I've been forced to reproduce without consent. My sperm's already been taken by force. Your precious femocracy don't want me dead, they want me contained where they can use me. But I don't like being used, and I'd rather be a fugitive than a gilded birdcage.'

'A gilded birdcage?' Off came the bra.

'You know what I mean.'

201

'OK,' said Naomi after a pause. 'I'll take your deal. Your sperm for your freedom.'

'When?'

'Now.' She shimmied out of the G-string.

Starry Eyes unbuckled his belt.

'Come in here, then.'

'Nuh-uh. Into the little baggy and through the pass-thru chute. Then I'll sneak you out through the janitorial access tube.'

'We've been over this territory before, Naomi. I'm not giving you it to sell, so you get your ass in here now.' He unzipped his fly and let his genitals spill out. Naomi couldn't take her gaze away.

'But I'm not sure it's my fertile time yet, and I don't have a freezer-baggie . . .'

'Then we wait,' said SE, starting to return his gear. Naomi waved her hands to distract him. Her tits bounced wildly.

'But what about Maddie! You said you offered her the same deal. You'll have to tell her to forget it.'

'No way. First come, first served.' He made his penis wave at her.

'That's not fair!'

Starry Eyes shrugged. 'Your call,' he said.

Starry Eyes was pulling hard on his rolling-pin-sized cock while Naomi dragged her body across the surface of the plexiglas, which squeaked a semitone-filled music of sweat and friction. She knelt and made kissy-kissies against the breath-clouded glass.

'Into the little baggy,' she whispered seductively.

'Turn around!' commanded Starry Eyes. Meniscus shuddered. He thought he had seen it all in the archives but this was much more intense than game-porn. The sight of Naomi's wide-open butt was causing revolt all through his ribcage and down the back of his right leg.

202

His skin burned and writhed from within, obeying laws that had nothing to do with humanity and everything to do with the Azure. He shut his eyes.

'Are you coming in here or not?' Starry Eyes said in a hoarse voice. Meniscus rocked from side to side, making Genghis squeak in protest. He kept his eyes closed. Naomi must not see his distress. She must not interrupt. This time he had to keep control.

There was a silence. Then, the unmistakable sound of the air seals popping open.

Naomi's voice sounded different when she wasn't speaking on the intercom. More nasal, Meniscus thought. He opened one eye to see whether she looked the same, and caught the view of her breasts and belly, decorated with a subtle Chinese-style scroll design that seemed to tell a story beginning at her neck and heading towards her groin. He didn't have time to interpret the images, though, because just then Starry Eyes took the back of her neck in his mouth and penetrated, making her eyes roll back as she grimaced and bit her own lip, drawing blood. That finally did it. Meniscus dived into the game.

This time when the hormone surges came, Meniscus could go into the game and use them. He could use the bugs' reaction, direct it where he wanted it to go. The story written in Naomi's skin was a dead story; but Meniscus's skin was alive and the bugs were the ink writing its future. He had blue magic now. He would use it.

He was going to change.

HIGH-RISK
DILDO

IT TAKES A COUPLE seconds before I realise the girl is the leader of the 'Boos, KrayZglu. By then she's given me a couple of good shakes and asked me the same question about six times.

'Where Psychopuppy at, bitch?'

'Psychopuppy?' She must mean Suk Hee. It's pitch black now, I can smell gun oil and I try to get out of the jacket but shit the zipper's stuck . . .

'Where she at?' Jabbing me with a nail extension.

'I don't know.' Even with my new panties on, it's amazing how compliant I become. KrayZglu is . . . shit, KrayZglu's for real and I'm not. We both know it. 'I think she got hit,' I blathered. I wrestled my way out of the jacket, throwing it on the floor like it's a python. 'She's at the hospital by now. She could even be dead.'

'I be crunchin' you you don't tell the truth. What the hell you be doin', I buy a liddle time from the cops 4 U and you tryin' on dingbat *outfits*? You a joke, girl, you better take me to Suck He Dick right the fuck away cuz she got some answering to do.'

She pushes open the door to Miles Moccasins and we go charging through the stuffed-together racks of clothes and shoes, KrayZglu breathing in my right ear.

'That wasn't Suk Hee in the picture,' I said desperately. 'It was doctored. Somebody set you both up.'

'Now why would somebody want to do that? Huh? *Shut up*, you hear me? Just shut up and take me to yo liddle *frinn*.'

The way she dragged out the last word, curling her lower lip away from her teeth like a snarling dog, made me seriously afraid for SHee After all, it's not like SHee knows how to actually *aim* her gun. Shit, her sleazy cousin Woo loaded it for her, meaning by now even if I'm wrong and she didn't get picked up by paramedics back in L&T, she's stuck somewhere out of ammo, hurt, and now KrayZglu—

'Git on out there!' KrayZglu snapped at me. 'We going to Guess!'

I started praying to whatever anonymous god might, against all evidence, be taking an interest in my shit as KrayZglu shoved my butt, literally, out the door. Just as I hit the marble floor and sprawled there like a fish, gunfire sounded to the right and the left, almost simultaneously. I heard girlz whooping and cursing, and male voices ricocheted back and forth as cops dived for cover.

Gravity's got me, I'm sticking to the floor, I can't get up.

'Gogogogogogogogogogogo,' huffs KrayZglu, and I'm slithering and flopping across the wide maul walkway like a motherfucking spasmodic caterpillar. I never knew you could skin your knees on marble until now. I reached the midpoint and cowered against a big round stone planter. KrayZglu darted up behind me and *banged* her gun once. I smelt it, and since my ears were pretty much ringing constantly now and hardly registering noises, it was the smell that made the shot seem real. It took a couple seconds before I realised she hadn't shot *me*, then her hot hand was on the back of my neck again, propelling me forward.

We reached Guess! and KrayZglu shoved a bunch of keys in my hand just like I did with Alex.

'Unlock the gate, quick, it's the red one,' she said, flicking her head back and forth to scan up and down the mall. She fired off a couple shots down towards Lord & Taylor and I was unlocking, ripping the security gate up with an effort that popped out most of the muscles in my back. I had my shoulders up around my ears and wasn't even trying to see who was shooting at us or from where. I guess I should have been able to deduce that KrayZglu had other girlz distracting the cops and drawing their fire but reasoning of any kind is pretty much two or three cognitive levels too high for me. I'm all senses, no thought.

The gate's up, KrayZglu's pushing me inside, then I hear the gate coming back down behind us. Darkness falls in Guess! as KrayZglu trips and falls on top of me. She smells like three auto mechanics crammed in the back of a Geo in August.

A pale green LED comes on. KrayZglu's checking her phone for text. She grunts once, types something back, her tongue sticking out in concentration.

'Come on,' she flings over her shoulder as she leaps up and makes for the stockroom. 'We got about two minutes max to get down to the maze before the cops catch on.'

Maze? I wasn't sure I heard her right, but I followed because I could hear voices approaching the security door and they didn't sound like fellow pussies. I followed KrayZglu up and down passages, ramps, through doors, all in the dark. Her gun's targeting light was the only thing I could see.

We reached a crossroads. KrayZglu stopped, whipped out a teardrop-shaped purple bottle and flung it into the darkness like a grenade. The moment it left her hand she was barrelling into me, hauling me back the way we'd come and then throwing me into the wall. I tensed, waiting for the explosion; but there was only the sound of breaking glass followed by a cloying smell.

'What was that?' I gasped, wrinkling my nose.

'L'envie,' answered KrayZglu. 'Throws off the sniffer dogs.'

She shined her light on a grate in the ceiling. Then she bent and offered me her back.

'Get up there. Go on. Climb up – take this – open the panel – come *on*, Casper, pay attention . . .'

Instructions had to be fed to me one baby step at a time. I kept dropping things and misunderstanding and apologising. At last the grate was open.

'Git down.'

I was sitting on KrayZglu's shoulders with my head and shoulders inside an air duct just big enough to crawl through. I could pull myself up and ditch KrayZglu, and she wouldn't be able to climb after me, although I imagined she could shoot at me through the hole. I hesitated. I didn't quite dare do it. I *should* have. But among other things I'm afraid of the dark. And she had my goggles and my gun.

'Git down *now*, girl.'

I know, I know. I'm the pussy of all pussies. Sorry, Suk Hee. I obeyed KrayZglu and slithered down. Now I had to give her a boost, and she went into the shaft first. Again I could have bolted, but I didn't. KrayZglu reached down and pulled me up. There was a lot of kicking and cursing on both our parts. KrayZglu's hands were slippery with sweat.

'Hurry up shit4brains.'

We couldn't really crawl; it was too tight. We squirmed and wriggled our way along, making so much noise that I really couldn't understand how we weren't getting shot at every time we passed a grate. It was a lot harder than Mrs Frazetti's aerobics class, and judging by the deep stitch in my side, I was sure that twenty minutes must have passed.

Just when I was about to go into claustrophobic freakout mode, KrayZglu took out another panel and we came back down into the plywood corridor, which was inventively decorated with obscene drawings in magic marker. We passed a grey access door that had *Mrs Field's* stamped on it in black ink. Until now, I'd had no idea where we were. Now I knew that we hadn't come nearly as far as I thought.

'Almost there,' KrayZglu said. 'I just got to catch my breath.'

She was sweating even more than I was. Hah! She didn't have an Energy T-shirt.

'Almost where?'

'The rendezvous.'

'With?'

'Duh? With my chix, cockless hot to trot thanx 2 GoldYlox.'

'I thought they were all captured.'

She didn't answer. She pulled out her phone and wiped sweat off her upper lip.

'And who's GoldYlox?' I said quickly. 'Is that the blonde you think Suk Hee had her boyfriend? Because I can tell you for sure it was a set-up.'

208

'No, stupit, that be Snowcone. GoldYlox ain't no woman.'

KrayZglu was speed-dialling. When the person answered, she snapped, 'I got the best friend. She a good hostage against the bitch. I'll be there in five – *what*?'

I could hear a voice jabbering on the other end of the line. KrayZglu looked grim.

'No shit. Somebody up our butt if they blocked the route already. OK. Can't go that way, I could get nailed for cop-killing. I go through the stores.' There was a pause; KrayZglu didn't look happy. 'Cuddles got there already? No, you better go.' There's another pause while the voice on the other end protests. 'You get yourselfs out, don't worry about me.' She's nervously biting her own thumb as she says it. 'That's a order, Maxine! Go now, take off while you can.' A blurt of noise from the phone. 'Calm down. I ain't beaten yet.' She hung up and went very still, her expression grave.

'Does this mean we're not escaping?' I said timidly.

'Shh. I have to think.'

I'm not surprised that KrayZglu's plan is ruined. I guess some people would say I'm a walking disaster, I make trouble wherever I go. I would argue that everything's already monumentally fucked-up but I seem to be the only one *noticing*. I don't *cause* trouble, I just kind of bring out latent trouble, like certain colours bring out the green in Keri's eyes.

Or maybe I just have a way of stepping in shit.

KrayZglu seems pretty angry.

'Somebody told the cops we was getting out through the truck tunnel, and they blocked off a whole bunch of the ways.'

I shrugged. 'That was probably 10. She's doing this for fun.'

209

'What your problem w/10Esha? She told *me* you were OK, it was Sucking Dick we had to worry about.'

'She said I was OK?' I was flattered. KrayZglu rolled her eyes.

'You wanna date 10 or something?'

'Look, I don't even know her!' I said. 'But she's got something of mine that doesn't belong to her and I need it back.'

'Yeah? What?'

'None of your business.'

'Everything to do with the 'Boos is my business. I am the boss.'

'I thought 10 was the leader.'

'She tell you that?' The pitch of her voice soared in outrage.

'Well, she led me to believe . . .'

'Fuck her! Bitch only in the squad because of her Uncle GoldYlox. She a nerd.'

'GoldYlox again, who is this GoldYlox?' Then I remembered: Uncle G. *I need the trux* . . . What truck?

'Never mind. Bottom line: none of this should've happened. *Your* friend should of kept her snatch away from *my* friend's boy.'

I shrugged. 'Your chocolate's in my peanut butter,' I quipped in a high voice, then changed to a deep voice to make dialogue. 'No, your peanut butter's on my chocolate.' KrayZglu just stared at me. I kept trying. 'It's the same damn difference, get it? Like one of those old Reese's Peanut Butter Cup commercials?' But she didn't get it. 'Look,' I elaborated. 'Why are you mad @ SHee? Why don't you just tell Snowcone to dump her doggy boyfriend?'

'You don't know him, so don't be talking about him.'

'And you figure it's worth another gunfight to settle this?'

210

'Look you little shit, don't you go with your attitude on me, let's remember who started shooting.'

'Um. What are you going to do – kill me?'

'I don't want to, but if your bitch don't rescue your skinny butt, I'll have to. I call it loyalty. Somebody going to pay for messing w/my Pookie's man.'

I groaned and rubbed my face in my palms, which were sweaty and smelled sour.

I sighed. 'Look, don't be mad, but I know Suk Hee isn't here.'

'You lying, is what.'

'No, I'm not. KrayZglu, she got shot. Right at the beginning. *I saw her.* She was just lying there bleeding.'

'Well, I hope she dead then.'

I launched myself at her like a Jerry Springer contestant – I mean, guest. We sprawled around on the floor with me kicking and biting and pretending to be stronger than I am, until KrayZglu got on top of me and pinned me in some kind of wrestling hold with my arm all twisted up behind my back. Suk Hee would know the name of the move, she watches all that WWE stuff.

'Fuck you!' I'm screaming. 'She was my best friend and she didn't deserve to die you stupid cunt!'

KrayZglu sits on me, both of us panting, me crying pathetically. After a while she gets up and moves away a little. I curl up on my side, my nose running, my stomach aching from sobbing. She still has a gun on me. A fucking gun, which to me was never more than a high-risk dildo, until today.

I wish they never invented it.

KrayZglu isn't very sympathetic. 'You are such a goddamn liability acting like that.'

'So fucking shoot me then,' I said. My voice sounded harsh and too deep.

'Shuthefuckup, or I will.'

211

I stopped crying. For the first time all day, I felt totally calm. Everything was really clear in my head.

'Go ahead. Shoot me with the fucking gun, you don't even know what this is about but go ahead and shoot if you want to.'

'*I* don't know what it's about? Yeah, right.'

'I'm serious. You don't know what it's about. I mean, 10 is right, what she says on her site about civilisation. Procreation got us into this. And language. Or we never could have exploited the new geography of the river valleys. We evolved to be tree people.'

'*Tree* people?' She started chortling. I didn't see what was so funny.

'Why didn't we stay? How much man-on-man violence could you get away with in the primeval forest? Without seasonal flooding and agriculture to increase the population there wouldn't be enough people to kill each other, would there? Never mind to invent guns & cartoons. All technology comes from man trying to kill or do better than nature. Man beating his fists against the mother goddess, whom he rapes and scorns.'

KrayZglu backs off me a little more, rubbing the gun against her sweaty forehead .

'You talking stupid now.'

'Oops, excuse me, my feminist slip is showing – I didn't mean that, how embarrassing and passé.'

She looks at me. She looks at me like I've seen people look at Cousin Woo's pit bulls. I'm too busy talking to realise this could be a chance for me to make a break for it. The words are tumbling out of my mouth like a fast downhill run.

'I know, I know, the noble savage ain't the answer, back to the jungle means I have a lot of babies and most of them die and all my teeth fall out by the time I'm twenty-seven, OK, maybe I shouldn't underestimate the shittiness factor of a hunter-gatherer lifestyle. Still. I think it would be better. Because the world would still be bigger than me and my pretensions, and that means there would always be hope. But I look around at this shoebox of a reality that somebody forgot to cut air holes in and contemplate my future existence & how can I not the fuck lash out?'

At the words 'lash out' her stare flashes onto my face and then away. I think she may actually be listening. I go for broke.

'I mean, take being a rebel chick. It's not all red lipstick and brass knuckles, am I right? Boys are expected to rebel and be hostile. Rebels are sexy – unless you're female. If you're a girl and you make trouble, you're just sad, I don't care what you see in the movies. I know because I've sat in psychologists' offices while they try to convince me I should play along with their vision, for my 'own good', because they say I can't win. And it's better to not fight and not lose than to fight and lose, they say. Sun Tzu would agree but none of that takes into account how I *feel*. And I feel like fighting. How many times is Maury Povich going to take a bunch of perfectly happy tomboys and give them make-overs so they look like Young Secretaries of America? How many times is Ricki going to try to reform girl gang bangers because it's so sad and pathetic to see a girl gone bad? We can kick-box in movies but only if we're cute and fluffy.'

'Fluffy,' KrayZglu snorted. 'Yeah.'

'Yeah, mothers in gangs better correct themselves and get in line because if their foetuses keep getting blown away in the crossfire then America might have to take a serious look at itself instead of just throwing all the black men in prison like it does now. It's the hypocrisy that kills me.'

213

There was a silence. I think she was actually developing some small amount of respect for me. I really do.

'Well . . . it's the fucking cops gonna kill *me* if I don't get my shit together. You finish with your ranting and your raving?'

'Maybe,' I said warily. 'What did you have in mind?'

'I have in mind to get out alive. Ain't no Sucking Hee here, and no Snowcone. It's only you & me – and somewhere our pal 10.'

I opened my mouth to agree with her, and then shut it because she was giving me a look. OK. I don't have to talk. She had all but told me that if I stuck with her, she'd lead me to 10, and then I could get the tape. Somehow. After all, I had a backpack full of power clothes I could use if ness.

'So do you want to follow instructions and come with me, and shut up when I tell you to – or you want me to leave you here by yourself?'

'Can I ask where we're going?'

She gave me a big, ironic smile.

'Laura Ashley, of course. *Darling.*'

WHAT'S THE MATTER WITH A LITTLE PARTHENOGENESIS?

MADDIE WAS FEELING shitty about things. She therefore devoted herself to painting her toenails, drinking vodka and eating a gift box of Neuhaus chocolate that she had picked up on the way home. She flipped through the Pigwalk Catalogue, recognising a number of the contestants from the promos they had on file at Babyshop. The Burmese chess genius with the sweet temperament and bewitching smell and those soft brown eyes (also available in green and indigo); the award-winning, kilt-wearing MUSE poet; the Insect Rights activist with the shy smile and manly-man hobbies including cross-country skiing, ice-fishing, and dogsled racing. (Hmm, thought Maddie, Y-plagues must be less virulent in the cold, that's worth checking out.)

They were all cute, they were all talented, they all gave great reasons for the continuation of their genes. But only a handful would be immortalised as pigs.

And not one of them got Maddie going like the SE in her own lab. The Pigwalk Previews were on and she was too drunk to bother skipping the commercials.

COME ON DOWN TO THE CARPET WAREHOUSE 40% OFF WET YOUR PANTS AND LIKE IT TRIPLE MAX EVENT!! FREE DONUTS AND LATTE!! FREE PARKING!! FREE KIDDIE ROMPER AREA WITH ALL THE LATEST GAMES FROM YESSYSTEMS!!!!!!! IT'S A ONCE A YEAR XXXTRAVAGANZA!!!!!!

The phone rang and she could see her reflection in the dark anti-UV glass of her living room's picture window.

'Maddie, it's Kaitlin.'

'Kaitlin, *finally*, I've been *dying* to hear from you.' Already she sounded drunk and she'd barely gotten started.

'OK, I have some stuff to tell you but first I want to know what's going on with you and this SE of yours.'

'Oh,' Maddie moaned. *'Nothing*, but he's driving me crazy, you know? Men are so . . . so . . .'

Zoom the cat looked up briefly from his exemplary efforts at auto-butt-licking and then resumed work.

'He's revolting,' Maddie's reflection went on. She grabbed her right big toe to hold it steady while she applied a coat of nail strengthener. Then she poured out her heart to Kaitlin. She didn't tell her about Meniscus, but she spilled just about everything else. 'It's crazy,' she finished. 'I could have Henshaw. All I have to do is look the other way. I can do that. I've been doing that all my life.'

She splashed more vodka into a plastic Roadrunner cup.

'I see,' said Kaitlin in a guarded tone.

'I don't know what's going on with me and my morals,' Maddie added apologetically. She bit into some kind of strawberry thing drowned in dark chocolate.

Kaitlin said, 'It doesn't sound like a moral problem, it sounds like it's a problem that you want what's in Carrera's pants. You think you want Arnie but you don't, not really.'

'Nuh-huh. Yes, really. I do want Arnie. An Arnie Henshaw kid is going to have a cool life.'

'Uh huh. So, if that's solved, should we talk about the—'

'Then again. Carrera has testicles the size of ellendales. He masturbates five times a day. There's something about him.'

LOSE WEIGHT AT SKINNYBITCH. ENTER OUR VIRTUAL COOKIE SIMULATOR OR HAVE YOUR THIGHS ZAPPED WITH OUR REVOLUTIONARY LASERS WHILE YOU EAT NOCALORIE CAKE.

'Should I try going to Skinnybitch?' Maddie asked with her mouth full. 'You're so slim, Kaitlin, how do you do it?'

'OK, wait. Wait just a cottonpickin' minute. In the antiparasite war waged by multicellulars against bugs, sex creates human culture and intelligence, which then tries to subvert and overturn sex. Right?'

'I guess.'

'Everybody's always trying to get away w/shit in this universe, especially us girlz. But why not get rid of semen while you're at it? Eliminate the middle pig and buy direct. What's the matter with a little parthenogenesis or even a little egg-splicing between girlfriends?'

'Egg-splicing is too expensive – I can't afford that.'

'And you don't want to, either, because it's less fun. I mean, you aren't getting any nutrition out of that chocolate and vodka, are you?'

'What are you saying? Are you saying I'm feeling some kind of primal lust?'

'Yup. Just ask your garden-variety evolutionary anthropologist: we're built for sex and all the bugs in the world can't change that. Bugs can be asexual but we can't. Your behaviour was predestined on the African savannah a long, long time ago.'

'Yeah, and what has my coffee table and toenail polish got to do with the Serengeti half a million years ago? Or the primeval ooze while we're at it? If we've evolved to make our own decisions about how we should evolve from here, then why—'

STAINMEISTER 40% OFF SMART-SHAG REPELS EVEN BLOOD AND GRAPE JUICE.

'—oh why are we such assholes?'

Maddie picked up her foot and blew on her toes. Looked at her reflection again.

'Freak,' she called herself. 'And I use the "we" part loosely, Kaitlin. I'm the one who's an asshole, you're just drunk.' Then she started laughing. 'I mean, I'm drunk, you're—'

'Never mind. Look, do you remember why you contacted me?'

'Shit, yeah. Come on, Kaitlin, quit beating around the bush and tell me what you found already.' She laughed ferociously at her own joke. Kaitlin managed a tolerant smile.

'Ready for this? Your SE has a major lack of antibodies against the bugs in Meniscus.'

'Major lack? That doesn't make sense. He's not sick. He must be making antibodies.'

'But he isn't. Maddie, he isn't making *any* antibodies for *any* of the bugs in Meniscus.'

'But he has to be,' Maddie said again, and saw Kaitlin shake her head in irritation. 'Kaitlin, those bugs are all over the habitat. Are you telling me that you didn't find any infection?'

'I'm telling you I didn't find any antibodies. How long ago was he exposed?'

'Long enough! Kaitlin, are you sure there are no bugs?'

'Ah, I didn't say there were no *bugs*. I said there were no antibodies.'

'That doesn't make sense.'

'*Is* he sick?'

'No! That's the whole thing I don't get. So why don't I see tissue damage on the I-MAGE? The bugs must be chewing the life out of him.'

'That's not for me to say. All I can tell you is that his histamine levels are normal, he's got no antibodies for *any* Y-plague-based organism that I know, including yours, and everything else looks perfectly normal.'

'No,' said Maddie. 'That's totally nuts. It's impossible.'

'That's what I thought. I've run every kind of analysis I know on your I-MAGEs and the juice you sent. The closest comparison I could give you is when we look at somebody whose immune system has been severely impaired or dampened. They don't react to bugs. They just roll over and die. And that's what I see here, with one important difference.'

'He's not dead,' Maddie filled in.

'Exactly. More to the point, the infection isn't taking hold. The bugs aren't reproducing. They are just – well – dying of natural causes, I guess you could say.'

'And you've never seen this before?'

Kaitlin bit her lip. 'Do you know his history?'

'No. Why?'

'This is the closest thing I've ever seen to what you could call natural immunity to Y-plague .'

'Kaitlin.' Maddie was shaking. She couldn't speak, she was thinking so fast. 'Kaitlin. Thanks. Thanks a lot.'

'But Maddie, why—?'

'Gotta go. Bye.'

'But —!'

Kaitlin's voice was squashed as Maddie killed the link. She grabbed her hair and tugged at it. She could still see herself reflected in the black glass of her picture window, and she was surprised that there was no smoke coming out of the ears of her reflection, because she felt like a 1950s television robot on circuit overload.

'Why do they want to kill him? Why do they want to kill him? Why do they want to kill him?'

Then Maddie started laughing.

'Hah, you idiots!' she yelled at the ceiling. 'You can put every bug in the planet in that habitat and I bet he'll live! Hah! Serves you right.'

But Jennifer mustn't find out. If what Kaitlin said were true, SE 4465 a.k.a. Snake Carrera was worth a fortune. Many fortunes. The fate of nations. If Jennifer knew . . .

Wait a second, did *he* know?

Did that big obnoxious bastard *know* he was immune? *I'll make you a deal. You let me go, you get my come.*

The smug shit.

'Hello, housekeeping?' Maddie shouted into her headset.

'Good evening, Dr Baldino. What can we do for you?'

'I need surveillance for my daughter. I've got to go out for a few hours.'

'We'll take care of it. Can we reach you at the lab?'

'Yup. But only call me if it's an emergency.'

'Dr Baldino, are you all right to drive? We can call you a car . . .'

Maddie breathed into her hands to assess how drunk she was, and smelled mostly chocolate. 'No, I'm good. No problem. Thanks.'

As the video image frowned and started to protest, she cut the link, giggling. Luckily, the ignition breathlyser on her car had been broken for a month. She lurched to her feet and pounced on her car keys. She might be drunk but she had the wits to fetch a turkey baster from the kitchen before she left. She checked on Bonus (asleep) and then caught a full-length view of herself in the black glass: dishevelled, pear-shaped, devoid of style. And quite possibly the luckiest woman in the world.

'A natural immune,' she said to the mirror. 'What if it's heritable? He could repopulate the male stocks, we could start again. If only I could figure a way to *steal* him, I'd have him all to myself to study . . . and stuff. But there's no time for that. If Henshaw succeeds . . . shit, I'm going to get a piece of this, even if it's just a piece of tail. Couple million pieces of tail, I hope.'

The moon outside was waxing almost to full. She always ovulated on the full moon. It was a good omen; she wouldn't even need to freeze the semen. No one else needed to be involved.

Maddie kissed the turkey baster and said, 'I'm bringing you just in case I decide not to let him fuck me.'

A DATE FOR
THE PROM

WE ARE JUST creeping past the back room of Kinney's when my phone rings. KrayZglu gives me an accusing look, seizes it and switches it to vibrate mode. Then she regards the number display.

'Who's Ken?'

'My little brother.'

KrayZglu sneers at me like I'm lying. 'Hello, Ken,' she snaps. Then, making a face as she realises by his voice that he really is just a kid, she passes the phone to me. 'No bullshit,' she mouths, flipping the safety off her pistol.

'Whaddaya want, Ken?' My voice breaking because the thought of the little shit has made me start to cry.

'Sun, I gotta ask you a question, it's real important.'

I take a big wet sniff. I wish I knew for sure that Ken could appreciate my George Clinton records. I think he should try because all that Scriabin and Weber can't be good for him.

'OK, booger-pie, I'm listening.'

'This is serious, buttnose. See, Jamal's got this ninth-level psionic Paladin with a vorpal blade—'

'What?' I interrupted, horrified. 'Talk about experience-points inflation! You guys have only been playing for six months, how'd he get to ninth level?'

'We started at sixth level because our first-level parties kept getting killed by bugbears and it was too demoralising.'

'What wusses. In my day we—'

'Shut up, nobody cares. See, he rolled an eighteen against a Mind Flayer and he says he's decapitated it but my character switched his vorpal blade for a −4 cursed sword in the last round, and so isn't he subject to the Mind Flayer's psionics?'

'Yeah, sounds like it. Why'd you switch his sword?'

'Because my character's a chaotic neutral monk assassin and I'm gonna use the vorpal blade to bribe this dragon with—'

'OK, OK, never mind, look, if you switched it you switched it, he's got to accept that.'

'See, Jamal, I told you! Sun says you've got to accept your butt is fucked. Hold on, Sun, he wants to talk to you.'

'Ken, I gotta go. Why doesn't the dungeon master settle it, anyway?'

'He had to go puke. We ate a pound of Skittles.'

KrayZglu grabs my arm and I hang up. I hear it, too: a thunder of bootsteps, coming down the plywood corridor from the direction of Bed, Bath & Beyond. We scoot into Innovations luggage and KrayZglu throws me behind a display of Jordache suitcases, then lands on top of me. After what seems an eternity, the footsteps pass and KrayZglu goes back into the stock passage. She makes me walk in front of her. 'You my human shield,' she said. It was hard to tell if she was joking or not.

Somehow she knows her way. We wind through the maze, passing store after store from behind. There are no lights. KrayZglu has her flashlight and I have my goggles.

As we pass Lenscrafters II, I hear men talking. Instinctively I turn and grab the bulb end of KrayZglu's flashlight to cover the light and then cringe, expecting to be shot. She switches it off and then grabs me around the mouth from behind. I can see shadows moving under the stockroom door. KrayZglu prods me in the ribs and we run for it. The next thing I know, she's pushing me into Laura Ashley.

'I thought you were kidding,' I said, following her out of the stockroom and onto the selling floor. We were surrounded by all the frilly-pinafore shit you could burn. 'Why would anyone in their right mind come here?'

KrayZglu overturned the cash register and pulled out a baggie filled with white powder.

'Want some?'

I shook my head. KrayZglu bent down behind the counter to snort coke. Wish it could be heroin, then her reflexes might slow down and I'd stand a chance, I thought. After a minute she came up for air.

'We keep stashes of what we need in different places.'

'And nobody finds it?'

She came out from behind the counter and sauntered among the circular racks of dresses. 'Nope. Thanks to Uncle GoldYlox, this is a bugged-out maul. We got everything we need to do what we do, and it be easy to

224

get to . . .' She started going through a rack of formal wear, as if she had all the time in the world. '. . . If you know where to look. Most people wouldn't look in Laura Ashley, would they?'

I just stared at her. KrayZglu had me all turned around, fucked up, scared. She's not my vision of a gang leader. As she stands there flicking long fingernails through hangers of pseudo-Edwardian dresses, occasionally stopping to pull one out, she looks totally comfortable. Maybe that's why she can pass so well here in the maul.

I said something to this effect and she laughed. 'I'm not some piss-ass fool steal from my own. Success is what I do. You come to my neighbourhood, look at me and my peoples, half of your look says food stamps crack babies prostitution such a shame, and half like scared scared scared we gonna come for your throat. Now you lookit me, all worshipful and shit, you want to be me, am I right? You don't *equate* me with where I come from. You think I'm a plastic bimbo you can copy.'

'No, I don't, shit, I'm on your side, I'm not some complacent middle-class stereotype—'

KrayZglu laughed so hard she had to wipe her eyes on a pink chiffon skirt.

'*What?*' I protested. 'I'm not, and I'm not gonna be . . .'

'*What*ever.'

'I'm telling you, I'm down with the struggle. As far as I'm concerned the downfall of all civilisation would be a good thing.'

'Whoa, see, you are *not* on my side because I don't have a side. What's with you people? You listen to a few joints, you think you know it all. I just want to get mine, KrayZglu's share of it. So quit trying the fuck to cuddle up to me.'

'I'm not—'

'Yes, you is. Me and my pussies run in packs. We hunters. You the prey, duffy.'

'Then why didn't you fucking shoot me back there?'

She looked at me like I'm scoping.

'I kill a Chinese kid, the Triads are all over me.'

I sighed. 'I can't believe it's still about race.' Nonetheless, I didn't see any point in mentioning that I'm not Chinese, I'm Korean. I'm too busy getting big ideas.

'All I'm trying to say is, you want to bring the system down, break out of the inner city and shit? And my friends and I are bored shitless with the suburbs, it's so white-bread and pathetic. So we should join forces. Military history shows that alliance is the only way to conquer. You can't just run in a little pack, the system's too big.'

KrayZglu reached over with her gun in her hand and patted me on the head. The metal thumped gently against my skull. She was chuckling.

'Just give me a chance,' I begged. I had forgotten that what I really wanted was to find 10Esha and get that tape off her before she could stick it on her site or blackmail my mother with it or whatever. I had forgotten because I was starting not to care about my normal life. KrayZglu stood there in front of me like an open door. In comparison with today, everything else I'd ever done was just one long dull hallway, day in, day out, A-cup bra, boyfriendless, nothing in my life matching TV – even Nair commercials are more exciting than my life. Everything I love is unreal. From a book or a CD, or so far away in the sky I'll never reach it.

Fuck it, I don't like the way these shoes are making me feel. Is my life that bad that I really want to be a junior pisshole in KrayZglu's gang? Hello, me? Contrary to the label on my sneakers, anything is *not* possible.

226

'I'm going to change,' I said suddenly. 'That OK with you? I got some stuff back at Miles Moccasins.'

'Whatever.'

Hmm. So she isn't clued in to the Miles Moccasin effect. I take off the sneakers, which in addition to messing with my concept of reality, are giving me blisters. I decide to go barefoot, but I put on a Tenacity T-shirt and a belt with the label *Lucky Muffin* – don't know what that means but it reminds me of Lucky Charms, my favourite cereal. Then I get an idea. I pull out a really sexy leopard-print *cuddly babe* tank top and say, 'KrayZglu, this would look cute on you.'

'I wouldn't be caught dead in that crap.' She holds up a white organza gown and pirouettes in front of the mirror. Her flashlight produces the only light, and it makes her look ghoulish. She smiles at me; her nostrils are red and flaring from the coke. I'm finding her pretty scary.

Then she says, 'You got a date for the prom?'

I shook my head, unnerved.

'It's only October,' I said defensively. 'And I'm a sophomore.'

'Well, I do,' she said. 'His name's Maleek and we going to rent a limo for the whole night.'

I gave her a weak smile.

'I need a dress, though, and you can never start looking too early.'

There's something weird about this conversation, I mean something *extra* weird, but I'm not getting a feel for what it is exactly. The coke is doing something spooky to KrayZglu. At least, I think it's the coke.

'Here's a nice one,' she says, dragging out something red and lacy. She clucks her tongue at the price tag. 'Maybe it'll go on sale.'

Then she reaches deep in among the prom dresses. Taffeta rustles as her face presses into the mass of fabric.

She gropes. Hangers clatter. I can hear the sound of plastic packing tape tearing.

I don't know if it's the Lucky Muffin effect or something else, but I step back instinctively.

'Oh, baby,' says KrayZglu to the fluffy skirts. 'Come to momma.'

With a jerk, she drags out an Uzi.

WHEN A GIRL'S GOT A CRUSH

THE SHRIEKS AND crashes of the fight dragged Meniscus from the game. The first thing he saw was Naomi. She held the sealed sperm receptacle over her head, just out of Dr Baldino's reach.

'No, let me explain! It's for my cousin in Tennessee. She lives in a trailer park and can't afford to get her own.'

Naomi's voice was a throbbing croak because Dr Baldino had her by the throat up against the wall of the habitat. The place smelled of *Samsara: For Us* and Naomi's sex with Starry Eyes, who could be heard bustling about the habitat whistling a happy tune.

'Bullshit!' Dr Baldino spat. 'Tell me the truth. What do you know?'

She glanced around with white, paranoid eyes. Meniscus backed deeper into the shadows on his side of

229

the habitat. His mind was still reeling. His senses felt wide open, and sight seemed to cross over to touch, sound to smell, so that the exultant expression on Naomi's face had seemed to register not so much in his eyes as in his very cells, burning into his flesh like a brand.

Now Naomi was choking.

'OK OK OK I don't have a cousin, they're for me, all right?'

Her face was streaked with tears. Meniscus had never seen Naomi show real emotion before tonight; now she was running the full spectrum. His skin crawled. The air seemed to shake and echo with the feelings of the two women. He could smell the emotion.

'WHY?' shouted Dr Baldino. 'Why do you want unlicensed sperm? Are you insane? WHY? Tell me WHY.'

Dr Baldino was shaking so hard that she reminded Meniscus of a hanging bridge oscillating beyond the point of maintaining structural integrity. She was going to break up in a minute and little Baldino-pieces would be all over the floor like in a Surrealist painting.

Starry Eyes was packing his duffel bag and shaking his head, not quite laughing but almost.

Naomi rubbed her throat. The words came out in an urgent whisper, 'There is no Arnie Henshaw. It's pure Hollywood: 4465 is the man doing the stunts on the video and it's his pheromones we've all been getting excited over, not Arnie's.'

Meniscus got the impression that this wasn't what Baldino expected to hear.

'What are you talking about?' Dr Baldino's tone was fierce, but she loosened her grip fractionally.

'Arnie's just the face – he's like a spokesmodel.'

'That's ridiculous. Hibridge have measures to authenticate models, Arnie can't just—'

'Hibridge are *behind* it, duh? I have a video, I'll show you, just let the fuck go of me already.'

'I'm ready to leave now,' Starry Eyes said, swinging his duffel bag. He had the bike leaning against his leg; it wasn't complete, but it rolled. 'I'm gonna disable the intercom just in case you was thinking of calling security after I go.'

Dr Baldino whirled, letting go of Naomi, who dived through the gap underneath Dr Baldino's arms and skidded across the floor, ending up at Starry Eyes's feet.

'You stay right where you are,' Baldino commanded. 'We didn't cut any deal.'

'No, but Naomi did.'

Dr Baldino glared at the younger woman.

'Yeah, I did,' said Naomi. She batted her eyelashes at Starry Eyes and said, 'I didn't call security. I wouldn't do that.'

Starry Eyes turned his back on both of them and made for the console beside the I-MAGE.

'You fucking bitch!' Baldino screamed. 'You knew it was a scam and you were going to let me fall for it. What's the matter with you?'

She lunged at Naomi, who scuttled towards Meniscus's bed on her hands and knees. Meniscus leaped back to get out of the way, and that was when he spotted Curator Gould entering the lab. She was flanked by a couple of big, bearded goons wearing antibug gear and body armour. Starry Eyes saw them, too, and snorted his derision at the guards.

'How can you move in that shit? Even little Squeak could dance circles around you.'

But for once no one paid any attention to Starry Eyes. Naomi and Dr Baldino were a writhing knot on the floor. Naomi was clearly the stronger and more agile of the two, but Dr Baldino fought dirty. She had Naomi by the nipples and was spitting in her face when Curator Gould came on the scene.

'Break it up, break it up,' cried the older woman, flicking on the sprinkler system and flashing the lights. Meniscus was trying to keep his distance from the action. He had too much going on inside his body already.

Curator Gould glanced at him once, taking in his bizarre appearance in such a way that he realised she must have suddenly remembered about the bugs. She signalled to the guards, and at the same time made a rush to shut the door of the habitat to seal the combatants, and the males, inside.

She was too slow. Without even seeming to try, Starry Eyes reached the door first and stuck his foot in it. He began to widen the aperture.

'This is an outrage!' Gould cried. 'Secur—'

SE grabbed her wrist and dragged Gould, spreading foul odours with every shriek, through the gap in the plexiglas and into the habitat.

'—ity! Make them stop! This is unacceptable!' she yelled even as SE hauled her past the bike and chucked her in a corner.

'I've had about enough of this,' he said. He turned to Gould and pointed his finger at her face. 'You. Tell your goons to stand down.'

'Or what? Or you'll rape her?' Dr Baldino had shoved her knee in Naomi's mouth and now sat on her chest, panting and sweating while Naomi bucked beneath her, heels scrabbling for purchase on the floor. Dr Baldino laughed hollowly as she reached into Naomi's cleavage and extracted the sperm packet. 'We should all be so lucky.'

Starry Eyes raked his gaze across her and opened his mouth to reply. Meniscus heard himself scream. The

232

stockier of the two guards had raised her arm, equipped with a wicked little miniature crossbow. Starry Eyes reacted instantaneously, dodging towards Naomi's splayed legs. He was almost quick enough. The dart missed his body but caught him in the forearm.

Like a doomed hero in an old cowboys-and-Indians flick, Starry Eyes plucked the missile out as he fell. His shining eyes rolled back and closed.

'Is he dead? Is he dead?' Meniscus wailed, throwing himself on the floor beside Starry Eyes.

'It's only a sedative,' Gould said to Dr Baldino, who had transferred her hostility from Naomi to the curator and now advanced on her menacingly, still clutching her sperm prize. 'He'll wake up in a few minutes. Pee-*ew*, it smells like a vet's office in here.'

Meniscus found the presence of mind to shove Genghis's shoebox under the bed as Jennifer whipped out a purse-sized air-freshener and sprayed the habitat liberally. The smell of synthetic lilacs filled the air.

'Unlicensed sperm?' said Gould, arching an eyebrow at Baldino. 'I'll just take that.'

Dr Baldino's fingers turned white, gripping the container. Gould signalled again to her lackeys, who picked up Baldino bodily and relieved her of the packet.

Gould's lips were even thinner and tighter than usual. She wore a smile that was just this side of a snarl. She pulled out some Peppermint Lifesavers and crunched viciously.

'I need not say that I'm shocked at this breach of security protocol. Infectious habitat wide open. It's beyond irresponsible.'

'I know,' said Dr Baldino, looking at Naomi as if this was all her fault. But the curator snapped back at her.

'I hold *you* responsible for your team, Maddie.'

Dr Baldino dropped her gaze. Gould continued, 'I'll

send a unit down to disinfect this place in the morning. Meanwhile, you two stay put and keep the habitat closed. I hope it won't be necessary to post Malone here on guard duty?' She indicated the guard who had fired on Starry Eyes. Dr Baldino shook her head wordlessly, still looking at the floor.

'Good. I'll send for you later, then.' Jennifer turned her back and marched off, taking the guards with her.

Starry Eyes stirred and moaned from the floor. 'You fucked it up for me, Baldino.'

Dr. Baldino ignored him. She picked up a spare MUSE headset and thrust it at Naomi.

'You. Outside.'

'But Curator Gould said to stay—'

'*Now.*'

After the women left, Meniscus and SE looked at each other. Starry Eyes yawned and slapped his own face, struggling to rouse himself.

'You were going to leave without me,' Meniscus said.

'Yeah, so?'

'I want to go with you.'

'Well, you can't. You'd get in the way, and then you'd catch something and get sick. You'd slow me down too much.'

'I wouldn't. I'm getting stronger. I'm going to become just like you.'

'Go back in your game, Squeak.'

'I mean it, I'll be like you.'

'That's the last thing you want,' grunted Starry Eyes, and wouldn't say any more.

'I don't want to step outside,' Naomi grumbled as she left the lab. 'There's nothing to fight over, you gave the shit away. We could've worked something out. Why'd you call Jennifer?'

234

'I didn't. Security must have notified her when we . . . scuffled. Or when you and the SE . . . you know. It doesn't matter now. What I want to know—'

'But I turned off the surveillance.'

Maddie gave an exasperated snort. 'That in itself could have alerted security. Now—'

'They showed up awfully quick. And what's Jennifer doing here at this hour? She lives in Toms River.'

Maddie narrowed her eyes. 'What exactly are you suggesting?'

'I'm not suggesting anything – it's just weird, you know?'

'A lot of things around here are weird.' She led Naomi away from the lab. They stood beneath the struts of the Dendrite Drop, now being tested for reopening. The noise would cover their voices, and Maddie knew that there were no cameras here because this was where Greta always smoked. Her Marlboro Light butts were scattered in the trampled grass along with empty Choco Squeezi Goo-goo boxes and a crumpled Bliss Fuzzy wrapper.

'OK, what's this about Henshaw not being for real? You said you have a video.'

Naomi squirmed a bit, as though now regretting the admission.

'Naomi, we have to team up. If you know something, you better tell me or the SE will be dead before either of us can get any sperm. Now: is there a video?'

'Yeah. There is. See, when I realised the pheromones matched I got curious, so I got my friend Bambi the bloodhound to do an image search on the Atlantis database. You know, to see what else I could find out about Arnie Henshaw? That maybe nobody knew? And Bambi comes up with this clip.'

'Show me.'

235

Tentatively Naomi put on the headset and Maddie took the video document from her and opened it.

Snake Carrera was a good forty pounds lighter and he sported a full beard. Maddie only recognised him by the contours of his bare feet as he paced up and down the castellation ramparts, thumping the glass with the side of his closed fists just as he did nowadays in the habitat. He was wearing Sylvester the Cat boxer shorts and a UCLA sweatshirt, and his hair was long and braided like an Indian brave's, with a shoelace tied around his head to keep it off his face.

'I ain't giving no sperm to no pig,' he said. 'You got the right to put me in prison for the thing with the sheriff, and according to my twit lawyer Angie you got the right to drug me, but you take my sperm without consent and the ACLU will be on you like gravity on a dwarf.'

'You're an illegal alien,' said a female voice off camera. 'Where are you from anyway? We've got Costa Rica, St Lucia and Greece from your skin paths, and that's just in the past month. You are committing a serious offence, entering Florida unbranded and unscreened. Frankly, you're lucky you weren't shot.'

The SE snorted, rocking back on his heels. 'Yeah, well, I broke the sheriff's rifle or I guess I would of been shot. You'd know that if you read the file.'

'I did read the file and all that posturing will get you nowhere here. This is a castellation. We know all about men here.'

'Not this one,' said SE. 'You tell Henshaw I don't mind working with him under the old terms, but there is no way in hell I am giving him my sperm for "experimental purposes", that's just fucked.'

'It's what is necessary if you want to participate in the Pigwalks.'

A look of desperation came over Carrera's face.

236

'I can't live in a castellation. I can't stand it here, this is a fucking prison, I don't need to be here.'

'Unfortunately, this is the way the world works. Now—'

'No!' And Carrera smacked the glass so hard that the image wavered. 'I'll tell you how the world works. I go out there, risk my ass doing Henshaw's dirty work, and what do I see on his promotional video? I see *me* fighting a shark, I see *me* out in the fucking jungle, I see *me* taking risks and I see *him* taking the credit. All I want is fair treatment. I'm tired of being hunted like an animal out there. I'm sick of you people trying to drag me in a lab and analyse me. I've got a right to live, and if it's not respected, then I'm sorry but His Preciousness Arnie Henshaw is going down with me.'

Naomi stopped the tape.

Maddie let out her breath in a whistle.

'Can you find this lawyer for me? Angie?'

Naomi grimaced. 'I already thought of that. She's dead. Hit and run.'

'Do you mean what I think you mean?'

'Turns out the SE started negotiating with Hibridge Castellation. They were using him in the wild as a kind of stuntman for Arnie Henshaw. It's him you see on a lot of the footage, only he's under a helmet, or else the stuff has been doctored really well. It's been going on for years. But lately he started getting uppity.'

'They get any sperm?'

'Enough to test. Not enough to seed a pig. Henshaw himself got into the middle of it. Arnie was holding him at Atlantis Castellation, where this was taped, until he was sent here. But I can't figure out what was the deal behind that.'

Maddie stared at her assistant in amazement. 'Well, Naomi, you know all about it!'

'When a girl's got a crush, she's got a crush,' said Naomi, blushing and looking at her feet. 'Anyway, maybe we should pool our information. I . . . I really like Snake, Maddie, I don't care what you say. And I think . . . I think maybe he could have been competition for Henshaw somehow. Maybe someone in Hibridge likes Henshaw better and was willing to remove the competition to clear the way for Arnie. Next thing we know, Carrera's on his way here.'

'They *want* him infected. But it didn't work.'

'Apparently he survived out in the real world for a long time.'

Maddie was dimly aware that Naomi had accomplished her goal of taking Maddie's mind off Naomi's sexual transgressions, but she didn't really care about that any more. She decided to keep the information about Carrera's Y-plague immunity to herself. Instead, she asked,

'How secret can this be? If you have the tape, who else must know?'

'Oh, it's secret all right. Bambi's the best bloodhound there is, and she knows every hiding place in Hibridge. She told me I owe her a hundred lifetimes of favours for this one.'

Still sceptical, Maddie took a closer look at the doc.

'But why would Henshaw send him to Jennifer? She's not what you'd call a player in the Modelling business, is she?'

Naomi shrugged. 'Maybe that's exactly the reason why. Who would look here?'

'Who would know that Jennifer has a live Y-plague under her jurisdiction?' Maddie countered. 'I'm amazed Henshaw could get that information. It's not widely known that all the Az79s came from Y-plagues originally.'

'Did they? Are you serious?'

'Yeah, of course. Naomi, hello? It was a safety measure built into the experiment. In case the organism got loose, there wouldn't be a public-health threat because women can't be infected. Otherwise there's no way we could have done this sort of work here at the Fun Park.'

'You know, speaking of the Fun Park, after Meniscus flipped out Jennifer was in a big rush to close the habitat to public viewing, even though he didn't really look any worse than usual. But it makes sense, if she wanted to hide the SE so she could expose him to Meniscus . . . Maddie – you don't think Jennifer somehow did something to Meniscus deliberately? So that she could close the exhibit, and control you?'

Maddie considered this.

'I've already accused her and she denied it. Besides, Jennifer doesn't have the know-how. If she could figure a way to affect my subject so that I can't even trace the cause, I'll eat my centrifuge. Something else is bothering me about that morning, though. Somebody *did* prevent you from reaching me when Meniscus went into crisis. I've been trying to figure out who did it and why. They made it look like the order came from my residence.'

'That could be done pretty easily,' Naomi said. 'I couldn't do it, but I bet anybody with access to Hibridge codes could.'

'But why?' said Maddie. 'Why block my communications for no reason?'

'Dunno.' Naomi frowned; then she snapped her fingers, her eyes flashing. 'Then again, maybe it *was* done from your residence. Maybe Bonus did it.'

'*Bonus?*'

'Yeah, she said she wanted to rescue that mouse, right?

239

Maybe she blocked you out because she knew I'd call you as soon as I caught her.'

Maddie stared at her. 'I never thought of that.'

'You should ask her. I bet that's what happened.'

Maddie shook her head. 'No, that's crazy. I mean, she had to know I'd be on to her sooner or later.'

'Kids don't think like that. They think they're smarter than adults, that we're just stupid marks.'

'Maybe we are. I don't know, I can't think about that tonight. Meniscus is the least of my worries right now.'

'OK, but while we're clearing things up, there's another thing I'd like to know,' Naomi said. 'I can't figure out why you were so mad just now.'

'Oh, can't you?'

'I mean, you didn't know that the SE was special, did you? So why should you care so much if I wanted to take a risk with unlicensed sperm? Why did you flip out?'

'I didn't flip out.'

'Do you want him too? There's something about him, isn't there?'

'No there isn't.'

'Oh, you are so in denial. Look, if it makes you feel any better, I've been lusting after him, too. Even before I found out that the pheromones matched. Although that did explain the attraction in a way. I mean, Henshaw sperm have never been an option for *me*, so imagine how surprised I was to find out that our SE is the real Henshaw. In a way. I mean, he's not as cute as Arnie but so what? I figure I'm cute enough to make up for him looking like a caveman. We could make a really cool baby. If you hadn't given my sperm to Jennifer.'

'I didn't have any choice,' Maddie reminded her. 'Besides, what did you ever do for me? When you found out about this scam, it never occurred to you to tell *me*, did it? You know it's breaking my heart that I'm forty-four and only have a clone.'

Naomi looked at Greta's cigarette butts.

'So am I fired.'

'Yes, probably. I don't know. I have to think.' Maddie ran both hands through her hair, rubbing her scalp as if she could massage sense into her own head. Then: 'Look, we'd better get back in there before Jennifer gets suspicious. From now on, it's you and me watching over the habitat, nobody else – no matter what the time of day or night. All right?'

'I keep my job?'

'Don't get excited. Jennifer's going to call me in to her office today. We could *both* be out on our ass.'

They went back inside. Meniscus lay on his back on his bed, engaged in Mall. Maddie had been hoping the SE would be passed out in the post-ejaculatory sleep she had read was characteristic of men, but no such luck. He was standing with legs planted firmly apart, his arms folded across his chest, staring at the door of the lab as they entered. Maddie tried to ignore him, but he kept his stare fixed on her in a way that made her feel squirmy.

He said, 'Like I said before you so rudely walked out, you really fucked it up for me, Baldino.'

Maddie continued to act like the SE wasn't there, and she dragged Naomi away from the plexiglas by the elbow to prevent her from talking to him. But she couldn't make Starry Eyes shut up.

'You think you can get away with this? What's to stop me going to your precious Curator with the same deal I offered you – that you fucked up, I repeat.'

Maddie knew that Jennifer didn't want any more children, she had three gorgeous designer daughters with her long-time partner Rachel and none of them had inherited her bad breath thanks to the pre-conceptual tweaking that money can buy. So she kept on ignoring the SE.

'Because they're watching everything that goes down in your lab now, Maddie, and you know I got – what you call it? – *poor impulse control*. Who knows what I might say or who I might say it to.'

What was this supposed to mean? Maddie again had the terrible feeling that the SE might very well *know* he was immune. He might tell Jennifer this. Jennifer might smell a lot of money and forget her allegiance to Arnie.

Maddie turned to face him, but she couldn't look him in the eye for very long.

'I'll deal with you as soon as I get myself organised, all right?'

It was growing light outside, and occasionally voices could be heard as people arrived at work and greeted one another.

Maddie glanced at the cameras. The computers would be tapped, and their voices could be picked up if Jennifer had activated the intercoms, which she undoubtedly had. Maddie cast about for a way to communicate with Naomi, settling on a pile of junk mail and a lipstick. She positioned herself so that the cameras couldn't pick up what she was writing, and scribbled a note to Naomi.

Must get them out of here. Away from J.

'You can't. They're hot, Maddie.'

'Naomi, *will* you shut up.' Maddie shrugged at the nearest camera.

'Oh.' Naomi bent and wrote, her tongue protruding from the corner of her mouth like a kindergarten child learning to edit video for the first time. Her handwriting was a sloppy, unpractised scrawl.

Thats crazy.

Maddie wrote back, There's more to this than you know. SE is supposed to die, but he's not going to.

How do U no?

Never mind. Do as I say and you can still have

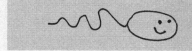

Naomi nodded and made an OK sign. Maddie wrote:

I need containment suits, the best portable system you can get your hands on, a rental van, a hotel room in PA and enough tranquilisers to keep Carrera quiet.

What about ￥￥￥￥???

Maddie wrote down a bank-account number and PIN.

'But don't get carried away,' she said aloud. 'Who knows how long this might carry on, and we don't want to run out of cash.'

Just then, the security check on the lab's door belched as it admitted someone. They both jumped guiltily. Maddie was sure that Jennifer had seen them writing secret notes and was coming down with more security to haul her ass out of the lab for good.

But the figure that entered was too tall to be Jennifer, and it wore no protective gear nor uniform. After a closer look Maddie decided it was a very old man who looked like a very old woman. He wore red overalls and a plaid L. L. Bean work shirt with Adidas cross-trainers, and there was so little of him to fill out the garments that he looked like an understuffed scarecrow. His hair was long and silver, braided in corn rows and liberally decorated with glittering databeads, so that when he turned his head, his hair chimed. He flashed blindingly white dental implants when he smiled.

Maddie was about to scold Naomi for inviting one of her weird friends to the lab when the man held out his hand and in a high, nasal voice said, 'Hi, Maddie.' When her face didn't register recognition, his whitewhite smile widened and he added casually, as if it should be obvious, 'I'm Bernie.'

EYEWITNESS NEWS

IT DIDN'T TAKE very long before my feet were full of little cuts from the grit and broken glass and pieces of metal that they picked up in the plywood corridor. I was distracted. When KrayZglu grabbed the back of my jacket to stop me, I didn't know why at first. Then I heard the voices.

They were issuing from beneath a stockroom door labelled Sony. It was more of a babble than individual voices: men and women, all talking at once. From beneath the door we could see a bluish flickering light. I flipped off the NiteEyes and blinked. I couldn't see shit without them.

KrayZglu kept her hand on me, and I could feel her breath on my hair. She was shaking. Then she let out a little snort.

'Shit, that scared me,' she whispered into my ear. 'I thought it was a doughnut confederation.'

Well, if it's not cops, who is it? I thought. But I didn't dare make a sound. KrayZglu must have read my mind.

'It's TVs,' she told me. 'And stereos.'

Then she made as if to go in.

'But it can't be! There's no electricity to this section.'

KrayZglu said, 'I just tell you the facts. Can't you hear the soundtrack?'

She was right. I distinctly heard the *Eyewitness News* theme. Now that I was paying attention, some of the voices even sounded amplified.

KrayZglu opened the door fractionally. The stockroom was empty except for a couple of pieces of styrofoam packing and a broken pair of headphones. I thought this was strange and wondered if there had been looting; but stranger still was the store beyond, visible through the half-open stockroom door. Every TV in the place was turned on, and about half of them were showing the maul. I glimpsed an aerial view, a parking-lot shot with a wind-blown correspondent, a scene showing the wreckage of L&T cosmetics, and what must have been stock footage of a normal day at the Plaza.

KrayZglu went first; I crept after her, still totally weirded out. There was a big TV facing us, surrounded by speakers, but there was no sound as what looked like grainy security-camera footage came on, silent and surreal. A ceiling panel opened and a gloved hand holding a Glock came out and took out the back of the guard's head at point-blank range. A moment later, Keri came toppling down, her skirt lifting to reveal Minnie Mouse underwear. She glanced around. Her mouth was full of cabling and she had some kind of high-tech equipment duct-taped to her chest. She saw the camera,

246

aimed her gun at it and screwed up her face. The image ended in static.

'This,' said Corky Meyers 'is one of the gang members. Keri O'Donnell, age seventeen.' Keri's yearbook picture came up. It had been taken while she still had braces. Bad luck. 'Police have not been able to locate her. She seems to know the insides of the mall intimately.'

I snorted. She knew the insides of the *dressing rooms* intimately.

A clip of Lt Swizzlestick, my old buddy.

'We will take out the shooter. If we can get her alive, that is our goal. But I'm not going to risk my officers' lives by treating this young woman like a princess. She is extremely dangerous and will be addressed accordingly.'

I wanted to see if my own picture was going to come up but KrayZglu switched to Channel 7, which was covering the status of the dead and wounded. I turned away. I was in no mood to find out bad news about Suk Hee. I turned my attention to a giant-screen TV, where Corky was continuing with her interview.

'Lieutenant, what effect does this information have on the theory that three salesgirls had their uniforms stolen by Keri O'Donnell, Sun Katz and Suk Hee Kim? If these three did not escape, then how is it that Keri O'Donnell has been seen recently inside the mall? And in that case, who are the girls who did steal the uniforms? And also, where are the other two members of the original trio?'

'Corky, we had considered the possibility that the three girls you've named had escaped using the uniforms, but as you say, it's now clear that Keri O'Donnell, at least, is still at large. We have yet to locate Sun Katz and Suk Hee Kim, although there has been an unconfirmed report by a paramedic that he began actually treating Suk Hee Kim at the scene, but during the second round of gunfire on the upper level, he had to abandon his efforts and when he came back, she was nowhere to be found.'

I changed the channel, quick, hoping KrayZglu had not overheard this bit of news. The last thing I needed was KrayZglu deciding she still had a chance to get hold of Suk Hee.

A commercial for Ben & Jerry's came on the giant screen. I'm sweating and chilled all at once. I check to see if KrayZglu heard what Lt Swizzlestick said but thank god she's still finding out about her fellow 'Boos and wiping tears off her face with the back of her gun hand.

I'm stunned.

Treated by paramedics and then disappeared? Dare I hope? It never occurred to me that it could have been Suk Hee who tied up the three cosmetix chix But now that I thought about it, there was a certain appeal to the ruse: tie up the three, take their uniforms and make it *look* like you escaped disguised as salesgirls. Only don't escape.

Why would we not want to escape, though?

Why would you want to shoot out a whole display of perfume?

Why ask Why? as the Budweiser commercial says. Suk Hee is a mystery to me.

The bottom line is this: she's not dead (I hope) and she's not captured. She's still here.

The ice-cream commercial gave way to a shot of two military helicopters spewing forth black-armoured men with automatic weapons. A wave of relief came over me.

'Well, at least we're not the only story,' I heard myself remark in a caustic tone. 'America must be in a war again.'

I wasn't actually that interested, but KrayZglu was.

'Oh, fuck,' she whispered, coming over and staring. The way she was quaking and shaking – from the coke, I guessed – was making me nervous and I moved away. I wandered towards the sales counter to see if the computer was up and running. It wasn't.

'I wonder how the electricity got turned on,' I said. From the area behind the sales counter, a row of digital handhelds confronted me, every one with its red light shining in record mode.

'I don't like this, it could be a trap,' I added. Then I saw a live picture of *myself* in one of the TVs. I stuck out my tongue just to be sure. It's a well-known fact that TV is more real than real life so when people say get a life what they really mean is, get on TV. Because either you're watching TV or you're on it, and if you're doing neither it's a little like Schrödinger's cat, neither alive nor dead till observed. So when I saw myself on the video screen I was pretty happy because it meant I was alive. Also, thankfully, it was not a shot of my butt, for once.

'KrayZglu, look—'

I turned to get KrayZglu's attention, but she was still gazing, rapt, at the big screen with the Special Forces or whatever. The Channel 2 reporter was interviewing Colonel Somebody-or-other, a wiry middle-aged black guy who had cut himself shaving.

'KrayZglu!' I hissed.

She waved at me to be quiet. For some reason she was shaking like she'd got a chill.

'Stupid cunt,' I mouthed, and went over to take her by the arm and *show* her that we were on camera. Then I caught the words 'bomb squad' and 'mall security' and a split second later, I noticed that the highway sign behind Colonel So-and-so's head said 17N-Mahwah.

It's one of the two highways that run past the Garden State Plaza.

Me and KrayZglu stood there like two pigeonshitstained statues in the park while text streaming across the bottom of the screen informed us that the events of today were believed to be a terrorist strike and that there had been an anonymous call

249

claiming there was a bomb hidden somewhere in the maul. It was due to go off in three hours. The bomb-disposal unit had little hope of locating it in that time and no demands had been made.

'Well, you heard it straight from Colonel Whosit,' said Tasha Cole, the Channel 7 reporter on the scene. 'This is being regarded by experts at the scene as a threat to national security and the situation will be dealt with accordingly. The mall has been successfully evacuated and there have been no more civilian casualties since the dead and wounded were removed from Lord & Taylor at approximately one-thirty this afternoon. However, apparently there are still an unknown number of gang members within the mall, including the shooter you saw on those live pictures from security cameras. The police are attempting to capture the girls responsible. It's hoped that the specially trained troops who have just arrived will be able to go in and get them. Denise?'

'Tasha, are you hearing any sentiments to the effect that these gangs are only getting what they deserve if they are trapped inside the mall when the bomb is detonated?'

'Well, nobody here is out to pass moral judgements, Denise. The impression I get is that these guys are just trying to do their job. At the moment we don't know just what the connection is between the shoot-out – which appeared to be a typical gang-rivalry incident – and the bomb report. Also, remember that if these girls did plant the bomb, they are key witnesses and should not be allowed to commit suicide. It's unlikely that they are working alone.'

'Who are they working on behalf of, then? And can you explain about the fire trucks and medical helicopters? What's been going on in there since the original shoot-out ended?'

Tasha's brow furrowed and she frowned as she held her earpiece in place.

'Well, the Bugaboos have obviously planned for this to some extent. I've been told that a special anti-terror unit cornered *them in the Eddie Bauer Home Store and they used mall merchandise, together with what's been described to me as "unconventional guerilla tactics," to avoid capture.'*

'Guerrilla tactics? In Eddie Bauer?'

'They doused a whole section of the store in cooking oil from Williams Sonoma. Then, they must have gotten hold of one of those battery operated novelty cars – a Ferrari, I understand – from one of the other stores. They set it on fire and drove it into the oil just as our officers were stepping—'

'OH!' cried KrayZglu. 'It bring tears to my eyes! My pussies be the greatest—'

She started doing a war dance, but I ducked around her to glimpse footage of gang members throwing something at the sniffer dogs, making them yelp and bark. The scene cut to Lt. Swizzlestick talking.

'—seasonal display of apples. Looks like they took the heads off a box of nails and stuck them in the apples. No one was seriously injured in this encounter, but see this crossbow? This was wedged in the handicapped stall of the Lord & Taylor's ladies room. It was set to fire when the stall opened. No, these girls are not nice. Our bomb disposal squad recommends—'

'Hey whoa, we didn't plant no bomb!' KrayZglu protested. 'That little thing outside Continental, that was just a distraction, shit you could make that in your kitchen sink, it wasn't no real bomb.'

She then started yelling at the screen and stuff.

'Anybody can make a phone call and say there's a bomb,' I said. I was thinking specifically of 10Esha and her 'art'.

'Yeah!' shouted KrayZglu to the TV, where a Right Guard commercial was showing. 'There ain't no bomb.'

'We better turn ourselves in,' I said. 'Just in case there is.'

'There ain't no bomb.'

'We better turn ourselves in,' I repeated.

'There ain't no bomb.'

This went around a few more times. KrayZglu seemed to be in some kind of denial mantra loop trance state. Finally I said, 'You know we're on video right now?'

KrayZglu glanced once at the bank of cameras and the screen showing us. Then she looked away. She seemed to be thinking.

'Hi girlz.'

The voice came from somewhere behind us. I knew it at once. I should have been expecting this, but somehow I never quite twigged it, until now.

I turned around slowly. There was a Watchman sitting on top of a hi-fi system. It cost $1799.99 on sale. Really cute. Filling most of the screen was 10Esha's face.

'Hi my pussies,' she said. 'You coming to the truck tunnel or not?'

'10 what the fuck?' said KrayZglu angrily. 'What's all this bomb shit? What bomb? We didn't plant no bomb.'

'You got to talk to GoldYlox about that.'

10 was looking even more smug than usual. I expected a big confab between the two of them, but KrayZglu just picked up the Watchman and switched off the screen. Then she herded me back into the corridor and shut the door, blunting the edge of the television sound. I was laughing nervously.

'You showed her,' I applauded. 'Where's she sending the signal from, I wonder?'

But KrayZglu was Popsicled, frigid, mannequin-still. She leaned back against the wall, which was decorated with obscene drawings in Magic Marker, and closed her eyes. She put her finger to her lips and I stopped laughing.

'What's the matter?' I whispered.

Slowly, like she expected to taste something bitter, she licked her lips.

'GoldYlox is here.'

'Here?'

'Here. In the mall. He came in through the air ducts. 10 gone out in the van to do the link-up, but GoldYlox come in.'

'10's out? Ah, damn, I'm fucked up a telephone post,' I moaned. 'My butt crack is going to be all over the Internet by tonight.'

KrayZglu showed no indication that she'd heard me. She'd turned all weird. Her hands made feathery stroking motions over her gun. Her teeth were chattering, and you could feel choppy waves of fear coming off her, like whitecaps on the Hudson.

'I need a hit,' she whispered. 'This be whipping my head.'

My butt crack's importance was diminishing in the face of KrayZglu's behaviour.

'So what's the deal with this GoldYlox guy? What could he do?' I tried to sound casual about it.

'You don't want to know.'

'Yes, I do. Come on, KrayZglu – you're freaking me. What's the matter?'

She let out a long groan and sank to the floor. She buried her face in the little hollow between her bent knees. When she spoke this time, she sounded less ghetto and more Sunday-school. She also sounded scared.

'10Esha is GoldYlox niece. He started the Bugaboos, a long time ago. It was kinda like R. Kelly starting off Aaliyah. We outgrew him a long time ago, we give him all respect but we went our separate ways, you know what I'm saying? So I don't know what he doing here now.'

'Maybe it's just a coincidence,' I said.

'I don't like the sound of this bomb thing. It's GoldYlox all over, Sun.'

253

My ears pricked up when she used my name. Was KrayZglu *consulting* me? Wow.

'See, the cops here today have been acting real *evolved*, you know what I'm saying?'

I didn't, but I nodded vigorously. 'Evolved, yeah, that's just the term—'

'We just starting to get some police cooperation, I mean I'm not saying we Boos is like the Mob yet, but we're getting some kind of dialowge going and that's the first step to control, you know? But when they see GoldYlox the police is going to get all tightass and righteous again.'

Police cooperation. I wondered what that meant. Did it have anything to do with the police basically letting me get away back at Sharper Image?

'So . . . are you and 10 on the same side, or what?'

KrayZglu's expression snapped shut like an unhappy clamshell.

'I thought she was one of us. Now I think maybe she working for Uncle G all along, and I don't trust Uncle G, see? He's not sophisticated like us. He's just a sneaky old counter-thief.'

'Counter-thief?'

She stood up. 'C'mon. I got a idea.'

STUPID PET TRICK

MADDIE STUMBLED TOWARDS Bernie Taktarov and took his hand in shock.

'Hi. You got my messages?'

'I'm here, aren't I? Don't have much time, though. My trailer's double-parked outside Gould's office so I have to be gone by 9 a.m. or she'll probably give me a ticket.'

Maddie laughed a little hysterically. 'You? Give *you* a ticket? She wouldn't dare.'

She was aware that she was acting stupid, wringing her hands and dancing from foot to foot, but she couldn't seem to stop. Fuck, what was she going to do? She never expected Bernie Taktarov to show up *here*. Besides, when she had first written to him the whole issue of the SE and his immunity and Arnie Henshaw had not even been part of the picture. Now she was terrified that she or

Naomi would spill something, and Taktarov would find out Carrera's secret, and she'd never get the sperm, much less the credit for the discovery. She had to deflect Bernie's attention. Keep him focused on Meniscus.

'Um ... we were just ... brainstorming what to do about Meniscus.' She turned to Naomi, silently willing her to not mention the SE or Jennifer. 'Naomi, this is our real boss, Dr Taktarov from the Board of Trustees. He wrote the original study that Meniscus was commissioned for and he approved our project. Bernie, my manhandler and assistant, Naomi.'

'I know who you are, of course, Bernie,' Naomi gushed. 'It's an honour.'

'You two are the picture of dedication,' said Bernie in a friendly alto. 'I wasn't expecting to find you here in the middle of the night. But, as they say, I saw the lights on and decided to take a chance.'

Maddie clocked the fact that he seemed a little nervous himself and dimly wondered why; then Bernie distracted her by indicating the I-MAGE display, which had been playing in the background all this time. He touched Naomi's arm.

'Now, dear, did you notice by any chance that game usage is related to the azure:human ratio as a function of temperature in association with blood levels of noradrenalin and dopamine?'

'Heck, doc, that fact had eluded me,' said Naomi, glancing at Starry Eyes and rolling her eyes as if to say, can you believe this weirdo? Maddie thought Taktarov was just showing off, too, because who could look at an I-MAGE without a MUSE and see sense?

'You're missing the trees for the forest,' he added. He went to the I-MAGE console and punched up a 3-D image of the equation. Naomi looked at it for a moment and then said, 'Aha, I was right. Pain does equal gain.'

256

'Cute,' said Bernie. 'But simplistic.'

'I was right to cut game access.'

Maddie flashed Naomi a warning glance, but she was rubbing her tattoos and shivering.

'That depends on your definition of "right". You thought increasing game usage was causing the Azure to multiply. What if it was the other way around?'

'Huh?'

'What if the peripheral nervous system created in the astrocytes was mature enough to start impinging on the CNS? What if the bugs are trying to communicate?'

'Naomi,' said Maddie, sounding rather shrill in her own ears, 'would you excuse us?'

Bernie turned to look at her and his databeads winked off and on.

'Let's go to my trailer, Maddie,' he said.

'Trailer? You actually live in a trailer? I thought you were kidding.'

Maddie grabbed Naomi by the elbow and hissed at her to get to work on the plan. Naomi hissed back that Maddie shouldn't be so hostile, she'd only been trying to distract Bernie from noticing Carrera and the overall state of confusion in the lab. They gave each other big, fake smiles as they parted. Maddie's stomach was doing nervous spins and she needed to shit.

Bernie was not kidding. Towed by a workmanlike old jeep, the trailer was big enough to sleep six. It had a pool table and a jacuzzi, and a macau named Sweden presided over it all.

'Are you all right, Madeleine? All these frantic messages, and –' he gestured at her clothes and hair '– and you're not looking too spiffy.'

'Bernie, let's cut to the chase,' she said to the bottom of her whisky glass. She ignored the fact that the Laphroaig was dancing an ill-advised sock hop with the vodka and Neuhaus. 'I need someone to take over Meniscus for me. I've got a . . . situation . . . with this SE they've saddled me with, and I need to take the SE away. Can you babysit my subject for a little while?'

Bernie's face fell. 'What about Meniscus's crisis? Surely you don't intend to abandon him now.'

'Oh, he's over that,' Maddie said airily, as if talking about chickenpox. 'And I'm not *abandoning* him, it's just that something really urgent has come up and I can't trust anyone else with it.'

'Well.' Bernie didn't look too happy and belatedly it occurred to Maddie that he was not just any colleague, he was a silent partner in Hibridge – eccentric, but powerful.

'I'm sorry,' she added. 'I shouldn't impose on you. It's just that everything is happening so fast.'

'I appreciate that. I've taken the liberty of reviewing your notes and scans on Meniscus, so I'm up to speed on what you've been doing here.'

'Oh,' said Maddie. She should have expected this. Bernie always did his homework.

'That's why I find it so hard to believe that you're looking to unload Meniscus now of all times. Surely this is the most important phase of your entire career, maybe your whole life.'

'Well, yeah, of course it's important. I've worked really hard on this organism, and I'm looking forward to interpreting all the data I've been collecting and hopefully publishing a really good contribution. But there's this SE, see, and—'

'Waitaminit waitaminit Hello? Are we talking about the same water buffalo here? Last I checked, you had an organism that stimulated an adult, Y-autistic male to produce functioning astrocytes that are now firing independently of the action of the central nervous system.

258

You had a subject who was pumping out norepinephrine, DHEA, pituitary hormone and a whole bunch of other goodies we don't even know what they are, in a pattern correlatable with Mall usage. You had a subject who should by rights be dead, yet there he is, alive, engaged in Mall, and from where I'm standing it looks like he's put on a lot of muscle, he *speaks* and he's turning fucking blue. Now what do you mean, you want somebody to babysit him while you go off and fuck around playing Cavepussy with Tarzan? Are you loopy out the wazoo?'

Maddie wanted to sit up straight in self-righteous indignation, but she found that Bernie's sofa had sucked her butt into some kind of inescapable trench, and instead she flailed around a little like Kafka's beetle on its back, then settled for tossing her hair back from her face and slamming her empty glass onto a coaster in the shape of a Great Dane.

'I am *not* playing Cavepussy, Bernie.'

'Then why would you walk away from a study that's going to put you on the cover of *Time* next year?'

Maddie stared at him. 'Could you stop exaggerating and blowing everything out of proportion? I am well aware that I have an obligation to the study, to Meniscus, and to you. But I'm only talking about a hiatus of a couple of weeks, and his condition is stable.'

'Stable? A couple of weeks?' Bernie's voice rose and cracked. 'Have you gone mental?'

'*I* don't live with a parrot named Sweden!'

'Macau, he's a macau. Maddie, Maddie. Is it possible you don't realise what you have here? Do you always drink this much? How could you miss it, it's staring you in the face?'

'What's staring me in the face?'

'Meniscus is an ambassador. He's a messenger from Them.'

259

'Them?' Boy-o-boy, not the conspiracy pronoun.

'The *bugs*, stupid.'

Oh, dear.

'We know we have co-evolved with the bugs. We think we are their masters, but why? It's just as easy to look at the historical record and say that They are our masters.'

Thus began Bernie's Bug Exegesis. Maddie kept drinking and ran through alternative routes across rural Pennsylvania in her mind as she planned her escape with Carrera.

'Because sex was only ever an invention of evolution, sprung out of the war against the micros, the parasites who try to pick the locks of our immune system. Throughout history they have been our invisible foes, and sex is our weapon in the chess game of lock-switching, which explains why almost everything we do can be traced back to sex in the end.

'Now, Maddie, I ask you, if the bugs are our partners, our shadow selves, and we have evolved Mind, then why haven't They? Or have They and we can't perceive It? Think on it. These bugs who have driven our sexual selection and our society, they sure know how to dish out drama. HIV that equated love with death as never before, the direct attacks on specific genes that followed as bugs, with the aid of their human agents, learned to make themselves useful and find warm homes for themselves by becoming weapons. With bubonic plague They attacked our civilisation but our civilisation, curiously virus-like in its behaviour, eventually took a page from Their book and prevailed, so that now They attack our identity with untouchable abstract brain plagues that make life so easy we get weaker and weaker. McDonald's and Disney and Virgin sprout up everywhere, like culture-destroying viruses that replicate and eat all complexity and make us predictable and compliant, and we blithely sit back and think micros are dumb. And that's not even mentioning this century's chosen means of economic warfare in the form of plagues. And *that*'s not even mentioning Y-plagues.'

'Can I have another drink? Ah, just hand me the bottle.'

'Now, the bugs can speak the language of chemistry. They know how to talk to your cells; and how to listen. For Meniscus they are acting as ambassadors between himself and himself. They are breaking the barrier between consciousness and the great subconscious.'

'You make it sound like they're something out of Saturday-morning cartoons. They aren't smart, Bernie. They're prokaryotes for chrissake.'

'They don't have to be smart, Maddie, because *you* are smart. Don't you see it? It's a case of negative space. You've created niches for them. And having amputated the superfluous gender, you are now free to move forward and fight the bugs on your own terms. Because, in a long-term evolutionary sense, thanks to sex we have these gigantic brains, these powerhouses of fantasy and logic and the whole discount superpackage, and we can do better than nature, I think, no I correct myself, *you* think.'

'You're right, I do think. To think otherwise I'd end up as a Christian Scientist or something, in court over the right to let my kid die from measles.'

'Yes, I know your type all too well. Your martial spirit is one of faith in the tenet that the power of consciousness can defeat the raw life-drive of the micro-organism, the ghostly dance partner we can't even sense directly. And now, with Meniscus and Mall, now you've made your great foray into the melding of the human senses with the abstract/non-sensing hitek bigscience that at present conducts its war against Bugs in the name of Woman.'

'Wow,' said Maddie. 'I thought I was just trying to keep up with my kid's laundry.'

'Don't be cute. You must see the implications of what you've got here. He's learned to make his fingernails grow – well, imagine it. If you could be physically informed by your empirical knowledge, if something abstract could find concrete form in your actions and you could *directly sense* your inner physical reality, now that would be some kind of a pastrami sandwich, you know what I'm saying? If you could sense what was happening in your cells, would you need a microscope? Radioactive tracers? An I-MAGE? Tylenol, for fuck's sake? Pregnancy tests, Maddie?'

'You wouldn't need any of it,' Maddie said softly.

'Do-it-yourself healing. If you've got the key to that, you'd better watch out for the AMA's hit squad because you're gonna throw medicine right over on its ass. Not to mention the implications for the species.'

'We won't be the same species any more, if Meniscus's DNA is altered by 10E.'

'No kidding. If the bugs seed themselves in human DNA, then his offspring will inherit his powers. And his infection. How do you feel about that idea?'

'I don't know.'

'You better think about it, because what you do from here on out matters. And I don't think you're in the driver's seat. I don't think any of us are.'

Maddie snorted. Bernie leaned closer and said, 'You gotta ask yourself the question: was getting rid of the boyz a stupid pet trick you fell for? Were the boyz really wiped out by human rational design or was *even that* all part of a plot by the bugz to take away our Biggest Gun? Are you now a member of a single-gender planned humanity that will be eaten alive by the pretty little critters who earn you your living? Or is it time to stop the war by mating with the microparasites and have you made Meniscus the white-veiled hymeneal bride?'

'Meniscus is in control of the game.'

'Is he?'

'It's still his body.'

'Is it? Have you asked him? Are you in control of your game? Is it your body. Do you know what you are, Dr Baldino?'

'I gotta go. Christ, I have a headache. What was in that drink?'

'Only Common Sense. What, leaving so soon? You haven't heard my theories about secret world domination by the Inuit.'

PIANOS ON THE TIDE

WE GOT INTO California Kitchen from the back, but it was all dark inside and after checking everything out KrayZglu led me into the restaurant area.

She sat down and said, 'You hungry?'

'I could eat a yak.'

'Help yourself. I'm not hungry. I can never eat on a job.'

I went over to the salad bar but I couldn't get into health food, so I decided to check out the kitchen. There were a couple of cold pizzas lying under what had been heat lamps; I picked one up and tore off a section. It was the best thing I ever tasted, and I don't even like pepperoni. I found some Coke and then, at KrayZglu's urging, went to the bathroom. When I came out, she was still sitting very quietly in a booth.

'Are you OK?' I said. She was being awfully low-key all of a sudden. Almost nice.

'Shoot out that camera,' KrayZglu said, not pointing but indicating the direction with her head. It took me a while to spot the camera, but I figured maybe this was some kind of test. So when I located the lens, I shot it. That part was easy.

'Now. Come here and sit down by me.'

She sounded like the Godfather. I sat down nervously. She was shaking her head at me in pity. 'Girl, you too stupid.'

I saw her hand with the gun in it come up from under the table, but I didn't react quickly enough. *Fuck.*

'Give me your piece.' She had some duct tape, which she wrapped around my wrists and then my mouth. She did it so fast I didn't even have time to squeak. 'Now, into the oven.'

The oven? What is this, Little Red Riding Hood?

I start hyperventilating.

'That's it, you climb on up there, I'll help you. In you go. I'll leave the door cracked like this so you can breathe, OK? But you stay quiet or else I'll turn this thing on, you git it?'

I nodded. I got it.

Then something whacked me on the side of the head and I went away. I had this weird little dream, set in Hawaii, about a guy who dragged pianos out of the sea and sold them to people. There was this beautiful image of piano hulks coming in on the tide, and a man with a long pole catching hold of them, and the ruin of their strings covered in seaweed.

I woke up with a headache and the taste of garlic in my mouth.

I couldn't believe it. I looked out through this teeny crack and I could see KrayZglu, tied to a chair in the middle of the restaurant. Ropes made Xs across her chest and wrapped around her legs. She was also gagged, probably with the same duct tape she'd used on me. Hah! The plot thickens. I wonder who has come along to give her her come-uppance. I assume it's 10, but there's no one else to be seen, which is strange.

A couple of minutes went by. KrayZglu was awake and looking around, but not struggling. She seemed pretty relaxed about the whole thing, actually.

Then I heard it. From out in the corridor. The sound I'd been dreading for days – OK, for hours, but it seemed like days. Only now I wasn't dreading it as much as I thought.

Police radios.

Two of them came in through the maul entrance. One was stocky and bull-like, the other tall and rangy. Both of them looked like they meant business. They were wearing riot gear and carrying AK-47s. I felt the strong urge to give up and go home – well, go to jail to be more accurate – but since I was tied up in the pizza oven I couldn't give in to my submissive reflex in action. I just had to watch.

With the arrival of the cops, KrayZglu was no longer acting cool. She was yelling from behind the gag and jumping up and down, the whole chair moving as she strained at her bonds. It took little leaps away from the table behind her and then back again. I saw the cords in her neck stand out. Her nostrils were flared and she was snorting with effort.

The tall cop approached her slowly, making pacifying gestures towards her. KrayZglu just shrieked through the gag and sweated and jumped around more. Then I noticed that there was blood running down her leg and pooling on the floor. When did *that* happen?

'Unit Four, this is Reichart, we need a medic on

standby at the West Entrance. We have an injured female adolescent, looks like a hostage but we're treating her with caution.'

I couldn't hear what the reply was, but the two men exchanged glances and hand signals, and the stocky one came around the counter and into the pizza-making area. Uh-oh. He checked under the counter and opened the fridge, but he walked right by my oven without noticing it was cracked open. I guess he didn't think anyone could hide inside a pizza oven. I am pretty small for a criminal. He then went into the back room and I could hear him opening doors and banging on things with the barrel of his gun.

While he was gone the tall guy was trying to soothe an increasingly agitated KrayZglu. She was going berserk, hyperventilating and crying and then struggling to breathe through her own snot. Finally the other cop came back, passed me *again* without noticing anything, and gave the all-clear sign. The two of them approached KrayZglu.

'Sorry about that,' said the stocky one to KrayZglu. 'I was just checking to make sure there weren't any surprises in the kitchen. My name's Bob.'

He bent over KrayZglu and wiped her nose so she could breathe, then started to free her. The other one put down his gun and helped.

I saw it happening but I couldn't believe it at first. Both KrayZglu's arms, which had *looked* like they were pinned behind her back, whipped around as if they'd been released on a spring. One buried itself in the groin of the tall guy, in the valley where the bulletproof armour met the top of his right leg. The other almost simultaneously made two cuts. The first slashed across the eyes of Bob, the stocky cop and then, while the blood was still spraying out, plunged into his throat. KrayZglu was on her feet as Bob was simultaneously falling. The taller cop fell back, blood gushing from his femoral artery, and KrayZglu lunged after him with the knife. He was going for his rifle, but as he turned to pick it up, she threw herself on his back like a monkey and cut his throat from behind.

It was over so fast I didn't have time to let my breath out. KrayZglu was laughing wildly and doing an obscene little war dance.

'My Bug Pussy got teeth, gentlemens and ladies of the jury. Come on in and—' She stooped and took Bob's assault rifle so now she had two, though it looked like she could barely handle the weight. She shot a round into the glass separating California Pizza from the mall. Then she vaulted the counter and opened the oven. She ripped the tape off so quickly that even though I didn't need an upper-lip wax, I got one. I think she took off part of my tongue, too, because it started to bleed. She dragged me out of the oven. There was blood all over her, though it didn't show much on the black leather.

'Here you go, bunny,' she said, and slapped the hilt of one of the knives into my hand. I should have stabbed her with it but I didn't dare. Instead, I dropped it.

'Oh, no you don't,' I gasped. 'I'm not taking the blame for this.'

The point of the rifle lifted my floating ribs.

'Pick it up. Take this one, too.'

'Aw, come on, KrayZglu. Ain't nobody here but us chickens, why can't you just give me a break, take me with you . . .' I didn't like the sound of myself begging especially when she'd framed me so neatly and here I was, goober of the century, believing I was being initiated into the Bugaboos. I should have known better. I'm too short, and I don't have the look.

I shut up. KrayZglu was looking unimpressed with my begging, but that wasn't why. It was because, over KrayZglu's shoulder, through an air vent near the pizza oven, I could see yellow smoke pouring into California Pizza.

They were gassing us.

Here's what I think about what happened. It's like, maybe one time in your whole life you get a real chance at something, and you're standing there looking at it. Like it's the proverbial open door and you stand there knowing you just have to go through it – it's so simple – just go through it and you'll be on the other side and everything will be different. And it's so simple that you want to turn around and say to god or whoever, 'You're kidding, right? This is way too simple. You can do better than this.'

At least, I had that urge. I don't know why I feel compelled to be such a wiseass. I don't know why I don't believe my own life even when it's happening to me.

That's when I found out I'm not the only inhabitant of my self. Because without me thinking about it, or willing it, or even taking a quarter of a deep breath, I threw myself backward and over a table. I dug the gas mask out from under some Wonder Wit pyjamas in the backpack and jammed it on my head even as KrayZglu was trying to grab me. She's a lot bigger and stronger than me but I was like a mad squirrel, and she couldn't hold me. I climbed backwards over the table and put the salad bar between us.

I started taking deep breaths. KrayZglu began to slow down. She was rubbing her eyes and weaving from side to side, almost falling. I stood there for a second and watched her come. She crashed through a pair of dessert carts and sat down in a peach-coloured vinyl booth. Then she slumped over.

I took her gun and her phone. I picked up the TV and took that, too.

Truck tunnel. Everybody was aiming for the truck tunnel, and escape. I had to find it. Back into the access passages.

So here I am running thru the maul's intestines like a GI bug (haha, v. funny Sun) carrying 10Esha's head in a box. She knows where I am but I don't know where she is. She knows where the cameras that can pick up my movement are; I'm only guessing.

I know I shouldn't listen to her. I know she's nothing but trouble. I switch on the TV to Channel 10.

OF MOUSE & MENISCUS

MENISCUS DOESN'T HAVE a fever yet but it's only a matter of time. He feels clear and high and he can see what those bugs are doing. All too clearly he can see it, but he's powerless to stop it because no matter how smart his body is now, an old-style Y-plague is functionally unstoppable.

Starry Eyes is royally pissed-off about the situation in general and Naomi in particular – a fact that she strives to ignore, driving him to complain and curse louder and louder. Occasionally he throws a wrench, or kicks something. Then he goes quiet. Meniscus turned his gaze outwards long enough to see that Starry Eyes was sulking, sitting on the bed with the duffel bag between his knees, the bike leaning skewed against Meniscus's system console. His shoulders were up around his ears, his large hands cradling his chin, his feet tapping a nervous beat on the tile floor. He didn't meet Meniscus's gaze.

Meniscus doesn't say anything. He is waiting for the two Doctors to come back into the lab. He is reeling from the sight of his clone-father's face. What are they saying to each other, those two? And what does it mean for the planets?

All these years he has remembered Doctor's face, the face of his father, the only face of love he has ever known. Probably his reverence for Dr Baldino arises from the fact that she has succeeded Doctor, who in his mind has grown and ascended to become a kind of higher power to whom he could appeal in time of need.

But Bernie Taktarov arriving in this way, at this time, is not exactly the cavalry. And when at last he returns, he is alone and has changed clothes. Meniscus looks at his outfit – clearance-rack Gimbels print dress and old-lady practical shoes – and his hasty, garish make-up, and feels weird and ashamed.

Doctor's smile for Meniscus is covetous.

'I've missed you so much. I wanted so much to come see you, but it wouldn't have been permissible in Dr Baldino's experiments. It would have disturbed your equilibrium.'

Inside Meniscus, bugs and hormones snarled and knotted around one another like rush-hour traffic. The game boiled under his skin. He didn't meet Doctor's gaze. He just said, 'You fuck.'

Doctor's smile wavered. He licked his lips and made a submissive nod of his head. 'I deserve that. But I had a higher purpose in mind.'

'So you said. "They are our future," you said. Some future.'

Doctor turned off the cameras and intercom. Naomi, busy calling up rentacar companies, didn't even notice.

With a furtive air, he approached the plexiglas. He whispered,

'When I said They are our future, I didn't mean Women. I meant the bugs.'

Meniscus charged the glass and Doctor cringed, stumbling backwards into Naomi's aloe plant. 'Get away from me!' Meniscus snarled. 'Just quit gloating, and get out!'

'But ... Meniscus ... don't you understand? It's all happening for you now. Your autism is cured! You can speak to me! You can do anything. The sacrifices we both made, they're worth it.'

'What sacrifice did you make, *Doctor*? I'm the one who's been sacrificed.'

'And that's been my sacrifice, too. I told you then and I'll tell you now, you wouldn't have had any sort of life with me. Now you're in power. Once you've developed your abilities, there will be no stopping you! Why are you looking at me like that? Don't you understand how thrilled I am for you? Don't you know that I've lived every day in the hope that you'd use the game to make this kind of connection? This is a miracle, son. We should be celebrating.'

Meniscus didn't answer. He was standing in the eye of a storm and he didn't want to venture out by speaking because he knew the winds would rip him to shreds. He stood glowering, looking through Doctor, and willing him to leave.

Bernie now turned to Starry Eyes.

'Tell him not to be so cruel,' he begged. Tears were welling in his eyes. 'In my life, I've Had It All, and I've lost it all. Career, manhood, mental health ... but I can't stand to lose my son. Not now, not when such wonderful things are happening. Tell him to have compassion for his old man.'

Starry Eyes looked a little freaked out at the term 'old man' as applied to Bernie Taktarov, but he went over and nudged Meniscus.

'Come on. Squeak, give the old . . . thing a break. It all turned out OK for you in the end, didn't it?'

'Tell him to go,' said Meniscus through clenched teeth. 'I don't want to see him.'

Starry Eyes looked at him for a while as if he was going to say something more, but then he shrugged and Meniscus, still looking at his own bare feet, heard him tell Doctor, 'You heard him. He doesn't want you here.'

'But what will happen to him? I'm all he's got. Dr Baldino doesn't know how to handle this. Meniscus, you have to agree to let me help you. It won't be for ever, just until you can get yourself acclimatised to the new bugs. And you'll need me to handle your legal situation with the company. I can do that. Even now, with my . . . problems, I can still do that.'

Meniscus scoffed at him. 'You think I'll just go on being compliant, but I'm not the person you think I am. I don't have a compliant bone in my body any more.'

'It's not a question of compliance, it's just—'

'I'm not a fool!' Meniscus interrupted, and he could hear Starry Eyes's speech patterns in his own voice. 'I'm not staying here. I'm not dying here. And it's too late for any of that shit you're talking about.'

Taktarov shook his head sadly. 'You're almost there, son. Don't let it all go to ruin now. We've come so far. Don't throw it all away.'

'Shut up!' Meniscus shouted, picking up a chair and brandishing it at Taktarov. 'I'm not listening to you. Take your fucking stones and get the fuck out of my face.'

'Whoa!' called Naomi, looking up from her screen. 'Calm down, Meniscus.'

Bernie cringed. New tears spilled over his white eyelashes.

'I'm sorry,' he whispered. 'I'm sorry, OK? I'm sorry.'

Meniscus put the chair down. 'You don't even know what you're sorry for. Just get out of here. Go away. There's nothing you can do here.'

Doctor seemed to shrink. He shook his head sadly, his whole body drooping. He fished in his handbag and pulled out a rumpled Kleenex.

'Uh, actually you could do one thing before you go,' Starry Eyes suggested as Doctor blew his nose. 'You could open up this door and let me out. I'm not holding anything against you.'

Doctor sniffed and wadded up the tissue. 'I can't even do that. I got kicked off the Board. They've closed me down. That's why I came here. I thought I could be of some use. Oh, it's all political – I'm no crazier than I was five years ago, but I guess my number just came up.'

'You must know how to open the door, Bernie.'

'They took my security codes, my system access, I got nothing except my trailer and Jennifer's going to have that towed any minute now. They want to institutionalise me.'

'Well, boo-fucking-hoo,' Meniscus said. 'You better go, then.'

'No, wait!' Starry Eyes said. 'You can still do something. You can deliver this order to *Cycle Freek* magazine. I need this stuff to come express.'

Taktarov took the sheet from the pass-thru chute and glanced at it.

'OK, if that's what you want.'

His eyes lingered on Meniscus. He started crying again.

'Stop looking at me, you nasty old shit. *Go away.*'

After Bernie Taktarov made his exit, sobbing all over Starry Eyes's *Cycle Freek* order form, Starry Eyes jerked his head at Meniscus and said, 'What was that all about? What's your problem?'

'Nothing!' Meniscus shouted. 'Fuck off!'

'Hey, whoa!' Starry Eyes huffed out the words, holding his hands up with palms out as though to make Meniscus back off. 'Let's not be rude here. I'm not your enemy.'

'Just leave me alone.'

'No, I won't leave you alone. I want to know what is up your butt. You've been acting weird ever since Baldino left. What is your problem with her? You in love with her or something? Or is it Naomi? You jealous? You wanna fight me? What the fuck is up?'

Meniscus grabbed his head and turned his back. He could feel the muscles of his back bunching. He wanted to explode.

Starry Eyes lowered his voice.

'Look, I'm outta here really soon but I don't want to leave it like this so either you tell me what you got to tell me or I kick your ass.'

'Yeah, I'd like to see you try,' growled Meniscus. Starry Eyes just laughed. Meniscus turned and charged him like a little bull. Starry Eyes spun off to the side and caught Meniscus's head in a guillotine hold, whipping him to the floor easily.

'You wanna fight? Huh? Huh? You really want to fight?'

Meniscus gasped for breath but couldn't find any. He started seeing stars and the light faded in and out. Starry Eyes let him go and he found himself on his knees, gulping air like a whale resurfacing from a deep dive. His throat was killing him.

'*What*, Squeak? For fuck's sake, tell me what's the matter!'

Meniscus grabbed Starry Eyes around the knees and burst into tears.

'Y-plague!' he gasped. 'In the uh-uh air f-f-freshener.'

Starry Eyes didn't say anything right away. Then he sighed.

'Well, I don't think it's going to hurt me. I've pretty much seen them all. They don't bother me.' Then he looked at Meniscus. 'But I guess you're screwed, Squeak. I'm sorry .'

All the anger went out of Meniscus, replaced by resolve.

'You have to take me with you now.'

'If I go.' The glum air settled back over SE and Meniscus realised this was what he was brooding over: his failed escape. Then SE said, 'How do you know it's a Y-plague? Could you, like, *smell* them in that air freshener?'

'I knew what they were as soon as they entered my body. Now I'm as good as dead. I don't know how to deal with them.'

Starry Eyes shook his head ruefully. 'These stupid women. They'll do anything for sperm. But if it's any consolation, you wouldn't be able to leave here anyway. Sooner or later you'd catch one. They're out there and they can lie fucking dormant for *years*.'

Meniscus nodded, and Starry Eyes's gaze faded to become a blank wall again. Neither of them spoke for a while, and Naomi's snores could be heard, faintly, through the plexiglas. Starry Eyes was still fidgeting like a motherfucker; what he was waiting for to happen, Meniscus couldn't imagine, because it was the dead of night and no one was around. But he had the deserted stare that fight chemicals gave you – Meniscus knew about that now, from Mall. Meniscus wanted to talk, but Starry Eyes wanted to kill. So Meniscus almost didn't say what he said next.

But Starry Eyes's voice was in his head, and that voice was becoming Meniscus's voice. The Starry Eyes in his head said, *Speak, you fucker, for all the times in your life you never said boo.*

He cleared his throat.

'I'm only alive now because of you,' he said.

'Yeah?' Starry Eyes wasn't really listening.

'Because of the way you knock me around, try to teach me to fight.'

Starry Eyes kept drumming his feet. He snorted a laugh. 'I tried, but some people are beyond help.'

Meniscus smiled. 'I used you. I learned to fight inside. I stood up to them. And you know what? They're not so bad. They can do things for us we can't do on our own. They can go places we can't.'

'Huhn.'

Starry Eyes was definitely not listening, or he wouldn't be so blasé.

'Shit, I'm hungry. I'm gonna wake up Naomi.'

'No! No, wait, don't wake her up yet. We gotta talk, Starry.'

'Wachoo call me?'

Meniscus shrugged. 'Nobody told me your name.'

'Damn straight, and nobody will. Talk about what?'

'About how I can change myself. My chemistry. The bugs talk to my cells for me. I can see inside myself.' He knew he sounded urgent, feverish – and he was, because the Y-plague was upon him and he was terrified.

'Yeah, I could see inside myself too if I could look up my own asshole.'

OK, so Starry Eyes just didn't get it and it was hardly surprising. Meniscus's own words sounded like shopping-channel mysticism to himself.

'Please. I've had a glimpse of something. Something *amazing*. And if I could only have a little more time, I could do more. I could explore, I could discover ... oh, fuck, what's the use of talking to you?'

He swung around and went to the far side of the habitat, away from Starry Eyes. He leaned on the glass and watched it fog where he breathed on it. He watched Naomi sleeping and remembered how the sexual response she had initiated had let him mate with the bugs, inside. And mating with the bugs had given him new perceptions, new power. If only there could be a way to stimulate himself to respond to the Y-plague.

'There should be a way,' he muttered to himself. 'In theory I know how the Y-plagues work. I know their methods. But how to fight them?'

He was bleary, hot, afraid, and he wanted to sink into Mall except he knew he was as clueless there as here. Starry Eyes was saying something.

'What?'

'I said, why don't you just do what my body does?'

'How am I supposed to do that?'

'Well, you imitated me when I came here. You started to act like me, look like me, talk like me. So why don't you fight the plague like me?'

'You wanna tell me how you fight it? See, you can't describe it because you don't have the physical consciousness I have. You don't know what your immune system is doing that's special. I bet nobody does.'

'That's not true. Naomi took a bunch of I-MAGEs, remember?'

'I don't know how to interpret an I-MAGE. That's what Dr Baldino does.'

'Well, we'll get her, then. I'll tell her she can have my sperm if she figures out what my immune system does, and then explains it to you.'

This 'solution' was so simple-minded that Meniscus didn't know where to begin in rejecting it. So he just said,

'There isn't enough time for that. I'll be dead before she can do it.'

'You're long on problems and short on solutions, ain't you, Squeak? You're so depressive, you want to change your attitude or you won't survive.'

'I'm not depressive! I'm running from death. There's a difference.'

'Ah, give me a break. I've been running from death all my life. One of these bitches could poison my cornflakes any morning of the week – don't know why they haven't, it would be easier than trying to kill me with bugs, I mean what's with this air-freshener shit anyway?'

Meniscus really wanted to cry but he knew that Starry Eyes would only scoff at him, so he didn't. Then, out of nowhere, a thought occurred to him.

'I would need to get the I-MAGE read-outs fed into the game. I'd need to see them, touch them. I'd need them moving around in my subconscious. Then maybe I could work with them.'

'Can't you weasel your way into the I-MAGE files from your precious game?'

'No. The I-MAGE's hardwired as an independent system. Nobody can just go in. I'd have to be patched in physically.'

Starry Eyes was thinking. 'OK,' he said. 'Just sit tight.'

There wasn't much else that Meniscus could do; the Y-plague had him by the balls, literally. With an effort, he turned his head so that he could watch Starry Eyes go over to Genghis's Oreo box and release him. Genghis came bounding out, running around the habitat in algorithmic switchback patterns that made Meniscus dizzy. Now Starry Eyes was waving to Naomi, who came switch-hipping over with a long smile on her lips.

'Honey,' Starry Eyes said, 'I think I found your mouse.'

Naomi put her hand over her mouth, squealed, and froze in place.

'Don't hurt her!' she cried. 'Oh, what am I going to do? Maddie will kill me – I told her the mouse was gone.'

Starry Eyes then blundered around the habitat, chasing the mouse. What on earth was he doing? For one thing, he could easily catch Genghis if he wanted to, since Genghis was half-tame already. But he made a show of not being able to.

Within two minutes the habitat was open and Naomi was inside.

'Yo!' shouted Starry Eyes. 'Look out!' He made a dive for Genghis, missed him by a mile, and the mouse shot through the open door and into the lab.

'Oh shit!' Naomi shrieked, and then, as if remembering herself, she suddenly started chanting one of her mantras. She ran after the mouse, making clicking noises with her tongue as though calling it. Starry Eyes trailed after her into the lab.

Meniscus was shocked. He almost sat up. Starry Eyes was out of the habitat.

'*Om tare tutare ture* – quick, corner her, Snake!' Naomi yelled.

'Got him – oops—' Starry Eyes hit the deck with a grunt.

'She's under the I-MAGE – *tutare ture so-ha, Om tare*—'

'Ha! Gotcha, buddy.'

Starry Eyes came up from under the I-MAGE console, holding the mouse. He passed Genghis to Naomi, who cuddled him.

'I think he damaged your equipment,' he said, holding up a piece of frayed electrical wire. Meniscus saw him moving something around inside his mouth with his tongue, and when Naomi glanced away, Starry Eyes spat a piece of red cable insulator over his shoulder.

'Oh, damn it,' Naomi said. 'She'll kill me, Snake, what – oh, *shit*, look, the monitor for the I-MAGE is down. What'm I gonna do?'

Starry Eyes shrugged, avoiding eye contact.

'I can take a look if you want,' he said. 'It might be just a simple thing . . .'

'N-no, you better get back in there. It's dangerous for you out here.'

Starry Eyes gave a grunt that said Naomi was ridiculous, and defiantly plunged back under the console. Naomi stood there telling him to get up and go back in the habitat. After about half a minute, he stood up, grunted again, actually *winked* at Meniscus, and then turned to Naomi. He said, 'What you going to do with the mouse, then?'

'Why?' Naomi asked suspiciously, clutching Genghis to her bosom.

Starry Eyes shrugged. 'I was just gonna say me and Squeak could take care of him, keep it quiet. Until you figure something out.'

Naomi beamed. 'You really are so sweet. You'd do that?'

'It's not for me,' Starry Eyes added hastily. 'Squeak's feeling pretty blue, though . . . ha ha, get it? Feeling blue? And Geng— I mean, this little mouse, might cheer him up some.'

There were tears in Naomi's eyes. 'I'm really sorry about before, Snake,' she said. 'I wouldn't have gone back on my word, but in this situation I have no choice.'

'Don't sweat it,' Starry Eyes said.

Naomi gave Genghis to Starry Eyes, then stood on tiptoe and kissed him. He grabbed her ass. She ordered him back in the habitat and he went. Meniscus watched, amazed. Why didn't Starry Eyes just make a run for it?

'Wachoo looking at now?' Starry Eyes said, reading Meniscus's expression. 'You better get to work. I could have been outta here just then. Genghis doesn't do you these favours for nothing, you know.'

'I'll try,' said Meniscus, and started hunting through the I-MAGE files.

Later he was vaguely aware of a delivery arriving from *Cycle Freek*. He heard Bernie Taktarov's voice, and tried to stay down in the game.

'No, you *idiots*!' Starry Eyes yelled. 'That wasn't in your instructions!'

Meniscus opened one eye. There were three burly women in the lab and they were holding Naomi, unconscious, between them.

'We couldn't read the order form too good,' said the biggest of the three.

'I'm sorry,' Bernie Taktarov put in. 'I was crying so hard it must have blurred. We had to guess what you wrote.'

'Well you guessed wrong. Shit. Are the cameras getting this?'

'No, of course not!'

'Then get her out into the rental car. Bernie, you drive. Get her out of here, I don't care where you go. The rest of you, go and wait in Bernie's trailer and don't let anybody see you. I'm working on another plan. Here, I'll write it down for you.'

'What about all these bike parts?'

'Put them there. No, don't disturb him. He's sick.'

There was a lot of commotion. Mensicus went back to the game, where he was searching for Starry Eyes's I-MAGE. A little while later he was aware of Starry Eyes coming to check on him. He felt the big man pick up his wrist to take his pulse.

'Fucking hell,' Starry Eyes whispered. But Meniscus couldn't spare the energy to think about what he might mean.

283

CHANNEL 10

I COULDN'T FIGURE OUT what kind of vehicle 10Esha was in. I thought at first that it was one of those FBI vans you see in movies, you know, the kind that look like a pizza-delivery truck from the outside but are actually wired to the nines to do stake-outs and shit. But the clear plastic tubing hanging from racks behind her didn't really jive with the FBI. She was rocking from side to side and the camera kept shaking, so wherever she was, she was definitely moving. Maybe it was like a cable-TV van or something. Something about it rubbed me the wrong way, but I couldn't put my finger on it.

'10, *please* don't broadcast that tape. There must be something you want that I can do in return. Are you pissed off about those reviews I wrote? What did I do to make you do this to me? What *could* I do to you, when I don't even know you?'

I was starting to cry and act pathetic. 10 just watched me with clinical interest, which fired my anger again.

'So help me god if you put that footage out there, I'll hunt you down and kill you.'

'Oh please girl, what is the big deal? So he didn't flick your bic, so what?'

'That doesn't mean I want everybody to see. Shit, 10, come on!'

'You could of shot him. Suk Hee prob'ly would have shot him. She'd say, "Gimme my gazz or else, sucka" and then if he didn't deliver, she'd blow him away.'

'No she wouldn't,' I snapped. 'She's usually really nice. I don't know why she went off like that today.'

10 looked away. 'Maybe she was building up to it for a long time. And maybe she was provoked. Either way, we got the job done.'

'What job?'

'The hook-up. Thanks to your girl Keri, the whole place is Bugged now. It's totally visible to the outside. Smile.'

I didn't smile. 'Aren't you going to ask me where KrayZglu is?'

'I know where she is – I filmed her getting arrested in the Toys-R-Us parking lot.'

'No shit.'

'You are way behind on your news, girl. You seen what's going on in the truck tunnel?'

I shook my head. The image of 10 vanished, replaced by a security shot of an underground loading bay. Maul personnel dressed in blue suits were unloading boxes and putting them on dollies. There were cops there, too, talking on radios and standing around. Seemed like there was a lot of new stock coming in.

'What are they doing?' I said to the air. The images on the screen continued to busily unload boxes of stuff. 'I don't get it. If GoldYlox is here to loot the maul, how come he's bringing stuff in and not taking it out?'

'Who said it was GoldYlox doing it? Besides, GoldYlox is a counter-thief,' said 10's voice-over.

'Counter-thief? Who would want to steal a counter?'

'Don't be funny. You know. Like counter-spy. He's a thief who doesn't steal things, he plants them.'

'So he did plant a bomb? Where is it? Is it really going off in three hours?'

'Stick around and you'll find out.'

'You're sick,' I said. 'I don't know why I ever admired you. You are absolutely sick.'

10's voice said, 'That is no way to treat somebody who trying to help you.'

The images cut, replaced by static. I smacked the Watchman in frustration and then saw that the battery was dead.

'Well fuck you, too,' I said to the TV. I checked my ammo and proceeded. But I didn't go far before I hit my next obstacle.

Mannequin torsos and limbs, some still dressed in last season's Esprit and Liz, lay heaped in the intersection ahead. I dropped a Gucci keyring on the floor to mark my trail and headed forward, intending to take the right-hand turning. Just as I reached the mannequins, a white leg with a black thigh-high on it came flying out of the pile at a bizarre, impossible angle. It only took me a split second to realise it was a plastic leg, displaced by something alive beneath, but that was enough time for the first bullet to hit the planking at my feet. I threw myself to the left with a startled scream. More bullets peppered the walls of the passageway as a figure emerged from among the plastic body parts. I aimed at

286

the chest, about to squeeze, and then my eyes registered the 79ers logo on the sweatshirt.

'Keri!' I managed to scream, my finger stalling on the trigger.

The shooting stopped and I saw her, pigeon-toed, blind, panting among the elbows and knees.

'Keri it's me Sun don't shoot!'

I lowered my own gun even though I knew she couldn't see me.

'Sun?' It was a whisper.

'Yeah, it's me. Could you put the gun down.'

She lowered it halfway. 'Where are you? It's pitch black.'

I took out my Yankee lighter and flipped up the goggles because I couldn't see anything beyond the heat of the flame. The scene looked a whole hell of a lot spookier in the flickering light. The mannequins threw anorexic shadows.

Keri looked like shit. She tripped over a couple of male heads and kicked a torso out of the way. She was knock-kneed and shaky, and her sweatshirt was blotched with drying blood.

'I shot them Sun,' she whispered. 'She said she'd kill me otherwise.' Then she started talking about how 10Esha had directed her through the crawl spaces and made her set up cameras and microphones 'in all these weird places' and if anyone tried to stop her, she had to shoot them.

'She took my inhaler,' she finished.

I didn't see what the inhaler had to do with it.

'I'm running on pure adrenalin,' Keri said. 'I can't stop. If I stop I'll stop breathing.'

'That's crazy,' I said. 'Your asthma's not *that* bad, is it?'

Keri exploded. 'You really don't fucking understand!'

287

'OK, OK, I'm sorry,' I said. I refrained from adding that I'd never heard asthma given as a defence against murder but there's a first time for everything. 'What are you doing here, then?'

'I was looking for the truck tunnel. I'm supposed to meet her there. That's her escape route.'

'Oh, is it?' I turned the light off and flipped my goggles back down. I felt tough. Really, really tough. I mean, shit, KrayZglu and her crew were dead or captured but for some reason I'd escaped. And KrayZglu wasn't around any more to make me feel like a grubby little chickenass nobody. Alone I was third-pair-of-underpants-in-one-day scared, but with Keri as audience I was positively bold.

Albeit trying not to think about the footage that showed her killing people.

'We really have to get out of here fast, Keri,' I said. I didn't want to mention the bomb because I thought she was out there far enough already, but I knew I needed to get her to hustle. She seemed to be preoccupied with herself, ragged breathing and all, so I added, 'Do you know the way to this truck tunnel?'

'Yeah but I can't make it breathing like this. Plus I've got a really bad headache,' Keri said. 'Do you have any Excedrin?'

I shook my head. I had to think of a way to get to 10. It's one thing to get killed or go to jail, but if that footage of me and Alex gets out then that would be a fate worse than death.

And 10 is playing with me. Why? Why is she doing this?

I've always wanted to be important. I've always wanted my life to have some meaning to it. I've always wanted what I do to matter. But now that it's happening I feel totally unprepared.

'CVS is just over there,' Keri said, pointing. 'I can get another inhaler or at least something to stop this attack. Are you coming?'

'What? Yeah, OK. Shit, you really can't breathe, can you.'

Keri gave me a dirty look. I took her arm and helped her along. But I have to be honest and say that it wasn't true altruism that moved me. Because, while Keri was raiding the pharmacy, I found an outlet and got the Watchman powered up. I sat down in the junk-food aisle and switched on Channel 10. Immediately an image of me sitting in front of a rack of Cheetos came up on the screen. I looked around but I couldn't see the camera.

'It's behind the umbrellas,' Keri informed me through a mouthful of Oreos. 'Put it there myself.'

'Your breathing is better.'

'Found some epinephrine and shit. Got another inhaler, too. Christ, I'm starving.'

I watched her grabbing packages of food off the shelves and my stomach rumbled sympathetically. She offered me some pretzels, but my guts still ached from the pizza I'd vomited back in California Pizza.

'I'm going to turn on Channel 10 again.' I said it as a way of convincing myself I had the courage to do it; I was afraid what 10 would disclose this time. But Keri didn't even seem to hear me, and that pissed me off.

'Keri! Did you hear what I said?'

'Mmm. Whuhever.' She was eating.

'Well, do you have any advice?'

She cocked her head and pointed at her own chest as if to say, *Me*?

'You wired the place for her. *I saw you*. Keri, you must have some idea what she's doing and why.'

Keri chewed and swallowed. 'She said, "I'm gonna elevate Bugaboo consciousness." That's what she said.

Something about the world seeing how she thinks. "I'm tired of my 'boos being misunderstood and abused," she said. "I want some credit for good works."

I gaped at her, and Keri rolled her eyes, whistled, and made a whirlybird gesture with her forefinger by her temple.

'You sure you don't want some Ritz crackers or something?'

I shook my head and, bracing myself, turned my attention to the TV.

'I knew you'd be back,' 10 said. She was smiling out at me, with her dark apple-shaped face and its dimples and its impression of goodness and wholesomeness coming on so strong I wish I could vomit but a tiny part of me is drawn to her, wishes it were true that she really is an ally in some unknowable way. Her glasses were foggy and wherever she was, it was dark. I had the impression that she was bending over in a confined space. The image was jogging and shaking; I figured she was still in the van. 'We need each other,' she added. 'Neither of us can win the way things stand. You got to start working with me, not against me.'

I wanted to snarl a defiant reply, but 10's face disappeared to be replaced by a new image.

My heart leaped.

Suk Hee's face had come on the screen. But it was not the Suk Hee I wanted to see. As I sat there looking hungrily at the image I felt myself freeze up inside.

Even on the fuzzy b&w monitor, she looked terrible. She had some kind of makeshift bandage wrapped crookedly around her head; it was darkly stained. Her cheekbones were lit from below with Hallowe'en-mask effect. Her skin was shiny with sweat. Her pupils were dilated and her eyes flicked back and forth as though she was reading something written on the lens of the camera.

Her lips moved in speech, but there was no sound on the security cameras, and the words came with no change in expression. She almost seemed to be chanting.

But there was something else, too – something I could sense without being able to identify it. It was that feeling you get when you're struggling with a math problem and you sense that you could get a hold of its parameters and surround it if you could only strain that little bit further, hold on to the variables in your mind: that sense of something perfectly familiar and ordinary lurking beneath the unknown. That sense that you should be solving this. But aren't.

I tore my eyes away from the box long enough to look at Keri. I wanted to share my relief that S-H was alive, relief that was viciously undercut by shock and horror at the realisation that Suk Hee was – apparently – not only wounded, but under 10's sick power. I wanted to feel the echo of my own emotions, in her. But Keri wasn't even watching the TV. She had moved off and was actually *trying on sunglasses*.

It's decision time, but I don't know what to do. I could pursue 10, but if Keri is right, she's already escaped the maul and is driving around in Uncle G's TV van, broadcasting. So I should just get the fuck out, before the bomb goes off.

But there's a little time before the bomb explodes, and 10 has been considerate enough to show me Suk Hee, so I sort of have to try and save her. At least, that's what 10 is trying to manoeuvre me into doing. I don't want to be manoeuvred into a trap, but at the same time, I can't walk away from Suk Hee.

What am I going to do? I don't know where she is. She could be anywhere. 10 might even be holding her captive. How the fuck am I going to find her before Uncle G's bomb explodes?

I don't know how I'm supposed to think. I wanted to say something but I couldn't even think of anything wiseass to say. I muttered, 'This sucks.' Then I started to cry.

After a while of me sniffling and gasping, Keri came over and put her arm around my shoulders. She said, 'Why the *fuck* do they have to put the price tags on the nose part, right where the damn thing sticks in your eye when you're trying them on?' Then she pulled out her gun and pointed it at the mirror. Before I could react, she fired.

I threw myself across the TV screen, instinctively protecting Suk Hee's image. Glass went everywhere. The shot echoed and re-echoed, as sure a way of alerting the police to our location as anything I could think of, other than sending up flares.

I stopped crying. Keri crunched over to the sunglasses rack and spun it mindlessly. I could still feel where her arm had been around my shoulder. I could smell her perfume and her Doritos breath and her mad and fearful sweat.

My ears were ringing painfully, but my head was clear now. I looked at the screen again, testing myself to see if I could bear it. I could see nothing in the girl's face of the Suk Hee I knew. There was just this broken doll's face saying the same words over and over again.

In fact, I could read her goddamned lips.

She was saying, '*I'll save you piggy. I'll save you piggy.*'

That's when I hauled off and slapped myself across the face.

'You idiot!' I reproached myself. 'You should guessed.'

It was probably too late now to do any good, but I knew where Suk Hee was.

MILLER TIME

MADDIE WAS STANDING outside Bernie's trailer, leaving instructions for Babysitterware, when Malone the security guard found her.

'Curator Gould wants you in her office. Now.'

'I was just on my way,' Maddie lied. 'Tell her I'll be right there.'

'I'll escort you.' Malone flexed her pecs and assumed the military 'at ease' posture. Maddie found it threatening. Malone had a neck like a pit bull's.

Maddie was tempted to run back into Bernie's trailer and ask for his help, but she was really drunk and not thinking too well. So she preceded Malone up the dark stairwell and into Jennifer's office.

'Well?' said Jennifer. 'Is he dead yet?'

'Who?'

'Don't be funny. I've got Arnie on the phone to me every five minutes.'

Maddie remembered that she had planned how she was going to handle this conversation, but the whisky/chocolate/vodka combination had driven the plan from her mind.

'Uh, he's in a pretty bad way,' she improvised hastily. After all, by the time Jennifer checked up on her story, she and Carrera would be gone. 'I know he looked OK when you saw him, but I think he's finally on his way down.'

To Maddie's surprise, Jennifer actually bought it. She had a look of catlike satisfaction on her face. 'Good.' She drew breath to continue, but just then Malone burst into the office without warning. 'Dr Gould, he's getting away!'

Maddie was on her feet before Jennifer could say boo. 'Who's getting away?' she cried.

Jennifer waved at her to shut up and said, 'What happened, Malone?'

'Dr Taktarov stole one of the Leukocytes.'

Maddie breathed a sigh of relief. For a second there she thought she had lost the SE.

Malone continued, 'It had an out-of-order sign on it but he got it started. He's zipped out the west gate and onto the Turnpike.'

'Well, go get him, then! He won't get far on the Turnpike in a little electric buggy.'

'It's outside our jurisdiction.'

'Malone, the man is a mental patient. Get moving before he hurts himself! And call the police.' Jennifer hung up and turned to Maddie.

'I'm not very happy with your conduct. What's gotten into you lately, Maddie?'

'What do you mean, Dr Taktarov is a mental patient? Dr Taktarov is on the Board of Directors, Jennifer. Show a little respect.'

'*Was* on the Board. He was canned three weeks ago. The Y-plague has gone to his brain. He's delusional and, to use the vernacular, basically screwy. He's been driving around in that trailer of his telling everybody that Bug Apocalypse is coming. They're having him put away for his own protection.'

'But . . . but . . . I need his funding for my experiment. NoSystems . . .'

'Yeah, no kidding. That's what I wanted to talk to you about. I've got an invoice on my desk for a $200,000 upgrade to your software. NoSystems refused his credit but for some reason the order was put through anyway. Are you sleeping with Ralf or something?'

'Of course not! Nobody told me any of this.'

'Well, you'd better not use it. I'm calling NoSystems as soon as they open and telling them to close our account. We won't need any of it when Mr Henshaw delivers, you know what I mean?'

'But you can't close the I-MAGE. Meniscus needs it—'

'Maddie, read my lips. *You have no more funding.* It's over.'

'Wait a second – give me a chance to go to another backer. There are people I can call, people who will be interested in the study. You have to give me some kind of grace period.'

'I don't have the budget for it. I'm going to have enough trouble getting NoSystems to cancel the order. You've already used it, haven't you?'

'Yeah, but—'

'Well, you're not using it any more. Get your subject off the game. Understood?'

Maddie nodded.

'Look, Jennifer, I'm not feeling too well. Can we finish this at a civilised hour?'

'Yes, of course,' said Jennifer briskly. She was whistling as Maddie slunk out.

'Where's Naomi, goddamm it?' Maddie gasped. Carrera gave her a blank look. 'Come on, just tell me! They're trying to kill you. Henshaw and some others.'

Starry Eyes gave a ragged cough, his muscles bouncing. 'You woke me up to tell me *that*? Fuck you.'

'I'm getting you out of here. Both of you. I'll take you to Dr Taktarov, you'll be safe with him. Her.'

'Meniscus can do what he likes, but leave me out of it. Can I go back to sleep now? Turn that fucking light off, will you?'

'You have to be the most maddening creature on Earth,' Maddie hissed, balling her fists and standing on tiptoe, chin out-thrust. Starry Eyes folded his arms and snorted.

'What, because I don't want to play dress-up? Let me call a few of the shots and then we can talk.'

'Not this Freedom thing again. Why should I give you that?'

SE shrugged. 'Because I'm not a fucking domestic animal.'

'No, you're a menace. You're lucky I'm here. They're out to kill you, but I'm going to help you. Now, where's Naomi?'

'I guess she split. I don't need any help. Just open the door for me, that's all I need from you.'

'I don't think so,' Maddie laughed. 'To judge from what I've seen so far, you'd be fucking everything you see.'

'I wouldn't be fucking you,' said Starry Eyes. 'In case you was thinking of asking.'

'I wasn't,' snapped Maddie too quickly.

'You sure? Why you come down here in the middle of the night dressed like that, anyway?'

'Because I happened to be awake.'

'Where's your lab coat?'

'I'll ask the questions,' Maddie said, but she was

296

twisting her hair around her finger and her voice had gone gravelly, and she was realising that she had no idea how to court a man. Especially in the middle of a sticky social situation like this one. Suddenly she couldn't meet his gaze.

'I see your bike is just about finished,' she attempted. She felt him watching her, and after a moment he snorted.

'This is a joke. I'm supposed to fuck you for what? Proof you're Naomi's boss and you get to fuck anything she gets to fuck? I thought hierarchies and dominance patterns went out with testicles. I thought you people were into *round* organisational structures now.'

'What you don't seem to appreciate is that your life is at risk.'

'That's rich, coming from you. We both know what I am. Your society doesn't want people like me. I don't fulfil your image of manhood. Because I'm a brute – right? I'm stupid – right? You think we don't hear what you say about us out there with your coffee and your meetings? I'm not that fucking stupid. You don't want me in your world because you know men like me would dominate the hell out of you if you didn't keep us marginalised.'

Maddie stalked back and forth in front of the plexiglas in fast whirly patterns, legs stiff, making *sss* noises of frustration as she hunted for expression.

'I know you've been abused by Hibridge. I know that. But I could help you. I could help both of you.'

'He doesn't want to fuck you either,' SE remarked casually, nodding over his shoulder at Meniscus without actually looking at him. Meniscus was heavily in the game, not even aware of them; he stood there with his shimmering blue-green skin, his newly hypertrophied muscles, his arched eyebrows and flaring nostrils like a character out of Greek mythology. His genitals had swelled to half again their former size and strained like chariot horses at the seams of his underwear.

'I'm not a total dickhead, you know,' the SE continued. 'You think I'm just like an animal in a zoo, you want me to survive but on your terms. I get sick and you try so hard to save me when what you never should have done was catch me in the first place. I don't want your pity. I don't want your help. And you can't make me comply. Got that?'

Maddie's teeth snapped shut. 'Yeah, I got it.'

She turned to go away. Her right ovary was swelling. She could feel it.

She turned back.

'I know what Henshaw did to you. I know about the sharks. I know the whole scam. They even killed your lawyer, in case you were wondering.'

'It was all a nice arrangement for everybody,' said Starry Eyes. 'Except I didn't die on schedule. I survived the plagues, and I've still got twice the balls as him.'

'I know, Starry Eyes, I—'

'Don't call me that. Only Meniscus can call me that.'

'Sorry. Carrera, OK, *Mr* Carrera . . . I'm sorry for what happened to you.'

'You going to let me out?'

Maddie looked at her hands. 'Please . . .'

'Oh, hell, do I have to fuck you, too? I mean, Naomi was one thing, but this . . .'

'Please. If you do, I'll let you go. I won't set off the alarms. Otherwise, if you stay here . . . things could get very bad for you. Very bad. They're going to take you away, sedate you, take sperm out of you until they've got a nice supply, and then kill you. Is that really how you want this to end?'

298

Starry Eyes shrugged. 'They want my sperm so bad, they can have it.'

Maddie, who thought the sperm thing was rapelike and who believed he felt the same, stood like a frozen gear on a bike. She had played her only card, and it didn't work.

'But . . .' she said. 'They'll kill you in the end.'

'And what are you offering? To make me your next guinea pig?'

'No. No!' Her eyes were full of tears now. 'All right, you can go, goddamm it, go be free if that's what you want and see if it does you any good.'

'Are you serious?'

'For your sperm. I'll do it. All right?' She was getting hysterical. 'You *said* you didn't care! So what's the big deal, do I have to beg you? You must understand. By letting you go, *I'm giving up my career for you.*'

Starry Eyes looked deep into her. 'Let's be specific, Doctor. You're giving up your career for my sperm.'

'You like that? You like that bitch?'

Maddie groaned incoherently. She did not like that. Starry Eyes's cock felt like it was somewhere in the vicinity of her trachea, plus there was the added factor of all those Jolly Ranchers not to mention the waffles not to mention the mid-cycle bloating she was prone to. Her right ovary was aching, huge, and hot gas balls were playing ping pong in her guts.

'Stay still.' The head of his cock rammed into her G-spot and Maddie let out a startled shriek. 'That's better, you *do* like that.' Starry Eyes coughed, hawked, and spat, thrusting absent-mindedly all the while. 'Ah, it's no use. Here, Squeak, you finish off. I just can't get off on this chick, you go on.'

'No!' Maddie cried, pulling away and turning around. Meniscus had left the habitat, anyway, and was wandering around the lab. At her eye level, Starry Eyes's large member was half-flaccid; he held it in one hand with a resigned air.

'That's not the deal!' Maddie spoke up from her doggy pose.

'Can't help it if I can't get him up for you,' said Starry Eyes in a snide tone. Maddie promptly spun on her knees and took 'him' in her mouth. She tasted her own juices, glistening clear and elastic along the shaft of Starry Eyes's cock. She nearly choked when he grabbed her head and started slamming it around like a basketball. She finally got control by putting both her hands on the shaft of his cock so that he couldn't push the glans all the way down her throat. Sucking wildly, she knelt and rocked and *prayed* he would come.

'Oh, yeah,' he said at last, and stopped moving. Maddie, whose whole jaw and tongue were aching with lactic-acid build-up, started to withdraw in exhaustion. Then she felt the little flood. Triumphantly she snapped her mouth shut around the semen and reached for an empty beer bottle.

Starry Eyes stood there reeling slightly while Maddie spat everything into the beer bottle and threw herself on her back on the bed.

'Go on!' she said. 'I left the outer door open. Just leave, and don't come back.'

Maddie didn't care what Carrera did any more. She lifted her pelvis as high as she could and shoved the neck of the Miller bottle downwards into her cunt.

Bernie Taktarov hadn't been captured by Malone; apparently he'd returned for his trailer and had nearly run over several of Malone's underlings while leaving the premises at high speed. Greta didn't want to come down and watch Meniscus, but Maddie promised her a bonus if she would just keep an eye on her subject and repel all boarders. 'OK,' she said reluctantly. 'As long as that other one's gone.'

'He's gone,' Maddie sighed. 'I'll be back soon; can you get here in five minutes?'

'That depends on traffic. I'll do what I can do.'

Maddie wasn't crazy about leaving Meniscus like this, but she had to go to NoSystems in person because she was getting paranoid. If Bernie was out of power and Jennifer was going to cut game access, she had to make a deal with Ralf. She needed remote access and she needed processing power, and all she had to offer was a share of the credit for the discovery of 10E, the consciousness bug.

Maddie pounded on the door of Ralf's office.

'Ralf! Ralf, it's Madeleine Baldino from Hibridge. Ralf!'

'She won't be in until afternoon,' someone sang from behind Maddie. She turned to see a willowy, grey-haired woman in a leopard-print dress. 'Do you want me to give her a message?'

Something in the woman's gaze gave Maddie the heebie-jeebies. She seemed too helpful, somehow.

'I have her number,' Maddie said, and fled. She had been stupid to announce herself. If it got back to Jennifer that she'd been here, Maddie was screwed.

She had no choice now but to use Ralf's 24/7 contact code. It might turn out to be insecure, but she'd been seen here, anyway. And she was on camera. As she called the elevator, she activated the MUSE link and requested return contact.

She made it to the side door of the building before a new threat appeared in the form of a diminutive black woman in a silk suit and expensive cross-trainers. The woman smiled and offered Maddie a business card as she approached. Maddie was about to barge past her and run

301

for the car when the writing on the card checked her.

There was no contact number, no title, no web address; just a Hibridge logo and the name. *Charlotte West*.

'I'm Blanche,' said the small woman hastily, as an awed Maddie started to stammer. 'Charlotte asked me to invite you to her place in the country. She'd like to speak with you.'

'Uh . . . maybe another time,' said Maddie. 'I'm kind of busy now.'

The answer came automatically. She knew perfectly well that she could not turn down an invitation to the home of one of the Board. But she didn't care. She barged right past Blanche, making for a heavy security door that led to the side parking lot.

'Uh, Dr Baldino?' Blanche called. 'I think you should look out the window before you go out there.'

Maddie snorted and shoved the door open, and then just as quickly leaped back inside and let it close again.

Educational Fun Park security were clustered at the entrance to the parking lot, cheek by jowl with community police, all drinking no-calorie SugaRRugaS shakes from The Left-Handed Molecule across the street.

They were at her car, they were at the parking garage exit, they were at the main entrance to the building.

Maddie spun around to see Blanche watching her.

'I think they want to talk to you in connection with the disappearance of a certain SE,' Blanche commented, walking lazily away from Maddie and spinning a Jaguar keyring. 'Mind you, if you came with me they wouldn't be able to do anything about it. Being a PA to Charlotte West is a little like having diplomatic plates on your car.'

302

WHEN PIGS FLY

'**W**HEN PIGS FLY' has to be twenty years old. It's an old-style arcade game with joysticks and big greasy buttons. It has cheesy graphics and features a smiling pig called Bernie that you have to take through various mazes and puzzles in order to fit him with his wings; then, in theory, you have to fly him out of the castle-like slaughterhouse while the slaughtermen chuck stuff at you using catapults and rocket launchers. It's a really dumb game, and even among vintage-video enthusiasts it's not very popular or it wouldn't be shoved into a dusty corner beside a broken-down Defender and a never-much-good Galaxon. But of course, Suk Hee being the champion of the underdog, she won't hear a word against WPF.

'It's better than Atari's Dungeonmaster from the 1980s,' she told me sparkle-eyed the first time she played it. 'It's so flexible and lateral. There's stuff programmed into it that you can find if you know how, but it's not at all obvious. There are whole secret domains in it. Magic items. Special powers. And there are *no cheat books*, Sun.'

I glanced at the graphics and winced. 'But it's so . . . old. The graphics are a joke.'

'Fuck the graphics, it's the best game ever!'

I tried it a couple times just to please her but I didn't get it, and I lost too many quarters on the first level. What a rip-off when I could play Guts 'n' Glory at home, for free, and get to save my progress. Because that's the other problem: you can't save the arcade game and go get a candy bar or whatever. If you stop playing, you go back to the beginning every time.

When I walked into Vinnie's Video Xtravaganza carrying 10Esha's head in a box, I could see right away that Suk Hee was a victim of this problem. According to the game clock, she'd been playing for seven hours and twenty-three minutes. That shocked me because I'd been totally unaware of how much time had passed since the shoot-out in L&T. And Suk Hee's condition was even worse in person than on the video. She was still standing, but just barely; she was leaning on the machine console only just supported by trembling legs, and her head was tilted at an uncomfortable angle. The bandage that I'd seen on the video was actually a pair of Lycra bike shorts that were still wrapped tightly around her forehead. The price tag was still attached.

When she saw me, she smiled.

'Don't worry, I can fix everything,' she said. 'I'm inside the game now. I can customise the programming. All those new goods that are coming in, those are because of me.'

'10 said it was GoldYlox's stuff.'

'Did she?'

'She implied it,' I said slowly. 'She said he's a counter-thief.'

Suk Hee muttered. 'He's got nothing to do with it. I started changing the mall hours ago, long before he came.'

'OK S-H, whatever.'

'I know you don't believe I'm taking control. But I am. I'm getting rid of stuff, too. I'm going to get this whole mall up and running to a higher standard, but first I got to get rid of GoldYlox before he kills us all. '

I'm thinking if I don't get her to a hospital soon, she's a goner.

'Suk Hee,' I said as gently as I could, 'video games aren't real. You can't affect the real world by playing a game. That's only, like, on TV and stuff.'

'OK,' she said sadly. I took her arm and whispered, 'Come on, it's time to go.'

'OK,' she said again, her eyes still involved with the game. 'OK, I'm coming.'

I gave a gentle tug but there was no moving her.

'Sun?'

'Yeah, S-H?'

'But you have to admit the gas mask was a nice touch.'

I let go of her like she was electrified. I took a couple of seconds to steady myself. Then:

'What gas mask?' I said carefully.

'The one you found. The Nike poster.'

'Oh, you must have seen that on a security monitor. Is that what you mean?'

'You know what I mean,' she said coyly. 'I had it put there for you because the gas was the only way I was going to be able to rescue you from KrayZglu. And sure enough, KrayZglu caught you. Didn't she?'

'Suk Hee, the *police* used the gas,' I said.

'I know. That's what I said. I'm having a hell of a time dealing with this GoldYlox situation. My cops are freaking. They can't use gas with him on account of they don't know where the bomb is and it will go off anyway. I don't want to get blown up but I can't see a way out. I really could use some help. I thought you understood that. Why else did you come looking for me?'

'Because I'm *trying* to help you, silly. I came to get you out. You need to see a doctor.'

'No, I need to win the game.'

'Suk Hee, I'm not sure how to tell you this, but you've been shot in the head. You *need* to see a doctor.'

'I'm playing until I win or die,' she said, lower lip thrust out.

I looked into 10's head. I could still see an awful lot of loading and unloading going on. According to the footage, a lot of the back corridors that KrayZglu and I, and then Keri and I, had passed through were now clogged with stockboys carrying clipboards and pushing dollies.

'Who are these people? Keri, do you know what this is about?'

Keri, munching, looked at the screen. 'Nope,' she said at length. '10Esha had a couple 'Boos with her when she went for the van, but that's it. Nobody came in.'

'Then who are they? Are they looting the place? Or do they work for the police, or what?'

'They work for me,' Suk Hee said.

Keri snorted. 'For you, S-H. Since when are you in the retail business?'

'Well, they work for the mall but I'm directing them for the moment. They're bringing the stuff.'

'The stuff.'

'Yeah, the new stuff. I *told* you, Sun, but you don't listen.'

306

'What about the old stuff . . . shit, they're clearing the place out! They're stealing everything! How are they gonna get away?'

'Because the cops look the other way.'

'*Your* cops,' I added.

'Yeah. But this has been going on back to before I started playing. The 'Boos have the cops trained. They're very clever, but then GoldYlox taught the Bugaboos a lot of important stuff and I taught some of it to the mall . . . well, for lack of a better word, the mall lackeys. See, 10Esha is smart. I think she's probably a genius.'

'Oh, and you're not?' snapped Keri jealously. Suk Hee shrugged.

'It doesn't matter what 10 does because if I can't win this game, the mall will always be the mall, the world will always be the world, and nothing will change. And I'm like a wolf.'

Keri snorted and rolled her eyes but I waved my gun at her.

'She means she's not calculating. She's a creature of instinct,' I said. 'Right, Suk Hee?'

'I'm just me. I don't know what I am. But I know I have to win this game or it won't be real. None of it will be real.'

I feel like everything we say is in code. I'm trying really hard to go along with this and make it into some kind of sense. Keri humming the theme to *Twilight Zone* in the background doesn't make it vastly easier. I try again.

'Suk Hee, what does new clothing stocks have to do with flying pigs? I'm not following you.'

'It's all about empowering the pig. But it's nothing more than truth in advertising. Like saying Maybelline makes you beautiful or Timberlands make you tough. I'm just making everything a little more literally true. You

307

get a concept, you can buy the product and the product is real. Like your underwear.'

It took me a couple seconds to figure out that she meant the Miles Moccasin effect. I kept my face deadpan. 'You're saying you did the underwear too.'

Keri said, 'Excuse me, pussies, but you're both fucking nuts. Are we getting out of here or what?'

'You're a murderer,' Suk Hee said to Keri. She said it in that casual, little-girl way that she has. Not a good idea. Keri started patting herself on the chest and breathing really fast. It sounded like a flock of seagulls when she breathed in.

'Easy, Keri,' I said. 'Where's that new inhaler?'

'I know I'm a fucking murderer!' Keri was screaming but almost silently because she couldn't breathe. Suk Hee blithely played on, not even looking at her. Tears coursed down Keri's face.

'Whoa, Keri, easy.' I watched her gun hand carefully. I think she still had some bullets. She squirted some inhaler and held her breath, looking at the ceiling. 'Suk Hee's been shot, remember,' I added significantly. 'She doesn't know what she's saying."

Keri sniffled and wiped her red face. I went over and hugged her, hoping that she couldn't tell how terrified I was that she'd just up and shoot me for the hell of it. Eventually she pulled away and made an effort to compose herself. She rummaged in her pocket for a tissue and something far more important fell out onto the filthy Vinnie's Video carpet.

I heard my voice shoot up in an ecstatic shriek.

'ARE THOSE CIGARETTES?'

Without waiting for her answer, I leaped on the package of Marlboro Lights but I'd been fooled. It was empty – no, worse than empty, it wasn't even box any more. The cardboard had been unfolded so that it lay flat.

'Goddam it!' I threw the thing on the ground and stomped on it. As it fell, the package turned over so that the inside faced up. Someone had written something on it in purple fineliner. I picked it up, intending to crumple it and throw it, but something caught my eye.

'What the hell is this? A floor plan? Where'd you get it?'

Keri shrugged. '10 drew it for me. See, those are the places where I had to install cameras or microphones. And this is where the wiring goes . . .'

I studied it. All the wires led to one place.

'Suk Hee, stop playing!' I commanded. Did she listen to me? Yeah, right. She didn't even twitch in response. I ran to the back of the *When Pigs Fly* console and there were the cables, leading back to neatly sawn holes in the plaster wall . . .

'You can't wire video cameras into a *game*,' I said. 'That's like something out of a TV movie. It's apples and oranges, and the game is too old, and the protocols wouldn't begin to match – it's a ridiculous idea. There's way not enough memory and besides, they're different species!'

But no one was getting it. No one cared but me. No one understood.

'No,' I heard myself saying. 'It's just too fucking silly. I don't believe it.'

But I thought I'd better look over Suk Hee's shoulder, anyway. I don't know what I expected to see, but what I saw was not cheesy 1980s graphics. It wasn't brightly coloured or moving around fast. The image was like something out of DaVinci's sketchbooks, very beautiful and elegant – but incomplete. It was a diagram of a wing.

'You have to make the pig fly,' S-H whispered. 'So he can escape the castle, see?'

G-MA

THE YELLOW JAGUAR persons-carrier thumped
from pothole to pothole on Route 46 as it
approached Parsippany, following the signs for
Dover. Parsippany was all knotted highways and
decaying strip malls. Smaller buildings were all but
invisible behind scrub forest and vines, while giant hulks
of stores with signs on stilts proclaiming names like
Sofabed Warehouse and Fur Palace presided over
cracked and pitted parking lots overgrown with sumac
and dandelions. Maddie saw deer grazing behind
JiffyLube and there was a maple tree growing out of the
roof of a former White Castle Hamburger. An eagle
perched on a billboard.

'Look at this shit,' said Blanche to Maddie. 'Somebody
should clean it up. When Governor Diaz ran for office she

said she was going to give up the Nature Reclamation Project but once she got in she conveniently forgot about it.'

Maddie, glowering in the front seat, said dully, 'What did you want her to do about it? There aren't enough people to repopulate these towns. Might as well put a positive spin on it and have a nature reserve.'

'She could put *stores*,' said Blanche as if it were obvious. She had removed her silk jacket, revealing hard biceps and armpit stubble and a DKNY push-up bra. 'I'd go shopping here if there was a good discount shoe outlet, say.'

Maddie shrugged. 'Retail is obsolete. Did you know this all used to be farm country, before they had stores?'

'I think we should go back to having stores,' Blanche said stubbornly. 'Those were the good old days.'

'And before that it was Indian country,' Maddie added. Blanche flicked cigarette ash out the window, irritated that Maddie was not interested in stores. Maddie was just thinking that it was pretty obvious why Blanche was a driver and not a manager when she noticed that the bulging bicep displayed a tattoo depicting a fish riding a bicycle.

'Are you really in Bicyclefish?' she asked. 'Or is that just for show?'

Blanche laughed. 'Like I would tell *you* if I was in Bicyclefish.'

'I just thought you sounded like a romantic. "The good old days" and all that. Do you think that includes men?'

'I watch the Pigwalks same as everybody else.'

'Got any kids?'

Blanche held up a thumb and forefinger. Maddie's guts burned with jealousy. Blanche glanced across at Maddie. She must be well aware of the effect of this kind of news. How did a hired driver get hold of enough sperm for *two* kids?

'Good for you,' Maddie said dully. She tried not to think about the contents of the beer bottle, even though a warm trickle was emerging sporadically from her cunt into her Cellulift leggings.

Well, what did it matter? She'd never get Meniscus out of the lab now, because Ralf wouldn't be allowed near her and there was no other way to get remote access to Mall.

Maddie was starting to wonder into what butthole of nowhere Blanche was taking her when the personscarrier turned abruptly up a pitted road beside an ancient billboard advertising a golf course. The road ended at an ivy-covered wall that looked old enough to belong to an early twentieth-century estate; but the iron gate in the wall was controlled remotely, and the security cameras were spanking new. As the gates swung soundlessly open, Maddie took in several acres of manicured lawn surrounding a mansion that would not have been out of place in a Jane Austen novel.

'This is like another world,' she said under her breath.

'It *is* another world out here,' answered Blanche. 'It's a better world.'

She stopped the car in a circular gravel drive and led Maddie around the back, to a walled garden with statues of white cherubs and a pissing-boy fountain.

There were seven children under the age of five scurrying around the garden, each wearing a different-colour-dress. Among them was a bent figure squatting in the shade of a rose bush; Maddie almost took it for a garden gnome but then it moved.

'There's Charlotte,' said Blanche, pointing. 'Good luck.'

She turned and walked away, leaving Maddie to approach the garden on her own.

The brown gnome got to her feet and took off her gardening gloves. She was plump, wrinkle-eyed and apple-faced. She seemed about four feet tall although she was probably almost five. She held out a pudgy hand.

'Madeleine Baldino, we meet at last.'

Maddie was so nonplussed that instead of greeting Charlotte properly she glanced around, looking for the real Charlotte, and then blurted, 'Why is there Irish Spring hanging from the trees?'

Charlotte looked startled, then laughed.

'It keeps the deer from eating the flowers. They have plenty of wild grass but they keep coming after my pansies. They don't like the smell of the soap.'

Maddie wasn't really listening. She was watching the children ducking in and out of a collection of cement mushrooms and watering each other with a dribbling yellow garden hose. She made herself look back at Charlotte. Yes, the kids looked like mini-gnomes – smooth-skinned, giggling apples. But not clones of Charlotte; for one thing, they would all be taller than their mother by puberty. Maybe Charlotte had a tall partner . . . well, partners, to be realistic.

Maddie realised that she was staring and said, 'I'm sorry, I was just admiring . . . the children.' She didn't say *your* just in case she made a blunder.

'My daughters? They're a handful, I can tell you.'

She gestured for Maddie to come with her around the back of the house.

'I've been wanting to talk to you for a long time,' she said in a low, controlled voice.

'I didn't have any choice but to go along with Jennifer's plan, Charlotte,' Maddie blurted. 'She forced me into it.'

'Call me Grandma,' said Charlotte, laughing easily. 'Or G-ma, for short. Everyone else does.'

In a kitchen the size of a Viking longhouse, one of Grandma's daughters made them Ghirardelli's cocoa. Maddie got an impression of rich and appetising odours, dark wood, gleaming copper and yellow firelight, and she counted four cats perched at various heights on cupboards and counters as they walked the length of the room. Softly, almost subliminally, Sarah Vaughn sang 'Misty'.

Pointing to a tapestry-upholstered comfy chair, Grandma settled herself at the far side of a polished oak table nestled in an alcove by the fire. She shoved aside a stack of newspapers and journals and glanced once at the display of a laptop before closing it. Then she curled her brown hands around the earthenware mug of cocoa and leaned slightly towards Maddie. As she was about to speak, the same woman who'd brought the cocoa interrupted by offering Maddie a plate of oatmeal chocolate-chip cookies. Maddie felt distinctly silly as she took two.

'So you've discovered a natural immune,' G-ma said. 'Congratulations.'

Maddie looked at her cookies.

'It's OK! Relax. We've known for years that there was a small underground of plague-resistant males who avoid castellations. There had to be; how else could you explain the presence of unregistered children around the world? These males somehow manage to hide themselves within society – or, as is more often the case, on the perimeter of society, like your SE – and, Nature being Herself, children are the result.

'We're always trying to get these males in for study because, of course, the very fact of their existence means that they are resistant to Y-plagues. But the number concerned is very small. I personally only know of two others who have ever been identified, and one of them turned out to be sterile when we caught him.'

314

'And the other?'

'Died,' said G-ma shortly, and sipped her cocoa. 'It was a bungled thing. He died during an attempt to detain him. But that was years ago, and after it happened we made it a policy never to try to force a male to enter a castellation.'

'That's interesting,' said Maddie in a guarded tone. She remembered very well Carrera's insistence that he be freed, on Naomi's video.

'As for *your* SE, we'd been watching him for some time. Using him as a surrogate was a stroke of genius because it gave us regular contact with him during which we could observe him without making him nervous that we were trying to study him. He was willing to work for us, but he always refused to cooperate with any form of biological testing. It was like trying to catch a cat to take it to the vet. You know how they disappear the morning you make a vet's appointment, and then after you cancel, they show up howling for Meow Mix? Well, it was a little like that.'

Maddie smiled. G-ma had a nice style of talking, and the cocoa was superlative.

'Recently, he got pissed off that we were using him to promote Arnie Henshaw. He wanted to go into the competition himself, but he refused to live in a castellation or be screened in any way – how unreasonable is that? He got a real bug up his ass, and Henshaw started to get nervous because his big opportunity was coming up and his surrogate wasn't behaving. So, without my authorisation, Henshaw tricked him and brought him in.'

'Does Arnie know about the immunity?'

'Of course not. He knew nothing about his surrogate's history.'

'Surrogate – you keep using that word.' Maddie forced herself to get tough. G-ma seemed to think she was a silly

315

little lamb. 'Is deceiving the public about the abilities of your Pigwalk candidates common practice, then?'

'Irrelevant question.' A hint of steel behind the soft voice.

'Meaning yes. But if Henshaw brought him in, why did you let him be sent to Jennifer? You must have known that Henshaw wanted him dead.'

G-ma leaned back and looked at Maddie cannily. 'Arnie Henshaw is worth a lot of money. If I had interfered, taken the SE for myself or brought him to a lab that does this type of work, I would have risked scandal for Arnie and lawsuits against myself by the Bicyclefish types. This way, Arnie's out on a limb. If there are murder charges, they go against him, not me. And if Carrera doesn't die – and it looks like he's going to survive – then, quite frankly, I can afford to sacrifice Arnie's reputation if the story goes public. But I don't see why it should. Nobody's heard of you or your work. That's the beauty of it. And it was on that basis that I recommended your lab to Arnie in the first place. Who would look in the Educational Fun Park for cutting-edge research? All I had to do was plant the suggestion in Arnie's mind that a plague-related death would pass unnoticed. When he begged me for more help, I gave him Jennifer's number. Henshaw did all the rest.'

'Wait a minute. You knew that I was using a Y-plague on Meniscus?'

'Bernie mentioned it, some time ago when your study was passing through the approval process. I remembered.'

'That was nine years ago . . .'

'Yup. I guess that's why I'm G-ma and you're nobody.'

While Maddie sat there trying to gather herself together, a big furry grey cat leapt onto the table, stuck his nose in her cocoa, and sneezed. She stroked the animal absently.

'Now. I know that you've rented a van, I know that

316

your assistant has been phoning up motels all over Pennsylvania, and I've just had a phone call from Jennifer Gould letting me know that the SE is *gone*. So I think it's time we talked turkey.'

'We can do that,' said Maddie shakily. G-ma thought she had abducted Carrera. How long could she keep up the charade? Long enough to escape?

'But I still have some questions,' she added. 'Like, how could you be sure the exposure wouldn't kill him?'

'I couldn't be *sure* about anything. I had a pretty strong hunch that he would resist any Y-plague you could throw at him, because he's been out there in the world for a long time and never checked into a medical centre. But if I was wrong and he did catch your bugs, well, frankly, he'd have been no more use to us, anyway. His days as a surrogate are over, by his own choice. And he was prepared to expose certain details that I didn't want to become common knowledge.'

'Like the fact that your pigs are produced on false pretences. Arnie Henshaw probably can't do *any* of the things he appears to be able to do. I've got to hand it to you, because I've never heard a whisper of this in all my years.'

'We're very careful.' Grandma looked at her with deadserious eyes. 'And I have my reasons for what I do. If Arnie Henshaw really were Superboy as he seems, do you think we'd benefit as a society from having hundreds of thousands of his descendants running around? We'd be all chiefs and no indians.'

'Well, this indian is finding the whole thing really bizarre,' Maddie said. She wanted to say *unconscionable* but she was scared of G-ma. 'What do you want to do with Carrera now?'

'What do you think, Maddie? See if you can put it together.'

'I think . . . I think you'd like to detain him, take his sperm by force and use it to make . . . to make . . .'

'Say it, Maddie – go on. To make Chiefs. To make Boyz. Y-immune males, and they'll all have my genes. I'll be the new Eve.'

Maddie hadn't gotten there yet, so when G-ma said it, she had to keep stroking the cat and trying not to laugh. Oh, fuck, was the only thing she could think.

'Before you act all shocked, let's not forget,' said G-ma. 'Men got themselves into this one. The first Y-plague was designed by a team of men. They find death sexually exciting. They have to, it's programmed into them. Otherwise why would they go out hunting mammoths when they could eat nuts and berries?'

Maddie wasn't sure about this line of reasoning but she was intimidated by G-ma so she said nothing.

'They were fucking up the world. Truly, Maddie, everybody's happier this way. And anyway,' she added, laughing, 'it doesn't matter because it suits *me*, and *I* profit by it, so I'm going to carry on going the way I'm going. Them's the rules of nature.'

'But that's so . . . so . . .'

'Ungrandmalike? Yes, I know. We're supposed to be so selfless, aren't we? After all, the only reason we chicks survive past menopause is because we contribute so much to the welfare of the tribe. Babies wouldn't have the luxury of developing such big brains without us. After all, they come out of their mama's cunt so weak and half-baked they'd have died for sure if we grandmas hadn't been around to help forage while mom was busy with her helpless little grub. And without big brains, none of what you take for granted would be possible, *so maybe you should just thank me*, Maddie Baldino, because I'm giving you back your right to exist. What else is there for a forty-five-year-old woman to do? We live in a cooling universe, for shit's sake.'

'Forty-four,' said Maddie automatically. 'And you're as loopy as Bernie if you really believe that.'

'People have believed weirder things and gotten away with it. Did you know that Hatshepsut the Egyptian warrior-queen believed the sky was the underbelly of a celestial cow? Did you know—'

'Never mind, I get the point!'

Maddie wondered how long she could keep up this charade. Sooner or later some camera somewhere would pick up Starry Eyes leaving the Fun Park on his own, and Maddie's lie would be revealed. She had to stall Charlotte somehow.

'You should think carefully about what you do next, Dr Baldino. By kidnapping Carrera, you may have got yourself some sperm to play with, but even if you manage to make yourself pregnant, Hibridge can claim custody of the child because the father is Hibridge property and the sperm were taken without Board approval.'

Maddie remembered the video that Naomi had played for her, and her lip curled. 'The father is *not* Hibridge property. He's a captive.'

'I could have you detained, of course. I could force you to comply with my wishes. But I would prefer to avoid the use of force. It's so male and clumsy. So I suggest you and I come to an understanding, a mutually beneficial arrangement.'

'What kind of understanding?'

'I want the SE within my supervision. I'll give you forty-eight hours to get him here. That's plenty of time for you to take what you need, sperm-wise, no questions asked. I won't pursue you for control of any offspring, out of you or any other woman, even if you get boys for yourself. I think that's a very generous offer on my part. But if I don't have the man himself within my control by this time Thursday, then there will be repercussions for you.'

'What kind of repercussions?'

'Maddie, do we really have to go down that road? I'm going to leave this matter with your good judgement. I'm sure that when you think it through you'll realise what's best for all of us. Now, do you need to use the bathroom or anything before Blanche takes you home?'

Maddie felt in a dream as the persons-carrier glided away from Charlotte's mansion. The air-conditioned car was cool and smelled of leather polish and Tic-tacs. Snatch Aroma Overkill was on the radio but Blanche changed the station when Maddie got in. Mahler came on, or something Mahler-ish with a lot of cymbals and gongs.

'Well, that was easier than I expected,' Maddie laughed. 'It's not that I thought Charlotte would be an ogress, it's just that when you picked me up and brought me here I felt like I was in a Mafia movie.'

'I hate WQXR, it's so pretentious,' Blanche said, frowning at Mahler. She started flipping through stations and fixing her hair as she straddled the middle of the country road, steering with her elbow.

Maddie didn't mind the driving. She was happy. Whatever Grandma might have said, when she saw that Maddie did not *have* Starry Eyes – when she had Maddie followed, as she undoubtedly would – then it would become clear that Maddie was innocent. And Maddie could get on with gestating the conceptus that, hopefully, would form inside her with the aid of the drugs and the contents of the Miller bottle. Maybe there would be several babies. Four was a nice number.

Blanche found the station she wanted.

'It's not about food, it's about us. Brigitte, you're a cognitive psychologist. Can you shed some light?'

'Well, I can help people shed some pounds.'

'But first this message from Don't Die-Yet Extreme Chocolate Sin.'

'Did she offer you cocoa?'

'Yeah,' Maddie snorted. 'Cocoa, can you believe it? It was good, though. Ghirardelli's of San Francisco, they make good chocolate. Is it me or is it chilly in here?'

She rubbed her bare arms and glanced at the digital temperature display on the dash. 72 Fahrenheit – that ought to be warm enough. But Maddie's arms were goose-pimpled and . . .

'Oh my god. What's that on my arm?'

Blanche smiled without taking her concentration off the road. She had taken a sudden interest in her driving, and she didn't answer.

'Have Your Cake And Eat It Too – it's a miracle. Available at a ShopQuik near you.'

Maddie stared at her right forearm. There were looping lines of dark pigment rising to the surface of her skin. They formed numbers.

666.

'Oh, this can't be,' Maddie said. 'What's she infected me with? 666, that's so corny, oh, come on now gimme a break it's a joke, right?'

Blanche turned on her direction signal and swung the car onto Route 46 again.

'Must have been in the cocoa.'

'What was in the cocoa? What are you talking about.'

'666 is the brand for a forty-eight hour terrorbug. You must have heard of it.'

'A terrorbug? That's just superstition – there is no such thing.'

'You know, Brigitte, I feel so much better about myself since I had my stomach trimmed. I can only eat about three bites of food before I'm full. Any more and I'll be sick. Now that requires discipline!'

'So all you need is three bites of Don't Die-Yet's Burn in Hell Chocolate Delite and you've actually had a meal that achieves what we in the trade call "negative calorie nirvana". That's when you burn more calories chewing than you take in nutritionally, and that's the beauty of Don't Die-Yet.'

Actually, Maddie had heard of the bug in connection with a recent black-budget project on invisible assassination. But it seemed so out of context here in Grandma's persons-carrier. 666 just wasn't the kind of thing you expected somebody to spike your cocoa with. Then again, Grandma had said she had forty-eight hours before there were 'repercussions'.

'Wow. Now what about Thanksgiving dinner? I mean, we can't eat chocolate for every meal . . .'

Maddie tried to sound casual but her voice cracked a couple times. 'So, what, I'm supposed to have, like, forty-eight hours before the horrible terrible terror strikes me? Yeah, right. What's it do, supposedly?'

'Oh, nothing much. Just makes you uncontrollably afraid of your own shadow, afraid of everyone you know, afraid of heights, the dark, food, mattresses, the floor, doors, windows, pencils, computers, cats, dogs, rabbits, furniture, plants, dust, toothpaste—'

'Cranberry sauce and stuffing and turkey loaded on one fork, a sip of wine, and then there's still room for a small piece of cake from The Left-Handed Sugar Molecule.'

'Yeah, yeah, I get the picture.' Shit.

'Of course, it only lasts for about two weeks, they say. But nobody's ever lived that long, they usually do stupid stuff like accidentally throw themselves under a bus while running away from a scary garbage can they've seen on the spooky sidewalk.'

'I don't believe you.'

'I don't care if you believe me or not. Where you want me to drop you off?'

THE HACKER CROSSOVER

'**Y'ALL ARE RUNNING** out of time,' said 10Esha from the TV. 'Did you forget you got a bomb in the kitchen sink?'

'Come on, 10,' I begged. 'Help us out. This is your game, isn't it? Gimme some kind of clue.'

'Help you out? I'm already helping you out by not putting your butt and Alex Russo's balls on the nine o'clock news. Shit, give you an inch and you take the international date line, girl—'

I switched off the set. 'Broadcast this,' I snapped. Then I took a deep breath. 'Let me think, let me think. 10's right about the time. We have to get her out of here, Keri. Suk Hee can't stay and play the game. We'll all go up in smoke and no game is worth that.'

'You want me to try to knock her unconscious or

something?' Keri must have replenished her bubblegum supply because her jaws were working like pistons on something purple.

'No!' I said quickly. Jesus, Suk Hee already had a head wound and it was scaring me large. 'We have to trick her. Make her think the game is over. Or cut the power supply . . .?'

'I control the power supply,' Suk Hee said. 'How do you think all the TVs were on in Sony?'

How did Suk Hee know this shit? I tried to ignore the chill that was going down my spine but it was tough.

'Then we have to help you win the game, fast. Aha! I got an idea. We can get the cheat book for *When Pigs Fly* and you can short-cut to a solution.'

'*When Pigs Fly* doesn't have a cheat book.'

'Yes, it does. I saw it in Borders a couple weeks ago. I remember because it was right next to *Devil and the Deep Blue Sea*.'

Keri said, 'Sun, there's no cheat book for this game. They didn't have cheat books in those days and even if they did, it would be out of print by now. Your brain's gone all weird.'

'But I've seen it.'

'You only think you've seen it,' Suk Hee put in breathlessly. She was hitting the red buttons on *When Pigs Fly* so fast that a sweat had broken out across her chest. 'Like that déjà vu stuff.'

I groaned. 'That's not what déjà vu is, Suk Hee . . . oh, never mind. I'm going over there. I know what I saw.'

Keri was sitting on the console of *Death By Auto*, unwrapping a Ring Ding. She said, 'I wouldn't go through the back passages. The cops are patrolling the area by the truck tunnel; that's why I couldn't get down there. And you'd have to pass through that section to get to Borders.'

'I'm going through the maul,' I said. It was dark out there now, but I had my goggles and I was prepared to gamble that with all this talk of bombs there was a minimum of personnel on the ground at this stage.

'You're crazy,' Suk Hee said. 'GoldYlox is out to kill everybody and I'm freaking. Why is he doing this to me? Why did he have to show up now? I'm so close to solving this game and if I could solve the game, he couldn't hurt me. I could deal with him. But I'm not ready yet. I need more time. My police are in a tizz and I'll never get the other locks open to change the stock.'

'Here we go again with changing the stock. I thought you were making pig wings.'

'Is that like buffalo chips?' Keri quipped. I shot her a quelling glance.

'Suk Hee?'

'It's all the same. Can't you see it's all the same?'

I couldn't, actually.

'Is there anything I could say or do that would get you off this game, Suk Hee?'

'No, there's nothing you could say. But if you can help me solve it and make Bernie fly, then that's another thing. Then I'm totally free for the rest of the day, I have no plans, we could do Pizza Hut.'

Keri came over and whispered in my ear. 'We could pistol-whip her and take her out, between us. Or I could go back to CVS and get some tranquillisers. But we gotta move. We gotta get out of here *fast*.'

I nodded. My worst fear was that Keri would open fire on Suk Hee in order to expedite things.

'Let's have use of force be Plan B,' I said. 'She's got a head wound already. I'm not sure what would happen if we tried to knock her out. Give me one shot with this cheat-book thing. If I fail, we'll do it your way.'

Keri looked unconvinced and I started getting ready to

duck bullets. At last she whispered, 'OK. But hurry the hell up.'

Even as I moved into the open, hugging the entrance to Sbarro's, a shrill alarm went off somewhere across the maul. I jumped and stopped breathing, and a couple seconds later the prickle of adrenalin charged the surface of my skin; but by then I had realised that the alarm had nothing to do with me. It was coming from Nordstrom, I think. Maybe I was getting lucky. Maybe the alarm would distract anyone who might otherwise notice me.

I moved out into the open and started to run.

Although it was now deep night, the maul wasn't really dark at all. The promenade was a geometric dance of light and shadow where helicopters with searchlights passed overhead. Potted trees cut savage, fractal patterns against the shifting curves of the maul architecture. Some stores had their security doors down; others were dark maws behind the sheen of plexiglas. In these latter bays I could see figures moving around with flashlights and stock dollies The burp and fart of police radios echoed from many stores away. I saw men with rifles running down a side corridor towards Saks and wondered if they'd gotten a bead on GoldYlox.

I made straight for Borders. I'm not a runner: too short, too weak, too sedentary by disposition. By the time I got to Easy Spirit I was ready to cough up a lung, and this despite not having smoked all day. I leaned on the display window and gazed at a dozen size 6 left-foot shoes, all in non-committal shades of taupe and grey, guaranteed to make your feet feel good. My feet were blistered and sore. A feeling of despair set in. I was letting myself down.

Behind me, a dog started barking. Oh, fuck, I thought uselessly, and threw myself forward again. Finally staggered into Borders feeling blue in the face with my throat and chest aching and my legs feeling like they'd been grafted on from a baby elephant. I reeled toward the computer-books section, which is between Business and Foreign Languages; I know it well because all the cheat books are there. I distinctly remember the WPF cheat book because I was thinking of buying it for Suk Hee for her birthday. Not that she would ever *use* it; but she's into vintage and she'd probably like to have it on her shelf, still honourably sealed in its shrink-wrap.

But I had a problem. There was no computer-books section. I was so out of breath it took a little while for this fact to sink in, but after I'd walked up and down a couple of times clutching an incredibly painful stitch in my side, I could come to no other conclusion. And it's a ridiculous conclusion: Computers is a huge section and it grows every year. But it wasn't there. Instead, there was some big display of the newest non-fiction blockbuster. This one was (stupidly) called *How to Trick Angry Bears into Accepting You as Their Very Own: A Manual For Little Girls*, by Snake Carrera, PhD, SE.

How to placate angry bears, my ass. The last thing I need to know about at a time like this is the friggin' stock market. I was so mad I picked up a copy and threw it. It hit the mystery section and took out a large stack of *Cat Who* paperbacks. Then I raced around the store looking for the computer books.

There weren't any. Not downstairs; not upstairs; not in Music & Video; not in the café.

I went back to the original section, thinking maybe I'd missed something. And here's the strange thing. The blockbuster display seemed *bigger*. And now there was a life-size cardboard cut-out of the author with review quotes and shit; I definitely hadn't seen *that* before.

How to Trick Angry Bears into Accepting You as Their Very Own: A Manual For Little Girls, by Snake Carrera, PhD, SE.

Author of *The Wild Side: Stalk and Kill in the Boardroom* and *Y ask Why?*

'Transformative' *NY Times Book Review*

'Snake brings down his prey again' *Rolling Stone*

'The essential business book of the decade' *Fortune 500*

Looks like some shit my dad would read.

I stood there looking at the author photo – some big Indian guy wearing a Metallica T-shirt astride a flimsy little racing bike – and feeling desperate. I took out my lighter and was about to torch the whole display when the book fell open, not to text or a graph or chart like you'd expect in a business book, but to a line drawing of a little girl surrounded by three bears of various sizes, each holding a wooden bowl and spoon in their paws. The girl looked knock-kneed and guilty.

I finally got it. Duh.

'*Goldilocks,*' I breathed.

I started flipping wildly through the book, looking for something – anything – that could help us.

But some of the pages only seemed like they had writing on them. When I tried to read them, the writing turned to gibberish, like in a dream. And there were a lot of diagrams that referred to things I didn't even recognise. I read a few sentences on one page and then couldn't remember anything of what I'd read. Finally I returned to the cartoon and its descriptor.

Taoism is probably the most misapplied philosophy to be adopted in lay circles during the past century in order to explain scientific phenomena. But in this case, the paradoxical nature of the immune system's gentle battle with the GoldYlox invader is most easily described in familiar Taoist terms. Goldilocks, to be successful, must taste the porridges and lie in the beds of all three bears until she finds the niche that suits her best – that of Little

Bear. Even then, she is not a threat to the Bear family or the house they live in. The body that has embraced the GoldYlox invaders and tolerated them, allowing them to move freely throughout the host, successfully obviates the fleeing of the invader to the SRY region and the subsequent damage/destruction of that site on the Y chromosome by the host's own immune system. Once the immune system has been self-activated to drive out the GoldYlox invader, there is no turning back. Damage to the SRY leads to the explosive reproduction of the invading organism, its migration to other tissues and, in most cases, to eventual death of the host. This casual process has been well documented elsewhere.

Cases in which the host immune system does not react to the invader are sometimes described (inaccurately) as 'natural immunity' and are few and far between. Rather than 'natural immune', which is misleading and implies pre-exposure and/or the presence of antibodies against the invader, neither of which is the case, I prefer the term 'wise' to describe this non-responsive immune system. The wise immune system accepts the burden of lifelong parasite, the presence of which characteristically results in a pathology consisting of defective amino-acid production leading to the unsightly, but harmless, staining of urine to an ink-black colour. This is the only known price to be paid for hosting the GoldYlox invader.

Excuse me if I don't grok how this helps us.

What does a medical example have to do with commerce? See Chapter Six for a full exploration of the Wise Bear Paradigm.

'This is too fucking pretentious even for me,' I said. My phone vibrated.

330

'We have a situation,' Keri wheezed.

'What happened?'

'Did you find a cheat book?' She sounded desperate.

'No, but I found some book about GoldYlox. What's going on, Keri?'

'You better come back. Bring the book.'

She hung up.

'Who the fuck are you?' I blurted. There was some guy hanging out in Vinnie's. Suk Hee was still playing the game, but Keri was talking to him. It looked like she was showing him how to make airplanes out of smoothed-out Ring Ding foil wrappers.

As I burst in, aiming my gun at his head and demanding explanations, the guy pointed at the manual I was carrying and said, 'What you want with my book?'

I laughed. 'Your book? I don't think so. I've seen the author photo and you don't look anything like Snake Carrera.'

'Snake Carrera, huh? Yeah, well I never said I was no author. The book's *about* me. Let me see it. What they saying about me now?'

'About you? *Who the fuck are you?*' I repeated the question with a vengeance, keeping the barrel steady on the hollow between his eyebrows.

'Go ahead and shoot me,' he laughed. 'Bomb's gonna go off if you do.'

'Don't shoot him, Sun!' Keri pleaded.

I was staring.

'You're GoldYlox? I don't believe it.' With a name like that, I'd expected a mountain of a Mohamed, something heavyweight with gold teeth and muthafucka boots. But GoldYlox wasn't much bigger than me. He was on the light side of black, like KrayZglu, and he had frizzy bleachblond hair and freckles. He was skinny and kept his hands in his pockets and his eyes down, smiling nervously with a narrow elf-face. He was kind of cute in a cuddly sort of way. His ears stuck out.

'What you want with my book? You better not be trying to kill me. It only gonna backfire on you.'

'Back off, GoldYlox! I'm nervous and I don't want to shoot you by accident.'

'You don't got to shoot me. I'm just taking a few diamonds, couple of computer games and a Gucci bag for my woman. No big thing.'

'No big thing?' Keri squawked. 'You neglected to mention the bomb.'

He gave an 'aw shucks' smile and looked at the ground, standing on one leg and swinging the other like an embarrassed little kid. 'Oh yeah. The bomb.'

I really didn't know what to say then. This was the guy KrayZglu was quaking in her Reeboks about. This was the guy Col Whosit was treating as highly dangerous. This was the scary terrorist.

Then again, if I can be a gangbanger I guess anybody can have a shot at being a criminal legend.

'There ain't gonna be no flying pig,' he said to Suk Hee. 'Game over. Give it up. GoldYlox is here and this mall belong to me now.'

I opened the book and started skimming.

'Says here you're a counter-thief. What's that all about?'

'I got the key to the golden lock, get it? That's why they call me GoldYlox. I can go anywhere. I can get anything. But it's not what I steal that scares them. It's what I leave behind. That's the counter-thief part.'

'What do you leave behind, then? Other than explosives.'

He laughed. 'Too much blackness. They don't like it.'

'They – meaning the police.'

'They don't understand me. They're fucking prejudiced cocksuckers, excuse my François.'

'It says here they'll kill a thousand innocent people without batting an eyelash, just to stop you. Is that true? How come I've never heard of you?'

'I like to keep a low profile, you know. My 'Boos do the hard work nowadays. I'm, you know, semi-retired. Chillin' out and wait for the good opportunities. Like today.'

'And you're 10Esha's uncle.'

'So? What about it?'

'She's pretty smart. Do you think she'd want you to blow up the maul?'

'I'm not the one who's gonna blow it up, girl! *They* are!' He waved his hands at Suk Hee. 'Her and her police chief, they think they're so smart. I say, just let me do my thing and we can all Rodney King it just fine. But no! They got to exterminate me and my kind. It's like, they just look at me and they want to kill me. Is that my fault?'

'Suk Hee?' I asked. I sounded a little too Jenny Jones for my own comfort but I was getting exhausted and I wanted this to be over and I was even missing Ken, the little poop. 'What do you say to that? *Can't we all just get along?*'

Her voice was tight. She didn't look up from the screen. 'You don't know the first fucking thing about it, Sun. GoldYlox has killed *men*. You ask him.'

'It was just some selective snipping and trimming of the male population, all for a good cause. And the cops started it.'

'You escalated it,' Suk Hee said. 'You always do.'

'Cops could have backed off any time. Not my fault they messed up they own house with friendly fire.'

'Sun,' said Keri, 'Do you know what the hell they're talking about?'

'I'm not sure,' I said, skimming pages. 'According to Mr Carrera here, we won't get anywhere with GoldYlox by fighting him, Suk Hee. I think we've got to enter into negotiations of some kind.'

'Tell the police that,' GoldYlox laughed. 'There's just no way they gonna negotiate. They too stupid.'

'Maybe if we had more time.'

Suk Hee said, 'I can't finish the game before the bomb goes off. There's just no way.'

'But you can change some things. You did those clothes. You did the gas mask. So I'm asking you, can you change the bomb?'

'Sun, with a little bit of time, I could win this thing. I could fly this pig to the moon and back. But not as long as the bomb is ticking.'

'The bomb's not dangerous,' GoldYlox sang. 'I keep sayin', but nobody listen to me.'

'The police are freaking. They've called in the army for godsake.'

'They don't got to do that,' GoldYlox insisted. 'It ain't that kind of bomb.'

'So you say, but why should we believe you?'

'True,' said GoldYlox. 'I'm not a expert in a three-piece suit with a cellphone and a bunch of assistants running around after me. So why should you believe me, even though I built the bomb?'

Keri said, 'If it looks like a bomb and it ticks like a bomb, it's probably a bomb. That's got nothing to do with your presentation skills. Although if you don't mind my saying so, those are seriously lacking.'

'Presentation skills? That's all you care about. It's all surface surface surface. Image is everything. It's all about labels.'

'Spare me—' Keri began, but I heard myself say, 'Shut up!'

I must have said it with some force because everybody looked at me. I was thinking hard.

'Suk Hee?' I said.

'Yes?'

'You know how you made those labels on the clothes real? Like the underwear?'

'Yeah, yeah, I keep telling you that's what I'm trying to do here.'

'Could you do it to the cosmetics department? Like, could you do cologne and stuff like that? And could you do some menswear?'

'I guess. Yeah. If you still need me to prove it to you.'

I turned to GoldYlox.

'You're going to have to cooperate.'

'Me? Cooperate with you? Why should I do that? You just want to get rid of me. You're just like all the rest.'

'10Esha set this up for us both. She's your niece. She put us into this.'

'So?'

'And you'll get blown up, too, you know.'

He thought about it.

'Well, what's your idea? Just out of curiosity.'

'We'll trick the cops. I think Suk Hee can pull it off. We'll give you a make-over and you can do a hacker crossover.'

Everybody kind of looked at me. Keri was now using the tone we normally reserve for Suk Hee's wilder ideas. 'Uh, Sun, what are you talking about? What's a hacker crossover?'

'You know, like when a hacker gets hired out by the government to break into their security system and show them the holes in their defence. We get the maul security to hire you to teach them how you did it. How you got in without being seen, how you set up the bomb, etc, etc. Then they'll be safe against guys like you for ever.'

'Good luck convincing the cops to talk to me,' said GoldYlox. 'We don't have the best relationship.'

'Hence the make-over.'

'Make-over? Like on a talk show?'

'But only if Suk Hee can do what she says she can do. Can you, S-H?'

'I can try.'

We had to go back to Lord & Taylor. It wasn't as trashed as I expected; work crews must have already come in and started to fix it up, although there was nobody there at the moment. I was jumpy as a snake on a disco floor. I kept expecting to hear megaphones and Lt Swizzlestick; but the choppers outside had gone away, and because it was the dead of night, I guess, even the highway was quiet.

'You know where you're going?' GoldYlox said in my ear, making me shiver.

'I'll know when we get there.'

But I wasn't at all sure. We went around a couple of ladders and sawhorses that had been set up where Clinique used to be, and then I nearly shot a dumpy little woman with thick black hair. She seemed to pop up out of nowhere, carrying about ten garment bags over her shoulder.

'Help! I'm only a personal shopper!' she cried. She had an exotic accent, I wasn't sure if she was Iranian or Saudi or what, but I lowered the gun. She gave me a reproachful look and then, with an obvious effort, smiled. 'I got Brooks Brothers suits for Mr GoldYlox. We weren't sure about the size or colour, so I brought a selection. What shoe size are you, sir?'

'Nine wide,' said GoldYlox, looking pleased as he took the suits. The woman sprinted off without another word.

I saw the display I wanted, then. It was new, it featured

video screens in an otherwise dark department, and it wasn't connected to any designer label I'd ever heard of. I took GoldYlox's elbow and led him over to the new display.

The voice-over was a sandy, sultry woman's voice, breathy and deep and exquisitely nuanced. The visuals were binary, flashing in aquarelles over old newsprint.

Imagine if you could change your face with a thought. Eliminate wrinkles. Repair ultraviolet damage. Rejuvenate thin lips and dark circles. Now you can do more than imagine. You can change, with Thought. Thought Skincare available now at Lord & Taylor.

'Sit down,' I said.

'I like a woman who takes charge,' said GoldYlox, making a big production of settling himself in the tall makeup chair. '*But.* I ain't sure about no Brooks Brothers suit. I got to stay true to my self, youknowwhatI'msaying?'

I wasn't really listening. I was nervous. Suk Hee is the one who's all into make-up. I don't do this shit. I picked up a huge fluffy brush and gave it a few test swirls in the air. Then I noticed the fragrances.

Instinct: pour homme.

I picked it up. On the black spangly box was a map of constellations – *Chinese* constellations, I might add – but they were in the wrong places.

'The sky doesn't look like this,' I said. 'You'd think that for a product that costs over 200 bucks they could at least get the constellations right.'

GoldYlox didn't much listen to me, and can you blame him?

But it bothered me, and I kept looking at it. There was something stamped on the box in a raised design, very subtly. If you held the box sideways to the light, you could just see that all the constellations were set in the outline of a man's body.

'That's odd. The stars are rearranged for you. I wonder if that's a metaphor. It's a little bit of a stretch, but what the hell.'

I opened the cap and aimed it at the back of GoldYlox's neck.

'Hey, wachoo doing with that smelly shit? No way— *ffff!*'

Too late. I'd already nailed him with it.

'Now. We're going to make you over and you've got to act the part, or we all get blown up. Remember, when you start talking to the cops, your sales pitch is that you can teach them to defend themselves against other thieves.'

'I'm not a thief. I'm a counter-thief.'

'Or counter-thieves.' I started rummaging through the moisturisers and toners. 'Thank god you're a guy and I don't have to do, like, eyeliner and stuff on you.'

'I don't mind eyeliner as long as it's subtle,' GoldYlox stated, preening in the mirror. 'Samuel L. Jackson wears eyeliner in his movies.'

'Does he? Well, *you*'re not wearing it. Knowing me it would end up all over your face. This make-up stuff is not really my area.'

'Well, *make* it your area, girl! This is a life-or-death situation.'

He's bouncing around in his seat as he says it, and somehow I don't think GoldYlox is taking any of this too seriously.

'Never mind, I do it myself. Here we go, Samuel L. Jackson eyeliner, see? It's like they read my mind.'

I looked at the security camera and imagined Suk Hee at the game controls. This whole thing is crazy, but I like it.

'You've got some freckles which we need to try to minimise . . .'

'What's the matter with my freckles?'

'They make you look untrustworthy. Now, let's see, we need something strong, but flexible; sneaky, yet with a heart of gold . . . hmm, hmm.'

By the time I was done with the make-up, our personal shopper was back with shoes, and GoldYlox had picked out an Armani suit that he found acceptable. We got him an Animal watch so he wouldn't look too corporate, and he rejected all the Italian shoes and ended up dragging me out to Footlocker for a pair of high-end Nikes instead. On the way, we passed Miles Moccasins and I saw that somebody had returned the wolf poster to the wall. I was so disconcerted by this that I almost didn't notice that GoldYlox had the keys to Footlocker, which had been shut up tight as a drum.

'What was that Suk Hee said about needing keys?' I asked him.

'I got the master key to the whole place. She trying to change the stock but she don't got all the keys yet. If she did, she could catch me.'

'What if she wins the game?'

'Then she's got the whole mall, bugs and all, and she can do what she want. But she can't win in time. And I ain't gonna just disappear for her convenience.'

I tried my 'Why don't we all work together?' speech that hadn't worked on KrayZglu, but it was all I knew.

'Tell you what,' said GoldYlox. 'Give me your hand.'

I felt suddenly nervous. I held out my left hand; it looked pale and square and inconsequential. GoldYlox wrote a number on it in the Samuel L. Jackson eyeliner he had palmed.

'That's my phone number. Call me sometime. We could go out.'

I wrinkled my face at him suspiciously. I've been here before.

'If you want to go out with Suk Hee, ask her yourself.'

'Suk Hee? Oh, your friend with the bike shorts on her head?' He laughed. 'Not my type.'

I felt my face go hot and I was getting into the whole flirting thing when I remembered something.

'What about your "woman"?'

'Woman?'

'Woman. Of the Gucci bag, woman.'

'Oh . . . uh . . . I made that up.'

I started to make a sarcastic rejoinder but my phone rang.

'Are you guys ready yet? Suk Hee says we all have to meet in the food court.'

'Last 10 showed me, the food court is full of police,' I said.

'No shit. I hope you did a good job with GoldYlox.'

There were loads of cops in the food court; they had materialised from Zales or from the stock tunnels or for all I know they just *sprouted* like those instant freeze-dried Martians on Bugs Bunny, that you can sprinkle water on and they grow.

We started to edge towards The Stuffed Jacket, but it was a long way to go and there was a hell of a lot of blue to stop us. Strangely, though, the cops retreated slowly before us. This made me nervous. I felt like a dumb white man being drawn into the arroyo by some Indians who were planning on ultimately using his toe bones for dice.

Keri came out of Burger King carrying a shake. They let her approach us. I can't figure out what's going on here.

'They're prepared to negotiate,' she said. 'Apparently 10 e-mailed them some footage of the bomb and they've decided to talk to us.'

Footage of the bomb? Where is the bomb, anyway?

I turn around and realise we're trapped. There it is, forming behind us: The Fat Blue Phalanx. All the smug self-satisfied maleness you can drink, and free refills at the station house. It's all I can see in cops, that patriarchal bullshit that will never yield to a contract of mutual respect. That grunting fuck-obssessed inability to deobjectify and treat you as a person, it's a subclass of male that will never, ever change, no matter what. There they are with their uniforms and their discipline, an abstract and codified representation of all the construction workers who ever whistled at you and there you were, too polite to pee in their toolboxes in retaliation, too polite to challenge them, walking away red-faced because the worst part of it is that you were wondering whether they were *really* whistling like they'd whistle at Caprice or if they were just being sarcastic and were even now laughing at you with your short skinny legs and flat ass. Besides, you're not supposed to let it get to you. You're supposed to have a sense of humour: they do. See them waving their cocks at each other and farting? You aren't allowed to break the rules of their society which say that you are a cold uptight lesbian bitch if you don't like their hohoho aggressive male ways so just hold your head high from your position of moral superiority and go home and tell your boyfriend (if you have one, which I don't) who if you're lucky will offer to go beat them up knowing you won't take him up on it because you know perfectly well he'd probably get his ass kicked, most of the boys you know are highly ass-kickable because they've been brought up nicely. They were brought up in the luxury of knowing the money power of the military-industrial complex would protect them from the dirt and grime of uneducated testosterone. It's thanx to our weak boyfriends that we have cops at all, surrogate cock and balls to maintain 'order', whatever that is. Or was.

And where does it really leave you as a prisoner of the suburbs? Fuming over some tiny incident the aggressors have already forgotten about, but you have the sinking feeling you've just sniffed the true underbelly and the aroma was not what you get in Calvin Klein ads. Scratch 'n' sniff, scratch 'n' sniff, peel the onion . . . will you ever get down to the reality of what this place is about?

And I know I shouldn't brand individual cops with the big blue brush but in my mind these guys are a symbol of the whole iron-cage Boy system that makes me always a victim, no matter what I do, it's a cage I can't escape. I'm the little princess. They dominate, they aggress, they protect.

There's Lieutenant Swizzlestick; he's talking to a plain-clothes guy who looks more like Mr Rogers than Shaft. I'm thinking maybe we got lucky after all when he steps forward and says, 'First thing we need is Keri O'Donnell. Then we can talk terms.'

Keri and me looked at each other.

I gave my head a little jerk.

'Are you sure?' she said.

'You better. There's a bomb here, Kerr.'

'I'll get you a lawyer,' she said. 'Don't worry. My sister knows people at Cornell.'

I tried not to laugh. I punched her on the arm. The cops did better than that: they grabbed her and threw her on the ground and frisked the hell out of her. I can't say I wasn't relieved when they took her gun and cuffed her.

'You'll have to hold my shake for me,' she told the nearest one.

Then they reached for me.

'No!' said GoldYlox. 'Leave her alone. Now let's go take a look at my bomb and I'll explain all about it. What time you got? I got twenty-two minutes before it goes off. That what you got?'

'Yeah, that's what we got,' said Mr Rogers.

Everybody gets a little twitchy at mention of the bomb. GoldYlox is wearing a long leather coat that swirls around his ankles when he turns. He starts swaggering away from The Stuffed Jacket.

'So let's go over to the fountain and check it out.' Nobody follows him, although the phalanx doesn't get in his way either. 'What? Let's go, people.'

'Our experts say—'

'Your experts already got it figured out that if they try to defuse it y'all are going to be taking a free trip into space without the benefit of the space shuttle.'

He folded his arms across his chest and gave a wily smirk.

'But I can only work if I got trust.' He gestured to the air overhead. 'And I can't take no more of this Britney Spears. We got to have some groove.'

I tried not to giggle. I was watching Mr Rogers closely because he seemed to be the one in charge – or the smart one, anyway.

'See this is all game for me,' said GoldYlox. 'Believe it or not, I'm doing you a favour here. I'm showing you where you're vulnerable. You still don't know how I did it, do you? Hah! Well, I'll tell you – but it's gonna cost you.'

We all made for the big fountain outside Saks. They hadn't turned it off; I wondered if the fuse was wired into the fountain's power somehow. GoldYlox is talking and gesturing enthusiastically, and Mr Rogers and the bomb experts are all listening. Occasionally they make sharp gestures with their heads or start to ask questions. GoldYlox is fielding it all beautifully. Funny how he turns out to be one of those people who love to explain their shit to other people. He's a total ham.

That Thought shit must be some make-up. I wish I'd palmed some for myself.

The bomb was ticking away and you could see and feel and even smell the tension in the air. It reminded me of an orchestra tuning up. A lot of radio action was going on, and I didn't see a single doughnut or Danish. I might have to revise my opinion of the police.

I have always had this weird thing which is that sometimes the things that normal people don't even notice completely freak me out, and conversely, I sometimes find myself in situations where everybody around me is going nuts and I'm like – in the diction of Mom – 'Why you panic? Why everybody race-a-round?'

This was one of the latter situations. I can't say I didn't believe there was a bomb, or that I was particularly brave or cool; for some reason, I just became really detached. The Fat Blue Phalanx dispersed into the parking lot. Most of the bomb squad went, too. GoldYlox was still playing relaxed and easy. I don't know what he said to Mr Rogers and Company, but he looked really cool while he was saying it, and in the end they stayed.

I watched the digital clock ticking and wondered how many hundredths of a second behind the reality was my perception of the numbers flashing. They zipped down to nothing.

There was a flash.

The fountain stopped. We could see the bomb inside it, a black suitcase, dripping wet. The suitcase began to vibrate, and then to quiver, and then the next thing we all knew, the maul loudspeakers gave a sharp *crack* and started jumping and trembling to the beat of the track KrayZglu had been playing: 'Bug You Up'.

GoldYlox was grinning. 'That's more like it.'

Mr Rogers looks like a man who isn't used to being made a fool of and doesn't much like it. You can see his ring around the collar. You can see his adam's apple move, and you can see the pulse in his temple swell angrily.

'But it looked like a bomb!'

'It is a bomb. Was a bomb. Doesn't make it a killer – unless you try to defuse it. Let it do its thing and you get a nice groove on. C'mon, get out your notebooks and I'll show you how it's done. But first . . .' and he looked straight at me. 'I got some doors to unlock, as a favour for a friend.'

I smiled weakly.

BICYCLEFISH

MENISCUS'S BED REEKED of the exhalations exhumations excavations and excretions of the seed ones. There were stains on the sheets and on the wall. He looked around and felt like a squashed slug, his vital juices splattered around him while he waited to die.

Pain came and went like a bird feeding its young. When it flitted away in search of more worms Meniscus was left bathed in beatific joy, a Caribbean sense of well-being that matched the Azure now creeping around his left elbow like a gauntlet. The universe was singing then, until pain returned to hacksaw its way through his symphony till he thought his teeth would fall out. He breathed shallow and harsh, sometimes hawking purple fluid that reeked of motor oil and cabbage.

Greta showed up, read his chart, clicked her tongue and shook her head. She called Dr Baldino to bitch about the fact that he was dehydrated and no fluid intake had been recorded for an entire day. He knew she saw a passive, empty hulk rocking back and forth on the bed doing fuckall, and she picked up her bag of crisps and her paperback romance novel in search of stimulation. But in truth she was the unwritten one, the blank page. Meniscus was the language that no one else understood. Teeming hordes built bridges and towers of chemicals in his body. His immune system primed to racetrack efficiency held thousands of surprises like embers waiting to be stoked to life. His fever was like a jungle because he was more alive than anyone or anything.

His tongue swelled. His eyes discharged. Greta, though failing to get authorisation from Dr Baldino, clicked her tongue some more and gave him fluid intravenously. But his muscles squeezed his veins convulsively, making the needle slip out. Smoke came from the metal needle. Greta changed delivery methods and slapped a patch on his butt instead.

Grey ooze dribbled from his penis.

Meniscus shat fungus. He knew it was fungus not only because it looked like a slime mould but because Greta left the intercom on when she was leaving one of several angry messages for Dr Baldino.

'You didn't warn me the subject was in crisis again, Dr Baldino! I'm only going to be able to stay a couple of hours. I hope you're going to be back before I leave because I can't get hold of Naomi and Dr Gould has already been on the phone to me and she didn't seem too happy about the situation, either. Please call me asap.'

After that, he lost track of Greta.

*

When Meniscus opened up his eyes, the fever was gone and there was only him and the mouse, who was busily consuming some of Starry Eyes's leftover Doritos.

He had to pee. The urine came out black.

He giggled, and then he shed a few tears, and then he picked up Genghis, who struggled to get back to the Doritos.

He said, 'I'm afraid, Genghis. It's that simple. I've come this far, through this much, and I stand with all the threads in my hand, every one alive, every one thinking, and all I have to do is tie them together and I will have a consciousness like no one has ever known. And I'm afraid to do it.

'I can glimpse what it would be like.

'I think it would be easier to die.

'How will I know I'm not just giving myself over to Them, like Bernie thinks? If each of these bugs is a tiny horse pulling my chariot, and I'm the charioteer, I've got to hold millions of little reins in my hands and drive the way I want to go.

'What if they run away with me?

'What if they run me off a cliff?'

Naturally, the mouse did not answer. Meniscus knew the answers, anyway. It was too late to go back. He'd neutralised the Y-plague. He was fully conscious of his physical processes, and he was in no danger from any bug known to man. He and the Azure were in harmony with one another.

He surveyed his planets.

'I don't need you any more,' he says to them. They are no longer planets, they're just a lame rock collection, and who cares about them? He can walk away.

Or can he? The habitat is closed. No one has been assigned to watch over him; no one cares about him, only about Starry Eyes. But he is still captive.

348

But he's not alone any more. He can see someone small standing beside the re-wired I-MAGE. She winds a length of hair around her forefinger and steps on her left foot with her right foot as she studies him. The first time they met, she turned his world upside down. Now he's about to return the favour.

'Hello, Bonus.'

She startles a little as Meniscus stands up, shrugging off the MUSE. Unwashed black hair hangs raggedly to his shoulders. His skin looks like hieroglyphics or maybe a circuit board. There are blue-green lines and points and irregular splotches drawn just beneath the epidermis. It looks like his veins have been rerouted by a civil engineer to snap to a city grid. But the lines are only pigment, the by-products of 79 metabolism. His feet plant on the cool tile floor and he feels his body go taut and then hesitate, like a car revving out of gear, muscles sliding over bones, wanting action but denied it – so far.

And Bonus smiles. Her eyes are the colour of a shady pond in summer, committed to neither brown nor green.

'I came for the mouse,' she said. 'Where's my mother?'

Meniscus, absorbed in self-appreciation, was startled into answering simply, 'She went to see Ralf from NoSystems.'

'Good. Then we can get the mouse out of here. I'm getting totally stressed, trying to keep the exterminators away. Let's go.'

Meniscus started to pick up Genghis's Oreo box, then hesitated.

'What are you going to do with him? Can he survive in the wild?'

'I don't know. I'll keep her until I can figure out what to do. Come on, I don't have all day here, are you catching her or not?'

'Your mother isn't going to let you keep him.'

'My mother doesn't know shit. Look, do I have to come in there?'

Meniscus picked up Genghis by the tail and deposited him in the box, then added a few broken Doritos.

'Actually, yes, you do.'

'Oh, right. I'm so stupid. You can't come out.'

Bonus went to Naomi's workstation and hoisted herself up onto the stool. She spun around a few times, then got down to business. 'Let's see, let's see, pass-thru chute controls, seals to adjacent habitat, seals to main lab . . .'

There was a soft *pop* and the door to the lab opened.

Meniscus stepped through. The lab smelled of incense and coffee.

'Now what?' he said.

'Do you know how to drive?'

'I've driven a simulator. Using the MUSE.'

'I'm not sure that counts. I think we could be screwed unless we can figure out—'

The outer door swung open and a head popped in.

'Hello? Dr Baldino? I got a message that you were looking for me.'

The body followed the head, and Ralf of NoSystems stood there. She seemed to hang in the doorway, her wiry body taut with surprise as she took in the sight of Meniscus and Bonus.

'It's like Bill Bixby turning into Lou Ferrigno,' she said, awed. 'The Incredible Hulk, only blue, not green. Christ, you look like some kind of genie.'

And for the first time, Meniscus answered her.

'The genie's coming out of the bottle, Ralf. You can help or you can get out of the way, but whatever you do, don't interfere.'

'Bonus, are you OK?'

350

'Yeah – what does it look like?'

'It looks like you're gonna be in big trouble when your mom catches you. Where is she? She said she wanted remote access to Mall, and I came to tell her that's impossible, maybe next year or in eighteen months, but not now.'

'It doesn't matter,' Meniscus said, moving back into the habitat with a prowling stride. 'Your game has served its purpose. I don't need it any more.'

He picked up Starry Eyes's crowbar and came out. Ralf's eyes widened.

'Just relax, OK?' she said. But Meniscus hefted the crowbar and started smashing the hell out of the I-MAGE unit. Sparks flew, plastic cracked, error messages came up, and finally the thing died.

'I don't need anybody to know what I did, or how I did it. That's my business.'

Ralf was pale with fright, and she started to back out the door. Meniscus followed. Behind her, the Gut Zoom gurgled and farted at a high decibel level and children laughed. A Fun Park employee dressed in a velour leukocyte costume ambled by, saw Meniscus, and stopped cold.

'OK,' Ralf said with cheerful terror. 'No problema, I'm outta here like last year, see ya layda—'

'I'll take the Kangoo, though,' Meniscus added, holding out a smoking blue hand. 'Where are you parked?'

Sweat burst out on Ralf's forehead. 'Section G.' She threw the keys at him and kept backing away. 'Do you know how to drive?'

'No.'

Bonus said, 'You'd better drive him, Ralf. Otherwise he'll kill people.'

'M-me? Yo, I don't *think* so . . .'

351

'Yeah, you better. Come on, you're wearing a Bicyclefish tattoo, what's the matter with you? Aren't you pledged to help shelter wild males?'

'Bonus, babe, he's oozing Y-plagues—'

'Which are no threat to you, you're not a man. I can't believe this, Ralf! You're always going Bicyclefish this, Bicyclefish that, you're so macho with your muscles and your moustache and campaigning for donations to keep the NFL running, and now you get a chance to do something to help a real male, and you're a total wimp.'

Ralf actually seemed to think about this. She looked annoyed; then she said, 'Oh, all right, goddamnit. But if we get stopped by security, he kidnapped me. And you, Bonus – you're staying here.'

'No way, I want to come.'

Meniscus turned and shook his head at her.

'You can't come. You have to take care of Genghis.'

'But it's just starting to get fun!'

'You can't come. Stay here and wait for your mother to get back.'

'Why do I always have to pick up the pieces?' Bonus moaned.

So the worst thing you can imagine, the thing that's kept you up all night watching snooker on satellite TV from Scotland in the vain hope that the camera's tight focus on the coloured balls against the green baize would soothe you to sleep, the thing that should have made you a stockholder in Mylanta by now what with the amount of indigestion pills you've chewed, snarling, in the wake of your unholy chocolate binges – not to mention the Bliss Fuzzies you've stolen off Naomi when she's at lunch and she knows you stole them and you know she knows you stole them but neither of you says anything because Naomi could lose her job if you reported her for keeping Fuzzies in her purse and vice versa – the thing that chases you around until you're a ghost in your own house a stranger to your own daughter a mystery even to Zoom the cat who spurns your lap in favour of the warmth on top of the fridge, that Thing has finally happened. In fact, it's happened and then some. The point of no return has blown out your butt and is behind you. Your shit's gone ballistic.

It was all starting to sink in in a sick way. Coming back from NoSystems on the wet highway with tail lights ahead of her gliding like pairs of identical twins, each with its separatebuttogether mate, Maddie had eaten half a pound-size bag of Jolly Ranchers, smoked five fake cigarettes and then opened the window to let in truck exhaust to replace the smell of her own farts. She had to get out and puke in the parking lot of an abandoned K-Mart.

'What the fuck am I going to do?' Maddie said to the battering ram that was passing-truck wind. 'I can't take Meniscus out of the lab now. He won't have access to the game, and anyway, Charlotte will follow me wherever I go. And if Charlotte finds out what Meniscus can do, she'll take him. Oh *fuck*. Why did I let the SE turn my head? Bernie was right. Why didn't I pay attention to my experiment? Everything I do is wrong. I'm fucked, I'm so fucked.'

Maybe she could drug Meniscus just long enough to get him away from Hibridge, and then negotiate with G-ma for her own life. After all, a cure for Y-autism was a big achievement. And Meniscus showed signs of other accomplishments, too. Even if Bernie was crazy, Meniscus had to be worth something.

There were eyes looking at her from behind the rusted dumpsters outside K-Mart. Fox, probably. Maybe possum. She wondered where Bonus's wolf was now.

'Anyway, it's Jennifer's fault for putting the SE in my lab. I never asked for this!'

That was a good point. G-ma should be strongarming Jennifer, not Maddie. They always pick on the little guy.

Maddie stopped examining the sixes appearing on her forearms, remembered the radio show, and said, 'Chocolate! That's what I need.'

She got back in the car, groped around in the bucket seat until she found a couple of stale Milk Duds, and ate them to kill the taste of vomit. Then she left incoherent messages with Kaitlin and Ralf begging for help. She checked her bank balance and found that Naomi had taken $8000 out of her savings account, leaving $7.34 behind.

There was nothing for it but to go back to the lab.

All the lights were burning as if Naomi were working late, and loud music spilled out. Maddie could hear the bass as far away as the Dendrite Drop. As she drew nearer, she recognised the song, and the band.

Spoonfed.

She looked into the security monitor and waited for the door to open.

But it didn't, because, the security display said, Maddie was already there.

Then she had a little epiphany.

'Fuck!' she exclaimed, uselessly. She should have figured this out long ago – it explained how Babyshop had failed to connect Naomi to Maddie during Meniscus's crisis. It explained why Wipeout.com kept no-showing.

She used her emergency code to override the door controls and stepped in.

The I-MAGE was black and silent. The habitat was wide open and vacant. Meniscus was gone.

'I'm going to kill Babysitterware,' Maddie said.

'It's not their fault,' said Bonus. She was sitting on the floor playing with Ollie the Elephant and Alpha the Wolf. 'I disabled the local network. No one knows I'm gone.'

'Where is he? Where's Meniscus?'

'Same place as the mouse.'

'What, dead?'

'You wish.'

'You let them go?'

Bonus smiled.

Maddie sank to the floor, defeated.

Maddie wanted to run an I-MAGE on herself to see whether there was a conceptus yet, and to make sure that 666 brand wasn't just some kind of sick joke. But someone had taken a baseball bat to the I-MAGE. The casing was warped and the panels smashed. The power cabling had been ripped out.

'Who did this?' She knew the answer but couldn't accept it.

Bonus shrugged. 'I didn't.'

'Meniscus? Meniscus attacked the I-MAGE?'

Bonus shrugged again and looked at the floor.

Maddie prowled among Starry Eyes's cast-off possessions. Wrenches, wire, plastic moulding and metal shavings were scattered across the floor, the only legacy of the SE except for whatever was still swimming up her snatch. They reminded her of tea leaves, they were still connected to him in some way, like fingerprints, like an exhalation of his breath into the room, though he was gone. Regret gripped her, winding around her organs like a sad snake in her belly turning over in its sleep. How could she feel so much for someone she didn't really know – hadn't even liked – didn't understand?

She sniffed. The habitat was probably still full of pheromones. She wasn't responsible for her own feelings.

She turned and looked at Meniscus's abandoned possessions. He had left even the stones behind. She picked up the malachite and slipped it into her pocket; but it didn't make her feel better.

I am loaded with infectious agents, she thought. And she didn't care. It was such a relief to know that the worst had happened, so what the fuck? It didn't matter what she did now.

Then again, there was Bonus to consider. And she didn't *really* want to die. Not yet. Not with fresh sperm sloshing around in there. It wasn't *fair*.

'I can't believe I was so stupid. Charlotte actually made me a fair offer, and I can't do anything about it because I jumped the gun and let him go. It's all Jennifer's fault. Goddamnit. And you wouldn't think it would be that hard to find a big obnoxious male wandering around New Jersey unescorted, but I'll never do it in forty-eight hours because I've got no fucking clue where he'll go or what he'll do.'

'Um . . . I know where Carrera went.'

'You? How do you know? You've never even met him . . . have you?'

'No, but I've been looking at his stuff and it's pretty obvious what he's up to.'

'His stuff?'

'Yeah – didn't you figure it out? You've been looking at it long enough.'

'Just tell me, Bonus.'

'It's a code. He's been using bike catalogues to communicate with his cell. He orders stuff and they send different stuff to what he ordered, and it's all coded messages.'

'I think your imagination has run away with you . . .'

'Bicyclefish, mother! He's been in negotiations with Bicyclefish and they're going to attack the Atlantis

Pigwalks. They were due to break him out tomorrow, but you let him go and beat them to it.'

Maddie grabbed her clone-daughter's shoulders.

'Are you sure?'

'I'm always sure. Do you—'

Bonus abruptly shut up. There had been a slight noise outside; now Jennifer was coming into the lab. Expecting to see Malone in her wake, Maddie picked up the crowbar.

'Charlotte told me about the SE,' Jennifer said with a big smile.

Maddie gave her a surly look. 'I guess you're happy now.'

'Delighted! Oh, I have something for you,' Jennifer said.

'Yeah, well I have something for you, too,' answered Maddie.

Maddie swung the crowbar and hit Jennifer in the wrist because Jennifer threw her hands up to protect herself. The curator gasped and then groaned, doubling over with her wrist clamped between her thighs.

'You broke my wrist, it's broken. Oh, oh.'

So Jennifer was going to make a big drama about a broken wrist, after all the damage she'd done to Maddie?

I don't think so.

Maddie took a baseball swing at Jennifer's head, and the crowbar connected.

Afterwards she didn't feel sorry. She felt a lack of any emotion, actually, including pleasure .

'Mom, what were you thinking? Didn't you know Charlotte told her Carrera is dead?'

'Charlotte *what*? Why would she do that?'

But Maddie only had to think for a moment to realise that it wouldn't serve G-ma to have too many people in on the fact that Carrera was a natural immune.

'What did she want, then? If she wasn't coming here to give me trouble, what . . .?'

In the dead woman's hand were two VIP tickets to the Pigwalks.

OBJECTIVITY

GOLDYLOX TOOK ME back to Vinnie's and had a 'Closed: Out of Business' sign put up.

'Nobody gonna want this place any more after this.'

'But GoldYlox, how are we supposed to get out of here? Did you make a deal with the cops? Aren't they going to arrest us?'

'I made a deal for *me*,' he said. 'I opened some doors for your girlfriend, because she's under time pressure with the game and she needed some help. So I figure you owe me, not the other way around. Funny how things work out, isn't it?'

I looked at Suk Hee, who was still playing the game like her life depended on it. I said as much to GoldYlox and he said, 'Everything depends on it. I got to go. I got a meeting with my attorneys. They're gonna reopen the mall tomorrow. If you stay here in Vinnie's, nobody gonna bother you tonight. But don't go looking for trouble. '

'What about 10? Where is she?'

He shrugged. 'Driving around somewhere, broadcasting.'

'But why, GoldYlox? What's it all about?'

'She got to make the link-up. You can look at her footage. Just ask her.'

I gave a little snort. 'We aren't the best of friends.'

GoldYlox flicked the cuffs of his coat and turned to go. 'You got my number,' he said.

Dating GoldYlox was the last thing on my mind. I went to check on Suk Hee. She had beads of sweat all over her face. I got her some Sprite from a machine at the back of the store. She swallowed some, but she still didn't look good.

It was a long night, watching Suk Hee play *When Pigs Fly* and considering what was going to happen to us in the morning. What if she failed? What did it mean? And what if she succeeded? Would every piece of merchandise in the store be real, like the cosmetics?

At 2:49 a.m. she started laughing and then leaned on the machine, crying and wiping her eyes and sort of looking real shaky.

'Suk Hee? Are you OK?'

'I did it,' she whispered. 'Look at him fly! Bye, piggy!'

I went to see the screen, but by the time I got there the only thing to see were the words GAME OVER.

'Whew!' I said. 'Does that mean everything's OK? Can we get out of here now?'

'Everything's OK. And it's over.'

She seemed to be having trouble breathing; not like Keri with asthma, just kind of overconcentrating on each inhalation. Must have been exhaustion.

'I just have to know one thing. Why'd you do it, Suk Hee? I know you didn't really blow Snowcone's boyfriend, so why'd you let them get to you? Were you upset about the picture?'

'No.'

'Well, what, then? What made you start shooting? Can you remember?'

'Yeah, I remember. It was the wolf.'

'What wolf?'

'My wolf, on my backpack. She called the wolf a dog. A wolf is not a dog. A wolf is wild. You can't touch the bottom of a wolf.'

I bit my lip. I was also biting back a rising anger, that she could be so stupid – what did it matter? How could she trigger all of this over what some girl said about a wolf on a button on her backpack?

She looked fevered, overly intense like a Siamese cat. Too smart, too beautiful, too translucent. She staggered a little and I grabbed her arm. This stupid maul was no place for us to be.

She looked into my face with the fixity of a five-year-old and said, 'I'm not sorry for the people, Sun. I'm not sorry. The pig was more important. I just *know* this. I know it.'

I didn't answer. Three salesgirls trussed up like calves. Terry's stomach exploding in blood and bile. Old ladies diving for cover. What was I supposed to say? Suk Hee is obviously Looney Toons but she's my friend and I love her.

Means to an end, right?

But what end?

'Look, we better leave. How should we do this?'

But all the energy seemed to have gone out of her. She leaned against *Asteroids* and yawned. 'If we wait until they open the mall tomorrow, we can probably slip out without being noticed.'

361

'Tomorrow's too late. Look at you. You need a doctor.'

She picked at a cuticle and didn't say anything.

'Come on, Suk Hee, work with me here. Don't you have any influence with the cops?'

'No. Only in the game, and that's over.'

'But you won!'

'Morphic Pig won. I'm only Suk Hee now. I'm not special. Let's just wait until the mall reopens, and then we can—'

'Nuh-uh. You need to see a doctor. Let me think. If all the stock has been changed like you changed the cosmetics and the clothes, then all we need is some kind of weapon. Or a disguise, even, like what you did with those girls in Lord & Taylor, only better because they'll be expecting something like that . . . what? Why are you shaking your head?'

'It's only a mall now, Sun. I told you: it's over.'

'But we have to get *out*, Suk Hee. Didn't you think about that?'

'I'm really beat. I had a plan but I can't remember what it was. I'm not up to it.'

They say female competitors don't suffer the testosterone drop that males feel after the loss of a game. Their chemistry is the same, win or lose.

But I feel like shit, and I am female. Not that you would know it, to listen to the sociobiologists. I've melted all Ken's toy soldiers on the radiators and girls aren't supposed to do that, either. I feel seriously deflated and I sure don't feel like we won, no matter what the screen said. And Suk Hee; isn't exactly acting like the big victor.

'All the more reason to get you to a hospital. Come on. I'll help you.'

I tugged at her arm, but she was heavy and limp.

'The world is basically over for us,' she said. 'It doesn't matter what we do anymore.'

'Yes it does! You make us sound like a one-hit band. There *is* a future, Suk Hee.'

'Maybe for you. I'm already on a downward spiral, though. It's OK. Tennis players and physicists peak young. What just happened here, it's all I'll ever do.'

'You don't know that.'

'Stop arguing,' she murmured. 'You're so obnoxious. What just happened *is* true. Remember that, no matter what happens after. OK? Don't forget me, Sun. I haven't forgotten the world, so you mustn't forget me.'

'Suk Hee! Hey!' I shook her to make her stay awake. 'You can't go to sleep. Not with a head injury.'

'I don't feel too good,' she said. 'I can't remember what I was supposed to do. You might have to find the shadow without me.'

Then she sort of keeled over.

LITTLE GREEK
SOLDIERS

ATLANTIS CASTELLATION COULDN'T have looked less like a castle if you had stuck a pink flamingo in front of an L. L. Bean tent and called yourself Count Dracula. From the outside it looked more like a golf course than anything, being a fucking big field with little chimneys and air vents popping out of it here and there, and some hoppy-hoppy rabbits to keep the grass short. The image's more sinister association whispered *concentration camp* but that was a tough idea to take seriously if you had ever seen what was inside. Meniscus hadn't, and he was scared. Leaving everything else aside, he would have felt overwhelmed at the idea of going into a real castellation if he hadn't already been taken completely out of himself by the events of the past twenty-four hours.

It was almost dawn, a sulphurous hour with the sea wind taking the edge off the garbage aroma and the noise of the nearest superhighway still subdued. Meniscus was standing in the shadow of a tool shed at the south end of the castellation grounds, surrounded by a dozen young men. They ranged in age from fifteen to twenty-two or so, and their range in colorations was a kind of travelogue, suggesting a sojourn in Africa followed by a journey north through Spain and thinking about a weekend in Amsterdam – a motley collection of genes, but they all had one thing in common. A little or a lot, they all looked like Starry Eyes.

It had taken extensive begging, pleading, and threatening before Ralf's Bicyclefish contact had agreed to drop Meniscus off at the assembly point for Carrera's Army. Snake Carrera was a Very Big Deal, according to Ralf. Meniscus felt like he was the last to know. Apparently Starry Eyes had been planning this event for weeks, ever since Arnie Henshaw had reneged on his promise to put Carrera in the public eye and help him avoid capture by Charlotte West. And as for his little army, it was all a family affair. He'd been building it for years, using Bicyclefish as a safe haven for his many sons – thanks to the cooperation of a handful of his many *daughters* and their mothers. Ralf herself was an aunt; she showed Meniscus a photo of her chubby infant niece in New Mexico.

'We're kind of like the Underground Railroad, only instead of providing an escape route, we provide long-term homes and education, disguises for Accidental males,' Ralf told Meniscus. 'We can't come out in the open, or we'll put lives at risk. But with a price on Carrera's head, we had to do something. When we put out the word that Carrera needed help storming Atlantis, these were the guys who showed up. We turned away the under-fourteens.'

Once they arrived at the designated spot, Ralf had faded off into the background, leaving Meniscus standing there in the pre-dawn mist surrounded by a lot of edgy young men, none of whom seemed to know each other. Across the field, cars and helicopters were arriving in droves, dropping off spectators at the tram station that was the only official entrance to the castellation. There was a buzz in the air, and Meniscus had to exert all his will power to contain his excitement; he was a long way from the habitat and Naomi's Cookie Hour. He kept his hood up and kept moving, hoping no one would notice him, but when Starry Eyes appeared carrying his duffel bag and eating a doughnut, his gaze scanned the group and halted on Meniscus.

'OK, listen up!' he said. 'Thank you all for coming, now we're gonna have a little test to be sure you're all legit. You know what to do. Use that wall there.'

As one, the men went up to the wall, unzipped their flies, and peed.

Meniscus watched as the wall was stained black as ink.

'Yo!' said Starry Eyes. 'What about you there? Let's see it.'

Meniscus let his urine fly and it, too, was jet black.

'Good,' said Starry Eyes. Then he cocked his head. 'Holy shit, is that *you*, Squeak?'

Meniscus threw his hood back and Starry Eyes's mouth dropped open, revealing half-chewed dough and rainbow sprinkles. Out of the corner of his eye Meniscus could just make out a faint blue smoke beginning to rise from the surface of his own skin. Starry Eyes was giving him a questioning look.

'I changed the Y-plague to make it more acceptable to the immune system. It's fairly innocuous now.'

'What about the blue stuff?'

'That's a consciousness plague.'

Starry Eyes thinks about it. 'To teach you to grow your nails and stuff . . .?'

'And stuff. Don't worry; you won't catch it. Your immune system looks the other way, just like with a Y-plague. So it can't bite you.'

'I just can't believe you're alive. My idea worked. It really worked! Shit, am I good or what?' He looked around at his audience for support, and the young men made enthusiastic noises even though they couldn't know what he meant.

Meniscus felt himself smile.

'I still don't think you should be here,' Starry Eyes said.

'It's where I belong,' Meniscus answered. Starry Eyes looked gratified.

'You're only gonna get hurt, Squeak. You better stick with me, I'll try to keep you from getting totally creamed.'

They went in through a service entrance, disguised as janitorial crew thanks to the security-pass-obtaining efforts of well-placed Bicyclefish members. Not being noticed wasn't as impossible as Meniscus would have thought: the castellation was staffed by a great many wannabeboys, and in their boiler suits many of these women and quasi-women could have passed as men; so, conversely, Carrera's army managed to pass as non-men. The operation had Meniscus's nerves on high alert all the same, even after the group split up and went in different directions, leaving him alone with Starry Eyes.

Though all but invisible from the outside, the castellation was huge once you were in it. They passed shafts and towers underground, mosques and churches with fake sunlight streaming in from on high; service areas and storage bays; atria to games halls; and block after block of apartments, all connected via walkways and ramps, ladders and stairs. Everything seemed squeaky-clean and perfect in the underground half-light; but up close, the castellation had a certain greasy look about it.

Starry Eyes talked him through what they were encountering. 'I think if you asked most guys they would rather have had a real castle, you know like in Europe and shit. With arrow slits and a moat and crocodiles. But they say this is the safest type of structure and it's got all kinds of smart fibres and junk built into it to protect the so-called aspirant pigs.'

He pointed out places where these micro-oganisms were evident, and now Meniscus understood the impression of greasiness. There was a thin gunge to be found growing almost everywhere, sometimes shiny, sometimes furry. The organisms, according to Starry Eyes, were souped-up racetrack versions of algae and barnacles and cheese mould.

'Smartslime,' Starry Eyes said, pointing to a glistening curtain of the stuff that hung from the struts supporting a catwalk overhead. An entourage of grey-haired women passed across clutching programmes; they nodded politely at the 'workers' below. He added in an undertone, 'Screams when it smells Y-plagues.'

They had reached the entrance to the restricted living quarters of the Pigwalk contestants, and the access hatch was covered with the stuff.

'We can't go in,' Meniscus said. 'We'll set off the alarm.'

Starry Eyes snorted. 'I been planning this a long time, Squeak. Watch this.'

From amongst a colony of bright security moulds growing on the access door he pulled out a small electronic device that looked a little like a nasal aspirator. He pocketed it and replaced it with an identical one from his tool kit.

'It will stop the slime from screaming,' he said. 'I hope. See, a chemical signal sets off the moulds, then they trigger an electronic sound effect as an alarm. I can't disable it, but I can turn up the trigger threshold so that we can hopefully pass safely beneath it.'

Meniscus knew where the Y-plague was inside him; he was carrying it like a horseful of little Greek soldiers. He sent it deep inside, away from the surface of his skin. He didn't know how sensitive the slime was, and he had to hope that all the other signatures emanating from him would confuse it.

Starry Eyes passed through, turned and grinned. It was working. Meniscus was getting scared. Starry Eyes couldn't know just how many little nouveaux Y-plagues were scurrying around in him, or he wouldn't be so confident. Mensicus called for more noradrenaline. The answering rush brought him fully upright. He could feel his eyes widen and his weight became springy on the balls of his feet, like a sprinter before a race.

'Come *on*, Squeak!'

He darted through the aperture and caught up with Starry Eyes, who slapped his back so hard that he stumbled forward.

'See? Easy. Once you're through that, you got no worries. Come on, we're gonna have some fun.'

Arnie Henshaw made the mistake of answering his own door. He didn't look too pleased when he saw Starry Eyes and Meniscus standing outside. Actually, he scarcely glanced at Meniscus because he was too busy correcting his course, trying not to trip over the furniture while back-pedalling across his apartment. There were a whole bunch of attendants in the room, all schmoozing enthusiastically, and Henshaw's promotional video was playing on the giant screen that substituted for a window in this underground home. A couple of chubby women with electronic clipboards were dancing.

'Arnie!' Starry Eyes enthused, sticking out his right hand jovially. 'Just wanted to congratulate you on being here and wish you luck—'

Henshaw managed to elude Starry Eyes long enough to say something in the ear of a tall black woman who had been eating an hors d'oeuvre and talking on the phone; she took one look at Starry Eyes and started herding people out of the room and deeper into the apartment.

'More food and champagne in the kitchen!' she bribed, waving at everyone with a cocktail sausage on a stick.

'Hi, Charisse!' Starry Eyes said, but she ignored him. Within seconds, the video was muted and the room was empty. From behind the door where the party had retreated, the music resumed; another door near the bar remained shut, but Meniscus heard giggling and the sound of a shower running.

Henshaw rubbed his hands together and slapped his thighs, laughing nervously.

'Yo, how's it going?' he said, fiddling with his sports watch. Meniscus knew from TV that this meant he was calling Security, but he didn't get it at first when Starry Eyes's own watch chimed. Arnie didn't get it either, because he kept trying to act cool while retreating rapidly as Starry Eyes came on, steady and deliberate – and he kept messing with the watch.

'Yes?' said Starry Eyes, holding up his own watch and pressing something on it. 'I'm responding to the call; oh, and your assistant has called security, too. Well, that's handy. Now, see, I'm now alerting all other units that the situation here is under control.'

Henshaw dragged the watch off his wrist and threw it across the room as if it were a scorpion.

'What the fuck do you want?'

Meniscus had been wondering this himself. Was Starry Eyes going to *kill* Henshaw? Meniscus sort of hoped he was. He wanted to see how the bugs would react. They seemed to thrive on violence.

'This is your last chance to make good,' Starry Eyes said. 'All I want is to be acknowledged for my full contribution to your career.'

Arnie glanced at Meniscus and said, 'I don't know what you're talking about. You must be insane.'

Starry Eyes gave a mock-rueful shake of his head and made a motherhen noise with his tongue.

'You don't want to do this, Arnie. Being a pig ain't worth it. You can still walk away with your head attached to your neck.'

Arnie was trying to work his way around behind the bar, where Meniscus imagined he must have a panic button or a weapon or something. Starry Eyes cut him off neatly. Meniscus was surprised to see that Henshaw wasn't actually any smaller than Starry Eyes – they were the same height, anyway, and Henshaw had been to the gym plenty of times. He supposed that their bodies had to look somewhat alike for the deception on the videos to be effective. But there was something about Starry Eyes that must have made Henshaw think twice about trying to make him move out of the way. Henshaw seemed to screw up his courage; then he struck a Bruce Lee pose.

'If you want it to come to blows, then I'll have to take you out. But I think you're sick to do this, Carrera,' he said. 'You know you could infect me. It's not a fair fight.'

'And was it a fair fight when you set the Florida State Police on me?'

'I only set the Clearwater Beach sheriff on you. It's not my fault you took a shotgun off the guy and got the state upset.' He flexed his traps and started practising some kind of huffy yoga breathing.

'What the fuck you doing now?' Starry Eyes seemed awfully at ease. His arms hung slack at his sides and he was glancing around the room as if appraising the decor. He actually seemed at one point to be watching Henshaw's music video.

'Getting in the zone. Come on, you want to fight or not? Let's get it over with.'

Starry Eyes snorted. 'You really wanna go that way? You know it's not gonna be good for you. I'm making you a fair offer, and it's more than you deserve. Stand up, come clean, and give credit where credit is due.'

From the hitherto closed door behind them a female voice called out.

'Hey, what's happening here?'

Meniscus whirled and saw no fewer than five young women, all stunningly good-looking, standing in a mutually protective huddle just this side of the open bedroom door. They weren't more than sixteen or so, and they weren't wearing much. Starry Eyes could pick them up in his peripheral vision, but he didn't even glance their way. This, in Meniscus's opinion, was the most extraordinary occurrence of all; but then, Starry Eyes was in a funny old mood today. Since the two men had entered the castellation they had encountered any number of anatomically perfect women with little on their bodies but skin art, and Starry Eyes had taken no notice at all. Evidently Starry Eyes, who was usually obsessed with pussy and beer and pussy, had better things to do.

'Go back inside,' Starry Eyes said coolly, still not bothering to face them. 'This is nothing to do with you.'

'Who are you? How did you get in here?' The girl

speaks with the utter assurance of high station, and everything about her backs up the impression that she has a right to do whatever she wants and everybody else better get out of her way. She's far too beautiful to be anything but a product of Design, and her breasts are *exactly the same size*, Meniscus notes with interest.

Starry Eyes does one of those special Starry Eyes moves, where he travels so fast he seems to leave lightning trails behind him, and you can't remember afterwards how he did what he did. In one instant he turns around, leaps over an armchair and charges the girls with his head down like a bull. They squeal and disperse into the bedroom. He closes the door, locks it, and turns to Henshaw. Inside, the girls start pounding on the door and yelling the foulest curses that Meniscus has ever heard.

Starry Eyes turns back to Henshaw, who has made another unsuccessful pass at the bar and now manages to pick up a lamp and brandish it defensively. Meniscus wonders if he's supposed to be doing something to help Starry Eyes and decides he'd better not, or he could piss off the big man and that was never a good idea.

'OK, fuck it,' Starry Eyes says to Henshaw. 'You had your chance and you blew it. I'll finish with you later.'

He jerked his head at Meniscus to follow as he stalked to the door. As they were leaving Henshaw recovered his courage and yelled, 'Yeah, you and whose army?'

Starry Eyes just laughed.

Henshaw must have found another way to reach security, because within seconds of their leaving, a coded announcement came over the PA system and a high-pitched alarm sounded. Starry Eyes checked his watch and directed Meniscus towards a service corridor.

'We gotta get out of this area, they'll be looking for us here. The uniforms are useless now, too, which means we got to be really careful.'

'Why did you do that? Now you've lost the element of surprise.'

'It was worth it to see the look on the fucker's face. Besides, I like to see everybody running around.'

Meniscus had to breathe hard to keep up. Starry Eyes led him down a series of deserted back corridors and through various sealed doors. At last they emerged from a narrow passage into a sort of window. A strong draught was coming in, carrying with it machine noise and men's voices. Meniscus grabbed hold of the wall when he realised that the 'window' opened out on a huge auditorium, the floor of which was ant-farm distant below.

Starry Eyes went right up to the edge and peered down. He seemed to be assessing his position. Meniscus looked over his shoulder and saw the glassy snarl of the famous HotWheelsMax capsule track. From this distance it looked like the curving tubes and catheters of a mad scientist's chemistry set.

'OK, Squeak, you better stay here. You'll be safe, and you got an easy escape route up that shaft –' he pointed '– and then just follow the purple water-pipes until you come out on the surface.'

'What about you?' Meniscus said.

'I'm going in. Keep an eye on the action at HotWheels.' And without another word, Starry Eyes leaned around the edge of the opening and grabbed hold of a roof strut. He dragged himself out into the arena and clung to the pocked wall, wedging himself in amongst the pipework. Grunting and sweating, he began to climb methodically sideways across the bowl of the ceiling.

This was Maddie's first Pigwalk, and the Sheldrake-Springer Memorial Exhibition Hall was wired pretty much every way you could shake a stick. The contestants were on view behind the scenes at all times (there were no less than fourteen Arni-cams recording every shit and sniffle) and the audience were also being observed for Hibridge market-research purposes. The signals were not only AV. An elaborate system of microbial sensors had been woven into the fabric of the building, encompassing plumbing, air ducts, and frequently touched surfaces like door handles. Guests, Pigwalk workers and contestants alike had to submit to total-body decontamination before the exhibition hall would even admit them.

If the 666 Maddie was carrying was the same one she'd heard about through the grapevine, it was unrelated to Y-plagues. That was why she was shocked when she got stopped at the very first perimeter. Bonus sauntered through, but when Maddie tried to pass the detectors, the whole place went up on alert.

'Step aside, please.'

The next thing she knew, she was being I-MAGEd in a side room. People going by could see her, and she felt herself turning bright red. She wondered if they could pick up anything in her reproductive tract yet, but didn't dare ask. The guards looked serious.

'Dr Baldino, I'm sorry, but we've found traces of dead Y-plague on your shoes and pants.'

'That's not a Y-plague, it's an experimental organism, Az79-10E. I can show you proof that it's not dangerous and anyway, I can change my clothes . . .'

'I'm not talking about the Az79; we've already looked into that and it's not a problem as an airborne agent, not in this concentration anyway. But you've got an archaic Y-plague, highly virulent. There's just no way you're going anywhere near any males, in those clothes or any others. You'll have to be completely decontaminated first and that would take days.'

'What? But I came all this way. There must be some mistake. I haven't been anywhere near any sources of Y-plague.'

'I'm sorry. You can't enter the exhibition hall. You'll have to watch from the VIP Lounge. It's environmentally sealed.'

'But my daughter's already gone through. I have to catch up with her.'

'We can locate your daughter and bring her to you if that's what you want. But she'll be perfectly safe inside.'

'I don't believe this,' said Maddie. 'Talk about bad days. This sucks.'

Meniscus looked at the tool kit that Starry Eyes had left behind. It included a schematic diagram of the castellation with various notations and highlighted areas where, Meniscus assumed, something was going to go off tonight. He studied the plans for the HotWheels track. He had never felt any inclination to fight, but when Naomi played the Pigwalk Previews on the lab screens he'd always been attracted to the idea of driving one of the car capsules. Maybe it was because he'd had a set of HotWheels not so many years ago, as a boy, when Doctor used to give him toys. He used to make elaborate spirals and loops of transparent orange tube track all over his habitat for his cars to race. Seeing the real thing held a certain thrill.

Like the toy, the real track was orange-tinted tubing laid out in gravity-defying loops, twists, and inclines; the cars looked like bullets and travelled through the tubes much like luge sleds on a downhill run, with a few important differences. First, they were motorised. Second, they could overtake one another. And third, they had a range of offensive and defensive weapons: 21st Century chariots. Meniscus knew that the drivers were at least as fashionable as the *mano à mano* fighters, for all that they were seldom anything to look at physically. The fighters carried condition on their bodies like thoroughbreds; but the racers looked like geeks. They were characteristically small, wiry – some of them even gaunt – and tense-looking; never relaxed enough to be handsome or funny. They trained with single-minded intensity and their average life span was about twenty-three even with the plague protection afforded by the castellation. Why women were interested in speed-suicidal fathers for their babies, Meniscus didn't know, but he had always wondered what the speed felt like, and the abandonment of hurtling down those tubes with your crazy motherfucking opponents trying to kill you if they could catch you.

He watched through Starry Eyes's binoculars for about an hour while the preparations got under way. Then he decided he was going to get closer to the track. It was a kind of physical urge, a hunger in his bugs. They liked the drivers, too. Maybe they *wanted* the drivers, Meniscus thought. Maybe the drivers would make good hosts. He checked out the schematic and made his way painstakingly towards an observation deck just above the HotWheels track, where he secreted himself under a set of bleachers and watched the action through a cracked-open storage-compartment door.

That's where he was when Starry Eyes showed up. Carrera must have traversed a quarter of the domed ceiling and then descended through the light rigging, because he emerged in the region between HotWheels and Lords of the Slide Rule. The security presence did not seem to notice him; they were all fixated on the action in the Lords of the Slide Rule battle pit, nearby, where the engineering contestants were being introduced together with their machines.

While the MC was still talking and waving her arms, Meniscus saw Starry Eyes come out from behind one of the contestant machines. He started chucking grenades into the ranks of waiting engineers. The robot eye saw him and the arm started to swivel around, claws extended to pluck him from out of the stack of ammo. Starry Eyes's hand whipped out and slashed a control cable; the robot froze, and the eye flashed from green to red in distress. Starry Eyes ran up the base of the arm, chucked two grenades ahead of him, then jumped off. Meniscus saw him land on the shoulders of a contestant, knocking him prone; then Starry Eyes picked himself up and started laying about himself with the starter flag, which had fallen out of someone's hand in the confusion following the initial explosions.

'Bicyclefish!' bellowed a big black woman in a security costume. 'It's a Bicyclefish action! Shut the event down!'

Starry Eyes pounced on the speaker and laid her out with a left-right-left hook combination that left Meniscus breathless. Halfway across the arena, Arnie Henshaw could be seen diving for cover, but Starry Eyes had marked him and was wading through the ranks of opponents in a wild effort to get to him. Meniscus watched in disbelief. Starry Eyes looked like a salmon headed up a waterfall. His face was plastered all over the stadium screens, eyes wide and wild, teeth bared, a look of unholy joy on his face. Then Meniscus lost sight of him, and the camera shifted view.

HotWheels was in the midst of a commotion; the starting gate was in chaos. A group of men were dangling in harnesses that had been suspended from the ceiling, preparing to enter their vehicles. The slick orange curves of the HotWheelsMaxTrax flashed with continuous video feeds, sponsorship ads playing across the twists, turns, slopes and loops of the elaborately suicidal racecourse.

The commentator's tower shook; a blast of static roared across the PA system, and a body could be seen hurtling from the tower and falling to the sand below. Then a man's amplified voice boomed out:

'*Come on you fucker Henshaw, come and get it piggy piggy. Let's see what you're really made of.*'

There was a rumbling noise as the engines of the cars were switched on simultaneously by someone unseen in the control tower; several of the drivers, still hanging in their harnesses, kicked futilely. A whole rank of the cars shot off with the noise of an angry hive plugged into a bass amp. A young man Meniscus recognised from the Bicyclefish meeting walked out onto the track carrying a really big stick and began shoving the would-be drivers around, so that they swung back and forth colliding with each other like the chrome beadings of an executive desk toy.

Meniscus looked down at the Lords of the Slide Rule battle pit and picked out Starry Eyes again; he was fighting his way through the crowd, trying to get to Henshaw. A fresh commotion went off just outside the VIP bar; some of Starry Eyes's kids had scaled the sides of the dome and were mooning the wealthy lunchgoers. Meniscus couldn't see the strategic value in this, and then concluded that Starry Eyes's sons were likely as insubordinate as he was. They certainly weren't going to help Starry Eyes, and security had already surrounded the kid at the top of HotWheels, so he wasn't going to be much use.

Meniscus was still trying to pick out Starry Eyes from the seething crowd when someone's calves and feet blocked his view. Meniscus clenched his teeth in silent frustration; then he gasped. The person bent down and opened the door of the compartment where he was hiding.

Instinctively, Meniscus rolled his eyes back, reaching for his MUSE. He was conditioned to respond this way, and had forgotten that there would now be nothing there. He was dragged out like a rabbit from a hole. Two beefy security guards studied him. They backed off as soon as they saw his skin.

'We got a freak,' said the taller of the two to the other, and into her microphone, 'Scan for buggage.'

A purple spotlight appeared from somewhere high in the rafters and focused on Meniscus.

'You'd better stand back,' Meniscus said. 'You could pick up my bugs and carry them to the contestants. Not that it will make much difference; I've already been in the air-conditioning system.'

The shorter one murmured something into her mike subvocally. Meniscus read her body language and felt himself panicking. He wasn't going to get out of this so easily. They were calling for reinforcements.

He didn't give himself time to think. He scuttled sideways and slid between the safety bars of the observation deck. One of the guards grabbed his sweatshirt but had to let go when he went over the edge. The air rushed up at him for a long moment and then he smacked into the curved exterior of the orange track.

The wind was knocked out of him, his head was rattling and his jaw felt broken. Actually, *everything* hurt. Well, he thought, nothing new there. He dragged himself up the track, glancing over his shoulder to see the guards firing darts at him. One of them stabbed him in the left kidney. He stopped climbing long enough to pull it out, and to neutralise its effect with the help of the bugs. They did a neat hat trick and turned the sedative into a straight painkiller, which helped a lot. A few seconds later he found he could even move his jaw, so maybe it wasn't broken after all.

Then he got himself over the top rim of the track and found that there were even more security personnel at this end of the event. They had divested the Starry Eyes lookalike of his big stick and caught him in a net. Now they were putting drivers in headlocks first, asking questions second. Legitimate drivers were standing around cursing and throwing their helmets, probably in frustration because about a dozen cars were racing around the closed circuit, having been ejaculated prematurely by Bicyclefish. Then Meniscus noticed that in the confusion several car-capsules had been left unmanned and unattended.

The other drivers must not want to attempt the course in somebody else's machine.

Another dart hit him, this time in the chest. He reeled.

The bugs turned this one to adrenalin, and that was when things got interesting.

'Is your relationship suffering from the five-year blues? Are you bored with monogamous sex, but afraid to admit it to your partner? Do you want a safe adventure?'

'I'm not really good at relationships,' Maddie said to the screen. 'I don't trust anyone. Especially myself.'

'Why not try a long weekend in the beautiful, secluded grounds of the Alpha Institute? We have every facil—'

Maddie switched views and got the intro for FFreeFFighting. The VIP lounge was nothing if not comprehensive in its coverage. Being locked in until Charlotte West could come and vouch for her wasn't much fun, though. Maddie looked again at the 666s on her arms. Had they set off the sensors? Or had it been whatever renegade strands of Az79 she undoubtedly had been contaminated with? No, that didn't make sense. The sensors were designed to pick up Y-plagues.

'Now if you were with us in previous seasons, you'll know

that everything has been building up to the final competition in FFreeFFighting, the pitting of the champions against multiple opponents. Our two semi-finalists, Arnie Henshaw and Pete Nam, have already defeated a series of opponents, but now each of them will be pitted against all of the men whom the other has defeated. Arnie has to fight the men Pete has already beaten, and vice versa. This means there will be a total of six men in the ring at once. Five against one. It's a very, very tough situation, and because neither Arnie nor Pete is expected to totally prevail, this particular event will be scored by judges.'

She switched back, wanting to see the HotWheels racecar driving, but the sex commercial was still on. Maddie sighed and took the 'skip sponsorship' option. She watched her account being debited $2.49 for the privilege of not watching the commercial. She stared at the Atlantis Runway logo instead while a reggae muzak version of 'I Can't Get No Satisfaction' softly played. Eventually, the logo cut to live-view again, but Tammy and Monica were nowhere to be seen, and the video image was jerking around like footage from a war zone. Maddie had to stare at the screen for several seconds before she even figured out what she was looking at.

It was the undercarriage of a HotWheelsMaxTrax racecar, and the camera was pointed up between the feet of the driver, who wore no helmet and so was free to shout obscenities into the camera as he negotiated a series of impossible turns at absurd speed.

Maddie sat up so fast she almost careered into the screen face first with her momentum.

Meniscus was driving the car.

In his wildest dreams, Meniscus never imagined he'd be here. It was better – well, it *would* be better than any game – if only he had any idea how to work the controls.

He pressed the 'load' switch and the car was automatically inserted into a slot in the top of the track; after that he had no idea what to do. Gravity took over and he started to slide down the course, rotating counter-clockwise within the tube so that he was soon lying sideways and hurtling out of control. He started flicking switches and pressing things at random. His eyes widened as the instrument panel lit up and started giving him way more information than he could deal with. The next thing he knew, his foot connected with the accelerator and the car shot away, leaving his stomach and most of his intestines behind. He felt his eyeballs screwing backwards into their sockets.

The ride looked smooth from outside, but when you were doing it the whole world vibrated so hard and so fast that Meniscus felt sure he could now appreciate string theory from the point of view of the string. Arms shaking with the force of the car's resistance, he steered through the first loop, grazing the penalty lights and setting off a fusillade of sparks and shrieks; after that he tried to hit the brakes but couldn't control the car's spin and he spiralled through the straightaway wildly. Vomit hit the windscreen and the interior wipers came on automatically, just in time for him to see that an impossible bend was coming up while at the same time the tube soared skywards.

There was no way he could react in time. Meniscus hit the curve, flipped, and felt the car turning in midair. There was a moment when the car hung perfectly balanced; then he felt his hair lift off the back of his neck as gravity reasserted itself and he was plunging head first back down the way he had come. When he hit the track again, his foot ended up on the accelerator and he was racing upside down. He was also going the wrong way up the tube.

Two other cars were coming towards him neck and neck, duelling as they drove; he could see them several loops away, getting exponentially closer as he raced back towards them headlong. He was short on prayer time so he mobilised all his weapons at random and then closed his eyes.

Meniscus heard a sharp popping noise as the cars parted and drove to either side of him; then there was a *whoosh* followed by a thunderous explosion and he lost all control. Their weapons must have missed him or he'd have blown up by now, and his offensives had been too late to hit them as well. Seemed more like everything had hit the *track*, because he was flying free of the shattered orange tube, hurtling end over end. He saw the stadium flash past like a pointillistic painting smeared in the rain, the faces and torsos of the audience blending in a sickening swirl. The roar of the combined weapons explosion dopplered down to a bass throb as he left it behind, and then the belly of the car hit the Lords of the Slide Rule sandpit and his helmet hit the top of the cockpit. He blacked out then; when he woke up he was vomiting again and the car was still moving. He saw people scattering as it ploughed through the sand and then *bang* into the judges' box, where it came to a halt with pieces of scaffolding and mauve vinyl-upholstered chairs collapsing on top of it.

'Wow,' he said.

Starry Eyes was yelling at him and hauling him out of the car. Meniscus staggered a couple of steps and fell over; his helmet came away in his hands in two pieces. Starry Eyes's voice didn't reach him until sometime later; for a while he was just kneeling in the sand while the world pitched all around him, throwing him up and down like some psychotic ocean. Legs and feet gave him a wide berth, including the booted feet of the blue-suited security personnel. Nobody touched him.

After a while he recovered enough balance to sit back on his haunches and get his bearings. All hell was breaking loose. Security had mobilised fire hoses and water cannons; the PA system was overloaded and a pack of German Shepherds wearing bug-detection devices was barrelling through the crowd, noses down.

Then Starry Eyes's words sunk in.

'Get out, get out, I need the vehicle! Holy shit, Squeak – is that you *again*? You're like the fucking cavalry. I think I underestimated you.'

Now Meniscus looked at the cloven helmet and said, 'Everyone does.'

The camera switched to a stadium view and Tammy came on breathlessly, babbling away, but Maddie wasn't listening. She was too busy screaming and beating the coffee table spasmodically with her palms.

'WE'VE NEVER SEEN ANYTHING LIKE IT!' shrieks Tammy, grabbing Monica by the shoulders and jumping up and down. Monica was white as a bone. *'WHO IS THIS CONTESTANT? WORD HAS IT THE HOTWHEELSMAXTRAX RACE HAS BEEN DELIBERATELY SABOTAGED TO SHOWCASE THIS VERY DARK, DARK HORSE . . . And now a message from our sponsors.'*

'What? Oh, you *bitch!*' Growling, Maddie changed viewpoints and got back into the FFreeFFighting page, where the commentators did not seem to have noticed the disruption in MaxTrax.

'. . . And if you're just joining us, the final bout between Henshaw and Nam has already begun. Both men survived the multi-opponent semi-final bout against the men the other had defeated – but they hardly emerged unscathed. Henshaw has come away with a groin injury and Nam has broken his nose, but in the semi-final they both scored about the same: 9.25 for

Henshaw and 9.31 for Nam. This is too close to call. We have to see them against each other . . . but Monica, these two look pretty tired.'

'Endurance is a factor, Tammy. This is where all those months of conditioning drills really come into play, not to mention extraordinary mental toughness.'

'Where's Meniscus?' Maddie shrieked. She changed viewpoints six times, but couldn't spot the blue man. Then, from the FFreeFFighting screen, she saw a flashing icon indicating that what she was watching had been previously taped.

'They've shut down the live feed,' Maddie said, leaping to her feet. She raced around the room, desperate to get out. That meant something too hot to show was happening. She had to see this.

The suite where she was being kept had been electronically locked, but Maddie had been inspired by Meniscus's apeshit behaviour. First she blocked up the sprinkler of the main room with chewing gum and masking tape. Then she found some cooking oil in the kitchen cabinet and poured it all over the *New York Times*, which she had spread under the curtains. She flicked open her cigarette lighter and ran behind the door.

When the smoke alarm started shrieking and the lackey who was supposed to be guarding her crashed through the door, Maddie shot out and charged barefoot down the deserted VIP hallway. At the elevators she ran into a small group of very old women looking flushed and chattering excitedly, fanning themselves with their programmes.

'Sorry!' said Maddie, and snatched the Exhibition Hall access tag off the blouse of the smallest and weakest-looking one. Before the others could fight back, she jerked open the door to the stairwell and lit off for the main arena.

She was only a moment's dash from the restricted floor seats, but even so, by the time she got there and showed her pass, the match between Henshaw and Nam was well under way. Tammy and Monica were commentating as though everything was fine; but in truth, the other end of the stadium was going berserk as the racecar sped from one event to another, wreaking havoc. Maddie craned her neck to see how security was responding; it looked like a lot of red-clad units were moving into position to seal the exits, but the runaway car itself had not been stopped.

'Their ratings have just shot up 200 per cent,' said the chubby woman next to her, fanning herself with her programme. 'See, I've got my MUSE right here with me and you can see the approval factor. It must have gone out on the Internet that there's a wild man on the loose.'

Maddie nodded mutely, still out of breath.

'How come you don't have any shoes, dear? That excited, are you? I came last year, so I know the score, you see. How'd you get your ticket?'

'Stole it,' Maddie said. 'Mugged an old lady.'

She leaned forward. Tammy and Monica could be heard on the nearest loudspeaker.

'And Nam is looking very strong, Henshaw's taken some hard shots to the body. He hasn't been able to kick, I'll bet he's feeling that groin injury – oh! Nam goes in for a single-leg takedown, beautiful!'

'Monica, that's a classic takedown and he's got Henshaw where he wants him, he's going for the mount . . . wait, what's this?'

'Nam's out! He's out cold!'

Everyone, including the chubby babe next to Maddie, leaped up and screamed.

'The Dim Mak does it again. Nam is completely unconscious, and Henshaw wins it . . . if our viewers will look

387

at the auxiliary screen, we'll try to pinpoint the moment when Henshaw employs his secret Dim Mak technique . . .'

Everyone is screaming and cheering. Henshaw, sweating copiously, staggers to his feet, arms clasped overhead in victory, and runs to the side of the ring for his coach's congratulations, leaving Nam lying on the mat. Maddie mimes the act of vomiting. Then she hears the roar of a car.

'Again, kids, don't try the Dim Mak at home, I mean it takes years of dedicated practice and a deep mastery of Zen to achieve it, but you never know, you could get lucky and then think how you'd feel if like your cat died . . . Oh, look out, here comes the mad Mario driver – he's plowed right through a phalanx of security – Tammy, does anyone have anything on this guy? Who is he, is he part of the event or what?'

'The whole thing's very mysterious Monica, we're trying to find out—'

'Fucking WATCH OUT!' screamed Maddie as the runaway vehicle came flying over a springboard that contestants were supposed to use in entering the FFreeFFighting ring, cleared the ropes by inches, and landed spinning and rocking from wheel to wheel. As the driver brought the car to a barely controlled halt, a sheet of glittering fake sand went up from the FFreeFFighting arena. With the engine still idling, Snake Carrera stepped out.

Somewhere along the line he had acquired a broken two-by-four about three feet in length. All of the men who had been standing around in costume waiting for final scores to be announced after their bouts were armed. Some had cutlasses, some nunchuks, and one even had a spear. A man with a two-by-four ought not to be much of a threat. But they all stood stock-still as Carrera surveyed them.

They all stood still – except for Pete Nam, who leaped

to his feet and fled. Everyone gasped and then started laughing.

'Well, well, nobody's ever accused Arnie Henshaw of cheating before, but I must say I've never seen anyone recover from a Dim Mak stun so quickly . . . although that's neither here nor there, the question is where did this intruder come from?'

'I think security are holding back because they're not sure whether this is part of the show,' said Monica. 'I think they should close in and grab him while he's surrounded. Does anybody recognise this guy?'

'Uh, we've got our researcher Jeanette working on this, but for now I just want to point out that the HotWheelsMaxTrax race has been postponed, obviously . . . those competitors are going to need counselling and, in some cases, hospitalisation. One of our favourites today, Jeremy Pasquale, has a broken collarbone and isn't going to be able to continue.'

'Right, Tammy, and over in Lords of the Slide Rule we've got – Oh! Look at that, the intruder has tried to attack the new champion, Arnie Henshaw—'

'Shit, Henshaw managed to duck and Bob Monk just took it across the shoulder blades; here comes Sticky Mhoptep with his samurai sword. I think we could have some serious blood here if this intruder doesn't surrender immediately . . . the other competitors are standing back to let Sticky deal with this.'

'Now we know that Sticky Mhotep has been formally trained in Japan and he's a proponent of Bushido, so I want to stress that if Sticky can deal with this situation without causing grievous bodily injury, I'm sure he will. But you should also know that he's fighting with a razor-sharp katana made by the legendary 14th Century mad swordmaker Senzo Muramasa, who was driven out of the guilds and his swords were banned because, according to legend, they caused the user to commit murder or suicide. This particular weapon actually *cut through the helmet of Toda Shagomasu at the Battle of Sekigahara in sixteen—'*

'Excuse me, Monica, we just got word from our researcher Jeannette that the intruder is not a Hibridge AS and is not indeed licensed to any castellation – earlier there was speculation that Frisby was making a raid on Hibridge but it would seem this is not the case. He's a wild—'

'OH! Down goes Sticky Mhotep, did you see that? The intruder just whacked him on the head with the two-by-four, then charged in and grabbed him around the waist and knocked him down. It's a beautiful piece of counter-timing but so unsportsmanlike. Sticky's on the ground, he's dropped his sword, and the intruder is sitting on his chest punching him, blood is flying—'

'So much for the famous sword – can't believe somebody doesn't stop this fight. Ah, here comes our ref, Mindy Park, and she's trying to pull the intruder off—'

'Yoo hoo,' recited Maddie numbly, shaking her head. 'Burger King. Show me your tits.'

'OW! Absolutely no sense of conduct, he's grabbed the ref by the hair and thrown her in among the competitors – here they come, and about time.'

'Yes, and Monica, the other FFreeFFighting competitors seem to have agreed to attack this maniac as a group, and they are wading in, there's Barney Rivera with his nunchuks flying and—'

Maddie watched as a black guy dressed in thousands of little silk ribbons came handspringing in, throwing flying side-kicks at thin air and whirling what looked like bladed bolas around his head. The bolas threw off streams of laser light. Carrera stood up, leaving Sticky lying semi-conscious in his own blood, glanced once at the black acrobat, then picked up the samurai sword and turned away. He's scanning for Henshaw, Maddie thought, but the blond favourite was nowhere to be seen.

The acrobat continued to perform wondrous feats of agility in a whirl of fluttering silk behind Carrera's back, without actually moving in to attack.

'Now who could say this is fixed? We're getting a lot of complaints coming in live but I have to tell you, folks, we have no reason to believe this intruder is a plant – and Bob "Boggy" Marsh is down, stabbed with his own spear.'

Maddie winced as the spear went in. She knew that the weapons were supposed to be blunt, so Carrera must have put a hell of a thrust on the thing to get it in between Boggy's ribs.

'Why isn't he using the sword? He's stuck it in his belt, but according to legend—'

'Oh! Here comes Road Dog, look out—'

Robert 'Road Dog' O'Reilly came barrelling out of the shadows, all seven feet and two hundred and eighty muscular pounds of him, charging at Carrera like a bull. Maddie's eyes widened in appreciation and she secretly thought: that bully will get what's coming to him, finally he's gonna meet somebody bigger and tougher than him. But Carrera threw himself on the ground and had slithered between O'Reilly's legs before the big man could check his forward momentum. Carrera had spotted his quarry. Arnie Henshaw was skulking next to the water carrier, half-hidden behind his PA and two trainers to judge by the towels hanging around their necks and the water bottles they were carrying. Carrera roared, his voodoo eyes flashing and his nostrils flaring wide. Henshaw legged it to get away.

'Boggy's seriously injured, the medics are coming in, and – yes, I was afraid they'd resort to this—'

Maddie sees the security contingent coming, carrying what look like fire extinguishers, nets, and what appear to be trank rifles. Carrera isn't stopping to worry about that. He goes after Henshaw, who now can't run away any more without looking like a dipshit. He turns to face Carrera, putting his hands up in the latest fashionable fighting guard pose.

'In case you're just joining us, we're LIVE at the Atlantis Runways with some ASTONISHING surprises as the Runway explodes into chaos thanks to the arrival of a destructive intruder. Is it for real? Is it all part of the show? Find out with me, Tammy Madsen, and Monica Ruaz, when we come back with MORE of the Atlantis Runways after these messages.'

'They're taking a risk showing this live,' Maddie's seat-mate informed her. 'It's too controversial.'

'Come on Henshaw!' Carrera was shouting. 'There's nowhere left to run. Let's see what you *really* got.'

Henshaw pointed at the Samurai sword.

'You want it?' said Carrera. 'Take it.'

He thrust the sword into the stage; it slid through leather and wood like butter and stood there, quivering in the brilliant light.

But Henshaw didn't go for it.

'No way, man,' he was heard to say, spreading his hands in a gesture of peace. 'There's been enough blood shed in the name of manhood. I don't do murder.'

Maddie gulped. To Carrera, the remark had to be a red flag to a bull. But he only shrugged.

'No weapons, then. If that's really what you want.'

Henshaw's handlers were looking at the stadium screens and talking on their hands-free phones and flashing what looked like baseball signs or maybe stock-market bidding codes at each other. His PA said something in his ear.

Henshaw gulped.

'OK,' he said. Listened to his PA. 'Standard extreme fighting rules. No biting, no eye-gouging.'

'What about Dim Mak?' screamed Maddie's seat-mate, but she was inaudible in the general din.

Maddie was watching the opponents in fascination. Carrera was bleeding, limping on his left side, and covered in sweat. Compared to the dancerly movements of Arnie Henshaw, he had about as much style as a polar bear.

'The sword's made him suicidal,' Maddie's seat-mate said. 'He never should have touched it. Arnie's gonna fuck him up. Nobody can beat Arnie. Ooh, I think this is gonna be over pretty quick . . .'

She was right; it *was* over quick. Carrera cracked Henshaw on the jaw straight away, and then, while Henshaw was still reeling, shot in and grabbed him around both legs, hurling him to the ground. Nam had done it with far more showmanship, but no more effectively; Henshaw was pinned. He thrashed, but Carrera flipped him over and wrapped one arm around his neck from behind. ('That's a nice figure four,' Maddie's neighbour informed her. 'Henshaw's not getting out of that.')

Security stood there watching while Henshaw turned blue. They were shouting into their radios; then Henshaw's eyes rolled up and when it was clear that Carrera was not going to let go they moved in. Just before her view was blocked, Maddie saw Carrera shift his grip and give Henshaw's head a sharp jerk.

Maddie saw Charlotte at the edge of the crowd, and jumped up.

'Charlotte! Charlotte! Over here! See, I brought him just like you asked!' But Charlotte didn't hear her. Maddie made for the fastest route to the fighting stage. It was easy enough to get there; all the guards had been mobilised to deal with the various insurrections around the stadium, and she was already almost on top of the action in the VIP section.

By the time she got there, Carrera was surrounded. Red-clad guards swarmed around him and he was netted in three layers where he thrashed like a tuna, until finally someone stunned him with an electric baton and he went limp.

When the crowd cleared, Arnie Henshaw was still lying there, his head bent at a strange angle.

THE SHADOW
KNOWS

SUK HEEP SUK HEE! Wake up! No, no, I don't like this at all.' I stand up and walk in a counter-clockwise circle three times, bashing myself on the head with my open hand. '*I don't like this at all!*' I'm singing. 'It's not going to end this way. No, no, no, NO!'

'You sound like your girl Keri. Have you gone 7-up too?'

The voice is coming from 10's head on the floor at the base of *When Pigs Fly*.

I run at the TV in a rage, getting ready to kick it.

'Hey, take it easy! I might be able to help you out.'

I go hopping sideways and smash my hip into a pinball machine in an effort to not kick the Watchman.

'You got to realise something, Pookie. Your girl's game be *over*. The world is just the world now; but that's OK 'cos you still got me and I'm not the bad dude you think I am.'

'Yeah? Well, why don't you prove it.'

'It has come to my awareness that certain things were changed by Suk Hee, in the game. She had a plan and she left stuff for y'all.'

'But she said the game's over. She said she has no more influence.'

'No more influence like, yeah, meaning your boots ain't gonna actually kick nobody's ass. But that don't mean there's nothing left for you in the mall.'

'You mean like a secret escape route? Like the truck tunnel? She said something about a shadow. Do you know what it is?'

'Go over to Macy's. Men's Casuals. I meet you there.'

'Why can't you just *tell* me—'

The screen went dark.

I growled. 'She's a real muthafucka, that 10. This whole thing has gone right to her head.'

I went to Macy's. First I lay Suk Hee down in the recovery position and covered her up with a shawl from my backpack. It had been a Miles Moccasins *Invincible* label but now it was just plain old Donna Karan. For dignity's sake I put a white Hermes scarf (formerly *Cunning*) around her head in place of the Lycra bike shorts. Then I went to Macy's.

The Men's Casuals department is dark and deserted. I wait for about twenty minutes and then I start thinking how I never should have left Suk Hee alone, what if 10 is using this as an opportunity to get to her somehow? Do I believe 10 is that evil? And how am I going to get Suk Hee out if she doesn't wake up – shouldn't I just surrender? And why was I listening to Jethro Tull on headphones when they taught us CPR in gym class?

The PA system crackled to life and I startled, flipping the safety off my gun.

'You're warm already, Sun,' said 10's amplified voice.

'I'm warm?' I stand up and start towards the nearest mirror, wondering if I'm flushed.

'Getting cooler . . .' sings 10.

Oh, now I get it. We're playing a stupid kids' game; I should have expected this. OK. I retrace my steps. With 10 singing, 'Warmer . . . cooler . . . getting cold now . . . HOT! Oh, that's much hotter . . .' etc, I stumble around Men's Casuals until I'm facing the wall in between two alcoves, each one containing a different brand.

'Hot hot you're very HOT you're on FIRE.'

I'm standing in between Dockers and Island Bay, not getting it. These are boring clothes. Even Ken wouldn't wear this stuff.

I turn around and look at the tables that hold stacks of shirts. 'Still hot, you're in the Zone.' I start opening the bunker drawers to see if there's something hidden here, maybe a machine gun or a carton of Marlboros or a pony I could use to ride out of here . . . nothing.

'This is a stupid game. What kind of a clue is this?'

I'm looking hard at Island Bay and Dockers. I'm looking for the seam where reality changes to some kind of code. There is a sprinkler overhead. Keri said something about sprinklers and 10; Suk Hee could control the sprinkler system, couldn't she? What did this have to do with a shadow? Hmm. The colour schemes of the clothes are olive, grey, yellow and navy. I rack my brains for national flags which have those colours . . . for associations of any kind. I pick up a shirt and look at the label. 100% cotton. Made in Taiwan. Crew neck? Crew? Gang? Posse? What does it mean, I don't get it. Islands, Bays, Docks – water – boats – Nantucket – aargghh!

'I don't get it, 10,' I said. 'Come on. Give me another hint. Some kind of clue. 10? Shit, this isn't *funny*.'

'That's the best I can do,' said 10. 'I'm trying to speak your language but you got to meet me halfway.'

'Why can't you just *tell* me?'

'Maybe because I don't *know*, shithead.'

'I'm going back to Vinnie's. Poor Suk Hee. We're gonna have to just surrender.'

'OK,' said 10. 'The world is over anyway, it's just we don't know it yet. By the way, this is the clip of you that went out. It was real useful, not that I guess you care.'

And on came a little music video of me and Alex in the stockroom. Ugh. She had added an Otis Redding soundtrack. I switched off the Watchman.

Time to give it up.

'Suk Hee! Wake up!'

She mumbled something at me and tried to turn over.

'This is no good, S-H. I'm going to turn us in. You should be in the hospital.'

That woke her up.

'No. *No*, Sun, please, don't. My parents will send me back to Korea.'

I didn't think this was the time to mention that they wouldn't be able to send her back to Korea or anywhere else because she'd be in prison.

'Promise me you won't go to the police. Not yet.'

'All right, I promise. But what about your escape plan? Tell me what to do and I'll do it.'

'I can't remember. I can't remember. It's gone.'

She leans against me and closes her eyes.

My watch says 6:37 a.m. and the maul doesn't open until 10:00. I have too much time to think, lying there on the carpet that smells of spilled sodas, checking Suk

Hee's pulse every few minutes and wondering what I'll do if . . . if . . . you know. I can't say it.

I'm just waiting for the world to wake up.

The world. It's supposed to be big, but it's very small. It was never 'out there', it was always in *here*. The dark purple carpet of Vinnie's with its scuff marks from thousands of sneakers of kids standing at the game consoles pouring themselves into the action. The fish-tank luminosity of the pinball machines. It doesn't matter how many movies you've seen where reality gets twisted because of some psychokinetic kid, or where somebody's dreams walk around on the street, or where a character violates a time paradox and everything goes bonkers. In those movies, there's always a neat solution. There's always some wise person to come along and explain things, give advice, help the hero fix whatever's wrong.

Well let me just tell you, it's a whole nother story when you've got the reality in your face. Talk about trying to assemble a barbecue with no instruction manual! Try and assemble this!

You'll notice I've recovered my feeling for the philosophical now that KrayZglu hasn't got a gun halfway up my nostrils. It's amazing how much better you can think when you are alone than when you are being scared shitless by some maniac. Not that KrayZglu was a maniac, she was just too real to fit into my schema, and I'm happier without that level of grunge because it's easier for me to develop theories in the absence of truth. Though I do still have a headache from that pistol-whipping.

I figure: there is a reason to it all. I don't know what it is but I have to believe it or else why wake up? Why be impelled towards consciousness?

How do I feel today. Everything's so sharp and fraught. Everything oozes meaning. I know I'm going to either forget or die. It's common knowledge. You can't be sixteen for ever. I've read all about this phenomenon and I'm ready for it. You adapt or you implode. You say haha and get on with it. It's a weird feeling to know this is going to happen to you, to know the ironic raised eyebrows and stifled giggles you share with your friends in the back of Chemistry class are a limited-time-only offer. They'll expire with the season, like bikinis in December unless you shop really upscale where they cater to the cruise market. This awareness is going to end. I feel like I'm dying, anyway. Burning up in my own re-entry.

Why should I bear my soul, anyway?

Why should I play host to this culture that wants to read me, digest me, spit me back out?

Isn't there a planet where free will isn't just a seventh-grade party game like spin the bottle?

Well. Silence. Annoyed silence, actually – exasperated silence. KrayZglu's gotten into my head. Just like Mom with her missing articles and displaced gerunds, there's KrayZglu like a Greek chorus going, 'You so full of shit you could open a K-mart.'

Janitors start arriving around 7:30; then employees around 9:30. The maul opens at 10:00. I wait until 10:47 because I want there to be enough people to disguise our movements. Then I get Suk Hee up – she looks worse, if this is possible – and we go out the back of Vinnie's and into the kitchen of Sbarro's next door, then into Sbarro's itself when the pizza-making guy isn't looking.

'Can I have a Coke?' Suk Hee says, so I buy her one and we go out into the maul. Her head has stopped bleeding but I'm hoping nobody looks too close.

It's a bright and sunny day in New Jersey. Suk Hee has clean forgot her escape plan. Good morning.

Geometry is a death trap, so is cleanliness, and this

400

maul is guilty of both. The arches and swerves are supposed to lull you into a feeling of safety and optimism. The use of white and greys is so obvious in its intention that I can't be bothered to comment. It's all too much austere grandeur. This maul is a roach motel for humans, it sucks us in and spits us out with pitiless regularity, and we like it. Visible poison in the form of tidy stacks of clothing, the roles we are meant to fit ourselves into. The lives we live that will never measure up to the commercials.

I turn on the Watchman, just to see if 10 is still watching us. But the video of me and Alex is still playing. Bitch.

Well, it's all gone to hell, though, and I feel good. I feel like a scavenger crow hopping down the highway from roadkill to roadkill. Maybe the road's been built for some purpose other than satisfying my appetite for guts and brains, but so what? I can still enjoy the feast.

I'm going to die here. I understand why Suk Hee made me promise. She's right. We're not going to jail, not like this. The bass line from 'Dock of the Bay' is carrying me home . . .

'Oh my god!' I hear myself squeak, and I don't sound like my usual tenor self. I sound like an excited little girl. 'Oh my god. Otis Redding.'

'What?'

'Island Bay, Dockers. Otis Redding. *Dock* of the *Bay*. How could I be so stupid . . . c'mon Suk Hee, move it!'

Off we scurry to Virgin like demented chickens.

I'm flipping through CDs like a long-fingered old librarian shuffling through the card catalogue. There it is, at the very back of the cabinet, filed right after Jésus Redcap. Otis Redding, the definitive collection. I whip it out, tear off the cellophane, grab the CD . . . nothing. Then, underneath the stack of CDs, I see a round shadow on the formica cabinet. It's a hole about two inches across, and something gleams faintly inside. I stick my fingers through and tug at the panel. The whole thing comes out, CDs flying everywhere, I bang my shins as the wood unexpectedly gives way. There's a crash and a roar of falling plastic. Shocked Chick Corea aficionados on the other side of the display yelling at me and pointing *Oh my God it's HER!* Yeah, it's me. The whole pyramid-shaped display cabinet pulls open. Underneath I see it, buried like an archaeological treasure. First a handlebar, with its attached brake cable, then a gleaming fender, then—

'Pull, Suk Hee! Pull hard!'

'Oh, yeah,' says Suk Hee, rubbing her head. 'Now I sort of remember.'

From under the Blues section we drag an enormous, shiny Harley Davidson with the words 'The Shadow Knows' scrawled across the fender.

CO$_2$

YOU CAN'T TAKE him,' Meniscus said quietly. He had come among the guards and officials and VIPs without being noticed, his hood covering his face, one leg dragging because he had after all wiped out in a Hotwheels car. Even when he spoke, they wouldn't have taken much notice of him except for the facts that his voice was so deep and he flipped his hood back from his face as he spoke. A puff of Azure smoke came wafting up.

Dr Baldino saw and blanched.

'Uh, I think we better treat this one carefully,' she said to the others. 'He's hot.'

Meniscus identified a tiny old black woman as the probable leader; she glanced at Dr Baldino and said, 'How hot can he be if he got through the detectors?'

'They haven't invented detectors for what he's carrying, Charlotte. Bloody Mary, just look at him, can't you see he's hot?'

'Smoking,' commented Charlotte.

'I am hot,' Meniscus said. 'And all of these men are going to be infected with my bugs. You were worried about a Bicyclefish bomb? Well, *I* am the bomb. So back off, and do as I say, and it will work out better for you.' It was fun, acting like Starry Eyes.

One of the guards has been scanning Meniscus from a distance and she gulps, 'It's a Y-plague all right. Haven't seen this one before, though.'

'My bugs aren't killers, they're transformers. But to survive the transformation, you have to know what you're doing, and none of these men here have a clue.'

'Meniscus!' cried Dr Baldino. 'Let's be reasonable. Let's talk this through.'

'Let Carrera go. I mean it.'

'Let him go, Charlotte,' Dr Baldino begged. 'It's the blue one you need to be worried about.'

Charlotte said, 'Take them both to containment and guard them. I'll be along later.'

'I'll go to containment if you want, but my bugs won't,' Meniscus said. He was smoking in earnest now. 'I repeat: let Carrera go, we'll both leave quietly, and nobody has a problem.'

Charlotte wasn't even listening to him. Security started to move in on Meniscus.

'You can't let this happen!' Dr Baldino cried, throwing herself in the path of the guards. 'It's going to backfire on you bigtime, G-ma. The bugs have been waiting for this for millions of years. They're going to take over human consciousness. We'll have to do what They want!'

'You sound like Bernie Taktarov,' G-ma said. 'That's why we had to have him removed. He lost the shoehorn.'

She gestured to the guards to proceed, but Dr Baldino was in full fury and wouldn't shut up.

'Don't you see what you're doing? This guy is going to go around wiping out what's left of men! He's going to infect them with his bugs, which are basically a fancy Y-plague. What's left of the male gender is totally fucked. We'll have no diversity at all. We'll only be able to make clones and egg-splices – it'll cost a fortune to make daughters. And we will have lost all our protection against microparasites.'

'My plague doesn't kill,' Meniscus said. 'It doesn't effeminise.'

'But it makes men into bug farms!'

'*You* made men into bug farms. *I* can give your children total-body consciousness.'

G-ma said, 'Sounds like a deal. And we'll keep the other one for boy sperm. Now everybody's happy.'

'I'm not happy!' Dr Baldino shouted. 'And what about my 666? You've got what you wanted; Charlotte, come on, don't play games, I don't have much time.'

Charlotte looked through her and walked away.

'What about my daughter? Charlotte! I do have a lawyer, you know.'

Meniscus didn't hear what Charlotte said about Dr Baldino's daughter, because about that time he was netted by security and picked up bodily for removal.

Meniscus said, 'You shouldn't look a gift horse in the mouth.'

Then he released his little soldiers.

It was easy to check in with the Event Broadcast on her MUSE and find out where Carrera and Meniscus were being held; the commentators had so little information to offer their enraptured audience that they kept repeating everything they knew, over and over. Maddie cross-referenced their testimony with the floor plan for the castellation, and found a handy access through the vent system.

The terrorbug ought to be eating at her by now, and her teeth were chattering – but she wasn't afraid of guards or heights or pain, only of the bugs that she knew were coming for her from the inside. Climbing into the claustrophobic space and crawling from room to room was relatively easy, and for once in her life she didn't care whose rules she was breaking. If only Bonus could see her mother now.

She found Carrera in an interview room normally used for media interviews. It was well catered and the air shaft was copious, though heavily filtered. As a testimony to his infectiousness, Carrera had been left alone. If he was surprised to see Maddie squeezing herself out of a hole in the wall, he didn't say so.

'Where's Meniscus?'

'Ran for it,' said Carrera. 'They're using smartslime to guard us. He changed his skin chemistry and slipped through. He didn't want to go, but I made him. He's got work to do out there.'

'I can't believe you're still alive,' she told him.

'They're not going to kill *me*!' he said. He sounded affronted. 'They're telling me I'm going to be the Next Big Pig. Can you believe it?'

'You don't want that?'

'Are you nuts? I've spent my whole life avoiding this shit, and now I'm all over everybody's System. They're voting for me. How stupid is that.'

'You're in a cell,' she reminded him.

'They want to make me chief pig or some shit. I heard them talking.'

Maddie grimaced. 'That's probably true. You caused quite a sensation out there. You must be a little flattered.'

He shrugged. 'I don't want it. I want out.'

'You should have run while you had the chance.'

'I had a score to settle.'

'Henshaw's dead.'

'Is he? Good.'

'You seem awfully cheerful for somebody who's being held captive.'

'I won't be captive for long. I still got the Bicyclefish explosives. They haven't body-searched me yet. I'm gonna send a chunk of this place up and get out. I'm just waiting for my moment.'

'I don't want to live,' Maddie said. 'The 666 is going to start working on me any minute now. Why don't you give me the explosives, and you leave? You can go out the way I came, through the vent.'

'You're skinnier than me.'

'Not in the hips I'm not.'

'That's true. OK – but remember, this bomb's been up my butt.'

Maddie wrinkled her nose. 'In the face of death, I think I can deal with your butt.'

Actually, she was feeling unconscionably alive. More alive than she had ever felt. She was finding it hard to believe that anything could kill her.

Starry Eyes dropped his pants and squatted, straining.

'Hurry,' said Maddie. 'They won't leave you here for long. This room's not secure.'

'Here you go.'

'How do you activate it?'

'There's an indicator at one end, a little window. It reacts to concentrations of CO_2. Breathe on it. A lot.'

'Are you serious?'

'Yeah.'

'It smells.'

'I told you—'

'Never mind, just get into that air vent quick, before I change my mind.'

He stalled with his shoulders still protruding. 'Hey, Maddie, tell me one thing.'

'What.'

'Did you really want to have my kid?'

'Yes. Badly.'

He gave her an awkward warm look. 'Too bad it didn't work out. I'm sorry.'

'I'm sorry too.'

He disappeared into the shaft.

'Sorry about the lie, too,' he called back.

'What lie?'

'There is no such thing as a 666. That's just a Nacrewell fashion marker they're using to scare you.'

There was a clang as an airlock door slammed behind Starry Eyes.

Maddie stood, holding the explosive, hyperventilating and trying not to breathe on it. Gingerly she set it down on the small table and backed away from it.

'It's OK,' she told herself hurriedly. 'I'll just go after him. I'll escape. They'll follow me and probably catch me. And him. I'll be indicted and tried for murder. With an axe. I don't have PMS. No way out here, Mads. No way out.'

She picked up the explosive again and looked at it. So innocuous. A little slimy, but otherwise innocuous.

The door opened and women in safety suits armed with CO_2 fire extinguishers rushed in.

Maddie held up both her hands to stop them. 'Please don—'

Meniscus felt the explosion under his seatbones because was sitting on the grass near the tool shed outside the castellation. Bunnies scattered, then resumed grazing.

Sirens went off. Overhead, a helicopter changed direction and prepared to land near the tram station.

It was dark by the time Starry Eyes appeared from a drainage ditch. He seemed unhurt. Meniscus walked the bike over to him, but he didn't even acknowledge the fact that Meniscus had saved his beloved contraption.

'What are you still doing here?' he said in an accusing tone.

'Trying to think how to break you out.'

'I already had that covered.' Starry Eyes swung onto the bike. 'Come on, we have to rendezvous with the other Fish at the Palace Diner. Map says it's about two miles from here. We better move. Right now they're busy evacuating people and sealing the place up. Then they'll start looking for us.'

Meniscus followed him at a jog. 'Us?'

'There's a castellation just over the border in Delaware I want to hit next. I figure I'll handle the getting-in part, the boys can make as much mess as they can and get some media attention, and you can sneak in kinda like behind the scenes. With your bugs. What do you think?'

They were approaching the highway and started climbing over guard rails and climbing entrance ramps the wrong way. Traffic honked at them and helicopters whirled overhead; but the castellation grounds looked undisturbed from the outside. An air ambulance took off.

'I don't get it,' Meniscus said, panting. 'I thought we were enemies now.'

'Why?'

'Because we're standing on opposite sides of the great divide. Because you're immune to my bugs, and my bugs are the future.'

'Look, can we talk about that abstract shit some time

when we're not about to get picked off by a friggin' helicopter?'

They ran, Starry Eyes pushing the bike because he had to keep lifting it over the dividers between roads. Then they reached the highway.

'This way,' Starry Eyes said, starting to mount the bike.

Meniscus saw her then. She was standing just below an overpass, the wind whipping her Spoonfed T-shirt around her slight body like a flag.

Meniscus stopped in his tracks. 'Oh no. It's her.'

Starry Eyes looked at Bonus, squinted, and said, 'Who?'

'Dr Baldino's daughter. *BONUS!*'

Bonus turned and saw them. She pointed across the highway and cried, 'The wolf! The wolf!'

Then she ran out into the road.

Meniscus was rooted to the spot in horror, but Starry Eyes took off and sprinted after her.

They saw the wolf, a shadow in oncoming headlights. She was coming toward them across the ten-lane Interstate, trotting head low to the ground as though following a scent. She reached the concrete median and stopped. Bonus stopped, too, dodging back from the slow-lane traffic. Water sprayed over her. A semi hit its horn; ahead, a Porsche pulled over and stopped. Starry Eyes started running down the highway. He cupped his hands and yelled.

'Hey, kid, get out of the fucking—'

The wolf set off again.

'No!' Bonus cried, darting out into the road again and waving her arms at the cars to stop. The cars were coming too fast, and a tractor-trailer was passing another of the same kind in the fast lane. The wolf hesitated, unsure whether to go forward or back. The truck's brake lights didn't even go on.

Starry Eyes scooped up the kid and dive-rolled onto the shoulder. The wolf drew her last breath.

One of Starry Eyes's big hands shot out and clapped across Bonus's eyes. She screamed anyway, even though she didn't see the small grey body go flying in the impact and the living shadow become just another piece of trash on the road. Meniscus saw it, though. It was so fast, and so unreal, that he almost couldn't believe it. Of all the things that had happened, this was the one that he couldn't take in as true.

Like suddenly stripping the make-up from a glamorous woman, the world reveals itself, thought Meniscus. Something beautiful becomes something ugly and sad.

Bonus is wrecked with sobbing. Starry Eyes stands up, holding her at arm's length to see if she's OK; she's covered in little scratches. She clings to Starry Eyes's right leg and beats her fists against his belly. Presently he picks her up and slings her under his arm like she's a piece of firewood he's carrying back to camp.

'Get the bike, Squeak.'

They start walking down the highway.

The driver of the Porsche gets out and starts towards them. Then she gets a look at Starry Eyes and Meniscus and recognition spasms across her face. She ducks back in the Porsche and roars away. Bonus breaks out in fresh sobs.

'Hey,' Starry Eyes says, shaking her a little. 'You see the licence number of the truck that done it?'

'452NLN,' she answers automatically.

'Right. So I'm gonna teach you how to fight, and we'll look up the driver, and when you get really good, you can go and beat the shit out of her.'

They reached a slip road, where the traffic was quiet and crickets could be heard in the long grass by the

411

roadside. The sun was coming up in a yellow murk. Ahead, it glinted off the sign for the Palace Diner and a whole bunch of bicycles already parked outside.

Carrera set Bonus on the bike, steadied her on the handlebars, and gave her a push. Wobbling, she pedalled.

WEAR A
HELMET

OH, I'M HAPPY. Out in the filthy, thick wind and the traffic, pissing everybody off with my bad driving. Synthetic structures surround us: somebody's ideas, somebody's plans, concrete highway-dividers for abstract ideas, motor oil staining the surface of the road, light glinting off dirty windows. Mosquitoes suiciding on my high-speed face.

We drove the bike right through the maul. Through the maul, across the parking lot, and onto Route 4 East, bound for New York City. There wasn't much anybody could do about it.

I get stuck in the bus lane and the bus is stopping in Bergenfield. Three lanes of traffic whip past on the left while we're stuck behind the bus heaving and wheezing at the curb. There's a stumpy-looking old lady in a print dress with her slip showing, standing at the bus stop with a bunch of plastic shopping bags. The Harley roars and burbles as Suk Hee and I eat bus fumes, and the lady turns and looks over her shoulder at me as she gets on the bus. She's gesturing to her own head, and then pointing to me.

At this point I'm so freaked out that if I still had ammo, I probably would have shot her. But I don't, and in a minute the bus is moving again but I'm still stuck behind it sucking carbon monoxide because I'm afraid to change lanes in the Harley. After a minute I look up and in the back window of the bus I see the same lady. She's got to be in her seventies, she looks Hispanic and she's wearing red lipstick. She keeps pointing at me and then making some kind of gesture around her head. She's mouthing something.

I figure maybe she's Dominican and this is a voodoo curse. I pull the Harley out into thick traffic and gun it. We pass the bus and the voodoo lady and I notice the gas gauge is low and figure maybe that was part of the curse.

Then, about thirty seconds later, it hits me. The words she was mouthing.

'Wear a helmet.'

I started laughing.

Then I wanted to cry.

A part of me was still on that bus with her. I can see her so clearly. Going home to her little split-level house where she rents out the basement, picking up her junk mail, entering her kitchen w/its outdated artificial wood cabinets. There'll be Ritz crackers in there, and Shop-Rite cola in the fridge. She checks the machine hoping maybe her daughter has called, but there's only a message from Agnes next door asking if she can come over and use the dryer because Agnes's is on the blink.

Suddenly *nobody* is looking like my enemy.

Because of this stupid woman, she knows nothing, *nothing*, she doesn't know shit, she never took physics, she probably thinks the Holocaust didn't happen. She's never even heard of supernova 1997ff, so she doesn't know that the universe is flying part at an ever-accelerating rate. All she knows is how to gossip with her friends and cook Thanksgiving dinner for sixteen and maybe a few other things that are *totally inconsequential in the scheme of things*. And yet, because of this stupid woman telling me to put my helmet on, I feel different.

I wish I could chop my head off. I wish I didn't have a neocortex. I bet that's why sex with Alex was so shitty, I bet it was my goddamned neocortex making me think too much.

Maybe it's not the world that's fucked, maybe it's me. Or maybe we're both fucked but who cares, it's all there is?

Maybe I *don't* want the world to end.

If it all goes to hell, what about the lady on the bus?

She seems nice, like if I rang her bell she'd offer me the Ritz crackers and flat cola. She'll ask me if I liked school, and I'd probably lie. She'd offer to buy whatever I was selling.

'I like the mint cookies,' she'd say.

Right about now I wish I were Catholic so I could cross myself but then again I'd be afraid to let go of the handlebars.

I love the world.

We were running out of gas and we weren't at Bogota yet. I was upset about this, because I felt sure that it was imperative we get Suk Hee to the hospital, and Englewood was still a few miles away. But we weren't the only ones having problems. The rest of the traffic slowed, too. Then it stopped.

Friggin' traffic jam. Probably a jackknifed tractor-trailer, plus rubbernecking, plus whatever. We can scoot between cars to some extent; but not much, because my motorcycle-driving skills aren't really up to scratch.

Overhead, a police chopper is cruising towards us.

Do they know? Is this some kind of trap?

Suk Hee looked pale, and kept touching the bandage on her head as if it hurt. I wanted to ask her what she meant.

No, I didn't. I didn't want to ask her. What I wanted was to go back to that moment when I'd come down to the bus stop and she'd been standing there with her little silk umbrella, talking on the phone. I wanted to go back to my life. I wanted to see Ken again.

The bike sputtered and died. I started pushing it, Suk Hee staggering beside me. Ahead, I saw what was causing the back-up. It was a charter bus, and it looked like it had overheated. A bunch of guys had gotten off and were standing around looking vaguely at the bus and talking. I stared at them. They were all *really* good-looking. I mean, all of them.

'Ooh,' said Suk Hee, perking up. 'Male models. Let's go find out if they're as dumb as in that zoo movie.'

'Let's not,' I replied, grunting with the effort of pushing the Harley. 'Come on. The cops are following us. I can't believe we have no fucking gas.'

The Harley was really heavy. We came to a turnaround point where the cops hide to catch speeders, and I was just about to push the Harley onto the road and give it up, when in the forsythia bushes opposite I saw the wolf.

She must have seen me first. She didn't move at all, and neither did I.

Suk Hee was squatting in the grass, holding her head, rocking from side to side. She was in pain.

This is not good.

Me and the wolf were eye to eye. She was grey and I swear I could have counted every single hair, white, black, and in-between. Her body was side-on to me, her back arched slightly and her tail pointed out straight. She was much smaller than I would have expected, but her paws were enormous. She had her head turned to gaze at me straight on.

Like I said at the beginning, we are all made of stars. I wished upon her.

Then I blinked, and she was gone. The bushes stirred where she had been; you could barely see it, but they moved.

Somebody started honking their horn, and with a start I realised that the traffic was moving again. The air was full of fumes. I heard sirens and a police car screamed into the turnaround from behind us and blocked our path. I covered my ears.

Next to me, Suk Hee was lying on the grass, very beautiful, just like always. The white Hermes scarf on her head was now completely scarlet.

The white and orange striped underbelly of some big vehicle passed so close to me that I thought I was going to get clipped, then came to a halt, belching exhaust in my face. I squinted up and saw the outline of a satellite dish and loudspeakers silhouetted against the sun. The voice that issued from the loudspeakers was all too familiar.

'How ya doin, Sun? You ast for it, you got it Toyota, nowuhtimesayin?'

I stood up and kicked the van. The flashing lights and sirens were too much for me.

'You're too little, too late,' I cried. 'Suk Hee needs a hospital, not a transmitting station.'

I turned back to SH. She looked so small and broken and . . . irrelevant.

417

It's not fair.

The cops were heaving their bellies out of their cars. You'd never know SH and I were wanted criminals, the lazy way these guys walked. One of them was pulling out a ticket book.

'Hurry up, Sun,' purred 10's voice. 'They gonna arrest you.'

I kicked the car again, crying.

'I don't care,' I sobbed. 'Fuck off. Is this the best you can do?'

The back doors of the van flew open. There was 10Esha, like the Wizard of Oz exposed from behind the Emerald Curtain. At the same time, the driver got out of the front and ran around the side of the vehicle. He was wearing a uniform and he had a stethoscope around his neck, its end stuck in his breast pocket.

I looked past 10 and at last I clearly saw the interior of the van from which she had been broadcasting all this time. I saw the clear plastic tubing that I'd wondered about before. I saw the instrument panels. I saw the plastic containers labelled with a red cross, and the laptop running video clips. I saw the defibrillator, the empty coke cans and the paper packages of bandages. I saw the oxygen mask and the video handheld.

'Are you gonna help get your girl's ass in here, or what?' 10 gave a heave and the metal bed/stretcher thing came tumbling out the back door, bounced, and began to roll. I caught hold of it just before it could run me over. The paramedic guy was bent over Suk Hee. Here come the cops, starting to look worried.

'10 what is this?' I whispered. I was shaking all over and I realised I was in danger of going to pieces. 'Will she be OK? Will everything be OK now?'

10's expression was inscrutable. She should play poker, not chess, I thought.

'Don't look a gift horse in the mouth,' she said. 'The game's over now.'

I swallowed and wondered how to take this.

Options?

I still had a few rounds and my gun. Surreptitiously I took the safety off.

Wear a helmet. Yeah, right. Suk Hee's the one who needed the helmet, not me. Still . . .

I put the safety back on.

The cops were so close I could smell *Chaps.*

I turned to the first cop and squeezed out my nicest smile. It was like pulling the trigger on myself. It hurt me, but I did it.

'Was I speeding?' I asked.

LOOK OUT FOR ...

COOKIE STARFISH

by

Tricia Sullivan

www.orbitbooks.co.uk